firelands

firelands

michael jensen

alyson books
los angeles

MANUFACTURED IN THE UNITED STATES OF AMERICA.

THIS TRADE PAPERBACK ORIGINAL IS PUBLISHED BY ALYSON PUBLICATIONS,
P.O. BOX 4371, LOS ANGELES, CALIFORNIA 90078-4371.
DISTRIBUTION IN THE UNITED KINGDOM BY TURNAROUND PUBLISHER SERVICES LTD.,
UNIT 3, OLYMPIA TRADING ESTATE, COBURG ROAD, WOOD GREEN,
LONDON N22 6TZ ENGLAND.

FIRST EDITION: SEPTEMBER 2004

04 05 06 07 08 **a** 10 9 8 7 6 5 4 3 2 1

ISBN 1-55583-840-5

LIBRARY OF CONGRESS CATALOGING-IN-PUBLICATION DATA
JENSEN, MICHAEL, 1963–
    FIRELANDS / MICHAEL JENSEN.—1ST ED.
    ISBN 1-55583-840-5
    1. APPLESEED, JOHNNY, 1774–1845—FICTION. 2. FRONTIER AND PIONEER LIFE—
FICTION. 3. GAY MEN—FICTION. 4. OHIO—FICTION. I. TITLE.
PS3560.E594F57 2004
813'.54—DC22   2004047667

CREDITS
COVER PHOTOGRAPHY BY CHIP FORELLI/STONE COLLECTION.
COVER DESIGN BY MATT SAMS.

For Brent Hartinger

At least we're crazy together.

the ohio frontier
november 1799

chapter one

Things were not as they seemed. It appeared as if black storm clouds were boiling up over the horizon, spilling into the valley like floodwaters breaching a dike. The storm almost looked alive, as if it had a mind of its own. Faster and faster, the clouds surged forward as I, the ever-steadfast Cole Seavey, watched resolutely from my stony perch at the opposite end of the valley

But as I watched, I saw that those were not black clouds racing toward me; they were passenger pigeons, huge flocks being blown violently through the firmament. Their numbers were staggering—masses beyond counting.

The clouds were not the only thing to be other than they seemed. To those who did not know me well—and none did: I made sure of that—I also appeared to be something I wasn't. For I was other than the dutiful son and devoted fiancé I had so long feigned to be. What was I exactly? The answer to that remained yet to be seen.

I had little time to ponder the question, however, as the wind propelling the birds and thrashing the trees below suddenly struck me with all its fury. The very air seemed to explode. I flung an arm up to protect myself as dirt, dried leaves, seed husks—anything that could be swept up by the tempest—whipped all about me in a mad frenzy. The storm had caught me at an unfortunate moment. I stood high on a treeless ridge overlooking the long, narrow valley into which I was about to descend. Luck wasn't entirely against me, though. An ancient forest of oak, hemlock, and poplar lay a half-mile from where I stood. Beneath their protective boughs, I knew I would find shelter from any storm, no matter how fierce.

Downward I plunged over the scree-strewn hillside. Rotten, fractured rock slid about under my feet, slick as melting ice. The last thing I needed so deep into this desolate frontier was to wrench an ankle, especially since I traveled unaccompanied by man or beast. Therefore I obliged myself to move with more caution.

The shriek of the wind grew louder, and a branch the breadth of my thigh smashed into a nearby boulder. Wrenched ankle be damned; I broke into an all-out run. I was nearly to the forest when something peculiar off to the left caught my eye. I thought it to be a girl sitting on the ground, as if pausing to rest whilst out on an afternoon's stroll.

I slid to a halt, nearly losing my balance in the process. Certain I was mistaken, I shielded my eyes and peered closer. Blond hair whipped about her head, obscuring her face, but it was a girl all right. Despite the bitter cold, she wore naught but a red dress that clung to her as if wet. I hurried to her side, mystified as to how she had come to be in such a remote place.

The girl leaned against a large boulder that afforded her little shelter from the wind. I wondered why she had not sought the refuge of the forest that lay so close at hand. Her eyes were closed and her head hung limply to the side as if she were asleep—not that such a thing seemed possible in this howling maelstrom. She was perhaps twelve or thirteen, and her bare feet were so dirty and rough-looking that it was possible to believe they had never graced the inside of shoe or moccasin.

"Miss?" I shouted, drawing nearer, but no answer was returned. This close, I saw I was wrong about the color of her dress. It wasn't red, at least not originally. It was white. All of the blood soaked into the material had misled me as to its true color.

From years of hunting, I was well acquainted with the gore that accompanied a violent death. Too, I had seen the bloody outcome of many drunken insults settled with musket, stiletto, and fisticuffs. Yet none of that prepared me for the violence that had been done in the killing of this girl. Her dress was rent in a half-dozen places, as was the flesh beneath. Indeed, her left leg had been so brutally slashed from thigh to knee that bone was visible, and blood yet leaked from the wound. Beyond doubt, she had died a terrible death.

She took a breath, startling me. Somehow she was not dead after all. I leaned my musket against a boulder, knelt down next to her, and pushed the tangled hair from her face. I placed my fingers against her neck. For a long moment, I felt naught, then a single feeble beat. She would die if I didn't act fast, and probably would no matter what I did. Another falling branch plummeted down, splintering to pieces disconcertingly nearby. I knew I had to get her to shelter.

First, I had to stop the bleeding from her thigh. I whipped off my belt—a fine, beaded item I had acquired in trade from an old Iroquois. I slipped the belt under her leg, pulled it high, and then cinched it as tightly as I could. Blood stopped flowing almost immediately, though she had lost so much already, I could scarcely believe more yet coursed through her veins.

The windstorm had not lessened; in fact, it seemed stronger. Above the shrieking gusts, I heard the sound of groaning. For a moment, I thought it was the girl, then realized it was the sound of the forest straining to remain upright in the gale. My musket blew over, landing hard. I wanted to have it back in my hand, to double-check the charge was yet secure, the firing pan aligned. But I sensed no other threat and thought tending the girl most urgent. I threw my pack to the ground, rummaging through it for cloth to staunch her bloody wounds. Given how grievously she was injured, it was hard to believe how ferociously she suddenly gripped my arm.

My eyes went to hers, now open, and in them I saw pure terror. But her eyes weren't on mine. They were locked on something beyond me. Very slowly, I turned until I could see over my shoulder. Fifteen feet away crouched a catamount in the shadow of the forest. My approach must have momentarily frightened the big cat away from its victim, but now it had returned, fearing I intended to cheat it of its meal. The beast was not mistaken.

It was moments like this that had earned me the nickname Cold-Blooded Cole. Staring back at the cougar, my pulse did not quicken, my hands did not shake. Some said it was not bravery that kept me so composed, but dim-wittedness. I don't know why I was not afraid at such times, but as far back as I could remember, I never had been. Perhaps to be afraid, one must have something he fears losing.

The big cat's eyes narrowed to slits, its tail snapping back and forth like a banner mounted upon a windy parapet. It bared its teeth, almost certainly hissing at me, only to have the sound swept away by the storm. I stood and yelled—all that was normally needed to frighten away one of these lethal, if cowardly animals. This cat didn't back off, however. The cougar was gaunt, plainly starving, so much so that its ribs were outlined beneath its skin. No wonder it had attacked the girl and now refused to give ground, even in this howling storm.

I needed my musket. I was a fine shot; all I required was one opportunity. But the animal hurled itself at me afore I could act. I barely had time to fling up my arm to block its charge afore we tumbled backward. I slammed onto my back, skidding over crumbling rock. The panther landed on my chest, its breath rank as it snarled. As hard as I could, I kicked at its underbelly, but not afore it savaged my thigh. We separated for a moment, but the enraged animal charged again. I scrabbled backward as we fought. There was no time to think as I fended off the cat's huge, powerful paws, blow after blow. At last its claws caught me across the face and my skin sang with pain. Furious, I struck out blindingly with my fist, felt the satisfying "crunch" of a solid blow landing on the animal's sensitive snout. The cat yowled as it slunk back but didn't leave.

Injured, I sank to one knee, the wind continuing to howl all the while. Grit continuously scored my face and my watering eyes burned even more fiercely. The ground shuddered as a nearby tree crashed to the earth. A second followed moments later, and I glanced over as it bounced off the ground. Hot blood ran into my eyes whence the cougar had clawed me.

Instinct warned me to glance up in time to see the cat launch itself at me in another brazen attack. I threw myself to the ground, and the beast passed inches above me. I scrambled upright, mopping blood and sweat from my eyes. The air was a whirlwind of dust and dirt as I searched desperately for wherever the cat had landed. That was when I saw it. Not the cat. The cat was gone. Where it should have landed was a *thing*—a monster, a devil out of the bowels of hell. Or at least that was what I thought I saw. My eyes were so blurry that it was hard be certain exactly what it I beheld.

I had a vague impression of something huge. Seven, eight, maybe nine feet tall it stood. It was two-legged, but had an enormous head that was a ghastly shade of black. Its mouth lacked lips and was filled with terrible, jagged teeth. Even from where I stood it reeked, as if left dead for days beneath a blazing sun.

I briefly wondered what had become of the cat; I assumed it had been frightened away by this beast. Then I had another, more unsettling thought. What if cat and monster were one and the same? Perhaps I had come face-to-face with a shape-shifter. I had heard talk of such creatures, but had ascribed the stories to timid minds fearful of the night. Perhaps I had been wrong to be so dismissive. Then, as if things weren't bizarre enough already, I thought I heard a voice rise above the wind.

"Cole," the voice called. "Cole Seavey."

"Gerard?" I said, barely able to trust my ears. "Is that you?" Gerard was my brother, my only living family, and the one person out here who could possibly know my name. But I was days from the frontier settlement where he dwelled. Nor had he known I was coming, and therefore it was unlikely we were meeting by happy coincidence. Yet, unless I imagined what I heard, who else could it be but he?

The creature stepped toward me, its arms outstretched, and I forgot all else. Trying to locate my musket, I staggered back toward the forest as another tree toppled. I feared getting too close to the woods and being crushed, yet I had no choice but to seek refuge amongst those swaying trunks.

A figure emerged from the woods twenty rods distant to my left. My heart leapt with hope that it was Gerard after all, but the figure's face was hidden by the brim of his hat. Struggling against the blowing wind, he yelled what sounded like, "Stop, damn you!"

I wasn't sure if he meant me or the beast, but neither of us obeyed. The man swung his musket up, taking aim at the creature. The percussive bang of exploding gunpowder rose momentarily above the wind, but the shot went wide and I saw the musket ball shatter against a rocky outcropping. The beast turned from me, charging the man as he attempted to reload. Immediately, I knew he was in trouble. I was handy with firearms; nothing felt as natural in my hand as my Virginia musket. But despite my years of experience, even I couldn't reload in much under a minute; this fellow didn't look anywhere near as fast as I. The creature would have him long afore he could get off another shot.

Intending to help, I started toward him, but the *crack* of another tree falling grabbed my attention. The report was as loud as a cannon, and I spun about in time to see a huge oak plunging toward me. I tried to dodge the tree, but there was no escape. Its limbs rushed at me like a bristling wall of soldier's bayonets. I suspected I was about to die in a most unpleasant way.

chapter two

Upon suddenly awakening, I at once sat up, striking my head against stone in reward for my haste.

"God's balls!" I cursed, rubbing my temple. Then I realized I yet lived, and felt bad for taking the Lord's name in vain, especially since I had miraculously been delivered from sure death. I was grateful to be alive, but where in damnation was I? Looking about, all I saw was a darkness as black as pitch.

"Hello," I called, my voice echoing faintly as if I were in a stone chamber. No one responded in kind.

Directly beneath me lay a pile of something hard, uneven and very uncomfortable. Gingerly, I fumbled about in the dark trying to determine what they might be. The answer was bones. Human ones, I suspected, judging from the size and shapes—skulls, forearms, ribs and all the rest that remained when a body has been stripped of the flesh that had once enlivened it.

I cast my mind back, trying to remember how I had come to be here. I recalled naught after the tree had struck me, and even what transpired afore was a jumble of fragments: the wind, a girl, the creature.

I felt certain that whatever had befallen now me had much to do with that hideous beast. It had surely brought me to this place. Judging from the skeletons beneath me, I suspected I wasn't the first.

I had been captured like prey, then brought here to be devoured. If nothing else, I only hoped I had spared the girl from sharing my fate. I wondered if either she or the stranger with the musket were here with me. I called out again, but no one answered and I presumed I was on my own.

Between the windstorm, the blood in my eyes, and the general chaos, I had not a clear picture of the beast. Despite that, it wasn't hard to imagine it killing me, tearing the flesh from my body, gnawing the bones—unless I acted first. What I did recollect most clearly was the rankness of the thing. I doubted I would ever forget that smell. I wondered how long I might have afore the creature came for me. Time enough, I hoped, to form some plan, as I wasn't one to passively accept my fate.

I shivered from the cold, then forced my battered body to slowly rise, being careful not to hit my head again. I also took care not to fall as the unsteady mound of bones shifted about beneath me. My feet soon found solid ground and I paused, assessing the extent of my injuries. My face was stiff with dried blood, whilst my body was just plain stiff. My left leg was grievously hurt where the cougar had slashed me, but at least my other limbs still worked, if not without obstreperous complaint. Even so, I doubted I could run more than a rod without crumpling into a heap.

I pulled my bearskin coat tight—a futile attempt to stave off the cold. The coat was poorly made, though the fault lay with me and my feeble sewing skills—sewing being one of the few talents I had never managed to master. The sleeves and collar, poorly attached in the first place, were quite in need of mending. Cold air seeped inside the coat like honey through a sieve, not that a little chilly air was going to stop me from escaping.

I shuffled forward some distance when at last I glimpsed light up ahead. Dizzy, I placed one hand against a wall cold and rough to the touch. I realized this place was a cave, though with the dead all around me, it felt more like a catacomb. My foot inadvertently kicked a skull, which clattered hollowly as it rolled across the floor. Wondering how many unfortunate souls lay here, I felt as if I were trapped in one of those grim German folk tales parents told to frighten their children: the sort of story where ogres ate children, and beasties of every terrible sort lurked in the woods. Such tales seemed to be most eagerly embraced by those who thought life to be wretched—all futility and despair, lessons and morals. I had always looked upon them with disdain, but in light of my own looming fate, I wondered if perhaps those folks had not understood life better than I.

Not that I had given up hope. I intended at least to try to fashion an escape. Some sort of protection—a weapon—was necessary afore I ventured outside. Bending down unsteadily, I grabbed the first thing I touched: the thigh bone from a rather large man. How just it would be, I thought, to brain the monster using a bone from one of its victims. Not that I planned on attacking it if I could help it. I was in no condition for a confrontation and hoped to escape undetected.

I felt a breeze from the direction of the light. Carefully, I moved toward it, feeling my way by touch. After several minutes, I came to the opening—a tall, narrow slot in the rock. I stepped out into the light. The sky was rough and raw, like skin scrubbed with soap too heavy with lye. The deep and biting cold made my eyes water. It seemed impossibly cold for November, though I knew not the vagaries of weather on the Ohio frontier; perhaps winter here arrived earlier and harsher than back in New York.

The sun hung halfway between noon and sunset, its light weak and watery. Even so, it took several moments for my eyes to adjust to the brightness. Once they had, I gazed out upon a huge, frozen lake extending in either direction as far as I could see. In fact, this had to be one of the great inland seas of which I had heard so much talk. It truly was enormous, as seemingly vast and endless as the sky itself.

I had spent my whole life in the wilderness, as far from civilization as a fellow could be. Or so I had thought. Now that I had ventured into these ancient western swaths, I understood that I had never seen true wilderness until these past few weeks.

A raven floated down from the sky, a splash of black against a sea of white. The sight of that bird in this desolate place heartened me, for the raven was a powerful, crafty creature and had long acted as my talisman. When in doubt over some matter, I looked to the raven for signs of encouragement, hints of how to proceed, clues to the future. Its presence wasn't all comfort and gladness, however, for ravens bore ill tidings as well as good. Only those willing to see the world as it was, unvarnished without false hope and easy promises, took the raven as their talisman.

I felt about in my pockets for the raven feather I carried at all times. To my dismay it was gone; I feared that an ill omen indeed.

The glossy, black bird landed nearby, cocking a yellow eye at me. I watched it warily, if hopefully, for if it greeted me with one or two calls, it was a favorable thing, but three meant it smelled death hovering nearby.

Quork, quork, it croaked, then seemed to pause as if trying to make up its mind. I watched it intently, waiting for a third utterance. The bird studied me a moment more, afore finally turning and hopping a short way over the ice. I nodded with satisfaction, for the raven had apparently come to give me encouragement and not to prophesy my early demise.

My eyes flicked about, seeking any hint of the monster. So far it was only me and the raven. With any luck, it would remain thus. It was funny how much of my life had been spent hoping for that very thing, for I was most certainly a loner at heart.

An empty, windswept beach spread outward from the cave mouth. The lake lay in front of me, blocking the way north. The way behind was obstructed by a hillside too steep for a man to ascend, even one like myself who, as a child, had been nicknamed Goat. And to the east stood a rocky headland. If I hadn't felt as weak as watered-down brandy, I surely would have been able to scale it. In my present condition, however, the only chance for escape was to go west along the shore where the way was flat.

It was from that very direction the monster staggered into view, bellowing and clawing at its head as if in a terrible rage. Startled by the beast's abrupt appearance, the raven beat its wings, lifting into the air with a cry of *caw! caw!* The fiend stopped clawing its head as we both watched the raven soar higher and higher. When the raven was gone, the beast slowly turned toward me.

The whole world seemed empty except for the beast and myself. I even forgot the stinging cold. Perhaps fifteen rods stood between us. This was farther than the first time I had seen it, but at least now I *could* see. With the flat lake behind it, the obscene creature seemed to loom even larger than afore. Arms at its sides, it stood there watching me, whatever pain it had suffered troubling it no longer. It had the legs of a man, bear paws instead of hands, and the head of only God knew what.

The creature looked patched together, as if made from different beasts—the way a gryphon is part eagle, part lion. Perhaps this was a new kind of gryphon, one heretofore undiscovered. I did not revel in the opportunity to be the one to have made such an abominable discovery. Or perhaps it was something worse, something not of this world: Something evil. On the whole, I was not one given to believing in such things—I prided myself on being rational—but this beast *was* unlike anything I had ever seen. Satan's work was writ in its every feature, and I felt as if I were looking at evil made incarnate. Even then, I couldn't bring myself to truly believe it was an actual monster and not something not of this world.

When the beast began hurrying toward me, such musings became entirely superfluous. All that mattered was escaping. I spun about, hobbling back to the cave which proffered my only chance to hide. I plunged into darkness, scrambling over the bones of my predecessors. I worked my way deep inside, wareful of cracking my skull against the stony ceiling. As I pushed further back into the dark, another breeze washed over my face. I nearly ignored it afore realizing it might come from a second way out. Quickly, but methodically, I ran my hands over the wall, searching for the breach whence the breeze flowed. Even if I found it, I knew it might only be a small thing, a fissure perhaps, carved by a runnel of water occasionally flowing from above. But it could be more.

The opening turned out to be level with my chin, a little bit wider than the width of my shoulders. How far back it went, I didn't know, and didn't have time to find out. What meager light entered from the mouth of the cave abruptly vanished, blocked out by the beast. The creature stormed forward, was nearly to me when it stopped, mere steps away. I froze, and swore I could hear it sniffing the air, though it was hard to believe it could smell anything over its own stench of decay.

The beast lunged, the bones on the ground cracking loudly beneath its feet. I crouched lower, pressing myself against the clammy dirt floor. I listened to the creature's claws rasping across stone as it searched for me. My fingers brushed the cool surface of one of the skulls. As quietly as possible I picked it up, then heaved it into the dark. Bone clattered against stone, and the monster went quiet. A long moment passed, then it crashed its way to where the skull had landed. With a vigor that belied my condition, I sprang to my feet and jumped for the opening. My fingers clawed for a handhold whilst my moccasins scrabbled for purchase against the cave wall. Finally, I hauled myself up. Once inside, I scooted forward on all fours as fast as possible.

Straightway the tunnel narrowed, and I was soon compelled to proceed by wriggling forward on my stomach. At least I knew the enormous creature couldn't follow after me. But afore I had covered more than a yard, I was yanked backwards. The beast had seized me by the bottom of my bearskin coat. Again and again, it made a horrible guttural sound as it pulled me toward it. I had to get free of my coat afore it was too late, but the tunnel was so narrow that it was almost impossible to move my arms. I shifted about until I lay on my back, repeatedly kicking at the monster's paws. All the while I slid closer to it, expecting at any moment for dagger-sharp claws to sink into my flesh. I kept writhing about, changing the angle from which my feet lashed out. My hands grasped at the sides of the tunnel, but there was nothing to grab.

Then I heard the most wonderful sound in the world: my bearskin coat ripping away at the sleeves and collar. I heard the beast stumble and fall. I couldn't help but laugh as I realized my poor sewing skills had saved my life. Wasting no time, I crawled forward, quickly putting myself out of reach. I had no idea if the tunnel led anywhere, and I didn't care. I had escaped the monster and that was all that mattered.

◆

After gradually widening until I could walk upright, the tunnel ended after perhaps fifty yards. It didn't end above ground, unfortunately, and I still had to find a way out. From somewhere ahead came the sound of rushing water and the hope of escape. The space in front of me felt and sounded vast, and I presumed it was a cavern. Hesitantly, I edged forward in the dark, probing the crumbling stone underfoot with my moccasin. Afore I knew it, the slope grew precipitously steep, I lost my footing and plunged pell-mell down the embankment. At last I hit bottom, tumbling forward with my arms outstretched. I landed hard, and bolts of pain wracked my forearms. I counted myself lucky this was all I suffered.

The fast-moving water I'd heard was close enough for me to feel the sharp coldness of it. After arising and rubbing the sting from my hands, I pushed on until I reached the banks of a river. After slaking my thirst, I followed the river upward whence it flowed, hoping to come across the spot where the water first penetrated the earth.

Without benefit of light, the way was difficult. I fell more than once. It was after one of those falls that I found the body. At first I didn't realize there was a body at all, noticing only the stench of death and rot and some other strange odor I couldn't identify: something that made me dizzy and nauseous. My first thought concerning the body was that I had probably found someone else who had escaped from the beast, only to die all by himself. Judging from the stench, he had been dead several weeks. Or maybe the body had naught to do with the creature and his presence foretold nothing of my own fate. So I hoped. Whatever the case, I desired to get away from the body and that other terrible smell afore I was sick.

I pushed on, losing all track of time. At some point the ground started to slope upward. Too, fresh air washed over me and, sensing escape was at hand, I grew eager and quickened my pace to a trot. I had gone perhaps ten feet when I was struck hard across the forehead and fell senseless to the world.

chapter three

I had struck my head on the stony ceiling of the cave. Or so I ascertained upon my again becoming aware of my surroundings. At this rate, the monster wouldn't have to worry about finishing me off. Judging from the fresh welling of sticky blood upon my forehead, I hadn't been unconscious for too long. I swore to God this was the last time I would suffer such a blow. After rising carefully and moving about, I gathered I had come to a grotto rife with stalactites and stalagmites. It was one of the former upon which I had managed to bludgeon myself.

Moving much more cautiously, I picked my way around and through the stony obstructions until I reached the far side of the grotto. The way continued to slope upward as I made my way through a labyrinth I hoped would eventually lead to a way out. At last I felt a breeze tinged with the smell of the forest and was certain escape lay close at hand.

I saw light seeping from above, but at first my fogged brain didn't realize I had truly found my way out. I moved forward until I stood directly beneath the source of the light. It was definitely an opening, though it was partially overgrown with plants, or so I assumed. Even worse, the opening was a good ten feet above me.

I had to find a way to reach it. Perhaps roots from a tree could be twisted together and used to hoist myself up, or I could stack rocks into a pile. A quick exploration conducted by feeling about revealed no roots or rocks, but I did find another surprise: every few feet the dirt walls were braced with wood beams. Clearly, people had been here afore me, and I wondered if the dead body I'd found had some association with the place. Most of the wood beams were rotten; one or two had even buckled causing me to wonder if the whole chamber might not verge on collapse. Clearly, the place was quite old. I returned to the spot beneath the opening.

"Hello!" I called. "Is anyone there?" I listened, heard nothing, then said, "I mean you no harm! I swear it!"

Still no one answered, though judging from the dilapidated condition of the place—as ruined as a harlot's good name—I wasn't surprised. I would have to find a way out on my own. Moving carefully in the dark, I searched for fallen timber to pile high enough to reach the hole. Instead, I tripped over what felt to be a stack of metal bars that I had somehow missed upon my first search. In fact, further exploration revealed the center of the chamber to contain a number of large stacks.

There wasn't enough light so as to guess at their nature, but after weighing a bar in my hand, I thought I knew not only of what they were made, but what this place had once been. The bars were lead and this was a storeroom beneath either a fort or a blockhouse. Only a fort or blockhouse would have such a large quantity of lead, which was frequently transported in bars, the easiest way to move the heavy metal. Merchants often sold single bars of lead to regular folk like myself who melted it down for molding into musket balls. In fact, I had a bar about a third the size of these in my pack.

My pack! My musket! And my traps! For the first since I'd been taken by the monster, I realized all I owned yet lay back in the ruined forest. God's balls *and* bloody hell!

All I now had to my name was my ragged breeches, a hunting shirt, two sleeves from a bearskin coat, and my moccasins. I wiggled my left foot. Make that, moccasin. There wasn't a single thing I had lost that I could afford to do without, but it was the loss of my traps that hurt like a wasp's sting. Not only had they cost me dearly, but they had been the means to what I hoped to become: a trapper, dependent on no one but himself. Just then, however, I wouldn't have minded a little dependence. Say a coat's worth, for instance.

All of the misfortune that had befallen me of late made me feel as if I were being punished by God or fate. Perhaps I was. After all, I had done things of which I was greatly ashamed. Foremost was that back home I had left a fiancée I had no intention of marrying. In fact, once I reached the frontier, I planned on having a missive sent to Rebecca saying that I had perished in a mishap. Then she would be free to marry someone who truly wanted to make a life with her.

I sighed, briefly felt sorry for myself, then decided: So be it. If cursing God or my luck or some other power would remove me from this place and restore my traps to me, then I would have cursed until no breath was left in my body. Since it wouldn't, I could either go forward or lie down and wait to die. And dying didn't suit me.

Using one of the fallen timbers, I jabbed at the opening over my head, pushing vines and whatnot aside. More light now shone through, but vegetation yet covered much of the opening, and down where I stood it was as dark as the underside of a soot-coated cooking pot. Even after I gathered all of the fallen timber, there wasn't a sufficient amount to pile it high enough to allow me to climb free. Instead, I collected all of the lead bars into a single stack. Climbing atop the pile of bars, I found I could just reach the edge of the opening.

Normally, I would have hoisted myself up with little effort, but I was so battered and exhausted, doing so now seemed nigh an impossible task. At first, I thought I might have come all of this way only to be thwarted at the end, but I was nothing if not stubborn. Eventually, and with great effort, I climbed free. As I lay there gasping on the dead grass, I spied a raven feather fluttering nearby. When I finally had the strength, I scooped it up, grateful my totem had been nearby all along. I struggled to my feet, more bone-tired than I had at first appreciated. I was also worse off than I had realized. My clothes were tattered rags, revealing nearly as much skin as they covered. My stomach growled interminably, and

I couldn't recall when I had last eaten. I was dizzy from loss of blood and lack of food. And I had no idea where I was.

Around me lay the ruins of a fort (or blockhouse), though the ruins I saw no more resembled a fort than a seventy-year-old crone did a sixteen-year-old girl. Where the roof had once been I now stared up at the flat, featureless sky of a winter day. As I thought about it, I wondered if I might not be mistaken about this having been a fort. After all, this part of the frontier had only opened up four or five years earlier, and these ruins were far older than that. Maybe Gerard would know.

The sun hung farther east in the sky than when I had last seen it, meaning I had passed at least one whole night underground since I'd first encountered the beast. As if to verify, my stomach again growled with impressive fervor. I looked about for some belly timber—any edible plant, animal, or bug—but saw nothing. What winter had not shriveled up or killed, it had driven deep into hiding, the exception being fools like myself who had not the good sense to come in out of the cold.

A bad bout of shivering set in, and I knew I needed to get moving. I pushed through the thick bushes beyond the fallen walls, then made my way up a nearby bluff. Despite how much time had passed, I knew I couldn't have traveled far from the cave. A mile or two at most. From the top of the trail, I hoped I might find at least a hint of my whereabouts—and those of the creature.

In fact, the bluff did afford me a good view—of the damnable lake and the rocky outcropping right next to the beast's cave. *This* was all the distance I had come? Hell, a suckling could crawl that far, if only to get to its mother's teat. If I were to shout, the damned monster might even hear me. With a start, I realized how exposed I was and dropped to the ground.

I quietly backed up until the shadowy forest again hid me. Now that I knew where the cave was, I knew which way not to go. But which way *to* go? My brief glimpse from atop the bluff hadn't revealed the direction the blown-down forest lay, and where, I fervently hoped, my musket and pack yet remained. Then there was the matter of the girl, though I could conjure no scenario in which she yet lived. Of course, I would search for her anyway.

Since I wasn't sure which way to go, I elected to head directly away from the beast's cave until I could later get my bearings. When a frozen creek presented itself an hour later, I was so spent I wondered if I had the wherewithal to break through the ice so as to slake my thirst. I found the most likely-looking spot, then tried to smash through the ice with my fist, then my foot. Alas, the ice was stronger than I. I scrounged about until I found a sharp-edged rock with which I attacked the ice, eventually cracking it like the shell of a walnut. The water tasted sweeter than the meat of any nut, and I drank greedily until my tongue went numb. A stand of withered cattails stood nearby. I broke them free of the ice and ravenously devoured the roots. Cattails and creek water—Lenten fare indeed. Wasn't I *quite* the frontiersman?

I caught a glimpse of myself in the water. Four parallel scratches started above my left eyebrow, descended over my eye and onto my left cheek. It was a wonder the cat hadn't blinded me. My face would be scarred, but I cared little. The scratches weren't terribly deep, and I thought over time the scars might fade enough to be not much noticeable—not that there was anyone in my life at present even to take notice. I splashed water onto my face, winced from the biting cold, yet washed out the wounds as best I could. I had no poultice of apple peels and ash with which to ward off infection; I could do no more than hope that the terrible affliction would not appear.

Now that I had washed away the blood, I studied my reflection again. My already thin face looked even leaner. My black hair had come loose from its binding and hung down to my shoulders. My eyes tended toward a brown so dark as to be black in certain lights—or, I was told, in certain moods. As always, my face was brown from being out-a-doors, yet showed a goodly number of freckles scattered over my nose and cheeks. I was rather darkly complected to have so many freckles, but it was a Seavey trait shared by all the men in my family. Handsome was a word I had heard frequently to describe myself, though, frankly, I couldn't see it.

Rebecca had thought me comely, however, and I had always felt bad for not feeling the same toward her. She was not unattractive, but had stirred nothing in me beyond a genial tolerance for her company. Frankly, no woman had ever stirred me much. I didn't dislike them, mind you, but found I shared little in common with them. It was like stabling horses and cows in the same barn. They got along just fine, but weren't apt to spend much time together.

Women were so different from me. Whereas my interests were hunting and being out-a-doors, the females I knew were oriented toward children and clothes and talking. Lord, could they talk, and my own reticence was not something upon which they looked favorably. Whilst it seemed true that most other men also had little in common with women, there did always seem to be an unstoppable attraction that bound them together like salt to the sea. I had yet to find a woman with whom I shared such a bond.

I shivered again as a cold breeze prodded at me. Perhaps now wasn't the best time for such self-reflection, though I doubted I would have much appetite for it, no matter how improved my situation.

When I'd eaten and drunk my fill of dirty roots and water, I pushed on. As I walked, my eyes tracked over the quiescent forest, mist from the river having coated everything in ice so that nothing moved in the gentle wind. Another hour passed, maybe more. The river fell away and I was again deep in the forest. The air was so cold that as I exhaled, a fine coating of ice deposited itself upon my upper lip. With each passing moment, it was becoming harder to think clearly, and I knew the cold was gnawing away at what little strength I yet possessed.

Like livestock freed from their pen, my thoughts took to wandering, and they went far and wide indeed. One minute I remembered crying when Mother died (I was six and had not cried since), the next I watched raptly as a tree limb swayed in the wind, and then I was wondering if I would ever see Africa. Africa! Soon I would be babbling like one of those addlepated soldiers who had taken a Lobsterback's musket ball to the head during the Revolution.

So lost was I in my thoughts that I almost walked right into the

Indian on the trail. He, in turn, was so wrapped up in studying something on the ground that he neither heard nor saw me coming until it was too late for either of us to flee.

He slowly rose and turned to face me. An enormous bearskin hung from his shoulders, but his arms were bare. Several feathers adorned his black hair, which was pulled back into a ponytail. Despite my wandering mind, or perhaps because of it, I thought the Indian had the most appealing face I had ever seen on a man. Several elaborate tattoos adorned his arms, and for some reason I desired to touch them. For a moment, I was worried I had said this out loud—not that he was likely to understand me anyway. Even so, it was an odd thing to think. I must have been more unbalanced than I realized.

My attention returned to the brave, who watched me intently. Few Indians remained in the area where I grew up, so my experience with them was circumscribed at best. In fact, I had met only one— the old man with whom I traded for the belt I had used on the girl (yet another item I was now without). Mostly, I knew Indians were angry and resentful toward settlers and would likely welcome the chance to avenge themselves on a solitary, unarmed white man lost in their territory. I absentmindedly touched my hand to head. I hoped it didn't hurt too much when he scalped me.

"It's good hair," I jabbered. "A fine trophy." To my surprise, the Indian smiled. I supposed he was imagining what he might get in trade for my hair.

The brave was taller than I—unusual for an Indian—and possessed broad shoulders that his hair would just touch when unbound. His skin was nut-brown—not red as implied by the slur "Redskin"—and his face was clear and smooth, untouched by the pox. A small tattoo of a turtle lay upon his right cheek, but most striking were his black eyes that, despite their color, seemed warm and inviting.

For all my incongruous admiration of his features, he was an Indian, I was a white man, and we weren't likely to end up swapping stories over a jug of barley ale. In all probability, one of us was about to die, and something told me it wouldn't be he.

I wasn't going without a fight, however. I may have been shorter, but I was heavier, more muscled, and, normally, strong as a bear. On more than one occasion I had taken on fellows who weighed half as much again as myself. Under regular circumstances, I'd wager I could have taken this brave two out of three times. These circumstances, however, were far from common.

Hoping to catch the Indian off-guard, I lunged at him, but my legs buckled beneath me. I fell to my knees just as the brave rushed forward to bury his tomahawk deep in my skull.

◆

My head throbbed. In fact, it hurt so bad, I could barely think. Not because the Indian had tomahawked me, but because I had struck my head on the ground when I fell. Even after I lay there dazed and defenseless, the Indian did not proceed to scalp me, stab me, or do anything else lethal in nature. Instead, to my amazement, he helped me, though everything had such a dream-like quality that I wasn't entirely certain my appraisal of the situation was accurate.

By now I shook so violently from the cold, I thought it possible I might shake loose a tooth. The Indian drew the bearskin from his shoulders, solicitously placing it over me. When I yet shivered, he vigorously rubbed my arms and legs to warm me. Next he gripped my hands in his own, rubbing them together as he blew on them. His breath was warm and smelled of sweetgrass. Needless to say, his actions were not what I expected.

At some point I must have drifted off, for when I next became aware of my surroundings, a campfire burned right there on the trail. But it wasn't very big and even after it blazed brightly, I still trembled from an iciness that felt as if it had chilled my very blood. The Indian studied me intently, then removed his shirt and deerskin leggings so that he remained clad only in his breeches.

Yet dazed and delirious, I wasn't sure what was going on. I thought maybe he planned on killing me after all and simply wanted to keep blood off his clothes. Who knew Indians could be so practical? Even though I doubted he would speak English, I tried telling him I meant him no harm, but he only shushed me, climbed under the bearskin and wrapped me in his arms. I was so astounded by this that I wouldn't have been surprised if next a beaver had emerged from the woods and declaimed the Lord's Prayer then and there.

Lying with his body pressed to mine, the Indian pushed us so close to the flames that I feared the bearskin would catch on fire. All the while, he kept kneading my flesh, as if determined to keep my blood moving on his own. Such tactics were not unknown to me and were commonly used to treat victims of frostbite. Little by little, the shivering subsided and my mind again drifted off.

The Indian must have shifted about because at some later time, I again became aware of his body pressed against mine. Groggily, I noted that he smelled of tobacco, but also something spicy, like cloves or coriander. I rather liked the scent. I also—rather bizarrely—liked the feel of his hot skin against my own. I felt safe, cozy even, as odd as that notion was given my current circumstances. But then an alarmingly salacious tingle began spreading outward from my groin. I hoped I might yet be asleep and having one of those arousing dreams that frequented me if I had not recently sought release by my own hand.

Afore I realized what was happening, I grew stiff. Whether I dreamt it or not, the Indian again massaged my body; and when his hand next drifted lower, he encountered my stiffening roger. I thought his fingers lingered there a moment, but then they moved on. For some reason, I imagined his hand creeping back and taking ahold of me. I even wondered what it might feel like, should release come from his touch. I ascribed such powerfully peculiar thoughts to how badly injured I was.

I became aware of a growing pressure in the small of my back. At first I was puzzled, until I realized that the Indian had himself become aroused—his roger was what I felt. *What the blazes is that about?* I wondered. This *had* to be a dream after all. I desperately hoped so anyway, because for some odd reason the feel of him against my flesh only inflamed me further. In fact, I feared I verged on releasing my seed—not something I wished to do in the presence of any man, much less a savage. Whether I dreamt or not, I struggled to drive away the hot, pulsing feeling in my groin afore it was too late.

I must have succeeded, for the next time I awoke I wasn't the least bit aroused, even though my flesh was hotter than afore. In fact, I didn't think I had ever been so feverish. I was desperately parched, the inside of my mouth as gummy as a drained honeycomb. The Indian knelt in front of me. He placed a cool hand on my hot forehead. "You are burning up with fever," he said. "You need someone with healing skills greater than my own."

Needless to say, I was startled to hear him speak English. Too exhausted to query him about it, I closed my eyes and listened to him hurry away. I vaguely wondered where he was going.

I felt so hot, so ill, so weak that I doubted I would ever rise again. As my mind drifted toward sleep, the final bizarre thought I had was that if the Indian's visage were the last thing I saw, that wouldn't be so bad.

chapter four

Waking from a deep sleep, I opened my eyes to find a snarling wolf bearing down on me. Yelling a warning, I reached for a musket that wasn't there, only to nearly fall out of bed. *Bed? Wolf? Where the blazes was I?* I hadn't lain upon a bed in nearly three months. Only then did I realize the wolf's head wasn't moving.

Like the jaws of a spring-trap coming together, the pieces snapped into place, and I realized I was in no danger. I was in a cabin and the wolf was dead and mounted over the bunk in which I slept.

Wildered in my wits, I sat up, trying to gather my scattered thoughts. Unfortunately, they wriggled about like so many tadpoles in a pond, and I couldn't really make sense of them. The last thing I remembered was the Indian rushing me. I must have escaped him, but for the life of me, I couldn't recall how.

Struggling to clear my mind from the cottony remains of such a deep sleep, I took stock of my surroundings. The cabin was small, if well constructed, and consisted of one room, perhaps twenty by twenty feet. The logs fit together snugly, and any gaps had been neatly patched with mud. The roof was low, a wood and mud chimney the only opening in the cabin other than the door. A betty lamp perched on a table threw off a bright circle of light.

A fire blazed in the fireplace, the flickering flames dancing upon the dozens of glossy furs hanging on the walls. Three chairs sat around the table whilst a fourth tilted back against a wall. The table, as well as the chairs, looked to be well made; I knew someone here had considerable skills when it came to working with wood. The cabin had quite a homey feel for something so far removed from civilization.

The door swung open and a white man carrying an armful of wood burst in. I tried to rise, but my whole body felt beaten and bruised and stiffer than untanned deer hide.

"What's going on?" he asked. "I heard yelling inside. Is something amiss?"

I shook my head, glancing at the wolf.

"Thank goodness for that," said the man with obvious relief, and I felt the fool for having yelled so childishly. I also felt annoyed as this stranger already had the advantage over me. For who respects a fool?

"I'm glad you're awake," the stranger said, apparently surprised to find me thus.

The fellow was chitty-faced, with a long, thin nose to match. He was tall—long-shanked and long-armed ("The Duke of Limbs," my father had always quipped about such chaps). He was only a few years older than myself and wore his brown hair pulled back in a ponytail that only served to accentuate his angular features. In fact, with that sharp beak of a nose, he reminded me of nothing so much as a hatchet given human form. He was clad in deerskin pants, a linsey shirt, and a proper vest—an odd combination for the frontier. He looked queerly bookish, and if it weren't for his tanned face and rough-looking hands, I would have sworn he was newer to the Ohio frontier than I.

"Can you talk?" he asked. "Or is your tongue as badly injured as the rest of you?"

"It might be the only part of me not to be aching," I said.

The man smiled. "Otherwise, how do you feel?"

Insane. Bewildered. Lost. But he need not know any of that. "Thirsty," I said.

He went to a bumkin standing next to a table. From a shelf he took down a large noggin into which he ladled whiskey that he then brought to me. "I've got apple brandy, if you'd rather."

I shook my head. "This will do…" Since I didn't know the man's name, I let my voice trail off.

"John," he said. "John Chapman."

"Thanks, John." I quaffed the whiskey. Whilst it was far superior to water—known derisively as Adam's Ale—it was still a piss-poor excuse for a beverage. I had drunk teas that were stronger, not that I was ungrateful for that which I could not even pay.

When I finished drinking, John quickly refilled my cup and I drank that as well. I wiped my mouth with the back of my hand, then said, "Sorry if I seem a bit daft, John, but where might this place be?"

"Well, this humble abode is my cabin, but Hugh's Lick is the closest settlement, though I think of that place more like a boil on the arse of the world than a town. It's about five miles from here."

Hugh's Lick? That's where Gerard was supposed to be living! It was about time a damn break had come my way. Frankly, after enduring freak windstorms, bizarre creatures, and Indian attacks, I was due a decent streak of good luck. I wondered if John knew Gerard. If my luck truly was holding, then he wouldn't. For if Gerard were yet in Hugh's Lick, being known as his brother might not be the best thing.

Gerard wasn't only my brother; he was also a rapscallion who had made our surname synonymous with "cheater" and "lout," something I had been trying to live down since we were both boys. Even so, he was my brother, and I at least owed him notice of my arrival. Especially since finding him was the pretense under which I had left my fiancée.

"Sounds as if you don't much care for Hugh's Lick," I said.

"I most emphatically do *not,*" John replied. "But then I pretty much dislike any place with more than four people. Any more than that is a pox that needs to be done away with."

"Then I best hope there aren't already more than three folks here," I said. "Otherwise you might toss me out into the cold."

John laughed, then said, "You needn't fear that."

"I'm Cole," I said, making no mention of my last name, nor the fact that I had a brother residing in the apparent pox that was Hugh's Lick.

"It's nice to meet you, Cole," he replied. "Though I can't say we was expecting newcomers this time of year."

Nor had I expected to be here, I thought. Only Gerard's first letter in years, along with my realization three months ago that I was going to have to go through with marrying Rebecca, had foolishly driven me to venture onto the frontier with winter looming. Once again, I didn't volunteer this to John. Instead, I only said, "It's nice to meet you as well." I paused, then added, "This might sound a bit odd, and normally I'm not so featherheaded, but I don't remember much at the moment. How, exactly, did I come to be here?"

"Been wondering that ourselves," John said. "Although, I suspect by 'here' you mean this cabin, whilst we mean 'here,' as in the middle of bleeding nowhere." I nodded my agreement whilst wondering whom he meant by "we." John continued, "Our friend Pakim found you injured in the woods. He brought you here for safekeeping."

"Pakim?" I asked. "That sounds like an Indian name."

"It is at that," John said.

"An *Indian* brought me here?" I asked. Vague memories of my encounter with the Indian surfaced in my mind. Had he not attacked me then?

"That's right," John said. "You sound as if you find that objectionable. Is that so?"

"What?" I asked. "No. I'm just confused. I do recollect an Indian, but I thought he tried to kill me."

"Are you saying that Pakim did this to you?" John asked, angrily gesturing to my injuries. "I hope not, because if you are, I'll know you to be a liar."

Taken aback by his reaction, I shook my head. "The Indian didn't do this. It was the—" My voice trailed off.

"The what?" John asked.

"The panther," I said, alarmed by how near I had come to speaking the truth. I couldn't announce that I had encountered a shape-shifting beast anymore than I could claim I had seen angels astride goats. Nor did I dare mention the girl for fear of casting suspicion regarding her attack upon myself. "There was a storm," I said. "A terrible windstorm that blew an entire forest down on top of me. Then a panther attacked. I wandered for a long time afore I all but stumbled into this Pakim fellow. I don't remember what happened after that. I guess I just figured, the way events had been unfolding, he would scalp me. He obviously didn't, and I owe him thanks."

John nodded curtly. "That you do. And you can give it to him shortly. He should be here soon."

"Honestly, John, my memory is piss-poor at the moment. I meant no offense. It will be my honor to meet your friend." I spoke sincerely, and John looked mollified. "By the way, how long have I been here?"

"Three days, by my reckoning."

Three days! I could scarcely believe so much time had passed. And with each passing day, I was less likely to recover my lost belongings, already a dubious prospect at best. Clutching the blanket to my waist, I rose on wobbly legs and looked about for my hunting shirt and pants.

"Careful," John said. "You're badly injured and had a terrible fever." He placed his hand against my face and some memory stirred, something about the Indian. "You're yet a touch warm," said John. "But nothing serious, I warrant. Gwennie had to give you some remedies she thought might make you yet feel odd, so you best not push yourself too hard."

I assumed Gwennie to be his wife, and she was right about my feeling odd. My head felt as if it were detached from the rest of my body. So much so, I had to resist the urge to check that it wasn't floating away. I hoped Gwennie was a skilled healer, as infections were more often likely to kill men than whatever caused the injury in the first place. My hand touched my face, and I flinched to feel how tender it was. "I must be quite the sight," I said.

"Well now, you don't look too bad," John said. He regarded me a moment longer, then laughed. "All right, that's a lie. You look like something chewed on you a good long while, then spat you out when you didn't taste so nice. But you look a far sight better than when you got here. And that was after Pakim cleaned you up where he found you."

Again some recollection about the Indian tried to come forth, but I couldn't quite fish up the memory.

"Sounds like I owe Gwennie my thanks, as well as Pakim," I said.

John agreed. "Gwennie knows her plants and ointments and whatnot, that's for certain. She dosed you good with laudanum and then spent the better part of the first day foraging in the woods for goldenseal. She said without it you were as likely to die as a babe birthed in January."

Laudanum was made from poppies and was quite powerful, while goldenseal was as rare as an honest politician. "Maybe I can repay her, Pakim, and you somehow," I offered.

John waved his hand. "I don't keep track of accounts, Cole. Nor do Gwennie and Pakim. I do the just thing and expect the same of others."

I knew then that John was a little naive. In my experience, expecting people to do the right thing was like expecting vipers to not bite. It simply went against their nature. Even so, I tried to follow my mother's wishes and do good by other folk. I just didn't expect much from them in return.

"I should get dressed," I said, again looking about for my clothes.

"I suppose you should at that," John said. "Only thing is your pants were ruined beyond saving. Gwennie has your hunting shirt. She's trying to mend it."

"Oh," I said, wondering what I would do for pants. Running about naked was fine for savages, but I wasn't about to do so. Especially not when it was colder outside than a hangman's smile.

"You look about the same size as Palmer," John said. "There is an extra pair of his pants at the foot of the bed."

I wondered if Palmer was John's son, though John didn't look old enough to have a son who could wear the same size pants as I. The pants were only deerskin, not nearly as warm as my linsey ones, but beggars couldn't be choosers, and I was clearly the former. "Thank you," I said. As I rose, a wave of dizziness nearly knocked me back down. Lord, I was as fainthearted as an old maid getting rogered for the first time.

"You're very welcome." John began folding an already folded shirt whilst studying me surreptitiously. "You say a cougar tried to make a meal out of you, Cole? Mighty odd that, cougars usually being such shy animals."

So John doubted my story. Why shouldn't he? I was telling half-truths, after all. Given that I didn't believe half of what I'd seen, I wasn't about to be honest either. The last thing I needed was people thinking I was off my nob. On the other hand, it did me no good to arouse the suspicions of the very person helping me. Therefore, I had to tell him something convincing. But first, I had to sit afore I passed out.

Once I settled back on the bed and my vision stopped bobbing about like a leaf upon a river, I debated what to tell John. I figured starting with the truth might lend the whole story a ring of credence. Such a tactic was a bit like trying to marry off a horse-faced daughter by telling potential suitors how pretty her eyes were (and, I feared, about as likely to succeed).

"It was a panther that attacked me, all right," I said. "But it was starving something fierce, and that made it much more ferocious than usual. It ambushed me from above. I fought it off, but got mauled good as you can see."

John nodded. "And somehow your supplies were lost when the cougar attacked you?"

Now I better understood John's disbelief. He wondered where my belongings were. Only an idiot, or someone running from something, would be out on the frontier with no supplies at all. My mind flew back to the bloody, dying girl, the erstwhile panther, the monster, and my fighting it. They weren't memories to be cherished in one's dotage.

"Something troubles you?" John asked, apparently seeing the look on my face.

I shrugged. "Just remembering what happened is all."

John looked chagrined. "I'm sorry," he said. "I have no business making you talk of such unpleasantness."

"You needn't apologize, John." Again, I thought of telling him about the girl, but I feared once I said anything about her, it would become obvious I wasn't telling the whole truth—a truth I couldn't tell him. "I'd stopped to eat," I explained. "So I wasn't wearing my pack when the attack happened. I had even set my musket against a tree whilst I wandered off for a look at the view. That was when the panther struck." I added the part about looking at the view to make my story sound more authentic, even though only a fool would ever walk away from their musket whilst admiring *scenery*.

"Well, that mistake you shan't make again," John said, apparently having no trouble believing I was the sort to do such a foolish thing. "Things are different on the frontier than back east, Cole. Here, every day there are a half-dozen chances to die. But not to worry. Every greenhorn makes that mistake once. Fortunately, you survived."

Me, a *greenhorn?* I had killed bears, slept under the stars for months at a time, and could survive in the woods with nothing but my wits. Who was John to disparage me? Especially since he looked more like a scholar than a frontiersman himself.

I abruptly realized how foolish my thoughts were. After all, which of us was it who had no pants of his own? And it was better he think me a greenhorn rather than a bedlamite telling insane stories about panthers that turn into monsters. Besides, he had a point. I *had* been stupid to lay down my musket, and without even the excuse of being a greenhorn—especially given that the poor girl had obviously been attacked by something.

"Aye, but it was a costly mistake to make," I said, followed by a long sigh. I realized how exhausted I was despite having just slept three days. "I lost everything, including the traps I planned on using to establish myself." I laughed ruefully as I stroked the deerskin pants. "Now I don't even own a pair of britches."

John said, "Those you can keep, Cole. I'm sure Palmer shan't mind. And we've got other things you can have as well. Maybe we can even scrounge you up a trap or two. We'll have you back on your feet in no time. That's a promise."

My twenty years on earth hadn't been easy. I was a loner, and most everything I owned had come by dint of my own iron will, with breaks from others so few as to be nearly nonexistent. Therefore, I couldn't help but be a little suspicious of John's generosity. Whether he had ulterior motives or not, I couldn't say for sure. But I knew one thing, though. John might not keep accounts, but I would not forget what I owed him.

"Are you all right, Cole?" John asked.

I nodded. "Just a bit of soreness is all," I said. "And John? Thanks. You've been very kind."

The rumble of approaching hoofbeats rattled the cabin, and John said, "That's Palmer and Pakim returning. Gwennie's likely to be with them, so if you're feeling up to it, maybe you should get dressed."

Even as I uncouth as I could be (quite, according to some), I had no desire to meet these strangers as naked as the day I had been born. Stiffly, I stood and pulled on the pants. Every muscle in my body barked in complaint, but I persevered. John also gave me a pair of moccasins and a clean shirt that I pulled on as a white man and an Indian woman entered the cabin. They were followed a moment later by the brave I had encountered on the trail. As soon as I saw his face, it all came back to me. I remembered everything—his rescuing me, the fire, my stiff roger, *his* stiff roger.

God's balls—it had all happened, hadn't it?

I blushed, something I hadn't done since the age of six. Then I remembered that nothing truly untoward had happened between the Indian and me.

Pakim saw me and smiled broadly. "See, Palmer! My prayers to Manitto have been heard. My friend is up and awake!" I doubted I had ever seen a face as open and trusting as his right then. And he certainly didn't seem to think me loathsome for the odd fashion in which my body had responded to his. Perhaps he understood I had been so injured as to be unaccountable for my actions. Of course, the question yet remained as to *why* it happened (on both of our accounts, now that I thought about it), but that was something to be pondered later, if at all.

The Indian was dressed much the same way he had been when I had run into him—a deerskin shirt and pants, his beaded bandolier bag slung over one shoulder, the shaggy bearskin coat he had wrapped me in.

"Everybody, this is Cole," John said. "He woke up a little while ago and was relating what circumstances have brought him to us. It we seems we have a cougar to thank for our unexpected visitor."

A fellow a few years younger than myself stepped forward and held out his hand. "Nice to meet'cha, Cole. I'm Palmer." Palmer was perhaps five years younger than John, which meant I was mistaken about his being John's son. Perhaps they were yet related—brothers or cousins—though I saw little resemblance between the two. Unlike John, his face was full and robust. Too, there was a freshness to him, as if his youth hadn't entirely passed into memory. Offsetting that innocence were blue eyes that looked both sad and wise, and I wondered what he had experienced to make them so. He wore his blond hair loose, and it was long enough to touch his broad shoulders. His crooked smile came to him easily—I suspected it was the expression he wore most.

"It's nice to meet you as well, Palmer. By the way, many thanks for the loan of your pants."

"Happy to oblige," he said. "Consider them yours. Let me know if there is anything else I can help out with."

Palmer may not have resembled John, but clearly he was cut from the same cloth.

For the second time, I was struck by a stranger's generosity and again found myself vaguely suspicious. But suspicious of what? There was nothing these men could want from me, certainly nothing material they could gain by helping me. As hard as it was to accept, they actually seemed to be decent, kind fellows. Why, I wondered, was it so hard for me to accept that? The answer, of course, was my brother, Gerard.

"And this," John said, "is Gwennie."

As if I hadn't enough surprises of late, here was one more. Gwennie may have had a white woman's name, but she was definitely an Indian. She was short and stout—and generously endowed with all the curves of her sex. Her long black hair was braided neatly and hung over one shoulder. Puckered lips which made her look as if she had a mouthful of sour cherries were separated by round, rosy cheeks. To complete her dour bearing, hard, black eyes bore into me like an auger into soft wood. Her entire countenance was one of wroth, as if I had already given her offense, but perhaps I was hasty and her outward appearance did not reflect what was within. She was friends with John, after all, and he was certainly full of good chirk.

"How do you do?" I asked, wondering if John had taken her to his bed as an Indian wife. Or perhaps it was Pakim's bed she shared.

"Pah!" she spat. Any lingering notion she might be like John and Palmer vanished like a blown-out candle flame. "What you care how I am?"

Clearly, she didn't like me. Given the permanent look on her furrowed brow, I wondered if she liked anybody. I couldn't stand people like this—ones who acted like they had a bellyful of green apples that made them too ill-tempered to be pleasant to the rest of us. On the other hand, John had said she had dressed my wounds and spent hours looking for goldenseal with which to heal me. No matter how gruff her demeanor, I wanted her to know how much I appreciated her help. No one could ever say Cole Seavey hadn't shown them the proper gratitude.

"I understand from John that you tended to my injuries," I said, as sweetly as if she were my own mother.

"'Tis so," she said curtly. A long-tongued woman she was clearly not. "Though last thing we need out here is another useless white man who can't provide for himself."

And I had thought porcupines were prickly! Even so, I pressed on. "Judging from how much better I already feel, your skill must be considerable. Never have I recovered so quickly from such grievous injuries."

I must have said the right thing as she bobbed her head slightly as if in acknowledgment. She reached into a pocket, removing a glossy, black feather. "I not sure if you want this from your breeches, so I save."

My raven feather! Very much did I want it. "Thank you, Gwennie," I said, reaching for it.

"You are welcome," she said gruffly.

I turned to face the Indian brave. He startled me by stepping close, slipping his hand inside my shirt, and placing it on my bare chest. All thoughts of raven feathers vanished like bats at sunrise.

Pakim stared at me intently for several long seconds. It was unnerving the way his black eyes locked onto mine, but I forced myself to breathe steadily. "Your heart is strong, Friend Cole. I think you'll live a long time yet."

He pulled his hand away, and none too soon. My damned roger, with a mind all its own, had begun to stir like a bear rousing itself from hibernation. As nonchalantly as possible I tried to arrange my shirt to cover it.

"Greetings, Pakim," I said. "I owe you my life."

Pakim shrugged. "Only to God do you owe your life, Cole. I merely hope for your friendship."

Needless to say, after all he had done for me, he had that.

"So what was the word from the village?" John asked Pakim.

Pakim sighed. "Not good. The hunting party returned last night. They killed a brace of gobblers themselves weak from hunger."

John shook his head with dismay. "Soon settlers and Indians alike will all be starving. And relations are already bad enough. We're one attack away from another border war."

"Is there trouble?" I asked.

"There was a drought this summer," Palmer said. "The crops failed, winter has arrived early and damnably cold, and most of the game has moved farther west. Already people go hungry. We'll all be eating bow-wow mutton afore spring arrives."

"That explains the starving panther," I said. "And why I saw so little game." Unless there never had been a panther, but only a shape-shifting beast. Perhaps it was starving, too, though, judging from the number of bones in the cave, I doubted it. Thinking of the bones, I wondered if any settlers had gone missing. I thought about asking, but couldn't see how to do so without raising questions about myself.

"My village is fewer than thirty," said Pakim, "and still we could not gather and raise enough foodstuffs to sustain us through the winter. I do not know what we are to do."

"We're all going to kiss the hare's foot is what we're going to do," said Palmer, referring to the unlucky soul who arrives late for dinner and finds nothing left but the rabbit's foot for his supper.

"Speaking of being late, Palmer, we should head into town then for the assembly," John said. "Murdock doesn't look like kindly upon laggards."

Palmer snorted in disgust. "I've had enough of Murdock," he said. "Nobody elected him leader."

John shrugged. "Well, he's the closest there is to one, and I don't particularly want to be on his bad side, so we're going. Cole, I imagine you'll want to stay here and rest. Perhaps Pakim or Gwennie will consent to keep you company."

Gwennie shook her head. "Other things I must do," she said, then turned to me. "But I return later to change your dressing."

"Of course," I said. I wasn't about to argue with anything this woman had to say.

"Then I will stay with Cole," Pakim said. "I will tell him how Gwennie got drunk last Yuletide and—"

Pakim didn't get to finish speaking because Gwennie snatched a hickory nut off the table and fired it at his head. "You tell story," Gwennie warned, "and one day there will be saltpeter in your food. Then no tender young maids will ask you to warm their beds at night."

I didn't think she was jesting.

Pakim laughed a loud, infectious laugh, as full of chirk as was

John. Oddly, I wished it had been I who made Pakim laugh. "Sister Gwennie," Pakim said, "you know I only have eyes for you."

"Ach!" Gwennie exclaimed. "Such lies you tell. You only man I know who thinks he can talk Brother Bear into giving up his hide without a fight." With that Gwennie marched out of the cabin.

"That's settled then," John said. "Pakim, anything we can bring you from town?"

Pakim wrinkled his nose. "The only thing I want from Hugh's Lick is tidings that it has somehow miraculously disappeared."

Hugh's Lick! Gerard! I had to go with them.

"Wait!" I exclaimed. "I'm coming, too!"

John and Palmer looked betwattled by my outburst, and I couldn't blame them for being confused.

"I forgot John told me we were so close to Hugh's Lick," I said. "That's where I was headed afore I was injured. There's someone in town I need to see."

"A sweetheart, I reckon," said Palmer.

"No," I said, a little too emphatically. I realized the others were waiting for me to volunteer more. "It's an old friend, that's all. Almost like family, you might say."

"Are you sure you feel up to the trip?" John asked.

"Yes. I know I'm a little weak, but I'm all right. Maybe Pakim can come, too?" The suggestion was out of my mouth afore I knew what I was saying, but no one seemed to think it odd.

Palmer shook his head. "Relations between whites and Indians aren't so cordial right now. Pakim wouldn't exactly be welcome in town."

I was relieved. And disappointed. And confused. Why by God's balls did I care if Pakim came or not?

"Cole can ride with me toward town," Pakim said. "You only have Elizabeth to ride, and walking will take you too long. I will wait nearby, then give Cole a ride home."

"Are you certain?" I asked. "I don't want to chance getting you into any trouble."

"I am sure, Friend Cole," Pakim said, already headed outside.

I liked the way he called me "Friend" with his deep, mellifluous voice. "Well, if you say so, Pakim."

"Besides," Pakim added, "somebody has to keep watch over these two. They still get lost between here and the privy."

The sun had already climbed above the trees that ringed the meadow like a dike. Frost coated everything, and I had to be careful not to slip. John had given me a mandillion—an old-fashioned soldier's coat—to wear. It was thick and warm and had two brass buttons affixed to each sleeve. Despite the cold, bright sunshine lit the clearing, and I noticed the woods felt considerably less gloomy here. I wasn't sure if that was really true, or if my newfound company was the reason for my lighter mood. Either way, I was glad for the change.

Pakim mounted a sturdy-looking horse that glanced at me askance and whinnied nervously. He told me her name was Midnight as he affectionately stroked her long neck. I was chary about approaching, worried her sensitive equine nose might pick up traces of the monster that yet clung to me. Pakim extended a hand and effortlessly pulled me up behind him. As I swung upward, pain shot through my battered body, and I yawped noisily.

"My apologies," Pakim said. "Are you all right?"

With teeth clenched, I nodded.

The four of us set out. Whilst I rode with Pakim, John and Palmer rode together on John's horse—named Elizabeth, he told me, for his oldest sister. It was embarrassing to admit, but I'd never afore ridden a horse. I tried to pretend as if I had, and Pakim was kind enough to say nothing as I struggled to stay upright. But when he had to grab me as I very nearly fell, he finally said, "Have you not ridden a horse afore, Cole?"

I admitted I hadn't.

"Squeeze tight with you thighs," he instructed. I did, promptly sending searing pain up both sides of my injured leg. I'd forgotten how badly the panther had mauled me. I gasped, doubting I would forget again.

"Hold on with your arms instead," Pakim said, lifting his up so I could weave mine through his.

I did as instructed, loosely wrapping my arms about his mid-section. He felt good, as solid as an oak tree. Pakim yet had that same smoky scent I had noticed when he had first rescued me. It was a good, masculine smell, and I drew in a deep breath of it. Then I wondered what the blazes I was doing sniffing another man like he was a lady I was courting. Clearly, I was not yet myself.

"Tighter," Pakim said. "I am not some old brave's brittle tobacco pipe." He laughed as he pulled my arms close about his body. As instructed, I held onto him firmly, but not nearly as hard as I suddenly desired. I marveled both at the warmth blazing from him and how good it felt to hold him this way. Again, I wondered why the hell I was acting this way. It was as if I had not only left my old life and fiancée behind, but my right-minded self as well. I relaxed my embrace some—but not too much.

John and Palmer also rode doubled-up, Palmer behind John, his hands resting on John's shoulders. They looked quite at ease with each other, and I wondered how long they had been friends. For a while the four of us rode along in a companionable silence, which pleased me; I felt surprisingly content and wanted to enjoy the experience. That three compatriots, much less complete strangers, were the source of these good feelings was odd, but I simply chose to relish them and leave it at that.

By now, we had been riding for quite some time. The forest canopy grew dense again; in only a few places did sunshine arrow down through the tightly interwoven branches. Where light touched, however, frost briefly sparkled, and I was glad for the splashes of cheerfulness—like laughter in a roomful of dour folk.

Pakim began to hum. Between his gentle voice, the swaying of the horse, and the stillness of the forest, I found myself actually relaxing. Then Pakim slid his hand over mine and began to gently stroke my skin with his thumb. It was a little thing, but I found it the most intimate touch I had ever felt.

I hadn't been afraid of the storm, the cougar, nor even the beast. Pakim's touch, however, scared me nearly to death.

chapter five

I pulled my hand away from Pakim's. His touch unnerved me greatly, but I had no wish to let him know. Instead, I simply said, "My legs are getting stiff. I think I should walk a bit." Pakim eyed me keenly and I wished he would stop, for I deemed him unusually perceptive.

After carefully dismounting, I turned and began walking. I wasn't sure what I thought about these odd feelings I was experiencing. It was like encountering a new taste that is neither entirely enticing nor off-putting, but definitely intriguing. I knew one thing, however: I didn't relish the idea of this odd Indian trying to divine my strange thoughts, especially afore I understood them myself. Fortunately, John and Palmer drew abreast of us, and John asked, "Is everything all right?"

Pakim answered first. "Cole needed to walk a bit."

"We're close to town anyway," said Palmer. "I reckon it not wise for you to come much farther, Pakim."

"I'm much obliged for the ride, Pakim," I said to the Indian.

He smiled and said, "I will wait for you." He studied me for a moment longer, as if still trying to deduce my thoughts. Finally, he rode away, and I had to will myself not to look back. Truly, I was behaving most peculiarly.

Palmer offered to let me ride in his stead, but it genuinely felt good to be walking and thereby working out the kinks in my legs and back. Despite the daylight, an owl hooted nearby, drawing my attention back to the woods. The forest, already dark and gloomy again, grew even more so as we approached town. Thick stands of ash, hemlock, and wild plum trees crowded the trail. Burdock, gallberry, and shinwood choked every gap between the trees, with the result that I could see no farther than three or four feet into the woods—woods that stretched in every direction for untold miles.

It was easy to imagine the monster watching us from only a few strides away, and I was glad when the town hove into view. It occurred to me that Pakim was now alone in these woods, and whilst I was sure he was quite capable of defending himself, he was at a disadvantage not knowing about the beast. There was nothing to done about it now, but hope all would come right.

Founded a year and a half afore, Hugh's Lick was a crude place, even by my standards. Even more than crude, the settlement looked exhausted, as if it had barely made it to the frontier afore wearily slumping down along the banks of a large river. A quick count revealed the town to consist of twenty cabins built in two opposing rows and one blockhouse, the latter being by far the largest and sturdiest structure in town. The purpose of the blockhouse, I knew, was refuge should Indians attack. It had been some time since the last border war, but it was common knowledge that people were yet uneasy.

So many trees had been cut down in town that I thought it possible to cross the whole of it simply by leaping from stump to stump. A few of them had been uprooted from the earth to make room for crops, but most remained upright, like decapitated bodies without the sense to fall over. What a gruesome bent my mind seemed to have taken on this day! I wondered if it were due to lingering effects from my encounter with the beast.

All twenty cabins sat situated along a thoroughfare that had been hacked from the trees. The blockhouse was at this end of town, looking like nothing so much as a mother hen keeping watch over her brood. The forest pressed up against the town from three sides, and I swore it possessed an actual malevolence, as if eager to reclaim the land that had been forcibly taken from it. I knew that come spring, this exposed, frozen earth would dissolve into a sea of mud that would discomfit all who tried to navigate it. Judging from the trash tossed outside the cabins—contents of slop buckets, pieces of rotten vegetables, and rancid chunks of fat—I knew that once July arrived the smell of the place would be rank.

In part, I had come to the frontier in search of a home, something I hadn't had since my mother had died when I was six. Yes, I had shared a house with my father and Gerard, but Gerard was Father's favorite, and they were complete without me. Where the home I desired might be, I didn't yet know, but I knew one thing for certain: It wasn't to be found in this sorry-looking pigsty of a town.

John explained that there were thirty families in Hugh's Lick, only two-thirds of which lived right near town. The others, he said, were scattered up and down the river, where they could stake out larger claims, grow crops, and run livestock in the woods. The most influential family in Hugh's Lick was the Burkes, though they weren't one of the families that lived in town. Their influence stemmed from there being so many of them—six grown sons, the oldest being Murdock Burke, and their sundry wives and children—and the fact that they had come to the frontier so well provisioned that they had become Hugh's Lick's general store. Rumor had it that Murdock had invested his entire life's savings, possibly thousands of dollars, in buying supplies and land around the town. Clearly, he had staked his future on the success of the place.

"People should be gathering soon," John said. "Murdock called for an assembly at noon to discuss what to do about food."

Palmer snorted. "I can't wait to hear what brilliant ideas he's got. Most likely it'll turn out he's got foodstuffs hidden somewhere that he'll sell on credit to everyone for five times their fair value. He's a bastard, that one."

"He better have more ideas than that," John said. "Personally, I think most folks—excepting us, of course—should make for Fort Braden afore the snows finally fall and they're all trapped here."

John had explained that the bitter cold, which usually arrived in February, had struck back in early October, though hardly a single snowflake had been seen. Now it was late November, and everyone feared that once the snow did arrive it would be with a vengeance.

I kept my eyes peeled for Gerard, but saw only numerous ragged-looking bantlings bundled up against the cold whilst they played stoolball together. No one came out to greet us, and those few adults I saw eyed us suspiciously—especially John and Palmer. For the first time, it occurred to me to wonder if my new friends might have even a worse reputation than Gerard, whose sole positive skills were his ability to woo innocent girls and his accuracy in throwing knives. Such a thing was hard to believe until I recalled that John and Palmer were friends with Pakim and Gwennie. Even I knew most white folk took a swindler of their own kind over the best Indian. The swindler might figuratively stab you in the back, but it would be a very real tomahawk that the Indian would use.

I would have to tread carefully amongst the townsfolk, but in truth I was already in too deep and owed too much to John and the others to throw them over to get in the good graces of this frontier riffraff. It figured that I would fall in with the outsiders amongst the outsiders.

A crowd began to gather in the space in front of the blockhouse. This was the area least riddled with tree stumps and the logical place for any meetings to take place. As more folks appeared, I surmised the meeting was about to commence.

"I don't see Murdock," Palmer said. "You reckon these folks got the gumption to start without him?"

"I don't know," John said. "But here comes a sight less welcome than maggots in my meat."

I glanced up as a white-haired fellow dressed all in black strode toward us, a half-dozen men and women scurrying after him. The white-haired man clutched a large bucket in his left hand, and the palm of a small, chubby-faced girl in his right. She stumbled alongside him, trying to keep up. His hurried pace and indifference toward the girl angered me. I stifled my urge to scoop her up so she could ride on my shoulders.

"Who's that ill-bred fellow?" I asked.

"That's Dilly," Palmer said. "And that's his five-year old daughter, Anna. She's second-sighted."

"Is she really? Or is it a sham to get a few coins out of folks?" Growing up with Gerard had imparted a strong sense of skepticism to my dealings with others.

John shrugged. "Who's to say? Folks around here seem to believe in her."

"I've heard she was born on Christmas Eve," said Palmer. "Girls born then are renowned for their unusual gifts."

"What does she do precisely?" I asked.

"Lots of things, if you believe Dilly," Palmer said. "Of course, you have to be able to understand him first. He's from the Northeast and talks *ah-fully* funny. Personally, I don't place much stock in divination. Supposedly, Anna can read the entrails of animals. Some whisper that she and Dilly dabble in necromancy, but I couldn't speak to that."

Everywhere outside the safety of the large towns and cities, divination, good-luck charms, and spells to ward off bad luck were part of the fabric of daily life. Priests, ministers, and other virtuous souls disapproved publicly of such goings-on, but even they always seemed to be around whenever someone reputed to have the gift was present.

Dilly came to a stop next to one of the tree stumps. He plunged his hands into the bucket, wrestled with something for a moment, then raised up the writhing form of a very fat, foot-long pike. He plopped the silvern fish onto the tree stump, its bony teeth gleaming menacingly as it thrashed about. One meaty hand pressed the fish downward to keep it from squirming off the stump. Next to it, he laid a stubby but lethally sharp-looking knife. Other settlers came out of their cabins, and soon there were more than thirty folk gathered about.

"I caught this heah pike 'neath a midnaht moon," Dilly said in his thick northeastern accent. "Annah's gonna read its guts so's to tell us what kind of wintah to expect the rest of the yeah." He turned to the girl, pulling her forward. "Come along, Annah," he ordered.

The tiny slip of a child looked scared to death. Her bloodless lips pressed tightly together as she shook her head no.

Dilly didn't argue. Instead, he leaned over the girl and snatched a doll from her right hand.

"No!" Anna squealed. "Please, Papa! No!"

"Are ya gonna do as I tell ya then?" Dilly asked.

"Papa, I'm scairt," Anna whimpered.

Dilly let go of the fish, picked up the knife, and sliced off a chunk of the doll's leg.

Anna shrieked as if it were her own flesh that had been cut.

I cringed, then glanced around at the crowd as they watched. A few people looked dismayed, but the rest seemed not perturbed in the least. The welfare of this child was of no more concern to them than that of their neighbor's dairy cow. Perhaps it was even less, for the cow provided milk for which they might trade, whereas the girl ate food they might otherwise have had themselves. I was as interested in divination as any normal man. In fact, I considered myself a fine reader of bugs. But this wasn't right. "I'm going to put a stop to this," I whispered to John.

He grabbed my arm and whispered back, "Don't. I tried once, and the town nearly strung me up. It only angered Dilly that much more, and he treated Anna even worse."

By now the sobbing Anna had relented. Guided by her father's hand, she used the knife to slice open the belly of the still thrashing pike. Bright red blood spurted forth from the fish, spraying both girl and tree stump.

"Go ahead, Annah," Dilly instructed. "Ya know what to do next."

With tears running down her cheeks, Anna put her hand inside the pike. Each time the fish jerked, the poor child jumped, but her father pressed her to continue. Soon the pike's organs—heart, liver, a bulging stomach, and all the rest—lay spread out over the stump. The pike lay still at last. A change had come over Anna as well. She no longer cried, and in some way I couldn't identify, she no longer even seemed present. It was as if she had taken refuge deep inside herself, leaving only this eldritch expression upon her face.

"Tell us, Annah," Dilly commanded. "What do ya say about the wintah?"

Anna gripped the pike's liver in her small, chapped hand. Suddenly, she started to shiver violently. "It's so cold," she said.

"And how long is the cold heah for, Annah?" he asked.

Anna dropped the liver and whispered, "Always."

Dilly grunted as if dismayed. "Now squeeze out the stomach the way I showed ya."

Anna had to use both hands to hold the pike's bulging stomach. Even then she couldn't grip it long enough to squeeze out the contents without her father's help. Despite my disgust with Dilly's bullying, I was curious and leaned forward to see what the fish had swallowed. A smaller pike, nearly identical to the first, slid forth.

"What does *that* mean?" a stolid-looking woman dressed all in gray asked.

"It can't be good," someone else said.

"Annah?" Dilly said. "Do ya see anything?"

The girl stared straight ahead, then abruptly looked up. We all turned to follow her gaze as a raven alighted on the bare, bobbing limb of a dogwood tree. Given the grim atmosphere of the day, I suspected this time the bird bore ill tidings. The very smell of them was in the air. The raven turned its head back and forth several times, then called out *quork, quork, quork* in its harsh, guttural tones.

"It called out thrice," said a burly fellow with a beard. "It scents death on somebody."

"Maybe it's Addy," whispered a woman next to me. "She's still missing."

"Or Firenzi," said another man. "Something is wrong with his blood so that he can't eat, drink, or piss."

"Then why doesn't the damnable bird fly around his chimney and be gone?" asked a woman who must have shared the belief that when a raven circled a cabin, someone inside would die.

The raven cocked its head. *Quork, quork, quork,* it repeated, predicting another death. The sound was clear and carried far in the frigid air.

Several people gasped.

"Does someone else suffer from a churchyard cough?" asked the bearded man. "I've not heard talk of anyone else soon to be buried."

Quork, quork, quork, said the raven. Then again, *Quork, quork, quork.*

"Make it stop!" someone shouted.

"We should go," a man urged his wife, but she stood transfixed as the bird foresaw more deaths.

The raven's gaze fell on John, Palmer, and myself. A long moment of silence hung in the air. Then again it called out, *Quork, quork, quork.*

By now people were starting to panic. Even I felt unsettled—for the bird had looked right at us. *Or maybe it had looked at someone beyond us,* I thought hopefully. Never had I ever heard a raven warn of so many deaths. It seemed the bird foretold of disease or disaster striking the town. Perhaps it saw the threat of widespread starvation that loomed deeper into the winter.

Someone threw something at the raven, but it only hopped to another branch afore issuing yet another menacing call. Others began yelling, and I thought people were about to lose control when the urgent clattering of hoofbeats over frozen earth finally drew everyone's attention from the raven.

A settler on a white horse raced into the midst of the crowd, yelling wildly. Several of the men who had been watching Dilly scurried toward the new arrival as I glanced uncertainly at John and Palmer. They looked as uneasy as I felt. Unease became outright alarm when a woman's shriek pierced the air. Other hysterical screams followed, quickly giving away to a tumultuous hurry-scurry amongst the townsfolk.

John, Palmer, and I hurried forward.

"That's Abe Lobb that just rode in," Palmer said. Abe, a burly fellow, looked to be in his thirties and sported dark, brown muttonchops on each side of his face. "His daughter went missing four days ago, and something tells me he ain't come home with good news. Maybe that's what the raven's calls meant."

Maybe, I thought. *But the raven had predicted far more than one death.*

By now several sobbing women rushed past us, leaning on each other for support. We reached a knot of men gathered around Abe, who reluctantly parted to allow us a view. The horribly mutilated body of a girl lay on the ground where Abe had placed her. I recognized her immediately, though I was aghast at how horribly she had suffered since I had last looked upon her.

"By God's own blood!" fumed Abe profanely, kneeling rigidly next to his daughter's body. "I'll kill whatever bastards did this to her."

Palmer turned away. "It's the awfullest thing I ever saw."

It truly was, yet I couldn't stop looking. Her arms and legs were missing and her throat was slit. It almost appeared as if someone had been in the process of butchering her. I felt horrible. I should have tried harder to save her. I should have thought of some way to spare her this blasphemy. I hadn't, and I felt ill.

I was about to tell how had I encountered the girl, how I had tried to save her, and even about the monster. Afore I could speak, however, Abe rose and held up something I couldn't see. "I found her hanging by this from a tree," he stammered, then threw whatever he held to the ground with disgust. "She'd been strung up like a deer and they...they..." Unable to go on, Abe broke down sobbing. Several of the men helped him into his cabin and that was when I stepped forward and saw what it was he had held up.

It was my Indian belt, the one I had used as a tourniquet when I had tried to save her.

◆

Once Abe had been taken away, the remaining men gathered about the dead girl. With a gentleness that belied their rugged, uncivilized appearance, they wrapped her body in a blanket, then carried her inside another cabin into which several women hurried. The men quickly returned, standing about and talking agitatedly. Even if Gerard hadn't yet ruined the name Seavey amongst these folk, there was no way I could tell them what I knew, not since it had been my belt around the dead girl's neck.

"It was the Delaware," said a short, dark-skinned man. "It had to be."

"Damned right, Benjamin," said another. "They've been harassing us ever since we showed up last year."

"You don't know that Indians did this, Owen," John said.

"And you know it wasn't?" sneered Owen, a red-faced, shovel-nosed man. "I've heard what a shrewd judge of character *you* are, Chapman." Owen turned from John to the crowd and said, "Hey, everybody, let's listen to Chapman here and see if Hugh's Lick ends up burnt to the ground like Franklin."

John's cheeks flamed scarlet, and I wondered what they were talking about.

"We've no way to know the Delaware are responsible for this," said John, his voice remarkably even. "To blame them without proof would be iniquitous."

"Who the hell even asked you, Chapman?" said Owen, taking a menacing step toward John. The two men stood nose-to-nose. "You think you're so smart with your fancy break-teeth words no one else understands. Well, we all know what sort *you* associate with."

"Bugger yourself, Owen Stern," Palmer snapped. He stepped forward, prepared to fight. John placed a hand on his arm to restrain him.

"Wouldn't you like that, you bleeding—"

"Enough, you two!" snapped Benjamin, his booming voice at odds with his small frame. "We need to figure out what to do."

"Chapman is correct," said a third man who spoke with a heavy French accent. His face was badly scarred from the pox—I wondered how long ago he had been ill. "We do not know that the Delaware did this. In these woods are other things besides Indians."

Everyone looked at him uneasily, and I knew I would have to speak to him later. "Poppycock, Dumont," said Owen. "It was Indians that did this and Indians that will pay."

"We should wait for the Burkes afore we do anything," said Benjamin.

"Well, the Burkes ain't here, are they, Benjamin Carson?" said

Owen. He grabbed the belt, studied it a moment and said, "Aye, it's Delaware, as sure as I'm a Virginian. I say we go over there now and do to them what they did to Lizzie."

"It isn't Delaware," I said, afore I realized what I was doing. "The belt, I mean."

"Who the feck are you?" asked a man who had to be Irish. "I not seen you hereabouts afore." Everyone else eyed me suspiciously, no doubt wondering how I had come by the bruises and cuts that adorned my face. It wasn't beyond reason that I might have acquired them whilst brutally murdering Addy Lobb.

"I'm Cole," I said. "Cole Seavey." I figured now was the time to tell the truth about my identity, even if it meant admitting Gerard was my brother. If I lied and were later found out, it would only make me that much more suspect of being involved in the foul business of the girl's death. These men wanted vengeance and something told me they would be none too particular about where they found it. "I'm Gerard's brother."

The reaction couldn't have been much worse if I had announced I was related to King George.

"Gerard's brother!" exclaimed the Irishman. "That explains your face, then. Somebody already gave you the beating you deserve."

"You right about that, Eoin," said another. "I'll be sure not to turn my back on you. We oughta flog you and be done with it."

"Another Seavey," hissed Owen. "Just what this accursed place needs." He strode over to me, forcing me to take a step backward. "Your bastard brother near about ruined me. Thanks to him, I had to send my wife and child back east, and I'm still barely surviving."

The other men muttered and glared at me, and I knew Gerard had been up to his old tricks. Even so, being linked to swindling Gerard was better than being thought a depraved butcher of young girls.

"What Gerard did isn't Cole's fault," said Palmer.

"I reckon he's no better," said Eoin. "Your father must be one sorry son of a bitch to have sired you two."

It was all I could do to keep from cold-cocking the bog-trotter on the spot, and I had no doubt I could drop the shitpike with one punch. But I wouldn't because that wouldn't protect Pakim and Gwennie from these troublemakers.

"That belt is Iroquois, not Delaware," I said, as firmly as possible.

"You're a Seavey," said the Irishman. "Why should we believe you to be any more soothful than your brother?"

"And you're an Irishman," I said. "Why should I give a damn whether you believe me or not?

"It's all of us you need to be worrying about," said Owen.

I shrugged. "I'm not my brother, and I am telling you the truth. That belt isn't Delaware."

"Assuming you are capable of telling the truth," said Owen suspiciously. "How did you come to be such an expert on Iroquois belts? Perhaps you're an Indian lover as well as a congenital liar!"

Ignoring his taunt, I said, "I grew up in upstate New York not far from an Iroquois village. There used to be a lot of trade. I know their handiwork." I exaggerated hugely. There had been a village, but it had been abandoned, and the only trade had been our scouring the empty village for arrowheads and whatnot. Even so, I knew for a fact the Delaware hadn't killed the girl. "And I'll tell you something else," I added. "The Iroquois are a damned sight more bloodthirsty than the Delaware."

"An Indian is an Indian," said Owen. "They're all savages."

"Regardless," I said, "that belt isn't Delaware. If any of you get hurt attacking the wrong foe, that will only make it that much easier for the Iroquois—or whoever perpetrated this foul deed—to attack you next. Someone powerful and bloodthirsty did this. Do you want to chance ending up like the girl?"

At the mention of the girl, the men all blanched.

"You can count me out," said Benjamin.

"He be right, Owen," said a stocky, bearded man.

"Maybe so," said Owen grudgingly, "but I reckon those Delaware heathens might yet know something. Maybe they seen the Iroquois skulking about, or even sicced 'em on us. And I aim to find out."

He turned and strode away, followed by a couple of other muttering men.

When we were alone again, I asked John, "Do you think Pakim and Gwennie will be safe?"

Palmer nodded. "Thanks to you. I only counted two others going with Owen. The Delaware village may be a small one, but I reckon there ain't no way he and the others would be bird-witted enough to take on them odds."

"Is that belt really Iroquois?" John asked.

I nodded.

"Well, thanks be to God you knew that," he said.

"You're probably wondering why I didn't tell you Gerard was my brother," I said to John.

"I had wondered why you didn't mention your last name when you introduced yourself," said John. "But I've dealt with Gerard, so I understand."

"Has Gerard cheated you then?" I asked.

Palmer laughed. "Naw. A skunk might roll in lilacs to cover its smell, but any fool can still see it's a skunk. Gerard only approached us once about speculating on land with him. We made it clear we weren't interested."

"Unfortunately, much of the rest of the town wasn't quite so discriminating," said John. "Gerard fashioned himself a lot of enemies with his cheating and lies. It was a wonder Murdock Burke didn't evict him at the wrong end of a musket. I'd be careful if I were you, Cole. Quite a few people here will believe you're no better than he, and they won't hesitate to seek their revenge against you. Owen for one."

"So where is my virtuous brother?" I asked.

John and Palmer exchanged stricken looks.

"Lord, Cole," Palmer said. "You're going to think us unspeakable whoresons."

I shook my head. "I doubt that, Palmer. Gerard is my brother, but I know him for what he is."

John shook his head. "You misunderstand. We should've told you right away. You see, Gerard is dead."

So hard was the blow that I found it difficult to breathe. Such news shouldn't have been entirely unexpected, given Gerard's penchant for making enemies. Yet I could scarcely comprehend it. If Gerard had passed, I was well and truly on my own in the world.

John and Palmer watched me, and tried, I supposed, to gauge my reaction. "Are you sure he's dead?" I asked.

They nodded solemnly. "Stich Burke, his best friend, was with him when he died."

Feeling unsteady, I sat on a tree stump.

"How did he die?" I asked, even though I figured some aggrieved victim of his had most likely stuck a dirk twixt his ribs. "Did one of those men at the gathering kill him?"

"No, surprisingly enough," said John. "Though they oft threatened to do so."

"He and Stich and Thomas Lloyd were out hunting about two months ago when the bitter cold first came," Palmer said. "Word has it their canoe snagged on a submerged log and sank. They tried to swim for it, but the water was fast and freezing and Thomas drowned. Gerard and Stich made it to the middle of the river, where they were stranded on not much more than a sandbar. They lost everything excepting what they wore. In the end, Stich was the only one who made it back." Palmer abruptly removed his hat, stiffly holding it in front of him. "I'm so sorry, Cole."

How alone I now felt in this ocean of trees.

"Rose is still here," Palmer said. "I reckon she'd be glad to see you."

"Who is Rose?" I asked.

"Rose is—was—Gerard's wife," John said. "Did you not know about her?"

I shook my head. "I haven't seen Gerard for a long time and only recently heard from him several months ago. He didn't mention he was married."

"Then you probably don't know Gerard had a baby," John said. "A girl."

I was an uncle? I had a sister-in-law and a niece? I was surprised how much the news gladdened me.

"Can I meet them?" I asked, rising quickly.

"Of course, " John said. He hesitated, pondering something, and I feared he had more bad news. "First, though, you should know that Rose is, well, a bit different."

"Different, how?" I asked.

"She's all but a draggle-tail for one thing," said Palmer.

"Palmer!" exclaimed John. "That's uncalled for and un-Christian as well. Rose may be a lot of things, but I have not heard word she is of the sort that sells herself."

A draggle-tail was a woman who allowed her skirts to drag behind her through the muck in the streets. Over the years it had come to also mean a woman who, so to speak, dragged her good name through the muck by selling her virtue. I glanced around at Hugh's Lick, again noting its dilapidated state. How could a place only so recently founded already feel so worn-out? To end up a draggle-tail in this pathetic excuse for a town was to truly be the lowest of the low.

Palmer looked abashed over his comment. "My apologies, Cole. I only meant to say, word is that she's had a hard life. And she acts like it. You might say she's kind of hard herself."

"Palmer is right about her not being overly friendly," said John. "You might as well hug a blackberry bush as try clasping her to your breast. We just don't want you to be disappointed if she doesn't act overjoyed to see you is all. Gerard made so many enemies that by the time he had died, I'm sorry to say, no one was particularly aggrieved about the loss. In fact, most townsfolk have sort of taken it out on Rose. Ostracized her, I guess."

"She's family," I said. "And that's all that matters. I should bring her something though." As soon as I spoke, I realized I had nothing to give her.

"Here," Palmer said, digging through the pack he carried. "I brought a jug of cider to trade for some pemmican. You give it to her instead."

"Palmer, I can't take this," I said. "I know how short you are on provisions."

"Nonsense," John said. "Frankly, I'm embarrassed we haven't

thought to bring anything afore now to help her out. With food running so low, even we have become stingy. Not very decent of us, I'm sorry to say."

Reluctantly, I took the cider from Palmer but hastened to say, "I'll pay you back."

I followed John and Palmer down the street until we had passed what I thought was the last cabin in town. I was mistaken, as a little further on and off to my right, I spotted what was less cabin than hut, and a poor one at that. It was half the size of John's place, and as raggedy-looking as a mangy dog near about starved to death. The logs appeared to have been barely trimmed afore being stacked on each other, and one or two were so far askew I worried the whole thing might collapse. As we approached, I saw it was so crudely constructed that I could see gaps between the logs.

John knocked on the door. When it swung inward, I saw that he was right: My sister-in-law did look hard, not to mention tired, gaunt, and scared as she clutched a small bundle I assumed to be my niece. Rose was a small, pale-complected woman, though whether her coloring was natural or due to illness, I couldn't say. Her eyes, set rather closely together, were cold and calculating, a notion reinforced by the way her hair was bound into a severe braid that gave her entire being a pinched air. But she did have a certain beauty as well. Not a gaudy beauty, like a showy sunset, but something softer, like fog on a lake.

"What in God's Blood do you polluted whoresons want?" she barked, and all images of fog and lakes was dispelled like so much foolishness.

The three of us were shocked. It was one thing to hear profanity and blasphemy come out of a man's mouth, but to hear it from a woman was doubly appalling. God's Blood referred to the crucifixion of Jesus, and to allude to such a holy event in such a cavalier fashion was enough to land you in the stock in some towns. What sort of woman had my brother married? Perhaps she *was* a draggle-tail.

Despite his embarrassment, John bowed slightly and said, "Good day, Missus Rose. I'm John Chapman and this is Pal—"

"I know who you are, and I've heard all about you," she said. I wondered what she meant by that. "Now, what do you bloody well want?" Just then she caught sight of me, and she must have spotted something of Gerard in my injured features, for her eyes narrowed and some emotion—grief? longing?—flickered across her face.

"I'm Cole Seavey," I said. "Gerard's brother."

She studied me a moment, then said, "I can see it in your face, if barely. You be so banged up, you look like someone beat on you with a hand-iron." She stepped aside and bade us enter.

The inside was positively wretched. It was even colder than I had thought, due not only to the chinks in the wall, but to the fact that no fire burned in the fireplace. Two small stacks of wood lay near the hearth. I realized the poor woman probably had barely enough fuel to cook with. As soon as I had the chance, I resolved to lay in a decent supply for her.

Such was the depth of Rose's poverty that the cabin lacked even a sleeping platform. Instead, she and her child apparently slept in the corner nearest the hearth, where I spied several ragged blankets piled in a heap. Other than that, the cabin's sole contents were a table, a chair, a hatchet, and a single pot for cooking. I saw no clothing beyond what Rose wore, nor none of the ordinary household wares usually found on the frontier—not even a plate from which one could eat. The place looked as if it had either been looted or everything had been sold. The latter, I realized, was surely the case.

"You needn't look so consternated," she said coolly. "It's not as if I'm likely to be asking you to stay with the likes of us."

"What?" I stammered. "You misunderstand. I meant no offense."

Many times had I reason to be embarrassed at my brother's behavior, but never afore I had felt such outright shame. Gerard had provided so poorly for his wife that she had been reduced to selling what little they owned just to stay alive. Anger and embarrassment concerning that was what Rose had seen on my face, not disdain for her and her child.

"We've got some things to tend to, Cole," John said. "Why don't you stay and visit a bit with Rose. Palmer and I will stop back by later."

"Is that all right with you, Rose?" I asked. I had no wish to intrude on this woman, although something told me she was not the sort to tolerate much that perturbed her.

She shrugged. "Suit yourself. I can't so much as offer you a cup of tea, though."

John and Palmer beat a hasty exit, with not just a little relief writ on their faces. And who could blame them? I had a feeling talking with Rose could be a bit like trying to kiss a snapping turtle.

Once they were gone, Rose practically flew at me from across the room. "So what are you come here for?" she shouted, shoving me hard. "To finish what your brother started, is that it? Drag me from a respectable woman to a guttersnipe? Going to ruin my baby's life as well?" With her face as red as dye made from madder root, she pushed me again and I collided with the wall behind me. "Well, what the feck is it you want, Mr. Seavey?"

I was stunned by her ferocity. All I could think to say was, "This is for you." Half-expecting to be brained with it, I handed her the cider I had brought.

The sight of the jar seemed to bring her up short. Her eyes flickered and I saw the dudgeon drain away as she realized her rage was misplaced, and that I had done her no wrong. If she had been a more civilized soul, she might even have apologized. Wearily, she took the cider and said, "I'll pour you a noggin-full."

"No. It's for you and the baby."

"So you won't partake of what meager hospitality I can offer you?" she said snidely. Apparently not all of her anger had gone.

"What? No. That's not what I meant." How had I managed to give offense so readily? Especially when I had intended only to leave that much more for her and the baby. Interactions like this were the whole reason I wanted to be a fur trapper: Traps I could handle; it was people who flummoxed me.

She gestured toward the chair, but I watched her warily. I wanted to make sure she wasn't about to shove me again. Finally, I sat.

"You married?" she asked.

I shook my head.

"Figures. Men always say there's nothing like a woman and a child to saddle them down."

"I'm sorry," I replied.

"For what?" she asked. "The fact that life is such a bloody awful piece of work? That fact I was fool enough to think a pretty package meant the gift inside was just as fine?" She paused and shook her head. "I knew someone as pleasing to the eye as your brother had to be trouble, yet I ran off with the sod anyway. God's Blood."

Again with the profanity. And she spoke with such bitterness that I couldn't imagine what I could say that might make her feel better. No wonder she had attacked me. "I'd hoped meeting you might comfort us both," I said as I stood. "Obviously I was wrong. I'll go and let you be." I started to leave, then turned back. "By the way, for reasons I won't explain and you likely wouldn't believe anyway, I haven't money or even any supplies. If I did, I'd happily give them to you. But I will come back tomorrow and lay in enough firewood for the rest of the winter, though I promise not to bother you whilst I do so."

She said nothing.

"Well, then. Best of luck, Rose." I turned to go.

"Don't you want to see your niece then?" she asked just as I reached the door.

I faced her again. "Truly, I would. Very much."

She unwrapped the top of the bundle she clutched, and I stared down at a small, pink head covered with fine black hair. The baby's face swiveled toward us, her tiny mouth opening as if about to cry. Rose quickly stuck her pinkie into the infant's mouth. Small, sucking noises floated up from the blanket.

"We named her Colette," Rose said.

"After me?" I asked stupidly.

"Well, there tain't no one in my family named Cole," she said.

I couldn't believe Gerard had named his baby after me.

"Would you like to hold her?" Rose asked.

I nodded, and she passed the baby to me. Once in my arms, Colette wriggled about for a moment, then settled in as if she belonged there.

"Give her your pinkie," Rose said.

I slid my finger in between the pink lips. Immediately, Colette's tiny mouth pursed eagerly, sucking for milk that wasn't there, and I realized how hungry the child must be. I wasn't sure how long I stood there holding my niece. It might have been a single minute, it might have been ten. It didn't matter. Once she had settled in my arms, I knew what I had to do. This wasn't just any innocent child, this was *my* niece. The only thing, the moral thing, to do was to make sure she was taken care of.

A sharp rap at the door interrupted my thoughts. When I glanced up, it was to find Rose studying me with a shrewd look. It was almost as if she knew what I was thinking.

"Someone's at your door," I said.

She stood, smoothed her dress and went to answer the knock. A short, whey-faced fellow limped into the room. He was so thin that his clothes hung off him in great folds. He looked older—perhaps thirty—and wore his brown hair pulled back in a ponytail. There was something of the lickspittle about him, and I wouldn't have been surprised to learn he had a passel of brothers who had made his childhood hell. His complexion was ruddy, though judging from the fug of alcohol that clung to him that had more to do with strong spirits than good health. Clearly, he suffered from what wags called barrel fever—the barrel being filled with whiskey or some other potent libation. He was also quite bruised and scratched, as if he had been in a fight. I imagined him to be almost unrecognizable to his familiars and wondered with whom he had been fighting. I suspected whomever it might have been, looked a lot better than this.

"Good day, Rose," he said. "I've brought you—"

He stopped speaking once he saw me, and I thought I saw wariness creep into his eyes.

Rose said nothing. Instead, she watched us speculatively, and I wondered why she failed to introduce us. Finally, I rose, and, carefully balancing the baby, held out my hand.

"The name is Cole," I said.

He still said nothing, his eyes darting from me to Rose.

"He's got the baby," the fellow said, as if that weren't already obvious to Rose. I wondered how drunk he was.

Rose rolled her eyes and said, "Tain't you the observant one. It's a wonder you do so poorly tracking game. Or is that because you're so slow loading a musket? I can't remember which."

The poor fellow flinched, and I wondered if he were somehow related to Rose.

"And what happened to you this time?" Rose asked.

The fellow self-consciously touched his bruised face. "An accident."

"What accident?" she asked.

"I told you two days ago, Rose. I got thrown off of Elphira."

"Guess I forgot," she said, and I suspected she lied. For reasons of her own, she obviously wanted to embarrass the fellow in front of me. Given what John had said about her being ostracized, I was surprised she would treat so poorly anyone who bothered to call on her. "Did you fall 'cause you were drunk or 'cause you are the most acclumsid man God ever made?" she asked.

"I don't drink more spirits than any other healthful man," the fellow whined. His point was undercut by the way he slurred his words.

Rose snorted, then, gesturing at me, asked, "Well, don't you recognize him, you git?"

The man again peered at me, seemingly puzzled that he apparently should know me, yet did not. I, too, was perplexed as to why this total stranger should recognize me.

"Can't say that I do," the man said.

"He's Gerard's brother," Rose said.

"O-h-h," the man said, appearing to be genuinely startled. "Last thing we was expecting was you here," he said.

"It's nice to meet you," I said to him. Colette, annoyed by the removal of my pinkie, began to wail.

"Shall I take her then?" the man asked, but I had already returned my pinkie to her mouth.

"It's all right, I think," I said. "I'm afraid I didn't catch your name."

"I'm Stich," he said. "Stich Burke."

"You were Gerard's friend then!" I said. "You were with him when he passed."

"That's right," Stich said warily, as if he thought I might blame him for the loss of my only sibling.

"John and Palmer said you were his best friend," I added.

"Gerard and I had an understanding." He glanced quickly at Rose, then said, "Can't say that he said much about you, Cole. Was he expecting you and forgot to tell me? Or had you two been in touch somehows?"

"No, he didn't know I was coming," I said.

"Since he's, sorry to say, dead and all, will you be staying long?" Stich asked.

Subtle this fellow wasn't. "I don't know," I said truthfully. "I haven't given it much thought. Would you mind answering a question for me?"

"Suppose it depends on the question."

"Did Gerard suffer? I've heard he died, but not how."

"He froze," Stich said matter-of-factly. "We both fell asleep. When I woke up, he was rock-solid. Couldn't so much as bend his arm, and Lord knows I tried since he was clutching our only ax." Stich must have seen the dismayed look on my face because he hastily added, "But there was a real peaceful look on his face."

"That's some comfort at least."

"Uh-huh," Stich said, scratching absentmindedly at his neck. Abruptly he turned to Rose and said, "I've brought you something."

Rose crossed her arms over her chest. "And I've told you, Stich, you shouldn't do that anymore."

"But you and the baby are starving, Rose," he said. "And you ain't got nothing left you can trade." Stich's eyes darted to mine. "Not that I wanted to trade with Rose, you see. She wouldn't take anything from me lest it seemed like charity. So we traded instead, like Rose wanted, but always on favorable terms to her, God's truth."

He licked his lips nervously as he waited for my reaction. Normally, I wouldn't think much of a man who would profit from a woman in Rose's situation, but even my brief interaction with her led me to believe the veracity of what Stich said.

"Anyway, Rose," Stich said. "Let me show you what I got."

Stich hurried outside. Rose came to me and took Colette from my arms. "That man is a whiffling if there ever was one. He's got nothing but air betwixt his ears, plus he drinks too much. His own family treats him worse than a dog. Worst of all, he followed your brother around like he was his indentured manservant. Stich didn't so much as break wind unlessen he first made sure Gerard approved of it."

Stich returned, carrying a large white hare. "I snared it for you." He paused, then blurted out, "And I want to marry you, Rose. You and the baby are starving. I'll take good care of you. And the truth of the matter is, you don't really have any other choice, now do you? Nobody else in this town gives two hoots whether you and the baby live or die."

Rose looked at the sleek, white animal proffered by Stich. Suddenly, I remembered how after I'd first bought my traps I'd set them out to make sure they worked right. When I'd gone to check on the first one, I found I'd caught a small fox. The creature, desperate to escape, had nearly gnawed off its own foot. When I'd arrived, it had looked at me with an expression that mirrored almost exactly the one I now saw on Rose's face.

I could see she desperately didn't want to marry Stich, but I knew Stich was right. She didn't have any choice, not if her baby was to live to see another year. But now that I had arrived, maybe she did have a choice.

"Stich, you needn't worry about Rose," I said. "She and I are family, after all, and she's my responsibility now. If she'll have me, I'd like to be her husband."

chapter six

I wasn't sure who looked more surprised: Rose, Stich, or myself. Certainly, I hadn't greeted the dawn with the idea of finding myself a wife, any more than I wanted to find a musket ball twixt my eyes. After all, I already had one fiancée I didn't want waiting for me back east. And Rose wouldn't be just an ordinary wife, mind you, but one with a viper's tongue *and* a child. But as far as I could see, there was nothing to be done except to marry her. As Gerard's only brother, I was well-nigh duty-bound to do so, and the existence of Colette truly left me with no choice—not if I was to live with myself.

"What makes you be convinced Rose would rather have you for a husband than me?" asked Stich petulantly.

Such a thing was so patent that even I felt embarrassed for the scuttish fellow. He might as well ask which you would want to carry you over the mountains: a sturdy mountain pony or an ill-tempered ewe. Injured as I was, I was still twice the man Stich would ever be.

Rose sauntered over to Stich, took the hare from him, and said "Much obliged for your calling, Stich. Be sure to my give regards to your family."

Stich blinked wetly, as if holding back tears. Without another word he scurried out of the cabin.

I turned to Rose. "I don't presuppose there happens to be a preacher in town, does there?"

"Not that I've heard of," said Rose. "Though these townsfolk beg and plead with God so often a preacher would find himself right at home here."

"Well then, we'll declare our intention to wed, and I'll take up quarters here. We can make it proper when a preacher next comes through."

"You're an eager one, tain't you?" she said. "Tell me, do you always skin the deer afore you've shot it?"

"What do you mean by that?" I asked.

"I haven't said yes to your proposal, now have I?"

"Then you best give me an answer and be quick about it," I said.

"Tain't you the rutterkin," she said. "Bullying me about as if your stones were too big to hang twixt your legs. If I do marry you, it won't make me your chattel, you know." Rose appeared to be enjoying whatever game she was playing, first with Stich, now with me. But this wasn't a game, and I was having none of it. I had tolerated her sharp tongue and treated her deferentially when she was my brother's widow. I wasn't an ironhearted man, but if I was to make Rose my wife, I wouldn't indulge such childish behavior, nor her vulgarity. My situation was desperate, hers was worse, and there wasn't time for games if we were to survive the winter.

"I've not time for this, Rose, nor do you from the looks of things. If you don't wish me for a husband, say so, and on my way out of town, I'll send Stich back to you."

Rose looked taken aback, but said nothing else.

"I'll take that as a yes then," I said. "Now skin the rabbit whilst I start a fire. And by the way, Rose: I'm not especially religious, but should you take the Lord's name in vain one more time, I'll build a ducking stool myself, haul you down to the river, and drop you in the water. The whole town would likely enjoy that sight."

Rose looked as if she were about to object, then thought the better of it.

After a fire blazed in the cooking pit, I looked around the cabin, discouraged by how little I had to work with. Making a life here would be anything but easy. Then again, not much in life ever was for folks like us.

I knew the first order of business was to lay in enough firewood to get us through the night. Tomorrow I would try to bargain with Murdock Burke to get sufficient supplies to keep us going until I could hunt and repair the cabin. The fact that I was the nefarious Gerard's brother was only going to make my bargaining that much harder. I was hoping John and Palmer might be willing to vouch for me if necessary. It was asking a lot of them, but I was desperate.

Afore long, Rose was slowly turning the spitted hare over the fire whilst I cradled Colette. The crackling of the flames and aroma of roasting meat so piqued my terrible hunger that I thought I could scarcely wait until the meat was cooked. The smell also served almost to make the wreck of a cabin seem hospitable. At least it did until Rose abruptly said, "I'll wager you're not half the man your brother was."

Rose's opinion about Gerard seemed rather changeable. Holding Colette, I glanced around the barren quarters my brother had left for his destitute widow. "I'll wager you're right," I replied.

"Despite everything," Rose said defiantly, "Gerard loved me something fierce. People said they had never seen a fellow so smitten as he was with me."

Bully for you, I thought. *Too bad he turned out to be such a lout.*

"He chose me over all the other girls in my family," boasted Rose. "I had five sisters, and people came from miles around to admire their beauty. Nevertheless, it was *me* that Gerard chose."

"That's very pleasing for you," I said. Lord, what had I done, tying myself to such a vain, foolish creature? How could she possibly boast about having had Gerard for a husband?

"He courted me for six months. Brought flowers and gifts near every day. My sisters near about died from jealousy."

"I see," I said exasperatedly.

"I bet you never treated a woman half as good," Rose said.

I gently rubbed a knuckle against Colette's downy cheek. "You're right," I said, thinking of Rebecca. "I can't say that I have."

"And I bet you couldn't either," she said defiantly. "I bet you don't have it in you to be good to a woman. That's why you aren't married."

Understanding dawned on me at last, and I realized I was thicker than the feathers on a goose's belly. Gerard had been anything but loving or reliable toward Rose, and she feared I would be the same, hence her transparent attempt to shame me into being as "good" as Gerard. It was a desperate gambit and only made it all that much clearer how dire Rose's life had become.

"Go on, then!" Rose said. "I dare you to swear by God's name you'll treat us as well as your brother did!"

Without looking up from Colette's peaceful visage, I said, "I swear, Rose. I swear I won't drink, or get mad, or hit you. I won't cheat others and ruin your good name. I promise I won't leave you or Colette. And I swear things are going to get better." No promises about love would be uttered by me, as I didn't make promises I couldn't keep. Frankly, I imagined my ardor for Rose was really the least of her concerns.

Rose was quiet for a long time. "Are you nothing like him, then?" she asked at last. "Are you truly decent? Because he was a bastard, your brother. He did precious little else 'cept dream up ridiculous schemes, practice throwing his knives, then drink until he couldn't stand up. He ignored his daughter, and sometimes he raised his hand to me. I thought the rest of my days were going to be a living hell."

Rose suddenly glanced up at the wall.

"Is something wrong?" I asked.

"I thought I saw something," she said. "A shadow passed over that gap between the logs like someone was out there. It wouldn't be the first time I've caught Stich skulking about."

After handing the baby to Rose, I grabbed the hatchet and went outside. Rose was right; someone was out there. I couldn't say whom for certain, as I only I glimpsed a solitary figure disappearing into a stand of gallberry bushes. Normally, I would have given chase, but in my current injured state, I doubted I would catch our spy. Besides, I figured I already knew it had been Stich eavesdropping, so what was the point in going after him? Moreover, something told me this wouldn't be the last time he and I crossed paths.

◆

After we had eaten, almost nothing remained of the rabbit but bones and whiskers, and I wondered how they might taste. "I'm going for more wood," I said to Rose. "When I return, we'll make mud to start daubing the holes in these walls." I knew doing so would be cold, tedious work, but not doing so would doom us to a winter of bitter cold nights that would sap us of our strength and, possibly, Colette of her life.

Finding firewood turned out to be harder than I expected. The area directly around the town was picked as clean as the bones of the rabbit we had just finished. In fact, I had to venture so far from Rose's that not only would I have to chop the wood, but I faced the arduous task of hauling it back with nightfall only a few hours hence. This day was getting grander and grander.

As soon as I left town, I sensed I was being followed. I checked to make sure my hatchet was at hand. Certain it was again an angry Stich, I chose to ignore him. If he had the wherewithal to confront me, I would deal with him then. And if he tried something less direct—say from the wrong end of a musket—he better make sure he didn't miss, for he wouldn't get a second chance.

Nothing happened, and after a fifteen-minute walk, I found myself skirting a gloomy woods. I felt as if I were miles from Hugh's Lick rather than mere minutes. To make my circumstances even more fortuitous, instead of a proper ax, I had only a small hatchet with which I needed to dispatch an entire tree. Trying to fell a full-sized tree with a hatchet was only slightly more likely to succeed than attacking a bear with said hatchet. It was *possible* one might succeed, but only a fool would try. Instead I moved from tree to tree hacking away at the limbs that were the least thick yet would burn for more than a minute or two. Consequently, I found myself moving deeper and deeper into the gray, leafless woods. My injuries were less healed than I knew, and I quickly grew tired.

After resting a moment, I resumed my work and that was when I saw it: something pink and steaming coiled on the ground. Closer inspection proved it to be the innards of some small animal, not unlike those Dilly had removed from the pike. I prodded the guts with my toe. The organs shone wetly as if freshly disemboweled. I wondered if Dilly might, in fact, be responsible for this, but the earth hereabouts was not disturbed by footprints, and the fallen leaves were neither crushed nor spattered with blood. It was almost as if the organs had fallen from the sky. Perhaps an owl had killed some small creature and dropped the remains here, though it was early for owls to be out hunting.

The sight of the entrails wasn't unsettling, exactly; as a hunter, I was well versed in blood and viscera. But their presence here made about as much sense as a harlot's in a monastery, and that did bother me. Such odd circumstances put me in mind of the beast, but a creature that size could hardly have passed through without leaving some trace of its passage. Unsettled, I decided to cut one more limb, then head back to Hugh's Lick afore things grew even more disconcerting. It was too late for that, however, as my eyes came to rest upon the bloody head of a beaver regarding me from the crook of the tree. Its eyes were gone, its mouth drawn back in a rictus of pain made all the more disturbing by its huge front teeth. I jerked my hatchet free from the tree and peered at the gruesome sight. It didn't take much in the way of perspicaciousness to figure that the head and intestines had once been united in the same body. Things were getting downright odd.

Branches to my left abruptly began snapping as if pushed aside by something large. I turned to look but saw only a misty dale thick with trees. The sounds continued, though they faded as if drawing farther away. I felt certain it was Stich playing tricks on me, and now I was outright annoyed at his antics. This time I gave chase, but I quickly fell behind. Stubborn as always, I pushed on. Eventually, however, exhaustion got the best of me and I could go no further. Once I had caught my breath, I realized I was deep into the forest.

In fact, I had gone and gotten myself lost. Which was probably the little shitpike's plan all along.

◆

Chasing Stich had been about as smart as burning one's blanket because you're cold. Given that the conniving sneak had already got me lost, following his trail any farther seemed dubious at best. On the other hand, I thought perhaps I could track him back to town, where I would thrash him until his own mother wouldn't recognize him. After all, Stich didn't seem like the cleverest fellow (observed the fool who was lost).

I did follow his trail, but that soon proved pointless as Stich's footprints vanished into a soggy, half-frozen marsh that spread afore me like a watery taunt. Now I was even more lost than afore, though at least I had the satisfaction of knowing that the little bastard's feet would be plumb wet and frozen by the time he got back to Hugh's Lick.

So I was on my own. Well, Cold-Blooded Cole couldn't fancy himself much of a frontiersman if he couldn't find his way to safety, even through these thick, unfamiliar woods.

But a half-hour later, dense fog had rolled in from the marsh, and I wasn't quite as optimistic I would live up to my nickname. I was cold all right, but not in any helpful way. The mist grew so thick that I was soon reduced to making my way through the woods practically by feel. Nightfall was only an hour away, and if I didn't find my way back soon, I would be in grave trouble.

A branch snapped somewhere behind me. I turned, peering into the fog, but saw nothing. A sudden gust of wind rattled the treetops. At the same moment, I thought I heard whispers nearby. I turned all about but couldn't ascertain from which direction they came, as it seemed to be all directions at once. The wind faded, then returned, its power redoubled. Bare branches clattered against each other, and over it all I thought I heard a raspy voice muttering unintelligibly." It was likely Stich trying to scare me away from Rose. Or perhaps it was only the wind in the trees.

A ghostly apparition appeared in the fog lumbering steadily toward me. The wind kept rattling at the treetops as if trying to shake something from their crowns. Unable to make out the features of the encroaching figure, I moved backward. There was something not right about it and just then I would have traded my manhood for a musket, or even a dull dagger.

Any hope that it was just Stich ceased as the thing came closer, and the fuzzy outline grew steady and became the body of a man, but with the head of a deer. To what sort of evil-ridden place had I come? Were shape-shifters as plentiful as bears in the forest? Still backing up, I stumbled and went down hard.

The demon reached where I lay, paused, then a familiar voice said, "Friend Cole? Is that you?"

"Pakim?" I asked hesitantly.

The thing straightened, and I saw Pakim's smiling face. He knelt down, sliding a deer carcass off his shoulders, and I finally understood. He must have been hunting, killed a deer, and slung the dead animal over his back. My relief was immense, to say the least, although much was yet unsettling.

"Are you injured, Cole?" Pakim asked with great concern.

"No, I'm fine." Should I tell him that I had thought he was the shape-shifting demon that had already attacked me once? Would he think me daft if I did? That was my fear and the reason, as of yet, I had told no one what I had seen. Besides, I hoped that perhaps the beast hadn't followed me from its cave. I hoped it was already leagues from here, and I need never tell anyone what I had seen. Then I thought of Addy's butchered body and knew my hope was a foolish one.

"I thought you were in the woods on the other side of town," I said to Pakim, "waiting for John and Palmer."

He nodded. "I was until I heard this young buck foraging nearby. I shot him, then trailed him until he died. My people will be glad for the meat."

I suddenly realized how much had transpired since I last saw Pakim only hours afore. For some reason, I didn't know how to tell him that I was going to marry Rose. The truth was, I didn't want to tell him, which greatly puzzled me. So instead of telling him about my impending marriage, I said, "I was cutting firewood."

Pakim glanced about, then, seeing no firewood, said, "I see."

"The wood is back..." I hesitated, as I tried to guess the right direction, "that way. I heard something and I came to investigate."

Pakim glanced the direction I indicated. "I see," he said again, a smile playing at the corner of his mouth.

"I couldn't have come that way, could I?" I asked.

"Not unless you walk on water," he said, and laughed. "Are you lost, Friend Cole?"

Grudgingly, I nodded. So much for not looking like a fool in front of Pakim.

"Come then. I'll show you the way back." He patted me on the shoulder. "There is nothing to be ashamed about, Cole. These woods are tricky. Most white men get lost sooner or later."

Well, I'm not most white men, I thought to myself. Except, apparently, I was.

As if sensing my thoughts, Pakim said, "You are exceptional though. You get lost much quicker than any of the others."

◆

By the time I hauled the wood back to the cabin (with Pakim's aid), Rose and Colette were gone. I assumed Rose had gone to gather material—twigs, straw, sand—for patching the walls. Pakim said goodbye, then slipped away afore anyone saw him. As for me, I intended to find the cowardly Stich and prove to myself that he had been the one responsible for what had transpired in the woods.

Walking into town, I encountered no one but a mundungus-reeking old woman wrapped in an elk skin and smoking a pipe whilst sitting on a tree trunk. She told me she had seen Stich talking with John and Palmer down by the blockhouse. I hurried to find them.

John waved as I approached. "You were with Rose a long time, but you don't seem to be missing any limbs," he said. "It seems she must have taken a shine to you." He and Palmer both laughed. Stich only glared.

Somehow I had assumed Stich would have told them the news about my marrying Rose, but clearly he hadn't. Come to think of it, his not doing so actually made sense. Why tell people when he clearly planned for me not to return from the woods so he could marry Rose in my stead? It might even have looked suspicious when I vanished, had he told people how I had usurped him.

"John and Palmer," said Stich, studying me with all the warmth of a stoat, "were just telling me of your unfortunate plight, losing your supplies and all." He clucked with false sympathy. "Not to worry, though, Cole. My family has extra of just about anything for sale and, as I was saying to our friends here, I'll be happy to put in a good word for you. I'm sure Murdock will extend you credit at the most generous of terms." He smiled slyly, and I again had to restrain myself from cold-cocking him but good.

He looked too pleased with himself by half, as if this revenge of his was particularly clever. I felt certain Murdock would indeed happily extend credit to me—at a ruinous rate that I would never be able to pay back. The result would be that I would be indebted to the Burkes' forever, essentially becoming their indentured servant. *That* wasn't going to happen any more than Thomas Jefferson was going to be emptying his own chamber pot.

"Much obliged, Stich," I said evenly. "But that won't be necessary." John and Palmer looked as startled as Stich. Afore anyone could inquire as to how I planned to make a future without a cent to my name, I said, "Say, Stich. Not more than an hour ago I was in the forest cutting firewood. I swore I saw someone in the distance who looked just like you. Might that have been you, after all?"

Stich looked baffled by my question, as if his being off in the woods was as likely as a bear wandering the streets of London. "No," he said flatly. "It wasn't me."

"You're certain of that?" I pressed. "I would have sworn it was you."

"Yes, I'm certain," Stich answered, sounding not a little peeved.

"And if you doubt my word, ask your friends here. We've been talking for more than an hour."

Palmer nodded. "You must have seen someone else, Cole."

I glanced at Stich's feet, which should have been soaked from crossing the marsh. They were dry, however, and I wasn't sure what to think. He could have had an extra pair of moccasins with him, but that didn't seem likely. I was stumped. Someone had been out there with me. I yet suspected Stich, but perhaps I was simply blinded by animus. To change the subject and put Stich on the spot, I turned to John and Palmer and said, "I suppose Stich has told you the news?"

When Stich immediately blanched and excused himself, I smiled inwardly.

John's and Palmer's looks of puzzlement gave way to an appalled astonishment when I told them about Rose and myself.

"You're going to *marry* her?" asked Palmer, sounding as shocked as if I had announced I were going to dip her in honey and use her to lure bears into a trap instead. "You're not having us on, are you?"

I shook my head.

"I can't say that I'm terribly shocked," said John. "She was married to your brother, after all. Nonetheless, I'm not sure you know what you're in for, Cole."

"Oh, I have a pretty good idea," I said.

"At least now I understand why you turned down Stich's offer for credit," said John. "He's been proposing to Rose for the past month. Now that you've displaced him, I'm sure he's going to want to get even. Putting yourself into his family's debt would have given him the perfect opportunity to ruin you."

"Well, in the end I may have to relent," I said. "You've seen Rose's *home*. Sadly, she's better situated than I am. Frankly, I half expect that we're going to freeze to death tonight."

"You won't, as you're coming back with us," John said. "All three of you."

"No, John," I objected. "I can't cadge off of you anymore. I'm not a beggar. I suppose I should go and talk to Murdock Burke now."

"Poppycock," said John. "I'll not stand by and watch you be husked like an ear of corn. There is plenty of space in our cabin, and we'll set you up with supplies somehow."

"Honestly," I said. "I appreciate what you're doing, but…" My voice trailed off as I watched John and Palmer stride toward Rose's. Apparently, I wasn't the only one who was determined.

◆

The first time I had lain eyes upon John's cabin, it had struck me as austere and spartan. But now, watching Rose take in its solid walls, bountiful furs (Palmer was quite a hunter himself), and actual furniture, the place suddenly seemed fit for a king.

"You two and the baby will sleep here," said John, indicating the bed—his bed—in which I had recuperated. "Whilst Palmer—"

"No," I said, interrupting. "I'll not hear of our taking your bed, John."

"Cole's right, Mr. Chapman," said Rose. "We can't burden you anymore than we already are."

John and Palmer both looked at Rose as if she were a tree that had gathered up its roots like a long skirt and gone strolling about the countryside. And why not look at her that way? The tart-tongued, foulmouthed, nasty-tempered Rose to whom John had introduced me to that morning had become a deferential, apprecia-tive woman. I scarcely believed it myself and wasn't sure which Rose was the true one.

"I appreciate your thoughtfulness, Mistress Rose," said John, sounding as if he half-expected her to yet sprout fangs that she would sink into his flesh. "But it's really the baby I'm thinking of. I think it would be best for her to not sleep on the floor any longer."

Neither Rose nor I had a reply to that. John had shrewdly appealed to our greatest fear.

"What will Gwennie say?" I asked. "Shouldn't you at least check with her first?"

John looked puzzled. "Gwennie? Why?"

"Doesn't she live here?" I asked. "I thought you had taken her as your Indian wife."

"I see," said John. He looked troubled, and I worried I had said something to offend him. "No, Gwennie doesn't live here, though she does live quite nearby. Palmer and I share these quarters."

I felt foolish for having assumed John and Gwennie were husband and wife, especially since it wasn't unusual to find groups of unmarried men sharing quarters on the frontier. Even the fact there was only one bed wasn't all that curious. Men, and women, often slept together to keep warm. The practice was called bundling and helped preserve precious stocks of firewood.

The five us were soon settled in for the night. Rose, Colette, and myself were squeezed into the bed, if just. I imagined we looked like a family of squirrels packed into their nest. (How had John and Palmer, two good-sized men, managed such a tight fit? There was bundling and there was *bundling)*. Since we occupied the lone bed, John and Palmer had each built a soft pallet from furs and slept on the floor near the fire.

When Rose and I first clambered into the bed, I wondered about any expectations she might have concerning intimate relations. I didn't particular fancy flourishing her (even now I couldn't help but think of her more as an unpredictable she-bear than a dutiful wife), and I especially didn't want to do so with John and Palmer sleeping so nearby. I need not have worried about Rose trying to consummate our relationship, however, as she appeared to be asleep afore she had finished settling into the bed. Even little Colette drifted off without prompting.

Sleep didn't come so easily for me. Not that I was surprised after such an overwhelming day. Had it really been only twelve hours since I had awoken a single man searching for his brother? Now I had no brother and was betrothed! Again! Was I mad? Did I really think I had a chance in hell of making a go of it? And with a child depending on me?

So many worries crowded in on me that sleep seemed as remote as civilization.

◆

I was a proud man, something John didn't seem to grasp. After breakfasting the next morning, we walked together in an apple orchard near his cabin. Apparently, it was a venture he shared with Gwennie, who had a great deal of knowledge about raising apples. She and John not only sold the apples to settlers, but the saplings as well. New settlers were eager to establish their own orchards and were more than willing to pay extra for trees that would begin producing that much sooner. And John had a notion to include me in their business.

"I have nothing to contribute, John," I said. "I've no skills pertaining to farming. I don't see what help I could be."

"I'm not asking for your help exactly," he said.

"No, you're not," I said. "It seems to me you're offering me a share of your endeavor and asking nothing in return."

"No," he said. "It's not really like that at all."

"Then what is it like?" I asked. What was he up to? He had to want something from me. I found myself again growing suspicious of him.

"Don't be unreasonable, Cole," John said. "Why don't—"

I held up my hand to cut him off. "Most times, John, I would be suspicious of someone so generous as yourself," I said, somewhat disingenuously. "But I truly believe you are nothing but a kind, thoughtful man. I, however, am not so noble. I am proud and probably not a little vainglorious. The truth is, I don't want your charity. Or at least I want as little as absolutely necessary. I'm a hunter and a trapper, and if you'll help me obtain a musket and traps, I'm certain I can make a go of it that way."

John sighed as if I were an unreasonable, wayward child. "Well, at least stay with us for the time being. That cabin your brother built isn't fit for livestock, much less women and children."

I certainly couldn't argue with that. Perhaps it was best to stay with him—if only until the weather warmed.

For now, however, the sky was cold and gray, with a dull cast to it like the blade of a plow dingy with age. As we strolled down a row of apple trees, I was struck by how even these trees—friendly, help-ful apple trees—had a foreboding air about them. How could an apple tree look menacing, for God's sake? It was like being afraid of a frog or a freshly-hatched chick. What was it about the frontier that felt so inhospitable? I was a hunter. I had grown up in the woods and always felt at ease there. But these woods were truly different.

When we reached the end of the neat, orderly row of trees, some-thing about John's whole undertaking suddenly struck me as odd. Earlier he had told me he and Palmer had been here a little more than a year and a half. Yet these trees had to be five years old at least.

"That's because Gwennie has orchards all over the place," John explained, when I posed my question. "She's a bit of a nomad, you see, roving around and planting trees."

"Mighty shrewd. Do you or the other Indians do the same?" I asked. It was Pakim I really wondered about, but since I didn't want John to think I had any untoward interest in him, I didn't mention him by name.

John shook his head. "Not really. I've learned a lot from Gwennie, and I more or less act in her place when it comes to the trading, but she does the planting. A lot of settlers don't like dealing with Indians, and Gwennie certainly has no interest in dealing with them."

"Why not? Has something inimical passed between them?" I asked. "Other than the usual ill will, I mean."

John looked thoughtful, then said, "Gwennie's a very private per-son, Cole. Actually, we all are. It might be best if she told you about herself, if and when she is ready."

I could understand that. Even so, I was rather intrigued.

"It's not like I get along with the townsfolk much better than she does," John added. "Except for a few of them, they all tend to think Palmer and I queer for living out here so far from town, not to mention our associating with Pakim and such an odd duck as Gwennie." He paused. "Then there's the stories about what happened back in Franklin—that's a former settlement back in northwestern Pennsylvania, though half of what people say about that are outright falsehoods. God's wrath on them anyway."

I was curious about what had happened, but given what John had said about being private, I thought I ought not to pry. At least now I thought I understood a little about why John was behaving so generously toward me—and it wasn't solely kindness that motivated him. He clearly didn't like most of the settlers in Hugh's Lick and wanted to win me as an ally. I didn't doubt he was a genuinely kind man; but he was a man, after all, and who didn't feel better with someone watching his back? It also made me less uneasy, for now I understood what motivated him, which made me more comfortable in dealing with him. Despite knowing that, I didn't wish to go into the business of raising apples with John.

As I pondered a way to turn the conversation to the subject of Pakim (even now I continued to act odd!) the frenzied sound of branches breaking violently reached us from the woods. Hopefully, it was too late in the year to be a bear, but that much racket couldn't have come from a creature much smaller. John, oddly enough, never carried a musket, and had yet to furnish me with one. I hadn't wanted to leave the cabin unarmed, but less had I wanted to seem presumptuous and ask for one. Now I regretted my manners.

"By God's blest mother, I hope that isn't a grizzly," said John.

The crashing sounds grew closer, and that much louder for the otherwise quiescence of the woods. John grabbed my arm, silently indicating a vale in which we could hide. Afore we could reach it, however, the short, squat figure of Gwennie hurtled out of the woods. Such a wildness possessed her that when she collided with us she barely even seemed to notice.

The three of us tumbled to the ground. No sooner had we fallen than Gwennie tried to scramble to her feet and keep running. John grabbed her and held her back.

"It's us, Gwennie," he soothed. "It's Cole and me. What's wrong?"

Gwennie panted, taking great gulps of air like a horse that has run to its limit. I noticed immediately that the sounds of pursuit had ceased. Which, of course, didn't mean we were safe from whatever had been after her.

When Gwennie finally stopped gasping, she grabbed John and,

sobbing, buried her face against his chest. John looked so utterly shocked I could only surmise that this was the first time the ever-aloof Gwennie had done such a thing. That, in turn, made me wonder what the hell had been after her.

Unfortunately, I had my suspicions.

chapter seven

Once Gwennie had caught her breath, we escorted her back to her cabin. It was a tiny place—really nothing but a cosh. In fact, it was just about the smallest dwelling I had ever seen a person make their home. So small was it that, swathed deep in the shadows of the forest, I might not even have noticed it, had I been passing by on my own. Inside there was space for one bed—albeit with a luxurious quilt—a Franklin stove in the corner, and a stool, with just enough room left over for Gwennie to belch if absolutely necessary. Her quarters may have been small, but it was the coziest place I had seen in a long time.

"Gwennie, tell me what happened," John pleaded again as she threw her few belongings into a satchel. "Tell me who it was, and Palmer and I will go deal with them."

Still unnerved, Gwennie looked at John askance, then grunted as if he were talking complete nonsense.

"Was it Boxner?" asked John. "If it was, then we've dealt with him afore. You know that."

Gwennie said nothing as she folded a blanket and placed it in her satchel. John looked genuinely distraught, as if Gwennie's departure was the worst thing that could befall him. If they weren't married or living together, then what was his attachment to this strange woman?

John turned to me. "What I *think* is going on—" he cast an annoyed look at Gwennie "—is that one of the settlers has threatened

Gwennie. It's happened afore. I'm guessing what we heard was some-one chasing her, trying to scare her."

I had wondered if it might not be the beast, but John's explanation made more sense—or so I hoped. "Do they harass her for any reason in particular?" I asked. "Or only for amusement?"

"It's land," said John. "Not only does Gwennie plant orchards, but she claims land as well. The other settlers don't like it. Jake Boxner, to name one, wants that orchard for himself." John turned back to Gwennie. "Was it Boxner, Gwennie? So help me, if it was I'll make him rue the day he set foot on the frontier."

Gwennie said nothing, only resolutely continued to pack.

This display of ire wasn't a side of John I had seen afore. Up until now, he had been nothing but jovial and helpful, generous and considerate. Such attributes were fine in their place—I was cer-tainly fortunate he possessed them—but it gladdened me to know he had at least a little vitriol in him as well. If I was to ally myself with him, I wanted to know he would fight when necessary.

"Fine then, Gwennie," John said, throwing his hands up in the air. "I'm going to assume it was Boxner. I'm going to get Palmer and we're going to go over and settle this once and for all." John stepped out the door, but afore he could leave Gwennie caught him by the sleeve.

"It not Boxner," she said.

"Then who?" John asked.

Gwennie glanced nervously toward the forest. "I not know, John," she said forcefully. "I not see them. Only know they were after me and not to buy apples either. But it not matter who after me. This not a good place for me any longer. I go."

"*Go?*" asked John. "Where will you go, Gwennie?"

Gwennie sat on her bed. "I've heard talk of place further west. Called the Firelands."

"The Firelands?" asked John, sounding as incredulous as if Gwennie had announced her new home was to be the moon. "Where did you hear about these Firelands?"

"From the other Indians."

"Since when do you talk to the other Indians?" he asked. "Or they to you?"

Do her own people harbor her ill will as well as the settlers? I wondered. *If so, why?*

"I not talk to the others," said Gwennie. "But I listen. Some of them talk about this Firelands. They say white men think it only a wasteland, but it not. Can find game there and water. They say it good place to start fresh."

I thought it could be for me as well. Assuming these Firelands existed and weren't wishful thinking on the part of desperate Indians, they sounded like exactly the place for me to take my traps and establish a trapping territory. Without any damnable Burkes around, I could build Rose and Colette a small cabin, and we could hide there away from the world. It would be hard, but I could start over.

John sat next to Gwennie. "You can't go, Gwennie," he said gently. "The orchards need you. If you're not here next spring, who knows what will happen to the trees?"

Gwennie smiled a little. "They blossom, then fruit, John. They not need me to do that."

"But what if there is blight, or something else goes wrong?" John asked.

Gwennie placed her hand over John's. "You know almost as much as I do, John. You not need—"

"That's a lie!" John exclaimed, leaping to his feet. "You can't go, Gwennie! You can't!"

Gwennie looked as startled by John's outburst as I. For the first time, it occurred to me I was witnessing an interaction I had no business seeing. Even so, it was interesting to know John's geniality only went so far, even with his friends.

John closed his eyes as if calming himself. "You're my family, Gwennie," he said. "You and Palmer. If you go, I don't think I'll ever have a happy day again."

"You can't ask so much of me, Chakoltet," she said.

John smiled. "But I *am* asking, Gwennie. In fact, I'm begging.

If you go, then who will call me Chakoltet? Only to you am I Little Frog."

Gwennie sighed, then slumped as if in defeat. "For you, John, I will stay."

"You know I would lay down my life for you, Gwennie," he said. "I've proven that afore. And we will protect you, I swear. Palmer and I and even Cole—won't you, Cole?"

What could I do but agree? Besides, I all but owed Gwennie my life, so of course I would protect her.

"I'll even start carrying a musket," said John. "And so will Cole. In fact, we'll go arm ourselves right now. How does that sound?"

Gwennie nodded weakly, as if she knew no gun could afford her protection from what she feared. Again I worried that what she feared wasn't a settler, but the same creature I had encountered. Perhaps she did not speak of it for the same reason as I: for fear of being thought daft.

"Come, Cole," John said to me. "The sooner we go, the sooner Gwennie shall feel safer."

Somehow I doubted that. "Maybe I should stay with Gwennie," I suggested. "Lest whatever was out there comes back." I also thought I could find out more about what had been after her.

"Good," said John. "That's good. You see, Gwennie? Cole's already keeping you safe. I'll be right back."

But afore he could go, two figures on horseback appeared in the distance, riding hard toward us. A few moments later, Pakim and Palmer wheeled to a stop in front of Gwennie's cabin. Their foam-flecked horses stamped the ground as they exhaled loudly into the cold air.

"There's trouble," said Palmer, breathing hard himself. "Bad trouble. Marda Witt's claim was attacked this morning."

◆

The news hung in the freezing air, as palpable as the billowing white breath of the horses. It was common knowledge that one Indian attack on a settler could set off a whole border war. John quickly explained to me that Marda Witt was a German woman who had been widowed the year afore. Since then, she and John had become fast friends, and she was one of the few settlers he actually liked.

"Does anyone know who was responsible?" asked John.

"Not that we've heard," said Palmer. "But everyone is speculating furiously. Indians, most people reckon."

"Damn, damn, damn," said John. "This could not have come at a worse time."

"It was not the Delaware!" exclaimed Pakim. "We did not do this!"

"Are you certain?" asked John. "Might not it have been one of the younger braves? We all know how angry they are."

Pakim shook his head adamantly. "They know what I would do to them if they started hostilities with the whites. They would be banished and have nowhere to go. I give you my word, John, it was not one of us."

"Whatever the case, we best get to Marda's," John said. "And try to keep things from getting out of control. Pakim, maybe you'd better go to the village and warn them to be on the lookout for any settlers bent on revenge."

"I already sent word with Red Oak," Pakim said. "And I am coming with you. I want to see for myself what happened."

John nodded, then turned to Gwennie. "I'd wager whoever was chasing you was trying to retaliate for the attack on Marda. Why don't you go to my cabin and wait with Rose and the baby?" John swung around to me. "Cole, we're going to need every man we can get if we're going to persuade the others not to attack Pakim's village. Will you come with us?"

"Of course," I said, wondering what in Providence I had got myself into. Murdered girls, inexplicable beasts, and now a brewing border war. I might as well have tried something less risky, like bear-wrestling or tending to pox victims.

John climbed up behind Palmer, I mounted up with Pakim, and we set out. Despite the urgency we all felt, the trail was poor and narrow and wended its way over a steep ridge. In addition, each horse carried two riders, which made the already arduous going to Widow Witt's that much more burdensome on the poor creatures.

At least this time I managed to stay upright on the horse without having to wrap my arms around Pakim. I rather missed doing it and wondered if he might invite me to do so.

"I hear congratulations are in order for you," Pakim said, as we rode.

"For what?" I asked, unable to recall any news for which I deserved congratulations.

"I have heard you are to be married."

Oh, that. "I am."

"Is that why you came here?" he asked.

Given that exactly the opposite was true, I had to stifle a laugh. "Not exactly," I said.

"I was curious about that," said Pakim.

Why? I wondered. The idea that he speculated about me was intriguing, if not also a little unsettling. And I didn't much care for unsettling.

"When we got to town the other day," I explained, "John told me my brother had died and left behind a widow and daughter. I thought it my duty to take care of them."

"I see," said Pakim. "Then it is a good thing you are doing."

Normally, I wasn't the sort to volunteer much about my private thoughts, so I surprised myself when I abruptly added, "Actually, I hadn't much planned on ever marrying at all." Why was I telling this to Pakim?

"Then you are even more generous," he said. "I myself have been married twice."

"Really?" Pakim must have been older than I realized. I wondered if he was married now.

"I was very young the first time," he said. "When I grew older, I eventually came to know myself better and understood living that way was not meant for me."

So what way of living was meant for him? Again, I felt oddly uncomfortable, yet my mind kept circling that idea, inordinately curious as to the reason why he felt thusly. Then Palmer brought

Elizabeth to a stop, and John said softly, "We're almost there. I'm going to check things out." He slipped off his horse and made his way to the edge of the clearing. "There is yet a whole crowd there," he said upon returning. "Pakim, you best wait here."

Pakim nodded. "But you have to be my eyes for me, John. Find proof that this was not done by the Delaware. Otherwise, I am afraid something terrible will happen."

◆

Something terrible had already happened. There was blood everywhere to prove it, not to mention the stink of death that hung in the air. As soon as we started across the Widow Witt's now-fallow field, we saw a large puddle of blood pooled on the frozen ground. It seemed to have come from a dismembered sheep whose organs lay over a wide swath of frozen earth. It wasn't hard to picture the beast that attacked me having done this.

As we approached the cabin and barn, red smears soiled the porch, as well as the cabin walls. Half-expecting to catch sight of the creature, I cast a glance into the woods. Again I weighed whether to tell John and Palmer about my encounter with the creature. Circumspection yet seemed the safer course, at least until I learned more about what had happened here. I suspected, however, I would be compelled to speak soon.

John explained that the Widow Witt, along with her recently deceased husband, had mostly raised livestock: a few sheep, two hogs, a cow, a horse, chickens, as well as several dogs to guard them all. We soon learned that not one of the creatures remained alive. In fact, none of them even remained in one piece, although the horse was, as of yet, still missing. The air stank of their blood and guts.

The Widow Witt, however, yet lived, and uninjured at that. She was a carroty-pated, wiry woman who looked as if she knew a thing or two about wresting a livelihood out of these woods. When we entered her cabin, she looked to be busy turning dried corn into meal by means of a stone mortar and pestle. Owen Stern, the belligerent fellow I had met back in Hugh's Lick, watched her as if uncertain how to proceed. He was the one Gerard had cheated, apparently all but ruining his life, and I didn't really fancy seeing him again. Unsettlingly, the Widow Witt seemed to take no notice of the blood on her floor, her dress, or on the table at which she vigorously worked with the pestle. Nor did she look at us.

"Do we know what happened, Owen?" John asked.

Owen turned, regarding us coldly. "Oh, it's you, Chapman," he said. "No, we don't, by God's blest Mother." He glanced at Widow Witt, as if concerned she might be offended by his profanity, but she seemed not to notice.

"Is she all right?" John asked. "She doesn't look hurt."

"Widow Witt's uninjured in body," said Owen. "I'm not so sure how she fares in spirit."

"Was she here"—John gestured outside—"when that happened?"

"I've inquired," said Owen. "But as her husband and I weren't what you would call cordial, she hasn't seen fit to converse with me. Why don't you try, Chapman? Make yourself useful for a change."

John knelt down next to the thin woman who glanced over at him. She was so lean that every muscle and tendon in her arms were visible. With a light German accent, she said, "Oh, don't look at me that vay, John. I'm not one of dose silly vomen who zink they vill be scalped every time they have to hike their skirts in the woods." She waved the wooden pestle at him. "I'm not daft, you know."

"I know that," John said. "But are you all right, Marda?"

She rubbed the pestle against her chin, her head bobbing her back and forth slightly as if considering the question. "Zings, they aren't so good right now," she said, suddenly driving the pestle down into the stone mortar. "I still miss Vebster so terribly, you know."

"We all do," said John. "But are you hurt, Marda?"

She shook her head. "This blood, it is not mine. I'm not hurt."

John touched her arm gently. "Good. I'm glad to hear that. Marda, can you tell me what befell your animals?"

Marda glanced toward the door. "You noticed, eh?"

"It was rather hard to not, Marda."

"Even so," she said, brushing a strand of red hair off her cheek. "I had hoped no one might remark on it. But you know people—alvays sniffing other people's cooking pots. People vill probably talk about it, von't they?"

"It's likely," said John. "Did you see what happened? Can you tell me about it?"

"Everything has to die, John. You know that."

John nodded. "Yes, I do, Marda. But how did your animals die?"

We all listened as the pestle grated noisily against the mortar. Finally, she said, "I'm sorry, John, but I can't say."

"Was it Indians?" John asked.

"I never saw any," she said.

"What did you see?" asked John.

She shot John an annoyed look, then glanced at me. "You're new," she said. "Vat is your name?"

"I'm Cole," I said. "It's nice to meet you."

"Marda," said John, drawing her attention back to him. "Did someone threaten to hurt you if you told anyone what happened?"

"Ach, John! You and your questions. No. No one threatened me. I can't tell you vat happened because you vill all zink I'm touched in the head. Some might even say I'm possessed by spirits. I'll not have that said about me."

"Marda, I swear to you no one will think less of you," John said. "We only want to make sure this doesn't happen again. Now won't you please tell me?"

Marda furrowed her brow in thought. "All right, all right," she said. "I tell you. It vas…"

"Yes, Marda. It was who?"

"Me," she said. "It vas me."

"You!" exclaimed John.

"Zat's right," she said hesitantly. "I vas tired of alvays feeding the animals, alvays milking them, alvays something. I can't do it all vithout Vebster. So this morning I vent outside and butcher them all."

"You're sure, Marda?" John asked. "You did all of that?"

"Enough already!" she said. "I tell you, and still you badger me. I'm tired and zink you should go now."

"Certainly, Marda," said John rising. "I didn't mean to upset you. I'll come by later for a proper visit, yes?"

"Zat vould be nice," she said, yet again driving the pestle into the stone mortar. For the first time, I noticed the mortar was empty of corn and must have been since we arrived.

◆

John, Palmer, and I stood outside Marda's cabin. Around us gathered other men who had heard the news and arrived to see the carnage for themselves. To a man, the others stared slack-jawed up into a tall evergreen towering over the barn. The tree was such a dark green as to be black, but it wasn't the tree's color that entranced us so. It was Marda's missing horse and the fact that the dead creature hung from a branch at least thirty feet above the ground. Or at least its front half the did. The rest had yet to be located.

"Lord have mercy," said Murdock Burke, as he looked up. "She says she did that, eh?"

John nodded.

"Poor woman is cracked," said Murdock. "Nuttier than acorn porridge."

This was my first encounter with Murdock. To my surprise, he was slight, but wiry, and with a surprisingly quick-witted air about him. He was also as bald as a robin's egg, though quite beetle-browed, as if to make up for the lack of hair above. In fact, I doubted I had ever seen such bushy eyebrows. Murdock acted with an air of nonchalance, but I stood closer to him than anyone. I saw the unease in his eyes and heard the slightest quaver in his voice. He was as scared as the rest, only better at hiding it.

I yet remained unafraid. Fear wasn't a large part of my nature, but, too, I at least had an idea what might be responsible for this attack. The others had to speculate about who or what could have wreaked such carnage, and that was oft-times worse than actually knowing. It was like hearing unexplained sounds deep in the night and thinking Indians were about to attack, but, upon investigation, finding the sounds weren't being made by Indians, but instead by possums rummaging through the rubbish.

Of course, sometimes the noise was Indians *pretending* to be possums.

Whilst I was not afraid, I did feel irritation, for whatever was happening here was a threat to my plans and, as such, was to be dealt with forthrightly and with whatever force I deemed necessary. I felt frustrated as well because I was hamstrung from taking any action. Both my lack of supplies and my reputation as a Seavey forced me to keep quiet and rely on others to puzzle things out. And I liked depending on others only slightly more than having a tooth pulled.

"It was the bleedin' Delaware," said Benjamin. "They're the only ones vicious enough to do such a thing."

"Again blaming the Delaware," said Palmer. "Do you blame them if your balls itch, too, Benjamin?"

"How do you reckon they managed to get the horse up the tree?" added John.

"I dunno," said Benjamin, glaring at Palmer as if he wished it were his dead body in the tree. "But they bleedin' did it somehow, didn't they? Or do you think this was the work of a white man?"

"I've not said that," said John. "But there's no proof it was the Indians either."

"Now there's a surprise—you stickin' up for the Injuns." Owen turned to Murdock. "What do you say? What do you think did this?"

Murdock was Hugh's Lick's founder; therefore, I figured the men would listen to him. If he declared the Delaware were responsible, I would have no choice but to tell them about the shape-shifting beast, despite the dubious reputation I already had as Gerard's brother. I would most likely not be believed, but to say nothing whilst the settlers waged war against the Delaware would be unconscionable—nor would a border war help my cause either.

Murdock pondered the sight of the horse for a long moment, stroked his black beard, then said, "Grizzly, that's what I think. It killed the horse, tore it apart, then climbed the tree with the rest. They cache meat, you know. For later. And a grizzly certainly has the strength to do such a thing, not to mention slaughtering the rest of the livestock."

"But, Murdock, bears are hibernatin' now!" exclaimed Benjamin.

"A rogue one, then," said Murdock. "That would explain such bizarre behavior. Aye, that's what it was. Rogue grizzly. Had to be."

It sounded plausible, if rather unlikely. All that really concerned me was whether the others believed Murdock or not.

"Why aren't there bear tracks then?" asked one fellow.

Murdock glanced down at the ground. The earth was a mishmash of overlapping prints, churned up earth, and blood. Obviously, the livestock hadn't died easily. "Look at this mess," said Murdock. "There ain't one good track from anything."

Maybe so, I thought. *But he doesn't seem to be looking very hard.*

"No!" said Benjamin. "I'm tellin' you it was the Indians, and we need to deal with them afore they strike again!"

Murdock spun about, grabbed Benjamin by the collar of his jacket and said, "You start a border war by attacking the Delaware, and I'll see to it that Pakim fellow gets to inflict whatever torture on your bodily self he wants. And the Delaware have some ways of killing that you don't even want to know are possible." Murdock may have been slight, but there was steel in him as well.

Benjamin's eyes practically bugged out of his head as Murdock released his collar. "And that goes for the rest of you as well. Is that understood?"

The other men simply nodded their agreement. Benjamin glared at the ground as if it were somehow responsible for his discomfiture.

I doubted Murdock truly believed a bear was to blame for this. Clearly, it was more important to him to avoid a border war than to find out what had happened here. Given how much of a stake Murdock supposedly had in the success of Hugh's Lick, I wasn't entirely surprised at his turning a blind eye.

"As far as we're all concerned then, this was the work of a grizzly," Murdock said loudly. "Anybody who says different has to deal with me. Also—the first man to bring me the head of the grizzly gets a ten-dollar piece. We'll put the head in town to show people we've dealt with the problem"

Except for myself, John, and Palmer, the men's faces lit up with anticipation. I knew by the end of the day there would be more than one dead bear dragged into Hugh's Lick.

"You and you," said Murdock, pointing to two men. "Gather up all the dead animals, skin them, and divvy up the meat afore wolves come nosing around here. Burn whatever is left. And, Owen, take Widow Witt to town. Find someone to take care of her. Tell them I'll cover the expenses."

As the group of men began to disperse, John motioned for Palmer and me to head back as well.

"Hold on a minute, Chapman," ordered Murdock. "I got a job for you as well."

John slowly turned back. "I suppose I can spare you a minute."

"You'll spare as many minutes as I tell you," Murdock snapped. "I don't know for sure what happened here, though I *do* think it was a grizzly. But I want you to get word to your Indian friends that if I'm wrong and they had anything to do with it, they'll have to deal with me."

John gave the impression of pondering the wisdom of Murdock's words, then shrugged. "I guess I could mention it. If I see them, that is."

Annoyed by John's perfunctory manner, Murdock shook his head in disgust. "Just remember, Chapman, if you keep company with a firebrand, you can expect to get burnt."

"What's that supposed to mean?" asked John

"It means things are going to change around here. You best think seriously about whom you associate with." Murdock looked over at me. "That goes for you as well, Seavey, if you know what's good for you. Yes, I know who you are," he said, reading my surprised expression. "If you aren't careful, you might be reunited with that foolish brother of yours, after all. Of course, the way people around here feel about you, that's likely to happen no matter what you do.

Not that I'm going to lose any sleep over it." Without waiting for a response, he stomped away.

◆

Pakim listened carefully as John described the carnage we had seen, as well as Murdock's promise of retribution should the Delaware be involved. The four of us stood far back enough amongst the trees to not be seen by the others, but not far enough so that the acrid stink of burning hair, feathers, and animal flesh didn't reach us. That foul odor was all these dark, dank woods needed.

"Could it have been a grizzly?" Pakim asked.

"It's possible," said Palmer. "A grizzly is the only animal I know of that could conceivably do such a thing."

"I'd agree, if it weren't for that horse's body up in the tree," said John. "That was downright bizarre, no matter what Murdock says about bears caching meat.."

Again, I wanted to tell them about the beast, but misgivings yet dogged me. John and the others had only known me a few days, and I was loathe to give them cause to start doubting me, especially since I was still so dependent upon them. Besides, maybe it had been a bear; I had no proof otherwise.

"Brother Bear does store meat," said Pakim, as if reading my mind. "Although never in such quantities."

"That far up a tree?" asked John.

"It *is* possible," said Pakim.

"Maybe it was something else," I ventured. "Something nobody has seen yet."

John looked at me dubiously and I immediately regretted speaking. "Is there something specific of which you are speaking, Cole?"

"No," I said. "Just wondering." Wondering how barmy and suspect I could sound.

"I will tell you what puzzles me," said Pakim. "Even if Murdock knows we Delaware were not involved, I am surprised he did not use this as an excuse to attack us anyway. I am no fool. I know the man wants us gone so he can take our land."

"I reckon he's a wily one, all right," said Palmer. "I'll wager he's got something up his sleeve."

"Do you think Murdock could have been behind this, John?" asked Pakim. "A couple of sturdy ropes and three or four men could get a horse up a tree. Maybe he is not using this against us because he has some other plan going on."

"That's possible," said John. "But, frankly, that doesn't sound like Murdock. Despite that schoolmaster look of his, he's the sort who believes in brute force. He takes what he wants, bugger the trickery. And I believe Marda would have told me. No, I do not see Murdock's hand in this."

I agreed with John. I had seen the surprise and fear in Murdock's eyes when he had looked around Marda's claim. "He certainly wasn't shy about threatening me," I said.

"Why would he threaten you?" asked Pakim.

"A couple of reasons," I said. "First, I'm Gerard's kin and seemingly everybody in Hugh's Lick bore a grievance against him. Then there's the company I'm keeping. Consorting with the three of you doesn't seem to bode well for my future in Hugh's Lick. That's according to Murdock anyway. Not that I care what Murdock thinks."

"But I reckon you have to care, Cole," said Palmer. "He practically owns this whole valley."

"I know," I said. "And that's why I have decided to leave."

chapter eight

The three men were clearly surprised by my announcement. "You're going?" asked John.

"I'm afraid so," I said. "Too many things are against me here. I'm not sure I could ever live down the reputation attached to my name, thanks to Gerard. Nor do I fancy looking over my shoulder for the rest of my life, waiting for some recreant like Owen to shoot me in the back. You heard what Murdock said about how people feel about me."

"We're going to be sorry to see you go," said John.

"I'm going to be sorry to go, but I fear I'm a dead man if I stay." My eyes darted to Pakim's face, but in the gloom of the woods I couldn't read what, if anything, he felt upon hearing my news. My gaze traveled farther back into the forest. I hoped the Firelands would prove more inviting than this place had. Recalling the slaughter at Marda's, it was hard to imagine how it could be worse.

"You know we'll give you what we can, Cole," said Palmer.

"I know," I said. "And I appreciate it. But even you can't replace all, or even most, of what I had. I suppose that's Providence's will."

"You lost everything when the cougar attacked?" asked Pakim. "Then afterward wandered until I found you?"

"That's right."

"You could not have roamed too far from the attack site. We should go back and get your supplies."

Pakim was right—I couldn't have wandered too far on my own. The knowledge to which he was not privy, however, was that the shape-shifting beast had carried me a not inconsiderable distance whilst I had been unconscious. And I had no idea just how far. "I don't know, Pakim. I might have gone a good ways. And it's been close to a week since then. Who knows if my supplies are even there anymore."

"Do you recollect anything distinctive about where the attack happened?" John asked.

The valley hadn't been particularly unique, but I did my best to describe the way it had been situated, the trees that had filled it, and any other details I could remember.

"I believe I know the place," said Pakim. "I will take you tomorrow. It is a long day's ride, and we will have to pass a night in the wild. But for the cold, I foresee no difficulties."

Nor did I. So why was I so uncertain about venturing out with Pakim?

◆

I was trapped—again. Lord Almighty, I certainly had developed a knack for ending up in sticky situations. And this was one predicament I saw no way out of.

Rose wanted to consummate our marriage.

My naked wife-to-be had just climbed into bed with me and proceeded to nuzzle my neck. There was no doubt what she was interested in, leaving me to feel like an otter caught in one of my own spring traps. Unlike an otter, however, I had not the option of chewing off my own leg, though trying to do so might prove an interesting distraction.

It wasn't so much the prospect of rogering Rose that gave me such pause. After all, I had been intimate with several women in the past. It was the notion that the act itself signified that she and I would now be man and wife, and avoiding that very thing was why I had fled to the frontier in the first place. I supposed I yet delayed because I hoped for some sort of rescue, though what form that could take I could scarcely imagine. A fire? An Indian raid? Here I was, supposedly rescuing Rose and all the while I desired to be rescued myself. Wasn't that ironical?

Thinking upon my imminent trip with Pakim, I suspected there were deeper, and heretofore unknown, motivations involved in my hesitation than simply wanting to avoid marriage. As of yet, however, I did not desire to know them, and I forced myself to stop pondering such thoughts.

John and Palmer were yet at Gwennie's; it occurred to me that perhaps they might be there at Rose's behest. I studied her in the dim light of the single guttering candle. She was an attractive woman, if rather thin after the hardships she had endured since Gerard's death. Rose's stomach growled loudly, and I knew she was as hungry as I. Despite how short John and Palmer already ran on supplies, they had insisted on sharing what they had. Divided up amongst two more people, however, the food didn't go far and each night everyone had gone to bed with rumbling bellies. Such romantic thoughts! A lothario bent on ravishing women I most certainly wasn't.

"What are you thinking, eh?" Rose asked, sliding her hand down my belly.

"About tomorrow," I said. "About whether or not Pakim and I will find my supplies." As soon as I said Pakim's name, I wondered what he was doing, but I quickly pushed the question from my mind.

Rose's hand cupped me gently, and I willed myself to stiffen. "Perhaps I can help you think on something else," she said.

"As you would like," I replied, running my hand through her hair.

Rose pushed herself up on one elbow as if preparing to slide down under the bearskin. Colette chose that moment to issue a quite vocal cry. Rose sagged, and I realized she was exhausted. In fact, I now suspected she was no more interested in fucking than I, and had probably only been doing so to please me.

"Let me," I said.

She smiled gratefully and slumped back down onto the feather ticking. "If it turns out she needs feeding bring her to me. Unlessen, of course, you're capable of nursing her yourself."

"I'm a man of many talents," I replied. "As of yet, however, nursing is not among them."

Colette wasn't hungry, only wet, and I soon had her changed. I rocked her for a bit and by the time she had settled back to sleep, Rose slumbered as well. I felt guilty for being so relieved at the sight of her inert form and wondered what was wrong with me.

◆

"There is nothing wrong with you," said Pakim, as we rode together on Midnight.

We had been riding since dawn in search of my supplies, and the sun only now sidled up from the horizon. It appeared to move sluggishly, as if it found it too bloody cold to be up and about. I myself was still only half-awake, and my mind felt as if it trailed a few paces to the rear of us.

Pakim wasn't responding to my feelings about Rose—something I wasn't prepared to share with him or anyone else. He referred instead to my comment that I had often felt ill at ease around others. "Because you are not like others does not make you a bad person, Cole. At least I do not believe so." He grew quiet as he guided Midnight over a fallen log crusted with ice. The horse slipped, and I gripped Pakim tighter until Midnight had regained her footing. Pakim smelled of marjoram, or sweet mint, as well as that spicy scent I had noticed afore. Whatever it was, I was coming to think of it as his smell. I doubted I would ever forget it.

There was now an awkwardness between Pakim and me, and I blamed myself. It had started the day we had ridden together to town and he had placed his hand over mine. I had been confused by his action, as well as my reaction, and had been uneasy around him since. He, too, seemed unsure how to behave toward me.

"Not every flower smells sweet," said Pakim. "Skunk cabbage, for instance. But it is very pretty to look at."

"So are you saying I smell bad?" I asked in jest. "Or that I look pretty?"

Pakim chuckled as he lightly jabbed me with his elbow. I liked that I had made him laugh and took it to mean that perhaps the awkwardness between us wasn't as bad as I feared. I liked even more the ease and familiarity conveyed in his gesture. I wanted him to elbow me again or, even better, place his hand over mine. This time, I wouldn't pull my hand away like some shy maiden.

Regrettably, Pakim didn't place his hand over mine, and we both grew quiet as we emerged from the woods into a clearing that, whilst barren and dead now, would be lush and vibrant come spring.

"Why do you care what others think?" asked Pakim.

"But I don't," I said emphatically. Pakim had misunderstood what I meant. I didn't care what others thought of me, I simply felt out-of-place amongst them. "Frankly, I don't give a damn what the townsfolk think about me. Their opinions hold no sway over me."

"I have noticed that about you settlers," he said.

I bristled at being lumped in with the rest of the riffraff back in Hugh's Lick. "Noticed what?"

"That you all tend to value your own opinions over those of others," he said.

"Is that such a bad thing?" I asked.

"Yes. If you all do only as you please, then it is disorder. All one must do is look at one of your towns to see the truth of this. Hugh's Lick, for example. Everybody just builds a cabin harum-scarum wherever they want with no thought to their surroundings or how the town might grow or how often the river floods. The entire settlement is disgusting and smells terrible. Nothing at all like a Delaware village, which is as much part of the land as a tree or a river."

I had to concede his point, at least about Hugh's Lick. After all, I had had the very same thoughts the first time I had seen the place. But I was still a little annoyed with Pakim. I was *not* like the others.

"So that is how you decide things about your life?" he asked. "Never taking into account other people's needs? Only doing what seems best for you?"

"Of course not," I said. "The whole reason I came to the frontier was because my dying father asked me to look for my brother."

I immediately felt guilty for the partial lie. After all, at least half of the reason I had come here was to avoid marrying Rebecca, and suddenly I was making it seem like some great sacrifice on my part. Now I was really perturbed by Pakim; I hated being reminded of Rebecca, *and* I had made myself a liar.

"Good," said Pakim. "You seem too good a man to be selfish like the rest of the settlers. All of our actions concern others, and their feelings should be considered." He paused, then asked. "Is that the way it is with me?"

"What do you mean?" I asked.

"What you said earlier. About not being comfortable around others."

I considered how best to answer without telling him the truth. It was ironical, but part of my unease with him stemmed from how glad being around him made me feel. No one else had made me feel that way afore. In fact, I was beginning to suspect I could feel very glad around him indeed, and that puzzled me.

Even more, I thought it dangerous for people to allow their hearts to become too attached to others. It tempted God or fate, whichever one believed governed the lives of men. I wasn't especially religious, but it seemed sinful to love anything more than one loved God, and I had seen many people who did so come to grief for their overly strong attachment. My feelings for my long-dead mother came to mind.

I realized Pakim still awaited my answer. "No," I lied. "I'm not uncomfortable around you. Even with you criticizing me thus."

Pakim laughed. "I, too, enjoy being in your company, Cole. By the way, we are being followed."

I knew better than to look behind us. Doing so would only tell our pursuer we knew of their presence.

"Do you know where they're at?" I asked.

"I'm not sure," he said. "Behind us mostly. I think there is only one, though several times I have thought I sensed another. It is odd."

I chastised myself for not having noticed we were being followed myself. This was exactly what I had meant about foolish behavior.

I'd been so busy wishing Pakim would touch my hand, I could have been scalped and never even noticed until I went to comb my missing hair. I had become as heedless and burdensome as a two-year-old brought along on a hunting trip. It was time to get ahold of myself!

"What should we do?" I asked.

Pakim quickly outlined a plan wherein he would furtively dismount, then come up behind our pursuer whilst I rode on to the next clearing where I would wait. When we subsequently passed through a dense stand of trees, Pakim slipped off Midnight, melting into the forest so abruptly it startled me. I rode on, casting my eyes back and forth, but neither heard nor saw a sign of Pakim or whoever followed us. Everything went according to plan until a thunderous boom reverberated through the forest. In a twinkling, a musket ball whizzed between Midnight's head and my chest. The terrified horse promptly reared up, sending me flying ass over teakettle. When I slammed into the ground, it was all the harder for being frozen.

In a daze, I lay there listening to the sounds of a struggle coming from nearby. I tried to rise, but such dizziness swept over me that I was forced to stay prone until the face of a white man suddenly loomed over me. It was Benjamin Carson, the son of a bitch who had wanted to attack the Delaware.

"Pakim!" I called out, fearing that Benjamin had already killed him.

Benjamin grimaced, stumbled forward, then crashed to the ground. Pakim hove into view, and I realized he had been behind Benjamin all along, pinning the white man's arm behind his back.

"You do not have much faith in me, if you think this half-wit could ever best me," said Pakim.

"He damn near managed to put a musket ball into my head," I said.

"Ah, yes," said Pakim. "Apologies for that. I meant to reach him a little sooner."

Benjamin groaned and sat up. He looked from Pakim to me, then sneered, "Traitor."

I ignored him and said, "I've seen him afore. He was at Marda Witt's place and advocated attacking your village. Murdock warned him not to start any trouble and said that if he did, then you could torture him any way you wanted."

Benjamin made as if to rise and run for it, but Pakim kicked him in the back of his right kneepan. The frightened fellow went down as if felled by a cannonball. Pakim knelt by his side, a transformation coming over him as he did so. Gone was the friendly Pakim who had tended my injuries. In his stead now appeared a stone-faced warrior.

"Too bad you did not listen to Friend Murdock," said Pakim. A fierceness shone out of his eyes that I found all the more frightening for the gentleness I was used to seeing there. Pakim looked ruthless, capable of anything, no matter how horrific. Perhaps those terrible stories of atrocities wreaked upon white settlers were true after all. "By the time I am done with you," continued Pakim, "death is going to seem a blessing sent from your God. But that will not be for a long while yet."

Benjamin's face went white, but to his credit—and my surprise— he kept his composure.

"First," said Pakim, "I am going to thrust splinters of pitch pine under your skin, then light them on fire. They burn hot, and it is like being cooked alive. Indeed, it *is* being cooked alive."

Benjamin's dread-filled eyes darted to mine. So much menace filled Pakim's voice that even I was afraid of him. I certainly hoped he was never my enemy.

"Then we are going to lift your scalp," Pakim said, reaching over and yanking on Benjamin's hair. The white man whimpered as Pakim ran his finger along his hairline, eyeing it speculatively. "Perhaps I will trade your hair for a new pair of moccasins or a pouch of tobacco. But first I will have to dry your scalp in the sun, scrape off the flesh, then soak it to make it soft and supple." Benjamin moaned in terror and bile rose in my throat. Pakim smiled menacingly. "The scalping will be very slow, and you will hear your flesh peel away from your scalp. It is a terrible sound and there will be much blood. So much you won't be able to see, not that that will matter for long because first I am going to eat your eyes!" As Pakim yelled the last part, he pulled a small dagger from his belt and lunged toward Benjamin's face.

The settler's composure cracked at last. A dark stain appeared in the crotch of his pants as he went stiff as board. His eyes rolled back in his head, then he passed out cold.

Filled with both dread and awe, I waited for Pakim to kill Benjamin. I wondered if he was really going to eat his eyes.

Pakim slipped his dagger back into its sheath, then caught sight of me and started laughing. "You thought I was really going to do all those things, did you not?"

"What?" I asked. "No. Yes. Well, aren't you?"

"Do you know how long it takes to stick a man full of pitch pine splinters?" he asked. "Too, your fingers get all covered with tar, and that gets on your clothes. Very messy. Besides, this one is too pigeon-livered to bother with. I would not honor him by letting him have the chance to die bravely."

"I see," I said, hoping no Indians ever tried to honor me. "What should we do with him then?"

Pakim took Benjamin's musket, examined it, then said, "No wonder he missed you. Cheap work." Pakim gripped the musket by the barrel, then smashed the stock against the ground. Next he gripped the barrel at either end and bent it into a 'U' shape with his bare hands. His sinewy build belied the power that lay within.

"I already sent his horse away," said Pakim, glancing up at the morning sun still low in the wooly-clouded sky. "He has got most of the day to make it back, depending on when he wakes. I doubt he will make it, but who knows? Now we best get going ourselves."

We passed the day wending our way through thick stands of gray, leafless trees that seemed to go on forever. Several times we climbed out of the forests as we ascended stony ridges shrouded in mists. So lonely were our surroundings that it was easy to imagine we were the only people in the world. It wasn't an entirely off-putting thought, but it was an eminently impractical one, and I pushed it from my mind.

Eventually, Pakim successfully guided me to the valley where I had been attacked by the beast. As if to confirm that I hadn't imagined it all, we immediately came across the shattered oak tree that had nearly crushed me when toppled by the windstorm.

"Never have I seen such devastation," said Pakim, surveying mile after mile of wrecked forest in the valley below. "It is a wonder you survived such a storm, much less the attack by the catamount."

Alas, my supplies were gone. The disappointment was crushing, but there was nothing to be done. I assumed the creature must have come back for my belongings, which meant they were at its lair, but even I wasn't desperate enough to risk death trying to reclaim them. Rose and I would have to settle for only near-certain death in the Firelands.

"It is most odd that your supplies are gone," said Pakim, sounding troubled. "Few people live in these parts, and the chances of their stumbling across them seem poor indeed."

I wondered if Pakim believed me a liar. He didn't look suspicious, only puzzled, but I still did not tell him what had truly transpired here. I preferred the look of bewilderment upon his face to uncertainty at either my veracity or my sanity.

"There was food inside," I said. "Perhaps the cougar dragged my pack back to its den."

"It is possible," he said. "But I think it more likely a passing Delaware or Miami found and claimed them after all." He still sounded doubtful, and I worried about what he might be thinking.

Pakim again glanced down into the devastated valley awash with dead trees. "I do not like the feel of this place. It is not natural," he said. "It is as if Manitto himself was angered and desirous of destroying something here, and that is why he sent the storm you encountered."

With relief, I realized it was the devastation wrought by the windstorm that had unsettled Pakim, and not my missing pack. I found his unease in this place somehow reassuring; I felt less foolish knowing he, too, felt the strangeness here.

"We should go," he said nervously—the first time I had seen him nonplussed.

A short time later, we departed the valley and again rode beneath the soaring, leafless trees as we headed home. We wouldn't make it back afore dark, but Pakim knew of a spot where we could spend the night. As I looked up into the tangled canopy of branches above, my own uneasiness grew, for they looked remarkably like dozens of skeletal arms waiting to grab us.

I wasn't the sort of man normally given to fanciful notions, but ever since I had ventured west, it *had* been hard to shake the feeling that these forests were different from those back home: more ancient and, somehow, more *aware* than something not human had a right to be. It didn't help matters that these forests also had at least one creature lurking in them that was unlike anything I had ever afore encountered.

"Why did you let Benjamin live?" I asked, mostly to distract myself from the foreboding atmosphere of the place.

"I do not like to kill," he said. "Since that man was no longer a threat, killing him seemed needless."

"But he is yet a threat," I said. "Could he not ambush us on the way back?"

Pakim laughed. "He could not trail us with stealth, much less harm us, even when he was armed with a musket and had the advantage of surprise. I do not think our friend now has any interest other than getting to safety afore something makes a meal of him."

"I still think you should have killed him," I said. "It would be one less white man for you to worry about later."

Pakim shrugged. "There will always be more white men, Cole. I am given to understand your people are like Brother Locust. You simply keep coming and coming. Each time we kill a white man, the multitudes that follow are only that much more angry. Do not misunderstand me; I will do whatever I must to save my people. I have killed when necessary, and I am sure I will have to do it again. But I believe it always best to be merciful when possible."

Should Benjamin make it back to Hugh's Lick, I doubted he would think Pakim merciful. In fact, I imagined that he would feel doubly enraged and wrathful toward Pakim and his brethren. I supposed Pakim and I simply saw things differently: I believed a man stung by a hornet should not shoo the insect away and let its nest go on unmolested. To the contrary, he should destroy every last hornet so as to ensure he would never again be stung. It was noble of Pakim to want to be merciful toward his enemies, but I feared he would regret it one day.

◆

We rode for some hours until we reached an encampment along a river where there was a wide, sandy beach scooped out of the forest. I noted the river had not frozen over and wondered why. Perhaps it was deeper than the one back at Hugh's Lick. This river was wide and slow-moving, hugged by the forest on either side. Except for the purl of the languid water, all was quiet except for the occasional breeze rasping the tree limbs against each other. The beach allowed for easy entry to the water, and I could see numerous charred stones where previous campfires had been lit along the shore. There was even a sweat lodge, which Pakim explained functioned as both chapel and gathering place for the passing braves.

No one else was present at the site, which was no surprise, as few folks traveled far from their homes during the winter. Pakim said the spot was busy during the summer, yet shared peaceably by all who passed this way, no matter which tribe they originated from.

I helped Pakim build a fire and heat stones for the pima'kan, or sweat lodge ceremony, he planned for the evening. He asked me to join him, but I declined. I had little use for religion—Pakim's or any other—what with their tedious rituals and rites, which seemed liked so much hokum. True, Rose's near-blasphemous tongue had brought out my righteous side, but those feelings were already again packed tightly away, like a sacred chalice that is brought out once a year for Easter Mass. Truth be told, I probably gave God less thought than a genuine heathen.

My feelings had been such ever since my mother had died—despite my father's endless prayers, multitudes of lit candles, and donations to the church. I did believe in God, but not a benevolent, merciful one who took note of the entreaties of men. My God was indifferent and uncaring and forced men to rely on themselves. And that was exactly how I liked it

No, if I were to expend some of my hard-earned coin on amusements, I preferred music and readings over a lecture on the evils of man. Too, religion seemed a private thing, and I would have felt awkward intruding on Pakim.

"Let me show you something most unusual," said Pakim. Though it was yet light, he lit a torch that he brought with us as he strolled to the end of the beach. There a small, foul-smelling spring gurgled up from the earth, its tainted waters flowing into the river. Right away I recognized its fetid scent as the same I had encountered underground during my escape from the beast. At least this time there was no dead body present as well. I wondered if there was a connection between this foul water and that I had found. They were quite some distance apart and yet it wasn't beyond imagining that they both sprang from the same source.

Pakim said something in his native tongue, then held the torch close to the surface of the spring. Almost immediately it ignited with a *whoosh*. The spring burned with a blue flame that extended all the way down into the river where it was finally extinguished. I wondered if the other foul-smelling water could also be made to burn thus.

"That is extraordinary," I said. "How do you account for it?"

"My people believe this is a holy place given to us by Manitto. We believe it is here to remind us that no matter how cold the world becomes, the warmth of the sun will always return with the coming of spring."

Speaking of warmth, I was quite chilled. Despite the unarguable uniqueness of the burning spring (as well as its headache-inducing odor), it provided precious little warmth.

Night soon fell, bringing with it bitter cold that abraded my throat every time I tried to breathe. Pakim built up a fire, then began slowly circling around it wearing naught but a breechclout—despite the cold—and I wondered if my newfound friend was entirely right in his mind. Watching him move about, I gathered the first part of the sweat lodge ceremony was to take place in front of my reluctant gaze. It seemed I was to intrude whether I wished to or not.

I was also going to feel awkward. How could I not, watching Pakim's lithe form moving about in the flickering light? He wasn't quite dancing, yet he wasn't simply walking aimlessly either. He was building up to something unusual, and despite my reluctance, I was curious to see what that might be. He began moving faster now, weaving his hands about in front of him in a dance of their own.

An unsettling wish to join him grew inside me the longer I watched. I pictured my hands moving along with his, my fingers, perhaps, brushing his skin. Our bodies would move in time with each other and we would draw closer. I imagined how hot his skin would feel, how good he would smell.

When I realized how intently I watched him, I averted my eyes, pretending to be suddenly very interested in the ring of stones that circled the fire. I shivered both from the cold and my impure thoughts. It was ironical that Pakim was the one tending to his soul when I was the one clearly in need of doing so.

How could Pakim not be freezing? I wondered, hoping to distract myself from my less wholesome thoughts. Trying not to impede his progress, I sat as close as I could to the flames, but Pakim seemed not to notice me at all. In fact, the more he moved about, the less present he seemed to be, as if his movements were taking his spirit to some place I couldn't follow.

Pakim abruptly stopped dancing, and retrieved an eagle feather and a wooden bowl from atop one of the stones circling the fire. The bowl was filled with something that smoldered fiercely. Pakim surprised me by turning to me and saying, "This is *ksha'te* or tobacco. We use it to send our prayers to Father Sky, to purify our bodies, and cleanse away all that is impure."

Pakim held the bowl in front of him, using the feather to fan the smoke heavenward. As he did so, he offered his thanks to Mother Earth for her bounteous gifts, then proceeded to honor the various grandmothers and grandfathers who seemed to live in each of the four directions as well as every frigging point in between. Since he needed more room for this, I moved farther away from the warmth of the fire. I quickly became damnably cold and wished him to skip a few of the lesser aunts, uncles, and next-door neighbors that he seemed intent to include. Even the Catholic Mass wasn't *this* involved.

Finally, he finished, then motioned for me to move closer to the fire. Whilst I did so eagerly, he knelt nearby and began deftly fanning the smoke from the tobacco-filled bowl so that it swirled all about him. He was close enough so that smell of the tobacco reached my nose. It was sweet, yet pungent, and made my eyes water.

Apparently the supposed cleansing effect of the tobacco had no impact on my spiritual well-being, as I yet wanted badly to touch Pakim. I did, however, quickly become light-headed. Either there was more than tobacco in the bowl, or this was a much more potent type of tobacco than with which I was familiar.

Pakim slowly rose, his body unfolding like a flower blooming, all the while fanning the smoke over himself. The tobacco must have affected my judgment, for I stared at him more openly now. My blood ran hot as he vigorously fanned the smoke, sending it across his glowing flesh.

I closed my eyes and turned away. What sort of deviltry possessed me? Had Pakim bewitched me somehow? Was black magic at work here? That thought seemed uncharitable. The man had saved my life, and I had thought him handsome the moment I laid eyes on him. Whatever this flaw in my disposition, it came from within and I would not cast blame elsewhere.

Perhaps the tobacco was affecting me more than I knew—my hands tingled and felt as if they were a great distance from my body. When I ordered my hand to make a fist, it did so, but only a long while after I commanded it to do so. When I looked again at Pakim, he in turn studied me, and I wondered if he had seen the lust in my eyes as I watched him dance.

"I am going into the sweat lodge now," Pakim said softly. "Join me if you wish. First disrobe and cleanse yourself with the smoke by breathing it in and letting it wash over your body."

"Certainly, Pakim," I said, once again staring into the dark. "Many thanks for inviting me."

I felt his eyes on me a moment longer, then he lifted the fur door to the sweat lodge and slipped inside. A hot, moist gust of air fragranced with sage billowed forth. I'd always heard how bad Indians smelled. So far my experience couldn't have been any more different. It was the white men who stank to high heaven.

I scooted closer to the fire, grateful to be away from Pakim and the confusion he stirred in me. It was time for me to think on matters more pertinent, though my thoughts were yet strangely fuzzy and slow in coming. Even so, I pondered my future now that we had failed to find my supplies. Truly, my situation was grim, and no matter how many ways I looked at it, I saw no good solutions. It was as if I were starving and held a rotten, maggot-filled apple in my hand, and no matter how hard I peered, I could find no place to bite.

My eyes wandered to the sweat lodge, and I wondered what Pakim was doing. My mind's eye pictured him kneeling in front of the glowing coals, sweat on his skin. I felt my own flesh begin to stir, become aroused, and I thought about seeking release whilst I was alone. Not knowing how long Pakim would be, I cast the idea aside and quickly deemed it best not to dwell on Pakim's doings any further.

I pulled my pack close to me so as to be able to lay my head upon it, then drew a bearskin farther over myself and faced the fire. There was a small wikwám where we would later sleep, but I thought it warmer here and decided to wait until Pakim emerged from the sweat lodge afore bedding down for the night. I was quite tired, however, and as I stared into the flames drowsiness swiftly stole over me like mist across a fen.

◆

A scream awoke me with a start. I sat upright, staring about in confusion as I tried to discern whence the screaming came. It came from the sweat lodge, and at first I thought perhaps I yet dreamed, but there was nothing about the experience that bespoke of a nightmare. No, I was awake, and I realized it was Pakim who had screamed. I sprang to my feet, rushed to the sweat lodge, and threw back the fur-covering.

"Pakim?" I called out, but only another scream answered me. Without waiting, I bolted inside. Almost at once, a staggering blow struck me across the forehead and I pitched downward into darkness.

◆

I knew I was not dreaming, nor was I awake. This was something altogether different. A huge, black entity hovered over me, but I did not fear it. I struggled to my feet, stepping out of its shadow, so I might see it more clearly. It was an enormous raven hovering over me, my talisman, and my heart was glad to see it. The bird was ten handspans from wing tip to wing tip, but somehow managed to float motionlessly in the air without flapping its wings. It simply hung there like the moon in the sky.

The raven began to glow, became the sun, and I was bathed in a golden light. All of my concerns vanished beneath that light. No longer was I troubled about my lack of supplies, my betrothal to Rose, or even my strange feelings about Pakim. Even when everything again went dark, I wasn't afraid. Unable to see it, I yet knew the raven would always be with me.

Light slowly returned, and I stood in a mist-shrouded forest. Pinecones and acorns and nuts of every kind dropped from the trees. When I saw my dead father walking through the woods, I called to him, but he didn't hear. I tried to follow, but now the nuts fell so furiously that I couldn't even wade through them. I called out to my father again and again, but he kept walking until I lost sight of him. I started to sob, convinced I would never see him again.

The forest vanished, and I found myself on the ridge where I had first encountered the windstorm, the girl, and the beast. The air was calm now, but all around me were the bloody organs of animals like those Dilly had taken from the thrashing pike. The ground was thick with hearts, kidneys, livers, and every other sort of viscera. Several white men walked up, though they did not notice me, and I could not see their faces. One knelt down, examined a kidney and took a bite. Blood squirted forth, dribbling down his chin and clothes. I shivered with disgust. He grabbed more organs, greedily taking a bite from each.

I glanced down at my feet, realizing that somehow my organs had been removed and now lay spread out afore me. The kneeling man knew this as well and crawled to seize my heart and eat it. That was when I saw his face and realized it was my own. I begged him to stop devouring my heart, but he wouldn't, and I threw myself on him. We grappled fiercely when he abruptly turned into a raven, caressed me with the tip of his wing, then flew up into the sky.

The world went black.

◆

Pakim regarded me with grave concern as we sat around the fire. In my haste to rescue him when he had screamed, I had rushed into the sweat lodge and struck my head on the joist across the doorway—I seemed to be making a habit of striking my head on low-hanging objects. I had knocked myself unconscious and, in doing so, had undergone those bizarre hallucinations

"Shall I fetch another compress for you?" asked Pakim.

I shook my head, then immediately regretted it. My very skull felt as if it throbbed beneath my skin. Nor had I yet to entirely regain my wits. I had only been unconscious for a few moments, yet those visions had felt much longer.

"I feel terrible that you hurt yourself trying to help me when nothing was amiss," said Pakim.

"It was the least I could do," I said. "Although you certainly sounded like you were in trouble."

"I was dreaming," he said.

"Not having a vision?" I asked. Pakim had told me that the one of the purposes of the pima'kan was to receive a vision.

Pakim shook his head. "This was not a vision. Only a nightmare. One I have had afore."

I waited to see if he would volunteer more, but he didn't. I thought about my own experience whilst I had lain there addled from the blow to my head. Perhaps I had had a vision.

"It is possible," said Pakim, when I told him I had seen something whilst unconscious. "Though there are less painful ways to go about having one." He laughed, and I relished the sound. He instructed me not to tell him the specifics of what I had seen—he believed such things were private—but he was greatly intrigued when I mentioned that my talisman was the raven.

"What made you choose the raven?" asked Pakim.

"It was more like it chose me," I said. "The first time I shot a deer, it was because a raven drew my attention to it. At first, I thought it only a coincidence, but whenever something good happened to me, a raven almost always seemed to be nearby."

"The raven is very important to the Lenape people," said Pakim. "Perhaps it is *the* most important animal because it brought the fire that keeps us warm during the winter and cooks our food."

"How did it do that?" I asked.

"It is a long story," he said. "Are you certain you are interested?"

I nodded, though, in truth, I was mostly interested in the chance to watch Pakim without feeling conspicuous.

Pakim added wood to the fire, then stoked it afore starting his story.

"The first thing you should know," he said "is that ravens were not always black. Once they were beautiful—every color of the rainbow—and the first raven was called Manaka'has, Rainbow Raven. It is said his beauty surpassed even that of the rainbow itself. Rainbow Raven had a voice that was sweet, and all who heard its song had to stop and listen.

"Now long ago, afore the age of man, the earth was warm all the time. But then cold and dark and snow came without end. Each day it grew colder and more snow fell, and soon the creatures of the earth feared they might perish. The animals held a council to discuss what to do and decided that a messenger must be sent to Kishelamakank, the Creator, to ask him to stop the snow and cold. But the animals could not agree who to send, and the snow only grew deeper whilst they debated. Soon all despaired. That was when Rainbow Raven said he would go.

"Rainbow Raven flew for three days. He flew up past the sky, the moon, and the stars. Finally, he arrived at the twelfth heaven, the home of the Creator. In his beautiful voice, he asked the Creator to stop the snow and the cold, but this could not be done, not even by the Creator. Instead, the Creator gave Rainbow Raven the gift of fire. He warned Rainbow Raven this gift would be given only once, and he must deliver it to earth afore the flame went out.

"For three days, Rainbow Raven flew back to earth clutching the burning stick in his beak. As Rainbow Raven flew, soot coated his beautiful feathers and soon he was as black as coal. The stick burned shorter and soon smoke and ash blew into Rainbow Raven's eyes and they became as black as coal. Next the smoke filled his mouth. His voice became hoarse and cracked and soon he could no longer sing, but only cry out harshly *caw! caw!* But he got the fire back in time and saved the other animals, and the fire he carried became the grandfather of all other fires.

"Despite his feat, Rainbow Raven was filled with despair because he could no longer sing and was no longer beautiful to look upon. The Creator heard his despair and decided to reward Rainbow Raven's bravery and sacrifice. He told Rainbow Raven that soon man would come to earth and be the master of all other animals except for Rainbow Raven who would be free of man's attention because Rainbow Raven's meat would taste of smoke, his voice would not be pleasant, and his feathers would seem ugly. But, the Creator promised, if Rainbow Raven looked closely, he would see that his black feathers reflected all the colors of the rainbow. And so it was."

"So the moral of that tale," I quipped, "would be to think twice afore volunteering to do anything dangerous?" The teasing words were out of my mouth afore I realized what I had said

Pakim studied me for a moment, and I was worried I had deeply offended him by speaking so impertinently. At least I did until he burst out laughing and said, "I had thought that myself, but never dared say so."

"I was only joshing, Pakim. It was a lovely story." And I meant it. Afore tonight, the only tales I had ever heard about Indians involved killing and torture. (Of course, all the stories I had heard about Indians had come from the mouths of white men, hardly an unbiased source.) I thought this story was wonderful and at least as interesting as those found in the Bible. Too, Pakim told the story with such obvious delight, yet with a reverence I rarely heard from preachers. The more I got to know Pakim, the more I liked him, and wished I had a way to tell him. There didn't seem to be the words for what I wanted to say, so all I said was, "Thank you, Pakim."

"You are very welcome, Cole."

Pakim rose, and as he did so, his bearskin fell away. Now he was completely nude. His body was compact and solid; there was nothing soft or curvaceous about him. He had narrow hips, and a flat stomach—and I couldn't believe how much I wanted him.

Apparently the feeling was mutual, for when I went to retrieve the bearskin for him, I saw Pakim was rather aroused himself. Never afore had I seen a man aroused, yet I doubted there was a power on earth that could stop me from watching now. Briefly I wondered whence this new inclination had come. Had it always been inside me, undiscovered, lying dormant like a strange bear hibernating for years on end? Or was it new, brought on by this strange place, this strange man? And what did this behavior mean about me as a man? That was a thought to be pondered later.

Pakim smiled and held out his hand, and I could have sooner stopped breathing than denied him. Maybe there were no words to express to Pakim what I felt, but there might be other ways. Afore I knew it, I was up, and Pakim's arms were around me. He clutched my back, and I slid my arms around him. His flesh was hot and hard, and unlike anything else I had ever touched. My mouth found his, and I could scarcely believe what I was doing.

Some part of my mind urged me to stop, but there was no doing so now. That right-minded, censorious part of myself was quickly shackled, then cast deep into a pit where I could ignore it. My hands moved frantically over all of Pakim's body. My mouth and tongue followed, and I was shocked at the hunger I felt for his flesh. He must have felt the same way, as he was equally frantic in pulling my body to his. My whole being throbbed, or perhaps it was only my cock. So intense was the pleasure, I could no longer tell the difference. I ground myself against Pakim, who ground right back. It felt a little like a battle, and that only served to excite me all that much more.

Pakim abruptly pulled away from me. Panting as I watched him, I feared he had changed his mind and wanted to stop, something I wasn't sure I could do. But Pakim didn't want to stop. He only paused long enough to spread the bearskin out beside the fire. Then he pulled me next to him, and took me in his mouth.

I gasped and clutched at him as the very center of my body seemed to ignite.

◆

The following morning, I awoke in the shelter where Pakim and I had passed the night. I had to piss, but the desire to stay warm overcame the urge to relieve myself, and I remained wrapped in the bearskin. Pakim wasn't in the hut, and I called out to him. Naught came back to me but the sound of the river rolling past. A fire already crackled in the pit, and I regarded it drowsily. Never afore had I experienced such well-being, such ease. That judgmental, reproving part of my mind seemed to be yet imprisoned. For such small things I was grateful.

Then I remembered Rose and Colette, my new responsibilities, and how my actions might affect them. Reproach burst forth from my mind like an army breaching a wall. What had I been thinking—lying with Pakim? I hadn't been thinking, that much was obvious.

This had to be put behind me. I resolved to say nothing to Pakim about what had happened the previous night, and if he spoke of it, I would claim my behavior an aberration, brought on, perhaps, by the tobacco he had burned, or exhaustion, or anything else that might still his tongue. I knew that it would all be lies, but I prayed he would not visit the topic. Would he say something to the others? I couldn't believe so. He would be as vulnerable to the same censure as I. Or would he? Perhaps the Delaware viewed these things differently. I had heard talk that some Indian men took many wives and that they divorced with heathenish ease.

Who was I to talk about heathens? I was betrothed to not one, but two women, yet I had lain with an Indian brave. It wasn't burning in hell that I feared, but disgracing myself and forfeiting my belief that I was a trustworthy, honorable man. Mistakes could be made once. More than that was either weakness or selfishness, not that there was much difference betwixt the two.

After many minutes of self-reproach, I realized Pakim still hadn't returned. Curious as to his whereabouts, and needing to relieve myself even more, I finally clambered from underneath the thick bearskin.

Darker clouds had moved in during the night, leaving the morning light diffuse and the river valley bleak. Snow looked possible; I hoped it held off till later when we were back safely. Pakim was nowhere to be seen, then I realized Midnight was gone as well. Had he awoken, felt ashamed by what had transpired betwixt us, and left without a word? Then I remembered his bandolier bag yet lay inside, and I knew he wouldn't have left without that. Perhaps he had gone hunting for our breakfast. Thusly satisfied, I found a spot far enough from the river's edge and relieved myself.

I was starving and thought it might be a nice surprise to have breakfast ready when Pakim returned. Whatever he might have caught (if anything) could then be our supper. I pulled on my clothing, including the wonderfully warm mandillion John had given me. I rummaged about the shelter until I found a goodly length of fishing line and a couple of hooks. Thanks to John and Palmer, I also now possessed a musket, which I slung across my shoulder. After all I had been through, I would not be taken unawares again.

I went down to the river to see if there were any freshwater clams for the taking. If not, I would catch a few trout and fry those up. The sandy beach afforded no likely-looking place for either clams or trout, and upstream looked the most promising to find a spot.

The trail along the river was narrow, crowded by bushes and shadowed by trees tilting toward the water. My surroundings made me watchful. Should someone, or something, ambush me the advantage would all be theirs. There was naught to be done but pay close attention and keep my musket at the ready.

I walked a few minutes afore I found a likely-looking spot with the deep, slow moving water favored by trout. First, I poked about, again looking for clams but found none, so I tossed my line in the water. Waiting for the first fish to bite, I cast my eyes about in search of a sapling to use as a stringer for the fish. That was when I saw the hand reaching through the bush.

Thinking it was going to grab my leg, I skipped away, grunting in surprise as I did so. However, when I saw the thick rime of ice coating the flesh, I knew the hand would not be moving under its own volition. The fact that the hand was frozen made me doubt I was in any immediate danger. Even so, as quietly as possible, I cocked my musket, then proceeded forward.

The hand was slender, the fingers delicate—and ended shortly after the wrist. Using the tip of my foot, I probed amongst the bushes and found more remains, all limbs and all charred and partially eaten. This had been done by no ordinary animal, but, I felt certain, by the beast. A breeze rustled the treetops, taking my attention from the awful sight. Beyond the narrow beach on which I stood was forest so thick that anything could have been in there stalking me.

Or Pakim. Bloody hell. He was somewhere back there and didn't know there was far worse danger in these woods than angry settlers. Leaving the fishing line in the water, I ran down the trail to find him and tell him everything. I cursed myself for not having spoken of this to him sooner. The footpath seemed more narrow than afore, more choked with branches that scratched my flesh, slowing me down. An image of Pakim being ambushed by the monster filled my mind, compelling me to run that much faster. So I did until I breathlessly emerged onto the riverbank where we were camped.

The beast had arrived afore me.

chapter nine

In fact, I ran bang-smack into the befouled creature. After we collided, I lost my balance and tumbled to the ground. Unfortunately, I also lost ahold of my musket and it clattered onto the stony riverbank. The firing pan sprang open, scattering black gunpowder everywhere. I knew I was in more trouble than a witch in Salem. At once, I scrambled away from the beast, determined to escape. I put twenty feet between us afore I looked back and saw it lumbering toward me as if dazed by our collision. I grabbed a handful of rocks from the beach, throwing them at its head as hard as I could. It growled in response, but the sound wasn't nearly as ferocious as I had expected. It held up an arm to shield its face, and even stopped coming toward me for a moment. There was a hesitancy about the creature, and I wondered if perhaps it had been injured. I should be so lucky.

For a brief span, the beast and I regarded each other. It was even more ugsome than I had remembered. And so huge! Then there was that black head and mouth filled with those awful teeth. Again I thought of the gryphon and how this creature seemed to be constituted from a whole host of savage animals.

The earth began to shake as something black and powerful shot past me in a cacophony of hooves and yelling. It was Pakim riding Midnight. I heard the monster grunt, then tumble backward after Pakim kicked it in the gut. Pakim rode on another twenty feet afore the whinnying Midnight bucked and lunged in such fright that Pakim lost his grip and flew forward through the air. As I watched, he hit the ground hard, then lay there unmoving. For the first time in as long as I could remember, I felt truly afraid.

Midnight bolted away, only halting her flight when she reached the cover of the forest. The terrified animal was clearly reluctant to leave Pakim, but desperately afraid of the beast, which yet stooped over, gasping and clutching its mid-section where Pakim had kicked it.

The beast stood twenty feet from me, Pakim another twenty feet beyond it, and Midnight even farther. Knowing the horse afforded us our only chance to escape, I chased after her, but the poor creature was so frightened that she reared and kicked out as I approached. I feared she would crack my skull with a blow to the head afore I could grab her lead.

"Come on, Midnight," I pleaded, dodging her slashing hooves. "It's me, Cole. You know me, you daft animal." She must have recognized my voice because she calmed enough for me to grab ahold of her lead. My inexperience with horses slowed me greatly and by the time I was mounted on Midnight, the beast was up and staggering toward Pakim's prostrate body.

Again I felt the entirely unaccustomed emotion that was fear. Driven by that dread, I dug my heels into Midnight's sides, then sharply jerking back on the reins when we reached Pakim. So abrupt was the stop that I nearly flew off the horse. I leapt from Midnight and, with an alacrity that surprised even me, grabbed Pakim under the arms and hoisted him up onto the horse. Once I was mounted, Midnight needed no encouragement to fly from the beast with all that she was worth.

◆

The old Indian woman entered the room, eyeing me suspiciously, as if I were a worm in her cornmeal. I wasn't sure if her wariness toward me was because of Pakim's injuries, the fact that I was white, or if, however unlikely, she somehow sensed that I had lain with Pakim. Frankly, I didn't care as long as she tended to him.

Almost as if he knew I was thinking of him, Pakim opened his eyes and smiled at me. We were safe in his wikwám—a Delaware house made of bark—in his village, which was where I had brought him after the beast had attacked us. It had been closer than John's cabin, and I had been impatient for someone with better healing skills than my own to tend to Pakim.

The woman said something in Delaware, handing Pakim a steaming bowl of what I assumed to be soup. From where I sat, however, the "soup" looked and smelled like nothing more than hot water. Pakim must have noticed my puzzled expression for he said, "It is only salted water and maybe a little fat. There is little else left for my starving people." Pakim then gestured to the old woman. "This is Guhn Na Hih. It means Snow Down the River and is a very beautiful name for a very beautiful woman. But I call her Aunt Snow."

I stood and bowed slightly. "Pleased to meet you," I said.

"You as well," she said in passable English. "Many thanks for bringing Pakim back to his people." Her words may have been ones of thanks, but her eyes said she still viewed me with great suspicion. Perhaps she simply looked at all white people that way.

"Thank you for the soup, Aunt Snow," said Pakim.

"You are welcome, Nephew," she said, handing him a cup she had also brought. "Willow bark tea. It will help the ache in your head go away."

Pakim touched the lump on his head. "I fear it would take a whole willow tree to do that. But this is a good start."

Aunt Snow reached out an unsteady hand in an attempt to pat Pakim on the arm. Pakim took her hand and held it in his own. "Everyone should have someone as fine and brave as my Aunt Snow," he said, squeezing her hand gently. "Even though she was a widow, she took me in and raised me as her own. I would be nothing without her."

Aunt Snow gave him a grateful smile.

"Were Gwennie and John Chapman sent for as I requested?" asked Pakim, continuing to speak in English, I assumed, for my benefit.

Aunt Snow nodded, letting go of his hand. She followed Pakim's example and said, "Yes, Nephew, but why you want Apple Woman here, I do not know." She fiddled with a seashell bracelet around her bony wrist. "She is bad. Not to be trusted."

"With all due respect, Aunt Snow, you are wrong. Gwennie is a good woman."

"Ha!" spat Aunt Snow. "She is not right. Why else does she see no one but two white men? Where are her children? Her people? Even they do not want her. Why? Because she is red on outside, but white on inside—not to be trusted. Now Blue Heron Egg, there is a fine woman. She is loved and respected by all who know her." Aunt Snow glanced slyly at Pakim. "She was asking about you, you know. She was very worried. Shall I send her in to brighten your day?"

"Gwennie and John should be here soon, Aunt Snow," said Pakim. "I have much to discuss with them."

"Pakim, you always have a reason not to see Blue Heron Egg," whined Aunt Snow. "You promised me you would think seriously about marrying her. I do not think you have told me the truth."

"I always tell you the truth," he said. He plucked the feather he always wore from his hair, absentmindedly picking at the quill.

"Will you marry her then?" she asked.

"As I have told you, I am considering it."

Apparently, Pakim didn't always tell the truth. Hadn't he told me two days ago that marriage didn't suit him? Perhaps he was only telling his aunt what she longed to hear. Even so, his words made me wonder whether he had been entirely soothfast with me. It took me a moment to realize I felt something else as well: jealousy. I couldn't recall the last time I had felt envious of another person. What was happening to me? First, I had lain with a man. Then I had been fearful whilst in the woods, and now I was jealous. I wasn't sure I much cared for these abrupt changes in my character.

Aunt Snow stamped her foot on the ground. "It is two years since you have been married, Pakim. Sometimes I worry you have forgotten your duty. You have been back for only a few months, yet every day you seem further and further from your people. You spend less and less time here. Have you forsaken us again, my child?"

Pakim's cheeks flushed, and for the first time since I had met him there was irritation in his voice. "I have forsaken no one, Aunt Snow. I have given you and everyone else my word."

"Then you need to marry and have children to help keep the village strong." Aunt Snow gestured forcefully with her hand.

"I *have* children," said Pakim.

Pakim was a father?

"But only two of them yet live and not even here!" she said.

Pakim threw the feather to the ground, then turned away from us for a long moment. Aunt Snow looked chagrined. Softly, she said, "If you marry Blue Heron Egg and have more children, they will stay here. You can watch them grow, teach the boys to hunt and the girls to sing. We need children here, Pakim. Without them, we will die."

"I will take care of you, Aunt Snow," said Pakim, turning back to us. "I promise. No matter how many more moons you live."

"You foolish boy, it is not me I am worried about. It is not even you."

They regarded each other dejectedly, as if tired of having this argument. There was also a sadness in the look, as if they were sharing a thought to which I was not privy.

"You say you always tell me the truth, Nephew," said Aunt Snow. "Then tell me—have you met someone else and you are afraid to tell me?"

Pakim regarded the cup of willow tea which he still held. "Yes, Aunt Snow. I have met someone else."

I glanced curiously at Pakim.

"Who is she?" asked Aunt Snow.

"Why does it matter?" he asked.

"You know why Pakim! Without family, we are nothing. When you came back to us, you said that you understood that now. There is—"

Aunt Snow held a hand to her mouth as if something terrible had suddenly occurred to her. "Pakim, you have not fallen in love with someone from our clan, have you? That would be *kulaka'na*!"

Pakim shook his head. "You can calm yourself, Aunt Snow. I have violated no taboos."

Aunt Snow frowned. "If she is not of our clan, Pakim, then where is she from? Tell me something about her."

I was interested to hear myself.

Pakim fiddled with the rim of the cup he held. "I have met someone new to these parts," he said. "Someone who has come a long way to make a fresh start. This person is very courageous and wants to learn our ways. I believe we could be very happy together."

Aunt Snow scowled. "You are being very vague, Nephew. What are you hiding?" Aunt Snow pondered her own question for a moment, then exclaimed, "You are talking about a settler! It is an even worse *kulaka'na*! You would love those who want to destroy us. You want a white woman!"

"Enough," said Pakim. His voice was not loud or angry, but there was ice in it. "I do not want a white woman, Aunt Snow. And I do not have to tell you my private business. All I need do is promise that I will do nothing to hurt the clan. And I won't. Now my head is throbbing. I need to rest."

Aunt Snow had been worrying her seashell bracelet ever since we had arrived. Suddenly it broke, sending tiny shells cascading to the floor.

Pakim made as if to pick them up, but Aunt Snow said dully, "Leave them. I don't need them anymore anyway." As she turned and walked out, she stepped on several shells, grinding them to a fine white powder.

Pakim stared after her, then said softly, "I told her the truth, Friend Cole. It is not a white woman for whom I care."

I had suspected as much. Pakim had been talking about me.

◆

John, Palmer, and Gwennie sat cross-legged on the floor of the wikáma. Pakim still rested in bed, but all four them were mulling over the revelation I had made. I had finally told them all I knew about the creature. I was especially worried about Pakim's reaction—since the beast had almost killed him.

"I'm sorry I didn't tell you sooner," I said. The wikáma suddenly felt cramped and confined. "But you knew naught of my character and I didn't think you would believe me if I told you I had encountered such a beast. I've seen the damnable thing three times, yet I scarcely believe it myself."

Everyone was quiet for a long moment.

"I understand," said John at last. "Especially given what you said about Gerard's reputation always making things harder for you."

"I reckon I do as well," said Palmer. "Though, in the future, I would rather you tell me when there is a monster in the woods afore I go out hunting by myself."

Gwennie sighed. "You like other white people, Cole Seavey. You worry about yourself first, then, maybe later, you think of others."

I thought that rather harsh of her. Then I noticed John staring at the ground and realized Gwennie had been talking to him as much as me. His having convinced her to stay yet rankled her deeply.

"Is there any chance what you saw *was* a bear?" asked Palmer. "Like Murdock suggested?" Having twice encountered the thing, I knew damned well it was no more a bear than I was. I looked at Pakim to see what he had to say regarding the nature of the beast.

"I only saw it for a moment," he said. "It did have some aspects of Brother Bear, and it certainly stank like Brother Bear, but it was no bear. Of that I am certain."

"It looked like it had bear paws," I said. "But it had the legs of a man, feathers on its arms, and the head of I don't know what. Something ungodly."

"What of its face?" asked John. "Can you describe it?"

"It was terrible," I said. "As if the gates of hell had opened, and this thing had come forth. The skull was huge, and covered with black hair. The brow was brutish, set with two black eyes and a mouth filled with nasty teeth."

"Is there anything else you can think of?" asked John.

I recalled the partially cooked and eaten arms I had seen by the river. The body Abe Lobb had brought into town had also been missing its arms and legs. Suddenly, I was certain what I had found had been the rest of the dead girl. I told the others about it, then added, "God Almighty. It must have been eating her."

"I think I know this creature," said Gwennie, and we all looked at her. "It called a wendigo. A most terrible thing."

"I've never heard of it," said John.

"Is it an animal?" I asked doubtfully.

Gwennie shook her head. "It is an evil creature. I hear of it once when I traveled far from here. The Ojibwa brave who told me about creature say it a beast of the north, of the cold."

"Have you heard of this thing, Pakim?" asked John.

"I have heard a rumor of an evil in the north that is so terrifying that people won't speak of it for fear of drawing it to them," he said. "I have never heard it described or even named afore today." The look on his face said he wished he still hadn't.

"Do you know anything else about it, Gwennie?" I asked.

"Yes," she said reluctantly. "It feeds on people."

That explained not only the half-eaten parts of Addy Lobb, but all of the bones in the cave as well.

"Did the Ojibwa tell you if the wendigo would leave of its own accord?" asked Palmer. "Or how to kill it? Or at least drive it away?"

"He told me none of this," said Gwennie. "The truth is, he was drunk when he start talking. His companions were very upset he say anything, and beat him afore he told more."

"Another thing," said John. "I wonder why the wendigo didn't kill Marda and eat her instead of her livestock?"

"Maybe it was going to," I said. "Maybe something frightened it off."

"We need more than maybes," said John. "We need answers."

Gwennie rose, brushing off her skirt as she did so. "We need to see the shaman Lennikbi."

◆

The bark canoe I rode in bumped up against a gravelly shore as bleak and gray as the sky overhead. We had arrived at the remote island on which the enigmatic Lennikbi lived. As we had paddled downriver, Pakim explained that Lennikbi, or Whitewood Tree, was the most revered figure of his clan. He was supposedly capable of curing the sick, foretelling the future, and casting spells for protection.

After climbing from the canoes, Pakim insisted we wait by the river for Whitewood Tree to come to us. Proper protocol didn't include barging in upon a shaman unannounced.

Each of us waited eagerly for Whitewood Tree to appear. Only Gwennie seemed not to expect him immediately. When he didn't arrive, John and Palmer eventually fell into conversation whilst Pakim wandered away. I sensed he wished to be alone and left him with his thoughts. Even so, I eyed him surreptitiously. I wondered if it were Pakim's children occupying his mind, or perhaps his aunt's recriminations over his lack of a wife. I hoped it wasn't the latter, although I knew it was foolish of me to do so.

For a brief time, I entertained myself by skipping stones along the river's surface, at least until Gwennie scowled at me as if I were a mangy dog eyeing her provender. That woman was crabbier than a boatload of German immigrants eight weeks at sea. Finally, I meandered away along the riverbank.

As always, it felt like the forest crowded in on me. How I longed for an open vista or a forest where the trees weren't packed together like shad in a fisherman's net. Perhaps I should consider pushing farther into the frontier. I had heard talk of there being prairies as wide as an ocean and rumors of mountains even farther west that dwarfed anything I had yet encountered. The thought of seeing some place like that set my blood to tingling, and I could almost feel myself being pulled westward.

A voice called out, fetching me back to the real world and my inescapable responsibilities. I turned and saw Pakim frantically motioning for me. Fearing that the wendigo, or whatever the hell it might be, had appeared again, I sprinted back.

"He is here!" exclaimed Pakim

"The wendigo?" I asked breathlessly.

Pakim gave me a confused look. "No. Whitewood Tree. And you are keeping him waiting."

And isn't that a bloody tragedy? I thought. Pakim hurried toward a slight man standing with John, Palmer, and Gwennie. I followed after.

White folk on the frontier tended to spend a great deal of time speculating about Indian shamans. They were reputed to be traders in the black arts, capable of monstrously evil acts. It was said that white children captured in raids on border settlements were sacrificed in terrible rituals performed by shamans. Given the outrageous things people said about their own neighbors, I had never put much stock in what they said about Indians, especially since most of the people who told such outlandish tales had never even seen an Indian for themselves.

That being said, I had to admit Whitewood Tree was one of the most ferocious-looking men I had ever laid eyes on. It wasn't hard to imagine him killing in any number of ways. He was smaller than myself, with black hair plucked into a towering mohawk. His weathered, angular face was elaborately painted and so tattooed he looked as fierce as a whole regiment of Hessians—those brutal and brutish mercenaries the supposedly civilized British had brought in to do their dirty work during the Revolution.

"Greetings Cole from New York," said the shaman when John introduced us. "Would you like to join me for a cup of tea?"

So much for being fierce and ferocious. A short time later, we were seated in Whitewood Tree's home. It was small, but comfortable, even if we were rather crowded together. It wasn't all bad, however: Pakim's leg and hip were pushed up against mine. I was hard-pressed to not to think about the last time our bodies had been in such close contact. In fact, I couldn't not think about it, and had to shift slightly afore anyone noticed I was becoming aroused.

All of us sipped tea from wooden cups as a plate of pemmican was passed about. Gwennie, Pakim, and Whitewood Tree talked animatedly in their native tongue. John and Palmer looked on politely, whilst I fidgeted, eager to get this pointless affair past us.

Clearly, Pakim disagreed with Whitewood Tree and Gwennie about some important matter. I knew not precisely what the three Delaware discussed, but given how intense each seemed, I guessed dealing with the wendigo to be the topic. Whitewood Tree waved dismissively at Pakim, who shook his head in disgust. So great was their disagreement that I wondered if any sort of accord could be reached.

Whitewood Tree rose abruptly and said in English, "I'll return shortly. I'm going to fetch Gwennie an herb that tastes wonderful with partridge. After Pakim tastes it, he will know better than to disparage my cooking skills."

Recipes! They were exchanging *recipes*! And this Indian was supposed to be a terrifying purveyor of black magic? I turned to Pakim and whispered irritably, "When in God's balls are we going to talk about the wendigo?"

"We will get to it shortly," said Pakim, patting my leg. "Please remember, Whitewood Tree is a holy man. I do not know how white people treat their priests, but we do not simply go to ours and demand what we want, as if they were nothing but tools to be wielded at our behest."

I felt the color rise in my cheeks. I really had to start thinking afore I spoke.

Whitewood Tree returned, handed something to Gwennie, then said, "I know you have come for some reason other than to visit an old man."

Pakim glanced at me with what I thought a rather smug look. "Yes, Whitewood Tree," he said, then proceeded to tell the shaman all that had happened.

When Pakim had finished, Whitewood Tree said, "From what you have told me, I fear Gwennie is correct: It is a wendigo. A most foul creature. The only thing that troubles me is Cole's having seen it change shapes. That is not something wendigos are known to do."

"It may have only been a coincidence," I said. "The wendigo appeared whilst the cougar attacked me, and I thought maybe it changed shapes. In hindsight, it seems as likely that the wendigo frightened the cougar away. I never saw it change shapes again."

Whitewood Tree considered, then nodded. "I believe you are correct. Do any of you know anything more about the wendigo?"

Each of us indicated we did not.

"You must understand that a wendigo is not an ordinary spirit sent by Kishelamakank, the creator." Whitewood Tree turned to me. "Do you understand how Kishelamakank works, Cole? About good and evil?"

Why was he asking me this? Did he think me an imbecile? "I believe so," I said. "Good is to be fought for, and evil is to be… defeated." I sounded foolish even to myself.

"But *why* is there evil?" he asked. "Why can't we only have good?"

If I had been talking to a regular preacher, and not some tattooed Delaware in the middle of nowhere, I would have said we had evil because Eve ate the apple and angered God mightily. Something told me that wasn't quite the answer Whitewood Tree sought. He had to mean something deeper, something philosophical. I took a shot in the dark. "I suppose that you can't have one without also having the other."

"Just so!" said Whitewood Tree. "Most often Kishelamakank sends evil spirits to keep things in balance. Babies die so that we rejoice in those that live. Crops fail so that we know hunger and appreciate when our bellies are full."

"So are you saying," asked John, "that the wendigo is here to teach us something?"

The shaman shook his head. "No. As I said afore, the wendigo is not an ordinary spirit. It is not part of Kishelamakank's plan. You see, it was once a man and has become a demon. Demons are not part of the Creator's plan."

Yes, yes, I thought. *Just tell me how to kill the damned thing.*

Whitewood Tree folded his hands in his lap. "You see, a wendigo is a man who has committed the most foul act a man can commit."

Whitewood Tree suddenly had my full attention. What *act* did he mean exactly? He wasn't referring to my having lain with Pakim, was he? I knew most folk took such a thing very seriously. Sometimes the penalty could even be death. But if this bloody shaman was about to tell me I was going to turn into some murderous evil spirit because I had been intimate with a man one time, then I was going to walk out of there that very minute.

"And what act might that be?" asked Palmer.

"It is the killing and eating of another human," said Whitewood Tree.

"You're talking about cannibalism," I said, not a little relieved. I may not have believed Whitewood Tree's poppycock, but still— who wanted to hear talk like that about oneself?

"Yes," said Whitewood Tree.

Everyone was quiet as we absorbed the news. I had heard tales of men lost in the wild who had been reduced to eating their companions, or snowbound families reduced to eating children. I had never learned of any of them becoming this wendigo creature, though I had been told they were never the same afterwards. Some folks even went crazy, eventually killing themselves.

All of that was beside the point. There was only one thing I needed to know. "How do we kill it?" I asked.

"It is very difficult," said the shaman.

"But it can be done?" I asked.

"Yes," said Whitewood Tree.

"Good," I said. "I'm an excellent rifleman. I haven't yet had a clear shot at the damned thing, but once I do, I vow I shan't miss."

"I'm sure you are a superb shot," said Whitewood Tree. "But it does not matter how many musket balls strike the wendigo. It will not die that way."

I thought Whitewood Tree full of claptrap. I had never seen anything that enough musket balls couldn't bring down. Out of respect for Pakim, however, I kept my tongue still.

"Then how do we kill it?" asked Palmer. "Drown it? Strangle it?"

"Burn it," said Whitewood Tree. "But I must speak honestly. I believe it is too dangerous a thing for you even to try."

"Then we do nothing?" I asked. "We wait for it to come after us? We wait to die?"

"All of life is waiting to die," said Whitewood Tree.

Maybe for you, I thought. *I, however, wasn't going without a fight.*

"Besides," continued Whitewood Tree, "this is not the wendigo's normal haunt. You see, it prefers the north, where it is usually much colder than here. I think it likely the creature will move on as soon as the temperature rises. The only reason for concern would be if the wendigo had called you by name."

"Excuse me?" I said, sitting upright. "What was that?"

"If the wendigo has called your name, it has chosen you for some reason known only to itself and will not stop until it has killed you."

Bloody hell, I thought, recalling having my name called during the windstorm. "It used my name," I said, and explained about the day I had found the girl. "I had thought it might have been Gerard calling me, but I know now he was already dead by then. And there is no one else out here who could have known my name."

"It called also my name," said Gwennie. John looked appalled.

"The day you were chased through the woods," said Palmer. Gwennie nodded.

"No!" exclaimed John.

"This why I want to go to the Firelands," she said. John flinched as if she had struck him.

I recalled that day, the strange feeling I had we were being watched. Perhaps something had been there after all. Could things get much worse? Why had I ever left New York? Marriage to the most foul-tempered of women couldn't be this bad.

"Then we have to do something," said Palmer. "Whitewood Tree, you said we could burn it."

The shaman nodded. "A wendigo is a cold-blooded creature with a heart of ice. That is why it fears fire. But you must burn all of the heart so nothing remains save for ash. If even a tiny bit remains, the creature will resurrect itself."

Whitewood Tree looked at each of us, in turn with myself being last. "A wendigo is fast and clever and powerful. More powerful than any man. To be completely truthful, it is said that the only way to defeat a wendigo is to become a wendigo. Only then will you have the strength to overpower it long enough to destroy its heart. It is believed that one wendigo cannot stand the presence of another, and they will always fight to the death."

"But becoming a wendigo means eating human flesh," said Palmer. Whitewood Tree nodded gravely.

"I've seen the wendigo," I said. "I believe I can kill it without having to eat anybody." Whitewood Tree eyed me doubtfully whilst the others looked at me with a mixture of fear and concern. I kept my face a mask of confidence. After all, who better than I to take on a creature with a heart made of ice? I hadn't been nicknamed Cold-Blooded Cole for nothing.

chapter ten

The following morning, back at John and Palmer's cabin, Pakim lured me away on the pretense of our going deer hunting. This, of course, made no sense, as it was the wendigo we should have been stalking. But John had, rather oddly, insisted I go, and I thought perhaps there was a matter about which Pakim and I needed to speak in private. I hoped it wasn't about the night we had passed together, for I had no wish to revisit the subject.

We had been walking for ten minutes, making small chat about how we had slept (I hadn't; consequently, I was exhausted) and what a foggy morning it was. Finally, we reached one of Gwennie's orchards, and Pakim came to a halt. I watched him for a moment, then, cold and annoyed, said, "Are you expecting the deer to walk up to us and wait whilst we shoot them?"

"No, of course not," said Pakim, looking uncharacteristically flummoxed. "I only needed a moment to think where we should go."

I had never seen such a poor liar. Two-year-olds denying that had taken a sweet whilst their parents had watched them do so were more convincing. Finally, I had had enough. "I do not think we should *hunt* today, Pakim. Indeed, I do not think you and I should ever *hunt* together again."

An odd look crossed Pakim's face. "But Cole," he said. "You and I have never hunted together at all."

I hadn't known Pakim long, to say the least. But he had not struck me as the sort to play such games. "Stop being coy, Pakim," I said, indignantly. "We both now we aren't talking about hunting at all."

"We are not?" he asked. "You know why I really brought you here?"

"I'm not daft," I said.

"But how could you know?" he asked.

"For one thing, hunting most often takes all day," I said. "And we've brought no provisions. We don't have a knife for gutting, nor anything to wrap meat in. Would you like me to go on?"

He shook his head.

"Yet you clearly wanted to get me away from the others for some reason." By now I had myself worked up into a righteous lather that he had thought me so gullible. "You must take me for a simpleton, Pakim, not to mention a reprobate to betray Rose again!"

Pakim again looked at me with an expression of bafflement. Then he began to laugh, which well and truly infuriated me.

"What's so damned funny?" I asked.

"You think I brought you here so we could take pleasure with each other."

"Didn't you?"

"No," swore Pakim. "I did not bring you here for carnal reasons. For one thing, it is a little too cold at the moment for me to drop my breeches. Perhaps you are made of stouter stuff than I."

"I don't believe you," I said, certain I was right. Of course, he wanted to lie with me again. *Didn't he?*

Pakim stopped laughing and looked at me intently. "You are calling me a liar, Friend Cole?"

There was a coolness in his voice I had not heard afore. "No, Pakim, I'm not. But I am confused. Why are we here?" I asked.

"I wished to talk alone with you. That is all."

I was speechless. He looked and sounded utterly sincere. He also looked angry that I had all but called him a liar.

"I'm sorry I thought so poorly of you, Pakim," I said.

"Me as well," he said. "It is a most serious thing to call a Delaware brave a liar."

Strictly speaking, I hadn't called him a liar, but I didn't think he would appreciate my trying to split such a fine hair.

"Is there anything I can say to make it better?"

Pakim thought for a long moment, then said, "You can perform Gubstcha Gokhotit."

My eyes narrowed suspiciously. "Gubster Gok-what?" I asked.

Pakim looked at me severely. "Gubstcha Gokhotit," he repeated. "It is a sacred Delaware ritual of apology. It is really the only way to prove that you truly meant no offense and desire forgiveness. But I would understand if you would rather not. Only a man who is genuinely capable of owning up to his errors would be willing. In my experience, I have met very few such men." He paused, then added. "Especially white men."

I couldn't believe Pakim was going to make me do this Gubstcha-whatever-it-was. On the other hand, I had impugned his character rather badly. I also didn't care for the implication I was like other men, white or Indian. "Of course I want to do this, Pakim. What must I do?"

"Do you give your word to do everything I tell you?" he asked.

I nodded.

"First we must find a high spot for you to stand," he said. "This is so the Creator can see you." Pakim looked about, walking to a large boulder. "This one is good," he said. "Next we need sacred feathers to carry your words to heaven. Mine will do." He plucked several from his hair. He jabbed one into my hair, then instructed me to hold the other two in my hands. "We really should shave your head," he said. I sputtered in protest, but he and said, "However, I believe we can make an exception this time."

Bloody well right, I thought.

"Next," he said, "we must decorate your face with the proper markings."

This was getting ridiculous. "Is this really necessary, Pakim?" I asked.

He gave me a look almost as forbidding as the one he had given Benjamin after he had tried to ambush us. "This is a sacred ceremony.

If you question me again, I am afraid there can be no forgiveness. It is your choice."

"I'm sorry," I said, seriously revising my opinion of Pakim. "Please, carry on."

"I am afraid I do not have proper face paint, so we must make do with something else." He rummaged around in his bandolier bag until he pulled out a greasy-looking pouch. "Bear fat," he said, and I groaned inwardly. Bear fat stank with a nauseating stench all its own. Even flies couldn't stand the stuff and settlers used it in summer to keep them away. I couldn't believe Pakim was going to smear it across my face, but he proceeded to do so with malicious gusto. "Up on the rock," he commanded, when he had finished.

I climbed up on the rock. "Now what?"

"You must offer your apology to the north, south, east, and west," he said. "A different grandparent lives in each direction, and each must be mollified. Proceed when you have thought up a proper apology."

I had a few choice in words in mind, but I doubted anyone would mistake them for an apology no matter how sweetly profferred. "Oh, Grandfather in the North," I said, whilst Pakim looked on sternly. "Please forgive—"

Pakim held up his hand, motioning for me to stop. "You must wave the feathers as you talk," he said. "That is how your words will reach the Creator in heaven."

"But I thought I was talking to the Grandparents," I said.

Pakim folded his arms across his chest.

"Fine," I said, starting again. This time I flapped my arms. "Oh, Grandfather in the North," I said again. "Please hear my apology. I meant no offense to the Great Pakim—"

Pakim again held up his hand.

"What now?" I asked, exasperated.

"You must stand on one foot. This is to show humility."

I would show him humility, preferably with tip of my boot. First, I would get through this because I had given my word, and no man would ever say Cole Seavey didn't make good on his word. I recited everything again, finishing up with, "I vow to always think afore I speak and to treat my betters with the deference they deserve." I paused, then said, "There. How was that?"

"Now you must gobble like a turkey," he said.

"What?" I exploded, throwing the feathers to the ground. "That's ridiculous! No! I won't do it. That's it, Pakim. I'm done. And if it's not good enough, then I don't give a damnation if—" I stopped because Pakim was clutching his sides as if he were in great pain. Or as if he were laughing himself sick. Then I understood: I had been had, and had good.

"None of that was real!" I hollered. "You were having me on, weren't you?"

Pakim kept laughing too hard to answer. All he could manage to do was nod as he staggered about cackling.

I was going to kill him. As soon as Pakim saw me leap down from the rock, he took off running. He was fast, probably faster than I, but I was mad, and that more than made up the difference. I tackled him from behind and we tumbled to the ground. He tried to get away, laughing the entire time, but I soon had him pinned down.

"You should have seen yourself," he gasped between gales of laughter. "I do not think I have ever seen a more ridiculous sight!" He started flapping his arms about, then added, "Gobble, gobble!" This launched him off into a fresh round of laughter.

"I never gobbled!" I said indignantly. If he liked laughing so much, then I would give him something to keak about. I would tickle him until he died laughing. I pinned his arms with my legs, then proceeded to tickle him with all of my might.

"Stop!" he pleaded. "Please, Cole! Stop!"

He would have to make me. And he did. Somehow he used his legs to flip me over and the next thing I knew, he had me pinned to the ground. I vowed to get him to teach me that trick later. "Shall we call it even?" he asked, perched above me.

"I suppose," I said. "But you really are a vile, ugsome serpent beneath the contempt of even the most loathsome sinner to ever walk the earth."

Pakim laughed, then pinched his thighs together, squeezing me between them. Almost immediately, a hot flame of excitement flared in my belly.

He smiled mischievously. "I will take your words as a compliment, Friend Cole."

"Only you would be presumptuous enough to do so," I said, feeling myself stiffen beneath his warm body. I tried to wriggle free afore Pakim could notice.

"You dare speak of my being presumptuous after *you* thought *I* lured you down here to burrow between your legs?"

"You have a point, I suppose," I said. "So what does Gubstcha Gokhotit mean anyway?"

Pakim smiled slyly. "Nothing."

"Liar," I said, pressing my fingertips into his sides threateningly. "Tell me."

"It means Foolish Little Owl."

"So I'm foolish, am I?" I said, with mock indignation.

"No, Cole. You are not foolish. But Gokhotit, Brother Owl, has always been very special to me. I think that will be my secret name for you for now on."

"Gokhotit?" I said, trying to pronounce it the way Pakim had. He nodded. "I like it," I said. "But you better not add the "foolish" part again or next time I might not go so easy on you."

Pakim smiled, then said, "I am glad you like it, Gokhotit. Would you like me to set you free now?"

No, I thought to myself. "Yes."

"You would not try anything underhanded, would you?" he asked.

"I guess you'll have to let me go and see," I said.

His hands slowly loosened their grip on my wrists. His black eyes, however, didn't leave my own, and we each studied the other for a long moment. With my arms free, I found my hand tentatively moving toward his face. Pakim closed his eyes as my finger traced the curving tattoo that lined his right cheek. My other hand slid under his shirt, causing him to shiver when I touched his hard belly. I moved my hand from his face to the back of his neck and pulled him toward me. I knew I should stop, that I shouldn't be doing this, but when our tongues found each other, I could no more stop what we had started than I could prevent the cold, dark winter from arriving.

◆

Pakim strode ahead of me as if he, too, felt guilty about what had transpired between us. Only then did I realize we had never discussed whatever he had wished to. The truth was, I didn't feel guilty for what we had done, or at least not very much so. What had happened had happened, and part of me believed that something which felt so right couldn't really be wrong, no matter what God or the church elders proclaimed.

The world was a much more complicated place than it had seemed a week ago, but it was also considerably more interesting. I certainly was finding I wasn't quite the man I'd believed myself to be.

Once Rose and I were wed, however, I knew I could not continue to carry on with Pakim. There were some bounds of propriety that even I would not cross. It was true that those bounds had thus far proved to be much more malleable than I had ever suspected, but even so,. I trusted I had reached their limits.

To my relief, Rose had not yet pressed me on our actually declaring ourselves husband and wife. But I wondered how much longer that would last. The answer turned out to be not very. As soon as I entered John's cabin, a shout of congratulations went up, and I was ambushed by John, Palmer, and a half-dozen other people.

"Here's the groom now!" shouted Palmer.

"Groom?" I repeated uneasily. "What's going on

"You're to be married, that's what," said Palmer.

John came close and said softly, "We had this planned anyway and decided to go through with it." He paused, then added. "In case something happens."

"I reckon you didn't suspect a thing, did you?" asked Palmer, handing me a noggin filled with whiskey.

I had to admit I hadn't. At least now I understood what Pakim had really been up to taking me into the woods. I wondered how he felt about being the one to lure me away from my own nuptials, especially given what liberties we had taken with each other only a short time ago.

"You and Pakim were gone an awful long time," said Palmer. "You must have had a successful hunt, although I don't see any game."

My eyes darted to the floor. "We lost the trail," I said, uneasily. "Speaking of hunting, whence did all this food come from?" I asked, gesturing at the table. Truth be told, there really wasn't that much, but given the scarcity of provisions, I was surprised there was more than water and nuts.

"Despite appearances," said John, "Palmer and I do have a few friends amongst the other settlers. Once we sent word that there was to be a wedding, it was surprising how much food turned out to be available."

Looking about the cabin, I recognized Aunt Snow and Marda Witt, as well as two other settlers and four Indians I didn't recognize.

"We wanted you to have a proper wedding," said John. "Or at least a close proxy of one. I hope you don't mind." He looked at me carefully, as if he truly worried I might object for some reason.

"No, not at all," I said, thinking regretfully of Pakim. "It's very thoughtful."

"Dumont over there even brought his fiddle. He's going to play for us later." John and Palmer smiled, plumb pleased with themselves. A knock at the door drew everyone's attention and John said, "That must be Rose and Gwennie."

Palmer ushered me to the back of the cabin whilst everyone else gathered about in a circle. The door opened and in stepped Rose. Her hair was piled on her head and decorated with something that looked like ivy. She wore a blue dress that was too large and certainly had to have been borrowed, but was fetching none the less. Gwennie came behind her, carrying Colette, and even looked slightly less stern than usual. Watching them approach, I steeled myself to become both husband and father.

The sudden pounding of hoofbeats drew everyone's attention away from Rose. John stepped to the door, peered into the distance, then said, "Pakim, you best come here."

Pakim did so, but everyone else followed as well. I had just stepped outside when three braves on horseback came to a stop in front of the cabin. Pakim talked to the braves, who gestured wildly and were clearly agitated. Given that they spoke in their native tongue, none of the settlers understood what was said, but when Aunt Snow began crying, we all knew something terrible had happened.

"The village was attacked about an hour ago," said Pakim, turning to us. "People are dead."

"Bloody hell," said Palmer. "Who was it? Settlers?"

"I am not sure," said Pakim. "There is some dispute. Some people saw at least one white man, but others saw what had to be the wendigo."

"Damnation!" said John. I saw him notice Gwennie glaring at him. She still hadn't forgiven him for making her stay.

"What is a wendigo?" asked a man whose name I didn't know.

John and Palmer looked at each other, uncertain what to say.

"It is a creature that Indians believe in, Mr. Alan," said Dumont, joining us. "A very *diabolique*—evil—creature."

I recalled having watched the Frenchman the day I visited Hugh's Lick. He had struck me as a calm, judicious sort, and I had thought then I could be friends with him. When the other settlers had blamed the Delaware for Addy Lobb's death, he had warned there were other dangers in the forest as well.

"Is this wendigo the same thing that attacked Marda Witt's claim then?" asked Mr. Alan.

"It very well could be," said John.

"Someone has got to warn the others." Mr. Alan turned and hurried away.

"What are you going to do, Pakim?" asked John.

"I've got to get back to the village," he said. "Red Oak says there is talk of attacking Hugh's Lick in retribution."

"We're coming with you," said John. "We need to find out who, or what, is responsible. I'm sorry, Cole. We'll have to marry you later."

"I understand," I said. "And I'm coming as well."

"Maybe it would be best if you stayed with Rose," suggested Pakim.

"But I've seen it twice," I said. "I have the most experience with it." That was true enough, but I also hated the idea of Pakim facing the wendigo without me.

Pakim considered, then nodded.

"Rose," I said, going to her. "I have to go. I hope you understand."

Rose was clearly frightened, but nodded her assent. "Be careful," was all she said.

By now the other settlers and Indians had all gone, leaving only Rose and the baby behind.

"Somebody needs to stay with Rose and Colette in case something happens here," said John.

"I will," said Palmer. "Now go, afore things get any worse."

◆

Smoke swirled up from Pakim's smashed wikwám. None of the other houses had been spared either. Broken jars, torn clothing, and foodstuffs lay scattered about. Injured Indians sat around with dazed looks upon their faces, and I saw two bodies laid out. Pakim was furious.

"What do the others say happened?" asked John.

"There is much confusion," said Pakim. "All I know for sure is that four of my people are dead, two braves are missing, and what little we owned is destroyed. The braves were out hunting, so there were only women, children, and two old men here. It all happened so fast, no one really saw anything. First, there was a fire that jumped from wikwám to wikwám. Barks Like a Badger says he saw a white man, but he is old and sees poorly. Morning Light swears she saw Woodcock Feather fly up into the air and be carried away. But she is old, and I do not trust her mind. Too, the village was yet shrouded in fog from the river. Most saw the creature you have described, Cole. Whomever it was could not have chosen a better time to attack." Pakim kicked at the ground angrily. "I do not know what to think."

"Whatever happened," said John, "the question is, what are you going to do about it. Is there still talk of attacking Hugh's Lick?"

Pakim laughed bitterly. "With what?" he asked. "Beads and feathers? Almost every one of our weapons has been destroyed. The two men who are missing are among our strongest braves. We could not attack a beaver lodge."

"What are you going to do?" I asked.

Pakim gazed around at the ruins of his village. "Even afore this, there has been talk of leaving. I would wager that is what we will do." He balled his hand into a fist as if preparing to lash out.

"Where would you go?" asked John.

"My mother's sister's clan lives a week's ride from here. I believe they will take us in. But it is a very hard, dangerous ride. More of us will die. But at least Murdock Burke can finally have our land, which he has wanted so badly."

A half-hour later it had been decided: Pakim and his people were leaving. Gwennie helped tend to the injured, whilst John gathered up as much as possible of the scattered foodstuffs. Pakim's people would need everything they could find to survive the journey. Whilst John and Gwennie did their work, Pakim and I worked side-by-side constructing several travois to haul the injured and whatever supplies John could save.

"I am sorry about your wedding, Cole," said Pakim. To free his arms whilst he worked, Pakim removed his bandolier bag and set it on a log.

"Don't be ridiculous, Pakim. It's nothing compared to this."

"I want you to know I admire you for helping Rose," said Pakim. "People talk about bravery being the highest attribute a man can strive for. I believe it is selflessness, and you are to be commended for having it."

"Don't go making me out to be some saint, Pakim," I said.

"I know you are not a saint," said Pakim. "But you are a good man, whilst many are not." He hesitated a moment, then said, "Cole, there is something I think you should know."

Uh-oh, I thought. "If you like," I said.

"It is about Friend John and Friend Palmer. They are different from most people. You see, they live together as a married couple. Excepting Gwennie and myself, people, of course, do not know this, but in light of our experiences, I thought you should know."

"I see," I said, absorbing the news. "Do they know we have...had experiences?" The notion that Pakim had been talking about me with John and Palmer made me nervous.

Pakim shook his head. "They know I have had relations with men. However, I would never talk about you without first obtaining your permission."

Pakim had been with other men? He had been married twice, had children, *and* been with other men? When the hell did he have time to hunt?

"I only thought you should know so you would not be taken aback when you realized it yourself," said Pakim.

A little too late to avoid that, I thought. I wondered which other men Pakim had been with. Were they white men or other Delaware? I hoped it had been with Delaware. Then I realized what foolishness I was thinking. What the blasted difference did it make to me who Pakim had relations with anyway? None as far as I could see, so I shoved the thought from my mind.

"Are you all right?" asked Pakim.

"I'm fine," I said. "Thank you for telling me about John and Palmer."

Pakim shrugged.

"I think I shall give up trapping for good," I said.

Pakim looked at me inquisitively.

"If I'm to be married to Rose, I think I'll have to be a farmer," I said. "Even though you and I both know I'm no farmer."

"I see," said Pakim, but clearly he didn't.

"My heart won't be in farming," I said. "Not like it was in trapping."

"You are a determined man, Cole," said Pakim. "I'm sure you will be as good a farmer as a trapper."

"I doubt it," I said, turning back to the travois. "Besides, it will mean nothing to me. Not like trapping has."

Pakim watched me a moment, then he, too, turned back to our work.

It was just after noon when the last travois was loaded with the injured, along with the salvaged provisions. As I watched Pakim gently help Aunt Snow climb aboard one of the travois, I wondered if I would ever see him again. It seemed unlikely. After all, assuming the wendigo didn't kill us first, Rose and I were going to go west to the Firelands, a place I wasn't even certain existed. Pakim was headed south and had to worry about keeping his people alive, both now and in the future. He wouldn't have time to be thinking of me.

That, I knew, was for the best. So why did it feel like the worst?

When everyone was set to go, I noticed Pakim looking for his bandolier bag and remembered his laying it down whilst we built the travois. I returned to the spot where I had seen it. I knew that inside the bag were the things most precious to Pakim: items from his vision quest, gifts from his father, symbols of his totem. I wanted him to have something from me as well. I took the raven's feather from my pocket and slipped it into the bag. It would say the thing I could not.

chapter eleven

Gwennie and Pakim embraced for a long moment. He held her tightly, whispering something in her ear that caused her to smack him on the back in mock indignation. He was grinning mischievously when he finally let go of her. John stepped forward, taking both of Pakim's hands in his.

"When Palmer and I arrived here, you befriended and helped us," said John. "We can't ever repay our debt to you, Pakim."

"Please tell Friend Palmer how sorry I am to not have said goodbye myself."

John nodded. "I will. And promise you'll come visit us when you can."

"I will try, Friend John," he said. "I will try."

Pakim turned to me, and I handed him his bandolier bag. I went to shake his hand, but he pulled me into an embrace instead. "Perhaps if our circumstances change someday, Gokhotit, we can both be trappers together," he said hoarsely. Then he turned and instructed his people to start their journey.

John, Gwennie, and I watched until the last of the Delaware had disappeared into the forest. In my mind's eye, I saw another figure vanishing along with the Indians: the strange, new person I had been becoming in the presence of Pakim. Perhaps the departure of that self wasn't a bad thing.

Weariness settled across me as heavily as a bearskin blanket. How badly I wanted to sleep, but there was much to be done. John, Gwennie, and I agreed that first we should go into town to let the settlers know the Indians had departed and were no longer a threat. John and I rode on Elizabeth, Gwennie on a sturdy little Indian pony I hadn't even known she owned. She said its name was Maboawikcham, which translated as Hiccup—a reference to the pony's odd gait, which made whoever rode it bob up and down repeatedly.

Once we reached the edge of town, Gwennie, like Pakim, had to remain in the woods whilst we actually delivered the news to the settlers. As we rode into Hugh's Lick, the first thing I noticed was a dead grizzly sprawled on the ground. It seemed someone had already laid claim to Murdock's bounty. A sad-looking young boy poked the dead animal with a stick. He solemnly informed us that Owen Stern had killed the bear—a sow—as well as its two cubs. It was that then that I noticed the two smaller black mounds nearby. The boy reported Owen had also earlier wounded another bigger bear that had escaped. I hoped the next time Owen went to take a piss he might encounter the animal who could return the favor.

We found the settlers themselves to be exhibiting an odd amalgam of relief and anxiety. Word had arrived of the Delaware's departure, hence the relief and the large crowd already gathered. But rumor of the wendigo's existence circulated as well, and more than a few people seemed fearful of this new threat.

"We don't really believe this nonsense about demons and this Winded Go creature, do we?" asked Owen, belligerently addressing his fellow townsfolk. "After all, I killed the grizzly that Murdock blamed for the attack on Marda Witt."

No one said a word, and it was clear they didn't believe the fiction that a bear was responsible any more than I had. Perhaps they weren't as idiotic as I thought.

Owen, noticing John's and my arrival, approached us. "You were friends with those red-skinned bastards," he said. "What's this foolishness about a demon prowling about in the woods?"

John and I exchanged wary glances. "It's called a wendigo and was supposed to have once been a man," I said. "A man who has become a cannibal. And once he has—"

Without warning, I found myself knocked to the ground. Someone had tackled me from behind and now lay on top of me repeatedly driving his fist into my skull. John and Palmer started yelling and grabbing at my assailant. Finally, they managed to dislodge my attacker afore I suffered any more damage than a stinging ear.

"I've seen it!" said a voice wrought with hysteria. "It tried to kill me!" At last I managed to stand upright. I was confronted with the beleaguered countenance of Benjamin Carson, whom Pakim and I had left stranded in the woods. "Did you and that red-skinned bastard know it was out there?" he yelled. "Did you know what you were leaving me alone with? *Did* you?"

Clearly, Benjamin was on the edge of insanity. His voice was shaky and panic-stricken, and he looked as if he had been through hell. His face was bruised and scratched, his clothes torn. His eyes brimmed with tears, and he couldn't stop shaking.

"What are you talking about?" asked John.

Benjamin gestured wildly at me. "This one—*Seavey*—and that Indian he associates with attacked me in the woods—"

"You attacked *us*," I said.

"Liar!" yelled Benjamin. "It was you—"

"Will you swear to that on your immortal soul, Benjamin?" asked Dumont, the Frenchman.

Benjamin glared at Dumont. "You don't understand! They tried to sacrifice me to that thing!" he said. "That's why they left me out there! They took my musket, my food, everything, and left me out there with that *monster.*"

Dumont placed a hand on Benjamin's arm. "Calm yourself, Benjamin," he said.

Benjamin jerked his arm away. "Calm myself?" Benjamin asked with a laugh. "Not likely after what I've seen."

"What did you see, Benjamin?" asked Owen.

"At first I thought it was a man in the shadows," said Benjamin talking quickly, as if he couldn't get the story out fast enough. "I was lost in the woods when I saw him. I called out, but he said nothing. As I drew closer, I realized he was the tallest man I had ever seen." Benjamin paused and licked his lips. "Too tall, really. I mean people just don't get that tall!" Benjamin's voice rose in pitch afore he regained a modicum of control. "But then the man stepped forward, and I saw he wasn't a man. He was a *thing*. It had a horrible black head and paws instead of hands." Benjamin paused, chewing on one of his fingernails. "You see, the thing watched me," he continued. "Watched me like it was hungry and I was something be put on a spit. I lost my nerve and ran." Benjamin shook even harder and someone placed a coat around him.

When Benjamin fell silent, everyone waited for him to continue, but he didn't. I saw more than one agitated look pass between unnerved settlers. Finally, Conor Mulcahy, the Irishman, said, "And what the feck makes you so certain this thing you seen was this wendigo? I thought it was supposed to be a man turned man-eating demon, not this mishmash of creatures you seen. To tell the truth, Benjamin, it sounds to me like you bloody-well might 'ave imagined the entire episode."

Benjamin slowly shook his head as tears finally spilled from his eyes. "It told me," he said. "It called out my name, said it was a wendigo and would be coming back for me and there was nothing I could do to escape it."

As soon as Benjamin said the creature had called out his name, John and I glanced at each other. I shrugged, telling John I wasn't sure what to think.

"Then it was gone," said the sobbing Benjamin as he turned toward the woods. "But it's out there right now. It's watching us. I know it is."

Each one of us scanned the woods uneasily.

"It told you it was a wendigo?" asked Conor. "Did it shake your 'and as well and offer to break bread with you? Why the damnation would a demon introduce 'imself to you?"

"I don't know," said Benjamin, crying harder. "I can only tell you what it did. And it's going to get me no matter what I do."

"Ach, you're daft, man," said Conor. "You got yourself—"

Suddenly, Benjamin shrieked whilst pointing toward the forest. Everyone took a step away from him. "It's back! It's come back for me!"

My eyes scoured the woods, but I saw nothing.

"Look! He's running away," shouted a woman, and we all turned. Sure enough, Benjamin sprinted the opposite way as if his life depended on it. Several times he glanced back over his shoulder, and it was clear to all that, at the very least, Benjamin truly believed something chased him. A moment later, he vanished into the woods.

"The man is obviously not in his right mind," said Dumont, the Frenchman. "I'll fetch him back afore he causes himself to come to harm." He took off running in pursuit.

"What the *hell* was that about?" asked Owen.

No one answered. We all watched the spot where Dumont had disappeared into the woods.

The minutes dragged by, and yet we stood there. A stranger stumbling upon us might have guessed us bewitched. Given the eerie events of the past several days, they might not have been mistaken. Finally, a woman said, "Perhaps someone should go after Dumont. Make sure he is all right."

"I'll go," I said. Afore I could move, however, Dumont reappeared from the spot in the forest into which he had vanished.

"I lost him," he said, breathing hard. "Never have I seen a man run so fast in my life."

If the crowd of settlers had been somewhat anxious about the rumors of Indian demons afore Benjamin's arrival, his hysterical behavior and story frightened them badly. The gray clouds scudding by overhead were well-suited to the pall that now hung over the crowd. Even the horses were skittish. White puffs of breath, from horses and people alike, rose into the frigid air, anxieties given corporeal form.

The settlers milled uneasily around the outside of the blockhouse, talking in hushed voices. Several men suggested getting up hunting parties to scour the woods for any unnatural creatures, and the feel of impending violence hung in the air. I could see the settlers were scared and wanted something to lash out against. It was the only way for them to stop feeling helpless. Seeing this made me doubly relieved Pakim and his people were gone.

The townsfolk seemed to have forgotten their questioning of John and me. I wished to leave afore they remembered—and made us the unwitting target of their fear.

"This must be what the raven foretold," said a woman. "It prophesied deaths. I venture the demon is going to kill us all. "

"And what about what happened at Widow Witt's?" asked a man I had not seen afore. "Might that not have something to do with all this?"

"Why isn't Murdock here?" demanded Owen. "He fancies himself in charge after all. In fact, why aren't there any Burkes here?"

"Perhaps Murdock knows something about all of this," called out a voice.

Owen nodded. "I think we ought make a call on him."

A chorus of voices yelled out in agreement

"No," said Conor "We should wait until Murdock comes 'ere. You know 'ow 'e doesn't want anyone but 'is family up at their place."

Whilst the townsfolk argued vigorously amongst themselves, I pulled John aside and told him I planned to go to Murdock's no matter what the others did.

"But why, Cole?" asked John. "We already know about the wendigo from Whitewood Tree. How could Murdock help us?"

"Supplies," I said. "I've decided that if I have to beg, borrow, or steal, I've got to get supplies from Murdock so Rose and I can clear out afore everyone here is completely wildered in their wits. These folks aren't going to feel safe until they've killed something. Maybe a lot of something."

"But why go to Murdock's now?" John asked. "Why not wait until later, after this lot has decided what course to take?"

"Because I want to go as soon as possible," I said. "There is no telling what's going to happen next and I, for one, don't fancy waiting around to see how bad things get. Something tells me it could be downright awful."

John nodded. "All right, then. I'll fetch Gwennie and catch up with you. We'll have to ride fast, though. Even then, we still might not make it there and back to the cabin afore dark. And I don't much fancy being caught out-a-doors with all that's been happening."

Just then snow began falling. It was the first snow of the winter, and the settlers regarded it apprehensively, as if it were another bad portent. Things were difficult enough without blizzards and drifts of snow to contend with.

"Excuse me, Mr. Seavey," said Dumont after John had left. "We have never been properly introduced." He held out his hand and said, "I am Dumont Lazare."

The Frenchman was short and stocky, so much so that I had been surprised at how fast he had run in pursuit of Benjamin. He was also most self-possessed. Despite the looming tensions and peculiar happenings of the day, Dumont seemed rattled not in the least. Even his dress—buckskin pants, a bright-red hunting shirt—were as neat as any Philadelphia gentleman's and bespoke of a man who was meticulous in all that he did. I quite liked him.

"Please call me Cole," I said, shaking his hand.

"Cole, afore you depart there is something I would like very much to show you. Would you consent to join me?"

"I've not much time, Dumont," I said. "Can it wait until later?"

"I think not," he said emphatically, so I followed after him. As soon as I saw him heading for the woods, I had a bad feeling about what he wanted to show me.

"I show this to you because you seem to know something about the wendigo. Too, you were the one with Benjamin leave as is. He saw the creature."

"Why not show the others?" I asked.

"They are already like an unthinking dog that is frightened by a thunderstorm. I do not wish to frighten them further. You, however, strike me as a man not ruled unduly by emotions."

We climbed steadily uphill until we reached a stone outcropping that hung over the river. Large snowflakes swirled around us, alighting on the rocky ledge. Below us lay a fast-flowing section of the river not yet frozen by the cold.

"I did not really lose Benjamin's trail," he said. "This is simply where it ceased."

I glanced down and saw he was right. The trail led up to the stone outcropping where we stood, then stopped. The only place for him to have gone was over the edge. That would have been disturbing enough, even without the large smear of blood spread out across the stone.

"Perhaps he tripped," I suggested, to explain the bloodstained rock beneath our feet. "He might have broken his nose or badly cut himself."

"That is much blood for someone who injured himself falling," said Dumont. "But I concede it is possible."

I walked to the edge so I could look down into the river. It was a drop of perhaps forty feet into deep, fast moving water riddled with boulders. Anyone who fell from here onto those rocks was almost certain to have perished. Even if it were the case that Benjamin had tripped, injured himself, and bled profusely, it still didn't answer the most obvious question: What had so frightened him that he then jumped to his death?

◆

Gwennie came to an abrupt halt and motioned for John and me to stop as well. Murdock Burke's claim lay somewhere not too far in front of us. "Something is burning," she said.

John and I sniffed the air. I smelled nothing mixed in with the steady stream of snow.

"Do you mean like a cooking fire?" asked John. "Murdock's claim should be just ahead. Perhaps you smell their supper roasting."

Gwennie shook her head. "It stink. Like rubbish burning."

Elizabeth whinnied uneasily, as if she, too, had caught some foul scent.

"We best be careful then," John said. "In fact, why don't we tie up the horses here and go on foot?"

As we made our way to the Burke's claim, John explained that Murdock had practically established a second town up here, but one solely for his kin. John had visited once and said there were five cabins, one for each brother and their families. The only one without a cabin of his own was Stich Burke, also the only one unmarried. Since he had neither the money nor the backbone to raise a cabin of his own, he had to live with Murdock, who treated him worse than the curs who skulked about Hugh's Lick begging for scraps.

I saw the smoke afore I smelled it. The thick, gray stuff snaked its way past the treetops like some sort of befouled mist. Gwennie was right—it did stink. This wasn't the smell of roasting venison or baked bread. It was the stench of burning hair and clothes. When we finally emerged from the woods and onto the Burke's claim, I understood why none of the Burkes had been in town.

They, too, had been attacked by the wendigo.

From the looks of things, the attack hadn't happened all that long ago. Amongst the ruined cabins, flames still crackled loudly, popping and hissing as they eagerly consumed Murdock's dreams. As at Marda Witt's, pieces of dead animals lay strewn about the claim, but this time there were human victims as well. A long-haired blond man lay face down in the dirt, a thin layer of snow upon his body. Despite the bitter cold, he was bare from the waist up, and three deep scratches rent his flesh from one side to the other. I checked his pulse, but there was none. I rolled the body onto its back and was appalled when I saw the violence that had been done to him. His face was missing beneath his nose. Lips, mouth, chin—all gone. It wasn't hard to picture the terrible bear paws of the wendigo wreaking such damage.

"God Almighty," said John, coming up behind me. "That's Wilmington Burke. And I found the body of Albers. They were the next two oldest after Murdock."

"Did he die the same way?" I asked.

John shook his head. "There isn't a mark on him."

I went to the body to see for myself. The man lay on his back, as if he had decided to take a nap. I wondered how he had died.

John looked about the devastation. "I don't see anyone else, and there should be at least twenty others. I fear they all perished in their cabins."

Gwennie returned after having finished her own inspection of the claim. "Look there," she said.

John and I looked where she indicated. A woman emerged from the woods aiming a musket directly at us.

"That's Virginia Burke," said John. "She's Murdock's wife. We've met once afore. Let me talk to her."

John walked forward, his hands held in front of him so she could see he was unarmed. "I'm John Chapman, Mistress Burke," he called out. "We met in town last year."

Virginia Burke had obviously once been a beautiful woman. And it was just as obvious that years of bearing children and living on the frontier had robbed her of that beauty. I guessed she was perhaps fifty—old, but not that old. Once-black hair was now mostly gray and wispy. Her complexion was sallow, her face deeply lined, and she was frighteningly thin, as if her last decent meal was far beyond recall. With the food shortage and such a large brood to raise, such was likely true.

Virginia's eyes lingered over the smoking ruins of her home. Then her eyes turned upward, examining the sky as if expecting to see something there. "You seen my husband, Mr. Chapman?" she asked.

"I'm sorry to say that I haven't," said John. "Are you all right? What about the others?"

"They're with me," she said, still eyeing the sky warily. "Those that yet live anyway."

John's eyes followed Virginia's eyes skyward whence the snow streamed down. "Are you looking for something, Mistress Burke?" he asked.

She shook her head slowly, her frightened eyes meeting ours.

"I believe it's safe for the others to come out," said John.

Virginia made what was supposed to be a laugh, but was more

of an anguished bark. "I shan't ever feel safe again, Mr. Chapman, but thanks for your opinion." She did, however, turn to the woods and call out for the others to join her.

A ragtag collection of women and children—perhaps a dozen in all—straggled forth. A towheaded boy, yet in the early transition from childhood to adolescence, came first. He clutched a tree limb and looked about wild-eyed as if expecting to be attacked any moment. Two women followed, supporting the slumped figure of a man between them. One of the women was the spitting image of Virginia, except younger and not nearly so thin.

"What in God's name happened here, Mistress Burke?" asked John.

"I'll be damned if I know," she answered. "I suppose it was the Delaware, though I never saw nor heard them."

"It was a monster," said a red-eyed young woman who had obviously been crying. "I saw it." Two small children, clearly terrified, clung to her skirts.

"Hush, Emiline," said Virginia. "You're talking nonsense."

"But I did," said Emiline. "And you did, too, Virginia. We all did."

"I said, hush." Virginia's eyes darted toward John and me.

But Emiline wouldn't be hushed, couldn't seem to help herself. "It was huge and had a black head with terrible teeth. It grabbed Stich and carried him away like he was nothing but a sack of earth apples." Emiline closed her eyes and said, "I shan't ever forget the way poor Stich screamed as that thing took him away."

"Shush!" snapped Virginia. This time she got Emiline's attention. "You're scaring the children."

They looked no more terrified then they already had when I first laid eyes upon them.

"Come with me," said Virginia to John and me. Gwennie, as usual, had disappeared in the presence of strangers. "Emiline, you stay here with the children.

"What Emiline says is the truth," said Virginia, once we were out of earshot of the others. "We were eating our supper when it happened. Something landed on the roof, skittering about like a bird— a *big* bird, mind you. Murdock got up to investigate, but the door wouldn't open. Simon and Carl joined him—the three of them all but threw themselves against the door. Still, it wouldn't budge. I swore I heard laughter outside too. Then the fire started."

The three of us looked to the still-smoking ruins of the cabins.

"Somehow the whole roof ignited," said Virginia. "The heat was horrible, and with the door blocked we had no way in or out. Chunks of burning wood were falling down on us. I thought for sure we were going to die when the door suddenly came unstuck. We ran outside and saw the other cabins were burning. Smoke swirled everywhere so it was hard to see. Wilmington was somewhere behind me when he let out a little yelp. By the time I got to him the lower part of his face was…" Virginia stammered as if unable to believe what she had seen. Having seen it myself, I understood her being at loss for words.

"It's all right," said John. "We saw. We know."

"Everybody was running about looking for whomever was attacking us. We all figured it was Indians, but there were none to be seen. And they weren't making that awful racket they usually do when they attack. All that ungodly screaming that unnerves a body so. No, this was almost silent, and that was even worse."

Virginia took a deep breath, brushed the snow from her hair, then continued. "That was when we saw the thing come out of the forest. Stich saw it first and went after it with his musket. I always thought that man was a white-livered poltroon. I was ungenerous—today he proved otherwise. He ran to within ten rods of the beast, then shot it. But the musket ball either flew wide, or had no effect on the terrible thing. As Stich was trying to reload, the creature savaged him something horrible, then carried his body into the woods. The poor man's screams were awful."

Perhaps I also judged the man too harshly, I thought.

"Where are Murdock and the others?" asked John.

"He and Albers and Robert went after Stich. Murdock told us to hide in the woods until they came back. I heard a scream about a quarter of an hour ago, then nothing until you appeared."

"Albers went with Murdock?" I asked.

Virginia nodded. "Why?"

"I'm sorry to say, we found his body, Mistress Burke." John gestured to where the figure lay.

"But he left with the others," Virginia said. "How did he get back here?"

The small boy who still clung to Emiline's dress squealed, "Look, it's Papa!" and took off running. Two men had, in fact, emerged from the woods. They leaned into each other, shuffling as they walked, as if either injured or exhausted.

"Stop, Andrew!" Emiline issued a bloodcurdling yell. The boy jerked to a halt as if God himself had issued the command. Emiline was clearly on the verge of hysteria. I think everyone felt that way.

John and I stood with the women who waited anxiously for the men to join us. They turned out to be Murdock and Robert Burke, and both men were ashen-faced, clearly shaken by something.

"Is Albers here?" asked Murdock. His hands were tucked under his arms as if he were freezing. It was cold out, but Murdock appeared to feel even colder than expected.

"He's not with you?" asked a woman I had not yet met. Something told me she was Albers wife and had not heard us tell Virginia he was dead.

Virginia gestured to where his body lay. The woman took several steps forward, then spun away. She neither cried, nor made a sound, but simply crumpled to the ground.

Robert squeezed his eyes shut. "He just vanished. He was right next to me, then he was gone."

"Did you find Stich?" asked Virginia.

Murdock shook his head. At least there was no wife or children to be devastated by the news.

"We're leaving," announced Murdock to his surviving family. "Now." He squeezed his arms even tighter to his sides, and I realized he was trying not to tremble. Something told me it wasn't the cold that made him shiver so. I had never seen a man so unnerved.

The others looked at him in surprise. "But where will we go?" asked Virginia.

"East," he said. "Fort Braden is two days ride from here,

though it will take all of us twice that long. We'll make for there nonetheless."

"But what about Hugh's Lick?" asked Virginia. "Our money? Our work?"

"Our work and money be damned!" said Murdock furiously.

Robert nodded. "He's right."

"What's going on, Murdock?" asked Virginia. "What happened out there? What was that thing?"

"I don't know what's going on," said Murdock. "But I know when a place is accursed, and this place is. We're *going*."

"But with what?" asked Virginia. "We've lost everything. We'll die if we try to leave!"

"We'll die if we stay," said Murdock. "I've cached supplies for an emergency not far from here," he said. "We'll take what we can carry and leave the rest." Murdock turned to face us. "In fact, I'd suggest you leave as well. Everybody in Hugh's Lick should. Things aren't right here."

Murdock removed the hat from his head and rubbed at his red-rimmed eyes. I couldn't be sure, but I thought they were welling with tears.

I needed no convincing. But I did require something from Murdock. "I need supplies," I said. "I know you aren't fond of me, Murdock, nor Rose, but there is an innocent baby involved. If you won't sell to me, we'll die. I can't—"

Murdock cut me off. "You can have whatever we don't take. No charge. In fact, anybody who needs anything can take it."

Murdock was giving goods away? Lord Almighty, he really was afraid.

As Murdock organized his remaining family, a half-dozen townsfolk led by Owen rode into our midst. Clearly, Owen had won the debate about Murdock's stricture against coming here.

"God preserve us," said Owen, looking about at the devastation.

"We're leaving," said Murdock to the new arrivals. "And not coming back neither. I'd suggest you do the same."

"You're serious?" asked Owen. "What about the money I owe

you?" Owen all but clapped a hand over his mouth as he realized what he had said.

"I don't give a damn about that, you dim-witted, money-grubbing stoat!" snapped Murdock. "And I never did. I only cared about building something, and now I only care about living. You do as you please."

Everyone was taken aback by the outburst.

Murdock addressed the other men. "I've a cache of supplies not far from here. More than I can carry. Once I've taken what I want, you can have the rest."

I think the fact that the purse-proud Murdock was so willing to abandon all that he had worked so hard for scared the other men as much as anything. More than one voiced a desire to flee with Murdock. First the Delaware had left, now most of the settlers would follow suit. At this rate, there was going to be no one left in the valley come tomorrow morning.

◆

"I've decided," said John, as we collected our share of Murdock's supplies. "I'm going as well."

It wasn't quite a fracas as the other settlers grabbed what they could carry, but there was definitely pushing and shoving taking place.

"To the Firelands?" I asked, seizing a bag of gunpowder.

John nodded. "Aye. I hate to leave here, especially with most of the others clearing out, but I don't fancy sharing the valley with whatever the hell is behind these goings-on. I don't know if a wendigo is responsible or not, but something out of the ordinary is happening, and I don't fancy Palmer and I facing it without you or Gwennie."

"It sounds like some of the settlers are staying," I said. "Owen Stern for certain."

"That's only because the grasping fool thinks he has a chance to take over Murdock's claims," said John. "Be that as it may, I don't like the feel of things here, and I certainly have no desire to cast my lot with the likes of Owen. I've started over afore, and I can do so again."

I was glad John had finally changed his mind. True, it had taken several dead Burkes, the total destruction of all their dwellings, the flight of the Delaware, not to mention everything else that had occurred, but he had seen the light at last. With any luck, by this time tomorrow, we would be well on our way to the Firelands.

I could only hope Whitewood Tree was wrong and that the wendigo would not follow after me.

◆

We left Gwennie at her cabin with her share of the supplies. She was going to pack what little else she had, and we had agreed to meet in the morning to head west.

"Are you all right, Cole?" asked John, as we made the trip from Gwennie's cabin to his. "You've been mighty quiet."

"I'm tired is all," I said, and it was the truth. I had scarcely recovered from my injuries, slept one night out of the past three, and we had been riding hard all day, going from John's cabin to Pakim's village, into town, and then to the Burke's claim. And always things got worse: More bad news, death, and destruction. I was glad evensong was upon us. I wanted this blasted day to end.

"After we pack, we'll go to sleep straightaway," said John. "We could all use a good night's rest."

I was so tired I only grunted my agreement. Snow had found its way beneath my collar and I pulled my coat tighter about my neck. The shock of the day's events had finally receded from my mind, leaving behind numbness and fatigue. My eyes burned with exhaustion, and my mind reeled with everything I had gone through in the past day, let alone the past week. I couldn't wait to leave it all behind for the Firelands. There, I fervently hoped, I would not only find my fresh start, but could return to being Cold-Blooded Cole.

"Do you think Palmer will come?" I asked.

"To the Firelands?" asked John. "Of course. Why wouldn't he?"

"I don't know," I said. "I just didn't want to presume anything."

It wasn't as if they were truly married and oath-bound to follow the other. Or, like Pakim suggested, did they see themselves that way? John and I had yet to discuss the nature of his relationship with Palmer, and I possessed a keen desire to know more about it. How did they keep it secret from the other settlers? Were they fearful of discovery? Did they feel bad about giving in to such base desires?

But I couldn't bring myself to query John about his curious relationship. I wasn't sure why. Puzzlement over my own feelings toward Pakim? Fear John would guess about my own seemingly mutable nature? Whatever the reason, instead of giving voice to my actual interest, I said, "Had you always wanted to be a frontiersman?"

John burst out laughing. "Forgive me, Cole," he said, yet chuckling. "It's just that I would have imagined myself living the life of a Dutch sea captain afore that of a frontiersman."

"Then how did you end up here?'

All signs of mirth vanished from John's face. As he wiped melted snow from his face, he seemed to be reminiscing about something I had apparently brought to mind. When he finally spoke, it was with a somberness that made me fear I had tread on unpleasant ground. "First off, let's be frank," he said. "Though I appreciate the compliment, I am clearly no frontiersman. It's true, I have acquired some, if not all, of the skills associated with such, but I lack the motivation of most of my neighbors. Namely, I have no desire to kill every animal or Indian I encounter. I do not wish to tame the wilderness until it is as domesticated as a Boston merchant's yard."

"You do seem a little out of place here," I said.

John grimaced. "Sort of like finding an onion growing on an apple tree, eh? You expect something sweet and, instead, get something considerably less palatable. Truth be told, I had no intention of being a frontiersman, Cole. It sort of happened. I thought I was going down one road, and I wound up somewhere else completely different. A little bit like yourself, I imagine."

"How exactly do you mean?" I asked.

"Well, clearly you intended to be a frontiersman, yet I would wager you had no intention of marrying the likes of Rose." John smiled. "That is one road down which I can't imagine too many men venturing."

"That is true," I replied.

"It puzzles me," said John, "whether we choose the road or it chooses us."

"How do you mean?" I asked.

John looked pensive. "Let's just say there are some roads which I tried very hard to avoid, yet every turn seemed to bring me back to them."

Was John referring to his relationship with Palmer? My logical self told me to let this conversation die, but I seemed not to be able to help myself. "You mean such as how to make a livelihood? Or where to settle?" *Or whom to love,* I thought to myself.

John nodded. "Be careful which road you choose, Cole," he said. "Sometimes you think you are doing the right thing, but it is wrong, only not for the reasons you thought." John shook his head and laughed. "Would you listen to me? I sound like a crooked fortune teller purposefully speaking in ambiguities. 'I see a mysterious stranger in your future! You should trust him—unlessen you shouldn't!'"

Only hindsight could answer such questions as John mused over. But for some reason I did feel compelled to tell him the truth about Pakim and myself, to ask him his advice, although to what end I couldn't say, as I wasn't likely to ever see Pakim again. Afore I could say anything however, we arrived back at the edge of the clearing where his cabin stood. I knew something wasn't right even afore Elizabeth started shying and bobbing her head about.

John's front door stood open, hanging from one hinge, banging back and forth with the wind. I didn't have to look inside to know that Palmer, Rose, and Colette were gone. I also knew they hadn't just gone for a stroll. The wendigo had come and had taken them all.

chapter twelve

We both ran for the cabin.

"Palmer?" called John, dashing through the door. I followed behind, but the cabin was empty. Inside was nearly as cold as out, the fireplace filled with nothing but dead ashes. A half-eaten plate of food sat on the table whilst an overturned cup lay on the floor. We both hurried back outside to search for signs of what had happened.

An inch of fine snow layered the clearing, a multitude of footprints stamped into the snowfall like indigo ink on white parchment. The prints were mixed up, and with evensong drawing to a close, it took me a moment to sort them out in the fading light. Tracks (other than ours) appeared to have been left three distinct times as indicated by how blurred each set had been left by the falling snow. The first set was the most blurred and therefore hardest to follow.

As best I could tell, events had unfolded thusly: Palmer had come out of the cabin, walked forward and backward a few paces, then made a circuit of the entire cabin. Several times he had stopped, facing the woods as if looking for something. It wasn't hard to imagine for what he might have been searching. Eventually, he had returned in-a-doors.

The second set of prints had again been Palmer coming out of the cabin, but this time, judging from the longer strides, it appeared he had been running. He had dashed outside ten or fifteen feet, then spun about. I did the same and guessed he had been looking onto the roof. I remembered Virginia's words about something skittering across the top of her cabin.

"I see something," said John, as he stood by my side. He walked to cabin, climbed up on a bench and peered at one of the logs. "There's a musket ball lodged here," he said. "Palmer was shooting at something." John sounded distressed.

"Well, he ran back inside," I said, following the footprints back to the cabin.

The third set had been made a short time later. This time, Rose had been with Palmer, and they had both been running. John and I followed them to the edge of the clearing where the snow ended and the forest began. Palmer and Rose were clearly going in the direction of town.

It was then I noticed a fourth set of tracks that had been made by neither Palmer nor Rose. I hadn't noticed them sooner because they had been made by a creature with an enormous stride and each print was so widely spaced that they didn't make an obvious pattern. The huge prints started on top of the cabin and had obviously been made when the creature pursued our friends. Studying one print, I counted the indentation of seven nails and three foot-pads on each foot. Never afore had I seen such a thing.

A few minutes later, John and I sped on horseback toward Hugh's Lick. Along the way, I tried to look for signs of a struggle along the trail or any more tracks, but John rode fast and night had arrived. At any moment, I expected one of us to be knocked to the ground by a low-hanging branch. John brought Elizabeth to a halt every few minutes, and we both called out Palmer and Rose's names. Only silence answered back each time.

Snow fell in fits and starts, as if the brewing tempest couldn't quite muster up the will to storm seriously. Clouds raced by quickly overhead, thick one moment, the sky all but clear the next.

We stopped and called out yet again, garnering the same result. With each failure to find Palmer and Rose, John grew more agitated. Just how agitated I realized when he drove his heels into Elizabeth's haunches with enough force to make the animal squeal afore again racing down the trail.

As we rode, I regarded John with a muddle of feelings. To a large degree, I thought all of us would have been better served if he remained as cool and calm as I. His fear, I worried, would drive him to make foolish, even deadly, mistakes. To a lesser degree, however, I felt for him as much fellow-feeling as I had ever experienced. Had it been Pakim missing, I knew I would have been greatly distraught, and without a doubt John felt more strongly about Palmer than I did about Pakim. They had been together for years, after all.

I feared for Rose and Colette as well. But it was a sense of duty I felt for them, and that was quite different from these new, strange feelings I had for Pakim.

"They couldn't have come this far on foot," said John, his teeth chattering from the cold. "We must have missed them. We have to go back."

The other explanation, of course, was that the wendigo had caught them.

"Let us go back then," I said, even though I feared it a waste of our time.

Again mounted on Elizabeth, we retraced our steps, calling out into the dark. The moon had yet to rise, so there was little light, but I peered into the woods looking for any sign of them. The wind kicked up, buffeting the treetops—a surprisingly loud racket in the darkness.

"Maybe Palmer tried to lose the wendigo in the woods," I suggested.

John immediately brightened. "It is much more direct to get to Hugh's Lick if you head straight through the woods. There's no actual trail that way, mind you, but Palmer could find his way through anything. I bet they are there already."

For his sake, I hoped John was right.

John swung Elizabeth about and set off toward town as fast as we could go in the dark. We rode in silence for a long while, and I knew John was consumed by his fear over what might have befallen Palmer.

Suddenly, Elizabeth reared up, refusing to go any further. Fearing the wendigo was about to attack, I raised my musket, peering into the darkness. John and I strained to listen, but I heard only the creak of the woods and, once, the "chit-a-chit" of a mockingbird. That particular mockingbird call was one of alarm, but I didn't know if the bird reacted to us or something else in the woods.

"What is it, Elizabeth?" asked John, stroking the horse's neck. "Maybe she's only caught scent of a wolf," he suggested hopefully.

It was a testament to our situation that encountering a wolf pack— for they rarely traveled alone—could be construed as a good thing.

"Maybe so," I said. "See if you can urge her forward now."

John tried, but no amount of cajoling could get her to budge. "The town isn't far from here, bugger it all," said John. "What do we do now?"

I was about to answer when the clouds parted, revealing the just rising moon and I thought I saw the silhouette of a man standing ahead of us on the trail. The moon was only half full, its diffuse light casting shadows as much as it illuminated. The man was tall, and something about his demeanor bespoke great power. I could make out naught of his features, which were all angles and shadows, assuming the man was not a shadow altogether.

"Do you see that?" I asked in a whisper.

"See what?" said John.

"Up there. I see a man. Or at least I think I do."

"Is it Palmer?" asked John hopefully.

There was something familiar about the figure, but I felt sure it wasn't Palmer.

"I don't see anything," said John. "But my eyes aren't good. Especially at night."

"Stay here," I said, swinging myself off of Elizabeth.

John grabbed my arm. "Are you sure, Cole?"

I wasn't sure, but something had to be done. Cold-Blooded Cole seemed to be the person to do it, otherwise we might freeze to death waiting for Elizabeth to overcome whatever it was that frightened her.

The wind continued worrying the trees, their limbs banging about in the night. I stepped forward on the trail and called out, "Is someone there? Show yourself, afore I shoot you."

No reply was given, but the figure walked further away along the trail. Or was it only a shadow from a tree? *God's balls, but this is queer,* I thought as I edged forward until I reached the spot where I thought the figure had last stood. There was no one there except the shadow of a tree. Perhaps my tired mind played tricks on me. Except I didn't think it was my mind. I sensed something palpable here. It was as if I had developed a new sense to go with sight and sound and smell. And this new sense told me there was something malevolent nearby.

"Yes," a voice whispered from behind. I spun around, raising the musket to fire. There was naught behind me but a tree swaying in the wind, and I realized it was the rustle of the branches I had heard. *Careful, Cole,* I instructed myself. If I let myself get rattled, I might do something foolish, like mistake Palmer or John for the wendigo and shoot. In fact, it wasn't beyond all likelihood that Palmer and Rose might be nearby, and I didn't fancy having to live with myself if I accidentally killed one of them.

Finally, satisfied there was no one there, that it had indeed all been a trick of the shadows and the wind and my own exhaustion, I headed back toward John. As I walked, I happened to glance into the woods, and this time I was certain: there was a man standing in the shadows of the forest. I couldn't see his face, but he was tall and wrapped in a black cape, a peaked hat perched upon his head.

A few clouds again gathered overhead, a light snow began falling, though faint moonlight yet reached the ground.

"Palmer? Is that you?" I asked. No response was forthcoming. "Who are you?" I asked.

The trees rustled in the wind and the shadowy figure made no reply. There was an utterly strange air about him, as if he were missing something fundamental—like a skeleton or a soul. I knew how fanciful I was being, but I had never seen such an odd figure afore. Even odder, the falling snow didn't settle on him, but swirled away as if repelled by him.

When I still got no response, I decided it was time to drop the niceties. I raised my musket, aiming it straight at the figure. "I've no wish to injure you," I said resolutely. "But there are strange things stirring, and you're making me uneasy. So why don't you show yourself?"

"Cole?" called John from the distance.

"Stay where you are," I said, briefly turning toward him.

When I looked back, the figure was gone, even though my head had only been turned an instant. I blinked my dry, tired eyes and looked again, but there was no one there amongst the falling snow.

"Seavey," whispered a voice from the opposite side of the woods where the figure had just been. This time it wasn't the wind in the trees I heard. "I'm coming for you, Seavey." The voice was cold as river mud, raspy and raw. I spun about, then it came from yet another direction. "I'm coming," it said.

"Who speaks?" I yelled. "Show yourself!" *What the devil is going on?* I wondered, squinting into the murky forest. To tell the truth, my sense of reason was rattled as never afore, and that made me as uneasy as the figure itself. Who was it? Or worse, *what* was it? And what did it want? If it was a wendigo, this wasn't the same creature that had attacked me when I found the girl. This was something different. Or was it? Perhaps Whitewood Tree was mistaken and wendigos could change shapes.

I slowly turned in a circle until the shadowy figure reappeared, this time on the trail behind me between John and me. It stepped toward me.

"Get out of here, John!" I yelled, knowing instantly that to stay was to die. "Get out of here now!"

A fierce gust of wind rattled the treetops afore swirling around me. But this wind was bitter cold, far colder than the air already stinging my eyes. And it had a taste somehow, metallic, a tang of iron or blood. Panic rose from within me as I stepped backward. Something wasn't right here, but foul and indecent. Then the cold punched inside me, inside my chest, wrapping itself around my heart. A terrible pressure enfolded that organ, squeezing, and I couldn't breathe. I tried to yell, but nothing would come. The pressure mounted until I feared I was about to pass out.

Then it was gone, and the bitter cold along with it. I gasped for breath, hardly able to stand. I glanced into the shadows, but the black-clad figure had vanished.

Without thinking, I turned and bolted. I became like a deer fleeing a wolf, all instinct and gut fear. I had to get away from whatever had so easily violated me. At first I couldn't run fast, but then the moonlight reappeared as I glanced behind me and saw the figure was back, bigger now, and giving chase. I heard it running harder, its very footsteps shaking the earth. I pushed myself to run faster, but I wasn't fast enough; I looked back and the figure was yet there. It was even bigger now, drawing closer with impossibly long strides.

A terrible stitch crept up my side, and I felt my legs flagging. Behind me my pursuer had become nothing more than a huge black shadow bearing down on me. It snorted like a beast whilst leering a grin filled with huge white teeth. I redoubled my efforts, willing myself to ignore the pain in my side, the terrifying shaking of the ground, the feeling my heart was about to burst. It wasn't necessary to look back again to know my pursuer was almost on me. And then it had me.

As I flew up into the air, I punched wildly, without thinking. It almost seemed as if it weren't me fighting, or at least not the me I knew. It was a more primal me, the animal me, and I fought like one, lashing out instinctively, even snarling like a beast.

"Cole, it's *me*!" John said, bringing Elizabeth to a halt. "It's John! It's all right! Stop striking me!" We kept grappling as he fought to grab my flailing hands. Little by little, my rational side reasserted itself, and at last I calmed my fists. I realized I had mistaken John and his horse for the creature, though my blood yet sang with fright.

"Bloody hell," said John. "Remind me never to pick a fight with you."

I looked behind us, but saw only the gloom of the forest at night. Nor did I any longer sense the malevolent presence I had earlier.

"What happened back there, Cole?" asked John. "Are you all right?"

I didn't know how to answer either question.

◆

It took me quite some time to regain my composure, not something I was well-versed in having to do. Fortunately, John had the decency not to pepper me with questions whilst we continued on to Hugh's Lick. If he had asked what had transpired, I wasn't sure what I would admit to. As I thought about what had happened, I could only ascribe what I had seen to exhaustion, the murk of the forest, and, whilst I was loathe to admit it, my imagination, though that troubled me as much as my having been so rattled. Ordinarily, I was decidedly *not* one to go around imagining things, though these were not ordinary times.

I had been genuinely afraid back there, and surely that accounted for the icy pressure I had felt in my chest. Perhaps the black-caped figure had only been a shadow after all, and that explained how it moved so impossibly fast. And the mocking voice had been the wind in the trees.

So why did I yet feel so unnerved?

A short time later we rode into Hugh's Lick and were very nearly shot to death for our trouble when the blast of a musket ripped through the air.

"Don't shoot!" yelled John when, point in fact, he should have said "Don't shoot again."

"Who's there?" called out a voice from within the blockhouse.

"John Chapman and Cole Seavey," answered John.

"Show yourselves and with your hands up in the air."

"Bloody hell," murmured John, as we both did as instructed.

"Do you see anyone else out there?" asked a voice I recognized as Owen Stern's.

"No, Owen," I said. "Now let us in."

The blockhouse door opened, and Owen frantically motioned for us to enter.

"Someone just attacked us," he said.

"Or something," said another man.

"It was the wendigo," said a woman. "It had to have been."

Owen glared at them both. "It was Indians. Or perhaps it was you two."

"Not bloody likely," I said. "We've just come from John and Palmer's. How long ago were you attacked?"

"Minutes," said Owen. "Which makes me mighty suspicious of you."

Hearing the blockhouse had just been attacked by someone, or something, made it harder to convince myself that my encounter had only been with shadows and wind. Had my assailant also attacked the blockhouse? But that wasn't possible, I realized. How could the wendigo, or whatever it was, have got from us to the town so quickly? No ordinary man or creature could have arrived here afore us.

"What's wrong, Seavey?" Owen said. "You look like Lucifer himself got his hands around that scrawny neck of yours."

"If I were as disliked as you, Owen," I said, "I'd worry about my own neck and not fret about others."

"Are you threatening me, Seavey?" asked Owen. "Cause if so, I'll—"

"Shut up!" exclaimed John. "Palmer and Rose are missing. Have you seen them?"

"Did you tell me to shut up?" asked Owen.

"*Yes!*" said John, with such fury that even I was taken aback. "Have you seen them?

"Can't claim that I have," answered Owen, yet glaring. "Not that I've been looking or would care if I did. Say, I know. Maybe that evil Indian spirit of yours got them. Maybe that's Palmer's punishment for being a sodomite." The word landed like a cannonball, and I saw a look of alarm cross John's face. "What?" asked Owen. "You thought people didn't know or talk about it? Hell, the two of you were just about everybody's favorite topic of conjecture. I'm given to understand it had been the same way back in Franklin, eh? Too bad there's only you and Seavey here to rescue your precious

Palmer. Those are odds I wouldn't want to stake my life on."

"Damn you," I muttered.

"Best watch your bone box, Cole Seavey," said Owen. "This is my town now, and what I say goes." Owen was so excited by the prospect of bossing other men, I could all but see his roger getting hard in his breeches.

"You have to help us find them," John said to Owen and the remaining settlers.

Owen roared with laughter. "You expect me to help you find Palmer? Why, John, I wouldn't help you find your catamite if the fate of the world depended on it. And consider that a favor. By keeping you two apart, I'm giving you a chance to give up your iniquitous ways. You'd best take it, Chapman. Otherwise you're going to rot in hell."

"Something is out there!" said an alarmed settler who was keeping watch. We all gathered around the slit windows.

"Where?" asked Owen.

"There. By the bushes."

I looked but saw nothing except shadows and falling snow. Then a figure staggered into the moonlight. It was Palmer.

chapter thirteen

I pushed my way past the gaping onlookers and knelt next to Palmer. His clothes were rent in a half-dozen places, his face scratched and bleeding, and despite the cold, he was sweating profusely. "Palmer, are you all right?" I asked.

Still panting as he tried to catch his breath, he looked up at me and said, "I'm sorry, Cole. ."

"For what?" I asked.

"For Rose and Colette," he said. "It got them. It got them both."

John appeared and knelt next to Palmer. "Leave us alone," John snapped at the gawking men. Together we helped Palmer walk the rest of the way to the blockhouse where he sat in front of the fire. A woman brought him a mug of tea and some scraps of food, but he didn't so much as glance at them. The other settlers drifted closer, wanting to hear what had befallen Palmer and Rose. John was justifiably annoyed that these people only moments afore had been unwilling to do anything to help find Palmer and now wanted to hear what he knew.

"I said, leave us alone!" barked John again.

"Don't you go telling us what to do, John Chapman," said Owen. "Or I'll see to—"

"Let us talk to Palmer, Owen," I said calmly. "Then we'll tell you what he said."

Owen eyed me coldly, grunted, then ordered the others to move away.

Palmer sat with his knees pulled up to his chest, his head down and resting upon his folded arms.

"I'm so sorry," he said again. "So sorry."

"What happened, Palmer?" I asked gently.

"It got them," he said. "The wendigo. It got them."

"Are you all right?" asked John. He tried to make Palmer look at him, but his distraught friend pushed John's hand away, refusing to look at us. "Damn it, Palmer!" said John. "At least tell me if you're hurt."

"I'm not hurt," muttered Palmer. "I'm fine."

He might have been fine physically, but he was obviously distraught over whatever had happened. As was I, though I showed not how I felt. How the hell could Palmer have let Rose and Colette be taken? I had trusted him to keep them safe, and I wasn't sure whom I blamed more for what had befallen them: him for allowing it, or me for leaving them in his care.

"The wendigo attacked the cabin, didn't it?" I asked.

Palmer finally looked up. His face was pale, his eyes wide and frightened. "Rose and I were inside talking when I heard something outside," he said. "I went to look, even walked around the cabin, but didn't see anything. I returned inside, and a while later something landed on the roof, then ran back and forth over our heads."

John and I looked at each other. That was how Virginia Burke had described the wendigo attack on her cabin. Palmer then related what happened each successive time he had gone out to investigate. It matched up near exactly with what I thought had occurred.

"We moved as swiftly as we could," he said, relating their final flight into the woods. "But with Rose carrying the baby, we couldn't run all that fast. Just when I decided that maybe we were safe, the laughing started."

"The laughing?" I asked.

Palmer nodded as he shuddered. "It was horrible. This mocking laugh, and it seemed to come from everywhere. One minute it was behind us, then to the side, then the other side. I didn't know which way to go. We were so deep in those accursed woods, it felt like I'd been swallowed alive. Then it started calling Rose's name."

I could well imagine Rose's reaction upon hearing that hollow, raspy voice calling her name.

"Rose was terrified," said Palmer. "It kept saying her name over and over, and she finally bolted into the woods. I followed after her, trying to get her to come back, but she wouldn't. Then I heard the wendigo smashing through the forest, coming for us."

"What did it look like?" I asked.

Palmer furrowed his brow in thought. "It had just gone dusk, so it was hard to see in the woods. What little I saw pretty well matched up with what you described, Cole. It was a mishmash of other creatures."

"No matter," I said, though I noted it looked nothing like what had just chased me. "What happened next?"

"When I knew it was close by, I put Rose behind me so I could try to defend her. The wendigo kept coming, one minute to my right, the next to the left, and always laughing and calling Rose's name. The trees were so thick and close together, I could scarcely see five feet. Finally, I reckoned I saw it and fired.

"I was wrong, though, because at the same moment I fired, I heard Rose scream. By the time I turned around, both she and Colette were gone. I was so frightened, I couldn't fathom what was happening. The wendigo started laughing again, and I knew it was going to come for me, so I started running and kept running until I got here." Palmer looked up at me again and said, "Cole, I'm so, so sorry."

"We'll find them, Palmer," I said.

"I can't believe I ran," he said, again cradling his head. "I left Rose and Colette in the hands of God-knows-what. I would have died to save them, Cole. I swear I would have."

"Stop it, Palmer," I said. "You did what you could. Frankly, Rose and Colette have a better chance since you came to get us."

"You'll go back with me then?" he asked. "Maybe we can get some of the other men to join us."

"These louts?" said John dismissively. "Might as well have asked King George to invite George Washington to tea."

"We'll go on our own then," I said. "We have to find Rose and the baby."

◆

It took us about an hour to reach the spot on the trail where Rose had bolted into the woods. Another quarter hour passed until we found the spot where Palmer had made his stand, and whence Rose had vanished. Steady snow had been falling for quite some time; any footprints Rose might have left were long obliterated.

"Take a look around," I said. "Mayhap there is something here that will give us a clue."

John held the torch we used for our search. Even with the light, trying to see far in the murk was feeble at best, like trying to push back the tide with your hands. Even so, we persevered, steadily working our way through the surrounding woods. The gloomy forest was so unsettling that I had to ignore the constant hum of uneasiness that haunted my mind. It was easy to picture getting lost here, wandering for days until driven mad by the foreboding gray endlessness of it all.

We had started up a narrow defile—a very small valley—when were rewarded by the sight of a betty lamp on the ground.

"What's that?" asked John, as I brushed it free of snow.

"That's our lamp," said Palmer. "The one I took outside to see what was on the roof."

"You brought it with you when you left?" I asked.

Palmer thought for a moment, then slowly shook his head. "No. I'm certain I didn't. I carried nothing in my hands but my musket."

"Rose must have had it then," I said.

"She had the baby," said Palmer. "I didn't see her holding the lamp, but perhaps she stuck it in her pocket."

"What's it matter who had it?" asked John. "It got here somehow. And it means Rose is probably somewhere up ahead of us."

John was right, I supposed. How the lamp got there didn't matter. But it seemed odd, and too much had been odd of late. I didn't like it.

"Have either of you been up this way?" I asked.

"No," said Palmer. "But I've been up on the other side of the ridge that's above us. It looked like this ravine opens up a bit afore dead-ending. I suppose there would be enough room there for the wendigo to hole up for the night."

The storm was worsening, and each of us now had a thick layer of snow on the brow of our hats and across our shoulders. None of us spoke of turning back, however. Palmer and I rode Elizabeth whilst John walked as we worked our way farther back into the defile. It was a place only a bear could find hospitable—dank, malodorous, and choked with blackberry bushes. We had to be a few apples short of a pie to be so foolish as to travel through such wilderness at night, especially whilst it snowed so heavily, but Rose and Colette were somewhere out here. We pushed on as far as we could, until the way became too choked with bushes, nettles, and every other loathsome plant known to man.

"What now?" asked John. "We'll need to hack our way through if we're—"

With no warning whatsoever, something huge hurled out of the woods. It collided with Elizabeth, knocking the poor squealing creature onto her side. Palmer and I were both thrown clear, the breath knocked from me as I hit the ground.

"It's the wendigo!" yelled Palmer.

The wendigo roared, and the ground shook from the power of it. Its hot, stinking breath washed over my face; with a visceral horror, I realized it was close enough to reach out and touch. Yet it was so dark I could see naught of its features, though that was not necessarily a bad thing. I scrambled backward, pushing my way into a blackberry bush, ignoring the thorns clawing at my flesh. From somewhere in the distance, I heard John yelling, Palmer yelling, and Elizabeth braying and thrashing about in the thick undergrowth. The wendigo roared again, and my whole body shook with power of it.

I looked to my left, saw a light bobbing about, and realized John still had the torch.

"Shoot it, Palmer!" John yelled. "Shoot it!

"It's too dark!" Palmer yelled back. "I can't see it!"

"To my left!" shouted John. "It's to my left."

John was wrong; the wendigo was here with me. Just then the beast seized me by the pant leg and started to drag me away. The sound of musket fire ripped through the air, and the wendigo let go of me. When I heard it move away through the bushes, I scrambled to my feet, grabbed my musket and went after it.

"Shit, shit, shit!" called out Palmer. "It's coming after me. I can hear it coming."

John reappeared. "Which way?" I asked him.

He held up the torch, pointing to my right. "That way, I think. Palmer? Where are you?"

But Palmer didn't answer. The wendigo roared from off to the side, but then I heard branches breaking in the opposite direction. All was confusion and chaos, and the wendigo seemed to be every-where at once. How did the blasted thing move so fast?

"Palmer?" called John. "Answer me, Palmer! Where are you?"

Something large lumbered through the bushes a few feet in front of us, and I placed a hand on John's arm to quiet him. We both lis-tened intently. When John started to speak, I forcefully clamped my hand over his mouth. Again he was letting his emotions rule him, and it was going to get us both killed. I motioned for him to remain where he stood. Creeping closer toward the source of the noise, I tried to peer into the bushes.

I thought I saw a dark figure shifting about, but couldn't be certain. Then an enormous black shape burst from the woods. It happened so fast that I only got a quick impression of it, but I felt certain this must be the wendigo. I did manage to get a shot off, but it went wide, and the wendigo clubbed me. I flew through the air, landing on my back.

The wendigo reared up to its full height, then dove toward me.

"Sweet Jesus!" I whispered at sight of the onrushing beast.

A musket fired from mere feet behind me. The wendigo grunted as if surprised, but kept falling toward me. The impact was bone-crushing. My lungs instantly collapsed, my nose filled with coarse fur, but the worst thing was the weight. It was incredible. I tried to inhale, but couldn't draw in so much as a mouthful of air. The wendigo lay sprawled on top of me, unmoving and apparently dead, thank God, but that wasn't so much comfort now that I couldn't draw a breath.

With every bit of my strength, I pushed up against the wendigo. The creature budged not at all. Bright flashes of light, like that from heat lightning, went off in front of my eyes. My whole body started to convulse, and I realized I was about to die.

◆

I inhaled so hard that it hurt. Again and again, I gasped, trying to get my breath, the freezing air scraping my already raw throat. The wendigo was off me, heaped to the side where it lay unmoving. Yet feeling unsteady, I looked up at the shadow hovering above me. "John?" I asked.

"No, Friend Cole. It is not John."

"Pakim!" I exclaimed, scarcely able to trust my ears. The torch had gone out, so I could see almost nothing. Pakim knelt right next to me and I could feel the warmth coursing off his flesh. "But where did you come from?" I asked.

"I was down by the river when I heard yelling," he said. "I came to offer help."

John appeared, starting in surprise when he saw Pakim. "Have you seen, Palmer?" he asked urgently.

Pakim shook his head. "No. I heard this commotion and came to investigate. What is happening here?"

Afore I could answer, a man's scream pierced the air.

"Palmer!" yelled John, bolting upright.

I struggled to my feet. "Where did that come from?"

The scream came again, leaving no doubt as to the direction:

farther back into the defile. But if the wendigo was dead here with us, then what was happening to Palmer? John, Pakim, and I plunged into the bushes and nettles.

"Palmer!" called out John. Pakim and I added our voices as well. John was in front of us, moving so fast that we lost sight of him.

"Wait, John," called out Pakim, but John paid him no heed.

"I see it!" yelled John, his voice moving farther away.

For several minutes, I thought we had lost John, but then we burst through the last of the bushes, nearly colliding with him as he stood at the base of a cliff stretching above us. The top of the cliff was lost in the dark of the night. John looked about, frantically searching for Palmer. "I saw it coming this way," he said. "I saw the wendigo. And I heard Palmer yelling. It was after him. But I lost them. They're not here and I don't know where they went."

I glanced up the cliff. "Could they have gone that way?"

Pakim looked upward. "I do not see how."

"Damn it!" said John.

"I'm confused," I said. "Pakim, if that was the wendigo you killed back there, then how could it have taken Palmer?"

"Maybe it was not the wendigo I killed," said Pakim.

After searching the area once more for Palmer, we hastened back to where the wendigo's body lay. Pakim was right: he had not killed the wendigo.

"It is only Brother Bear," said Pakim. "And it had already been shot once. Quite some hours ago I would say."

"Owen Stern," I said. "I'd wager anything this was the bear I'd heard he wounded earlier trying to collect Murdock's bounty."

"Then where's Palmer?" asked John. "What's happened to him?"

I didn't bother to answer John. He knew what had happened to Palmer. We all did: the wendigo had him.

chapter fourteen

The snowstorm worsened, and Pakim and I insisted we return at once to Hugh's Lick. John, frantic to find Palmer, protested so vociferously we finally had to wrestle him onto Elizabeth where he, at length, fell silent. In fact, he became all but catatonic, and I knew he imagined all of the terrible things conceivably befalling Palmer at that very moment. I understood John's feelings, but I knew we did no one—not Rose, Colette, or Palmer—any good if we acted hastily and perished in the woods.

Whipped by the wind, the snow fell so thickly that I considered it a bit of a miracle we finally made it back to the blockhouse. Relieved to be back, I slid down from Elizabeth only to find the wrong end of a musket pressed against my neck.

"Owen!" yelled the person holding the musket. "Owen, get out here and tell me what to do!"

As if wendigos and bears weren't enough lethal complications to occupy my mind, I again had to worry about some harum-scarum fool shooting me without even meaning to. "Don't shoot," I said calmly. "It's only John and Cole come back."

"You would be well advised to listen to him," said Pakim menacingly. I glanced over and saw he had his own musket leveled at my assailant. "Or I shall place a musket ball in the back of your skull."

Owen Stern barged out of the blockhouse, followed by two men and a woman. "What the hell is going on, Martin?" demanded Owen. "I leave you out here for half an hour, and you about wet yourself. I have half a mind—oh, it's Seavey and Chapman come back," he said, catching sight of us. "And you've brought your redskin rubbish with you. Well, we're not taking you in again, so go back to whatever place your polluted ilk come from." Owen turned to Martin, the fellow with the gun. "Shoot them if they don't leave."

"We've seen the wendigo," I said. "Not far from here. We've three muskets between us. Mayhap you should think twice afore sending us away."

Owen stepped toward me. "Don't you tell me—"

"I think he's right," called out one of the men. Several more had joined us and they eagerly added their agreement. I could sense how frightened they were. With everyone watching, Owen reconsidered kicking us out. The man may have been a top-notch bastard, but he was no fool. He knew he wouldn't stay the new leader of Hugh's Lick's remaining settlers long if people vehemently disagreed with his decisions.

"All right," he said. "But that Indian is not coming in the blockhouse. He stays over there." Owen gestured to a cabin directly across from the blockhouse.

"I'm staying with him then," I said.

Owen shrugged with an exaggerated motion to make sure I knew he cared less about my fate than that of an ant upon which he happened to trod.

"But John stays in the blockhouse," I added. "And I want him to be fed."

Owen looked as if were about to object, but one of the women came forward. Pakim and I slid our catatonic friend to the ground, and she guided him into the blockhouse. Owen gave us a final disgusted look afore he, too, went back inside. I felt completely out of place amongst these people—a horse trying to find company amidst a herd of stinking goats.

Pakim fed and watered Elizabeth and Midnight, then joined me in the cabin where I had started a fire. I burst with questions about what had happened to him, how had he found us in the woods, and most importantly, why had he come back. This time, however, I asked none of them, for I had no wish to appear any more overly eager than I already had. Nor did Pakim ask me any questions of his own. He seemed distracted, and I could imagine any of a dozen different reasons why.

By the light of the fire, I saw he had been injured during our encounter with the bear. "You're hurt," I said, gesturing to the tear in his shirt.

He glanced down, saw that he was, and seemed not unduly concerned.

"We should tend to it," I said, and set about doing so. The cabin belonged to one of the families that had fled with Murdock. Like the others, they had gone in a hurry and consequently left quite a few things behind, including a hake in the fireplace from which we could hang a pot. Unfortunately, there were no pots to be found, but I did find a blackjack—a leather drinking mug coated with tar—that would work in a pinch. I filled the blackjack with water from the bumkin outside, then hung it over the fire.

"I'd wager you have something in your bandolier bag we could use to tend your injury," I said.

Pakim retrieved two small packets. One had comfrey, the other yarrow. Both were good in treating wounds. I also found an old shirt that had been left behind and tore it into several strips. The water boiled quickly, and I added some of the yarrow root, then soaked the strips of cloth in it.

"Take off your shirt," I said to Pakim.

Pakim shucked it off, then sat cross-legged in front of the fire. "You need not mother me, Cole," he said. "I can tend to my own injuries."

I ignored him and set to work cleaning the deep scratches over his left breast. The wound had bled freely, and a smear of dried blood ran down to his waist.

"You're lucky," I said as I worked. "None of the scratches touched your tattoos. It would be a shame to see them ruined."

Pakim, normally so effusive and happy-go-lucky, only grunted, and I wondered what he was thinking about. His face gave away nothing; his entire countenance as inexpressive as the turtle tattoo upon his cheek. I applied the comfrey root, now pounded to a paste, to the injury. Whilst I waited for it to dry, I admired all of Pakim's tattoos. It was the first time I had had a chance to observe them up close. Yes, we had passed one night together, but I had been too pre-occupied with the rest of his body to pay his tattoos much mind. Truth be told, I was again more interested in the rest of his body, but hoped to distract myself from those baser desires.

In addition to the turtle tattoo upon Pakim's cheek, a tattoo of a snake started on his right shoulder then undulated down his back, finally wrapping around his chest. Like the turtle, the snake was a dark green and made me think of the wide, slow-moving rivers that moved through the deep woods. The snake looked neither fierce, nor sinister, not like the wicked-looking serpent etched in the Bible from which my mother had read when I was a boy. Instead, Pakim's snake looked placid—even wise, as if it were privy to some knowl-edge to which the rest of us were not.

"We do not hold Brother Snake to be evil," said Pakim, when I commented on this. "We think he is wise because he always seeks to avoid confrontation. He stays concealed, but if discovered gives warning by hissing or rattling his tail. He only attacks if he must."

I found myself reaching out and touching the snake. I traced its way down Pakim's shoulder and over his chest. Pakim said nothing, only arched his back slightly at my touch. His skin was hot, the mus-cles hard beneath my fingers. When I found myself remembering the times we had lain together, I felt my roger go stiff, and quickly pulled my hand away.

Pakim gave away nothing he felt, if indeed he felt anything at all.

"It's beautifully drawn," I said. "Who did it for you?"

"We called him He Who Stutters," said Pakim. "The spirits took away his ability to speak easily, but they gave him the skill to draw with a hand steadier than any other man in whole Lenape nation.

Our braves were renowned for their tattoos and the wisdom and strength each man drew from his during battle.

Given how few braves remained in Pakim's village, I wondered about the tattoos' efficacy in battle, but judged it wisest not to point this out. Effective or not, they were extraordinarily beautiful.

A third tattoo of an eagle had been done on Pakim's abdomen.

"It is Chauwalannae," said Pakim. "Brother Eagle. He is my Guardian Spirit."

"And mine is the raven," I said, ridiculously pleased that both our Guardian Spirits were birds. "Is the eagle wise like the snake?"

Pakim thought for a moment. "All of Kishelamekank's creations are wise," he said. "Or at least wiser than men. But Brother Snake is especially so. Brother Eagle's strength is that he can fly high and see everything happening on earth. He is Wapalanito, the spirit helper for East Grandfather and carries our prayers and thoughts to the world above. Nothing can be hidden from Wapalanito, who can see into the hearts and minds of men."

I wondered what Brother Eagle saw in Pakim's heart right then. I knew what he would find in mine. "Well, I think you were wise to choose the spirit you did," I said.

"Why?" asked Pakim.

I didn't know why. It was just something I said in hopes of keeping Pakim's thoughts away from whatever troubled him.

"I did not choose Brother Eagle," said Pakim. "He chose me during my *linkewhelan,* my vision quest. He chose me because, like Brother Eagle, I have flown far from home afore finally coming back. Mostly, he chose me not because I see well, but because I needed to learn to see."

"And did you learn to see?" I asked.

"Sometimes I think so. Other times I am not so sure. Always, though, I try to see more clearly."

Pakim grew quiet, and I resumed tending to his injuries. The comfrey had dried over the scratches, but dried blood still ran down his chest and stomach. I dipped another strip of cloth into the hot water and began washing it away. Blood had seeped under the waist of his deerskin pants, and I gently pushed them lower as I worked. Eventually, I realized the trickle ran all the way into the dark patch of hair above Pakim's manhood. I wasn't sure if I should continue, but Pakim said nothing and I hurried to finish. By the time I was done, my face was flushed and I was not a little aroused. From the looks of Pakim's crotch, he felt the same.

"I could do you," he said.

My heart thudded in my chest. "Do me?" I asked.

He nodded. "I could give you a tattoo. My hand is not as steady as He Who Stutters, but it is not bad either."

"What would you do?" I asked.

"Whatever you like," he said. "But I would suggest Brother Raven. That way you always have your Guardian Spirit as close to you as you can."

Now it was I who sat with my shirt off whilst Pakim sat across from me. He dipped a clean cloth in the blackjack, then leaned close as he washed the area of my chest upon which he would place the tattoo. His distinctive scent of sweetgrass and sweat enveloped me as he worked. It only took him a moment to finish washing the area necessary, and I was relieved when he pulled back.

Pakim dried my chest, then worked on the drawing for the next twenty minutes. Using a piece of charcoal, he drew on my body, pausing frequently to blow away dust. Never afore had I been so aware of my skin, of how alive it could feel. Pakim ran his finger over my flesh, making a smudge here, erasing something there, exciting me no matter what he did.

"Sit up straight," he said, and I obeyed. He placed a hand on my belly and told me to inhale as he regarded his work. The touch of his fingers was like a match to kindling and it made me shiver. "Are you cold?" he asked, and I shook my head. He reached over, made another mark on my chest, then said, "I think that is all."

I glanced down, but only saw a jumble of curving lines. Pakim rummaged in his bandolier bag, removing a small needle made of deer bone and a pouch filled, he told me, with the ash of a poplar tree. It was the ash that would give the dark-green color to my tattoo.

Pakim had me lie on my back, then used the bone to repeatedly prick my skin. Each jab felt like the sting of a bee, but I bore it without complaint. He pricked a half-inch of skin at a time, then stopped and wiped up the blood. Next he sprinkled the ash over the pricked skin, placed a leaf over it, and pressed down. Then he did another half inch. Each jab caused me to tense, then relax, and over time the relaxing part became deeper and deeper. My limbs fell as slack as the branches of a weeping willow whilst my breathing slowed to that of a hibernating bear. Soon I ceased even to notice the pricking part at all. I thought I had never felt so at ease in all my life.

Perhaps it was the sage Pakim had sprinkled in the fire. Or perhaps it was the nearness of him, but at that moment I was not *happy*, exactly, but content. It wasn't that feeling of contentment after having finished a hard day's work or the satisfaction that comes of a particularly good hunt. It was more a feeling that all was right with the world, and the world was right with me.

I knew it was horrible of me to feel pleased now, of all times. It was ironical as well, as I hadn't felt this good even when there weren't Indian demons and death all about. Most of my life I had been neither content nor dissatisfied. I simply *was*. It was best that way, or at least I had thought so then. Now I wondered.

I held onto this new feeling with the utmost gentleness, for I knew it to be a fragile thing. I knew that if I allowed myself to dwell upon the problems awaiting me, this contentment would vanish with the abruptness of a hummingbird darting away.

I realized Pakim had stopped pricking my skin. I opened my eyes and found him gazing back at me. "You are a handsome man, Cole. At least for a white man." He smiled.

I smiled back. "I know damned well my face looks like an entire regiment of soldiers shod with hobnail boots has marched over it."

"Perhaps you don't look your finest at the moment, but I still say you are handsome." Having finished pressing in the last of the ash into my skin, his fingers lingered on my stomach. I watched as his hand rose with each breath I took. It was erotic somehow, our slowly moving in time together, even more intimate than if his hand had immediately slid betwixt my legs. Our eyes met again, and we watched each other for a long moment. When he finally went to pull his hand away, I reached down and took it. I hesitated a moment longer, knowing I should not do this thing, but wanting it anyway. I pressed Pakim's hand lower until he knew exactly what I sought.

Pakim's mouth found mine, and I pulled him as close as I could. Somehow my pants slid down, and his hands seemed to be everywhere at once. Thusly naked, I thought I would be cold, but so much heat poured off Pakim that I began to sweat. He ground himself against me, and I ground back with equal zeal. With both of us soon slick, the sensation of his bare flesh against mine was delicious, and I moaned out loud.

We kissed each other harder and harder, as if each were trying to overpower the other. The struggle only excited me more. This was no seduction. This was two men, two warriors, each trying to take what they wanted from the other. Yet kissing me, Pakim pinned my arms at my sides. I struggled that much harder, but he didn't yield except with his tongue, which gave way to mine. Finally, I surrendered, but not in defeat, for I knew he would share his body with mine.

My surrender wasn't to him so much as it was to me anyway—my desires and to this newfound need to be touched by a man. I marveled at the experience, something I knew I could never have with a woman because a woman could never take me this way.

The truth was I could not have it with Pakim either, except for this last time. It was wonderful to feel so right, but I had Rose and Colette to rescue and care for. I knew now there was more involved in my decision than my responsibility to them, however. I feared that being involved with Pakim—that yearning and caring so much for him—would permanently rob me of the cool sense of reason that had earned me my nickname. It was easy to be unemotional and detached when I had nothing at stake. It wasn't so easy to be Cold-Blooded Cole when I cared so desperately about another.

Pakim drew himself into a sitting position so that he straddled me, and all other thoughts fell away. I took him in my hands and began pleasuring him. He leaned forward, his breaths coming in short, ragged gasps. He gripped my shoulder, clutching it so hard as to almost be painful, but I cared not, for I loved knowing I could move him so. I knew he was close to release when he arched backward, quetching and moaning as if in great pain. I worried Owen's sentry might come to investigate, but I heard nothing except Pakim's gasping. Release came at last, hot liquid spattering my sweaty chest. Pakim slumped forward, his forehead resting against mine.

Finally, he sat up, shifting his weight. I glanced down, saw his seed glistening on my chest. It glowed reddish in the firelight, as if the very nature of our singular act had somehow altered its ordinary color. Pakim leaned forward, kissing me deeply. I kissed him back hard, desperate to have him as close as I could. For some reason I felt overcome by grief. I supposed it was knowing this would be the last time we lay together, and I couldn't bear the thought.

Pakim finally pulled away, his breaths yet coming in short gasps. I was struck dumb by how handsome he was, how natural it felt to lie with him this way. I felt as if I had been holding my breath for years and only now was I able to breathe again. When Pakim once again left me, the loneliness would be tenfold worse than when the gravediggers had taken away my mother's body. How was I supposed to live without him—without this feeling—for the rest of my life?

I wasn't so smitten that I imagined my life wouldn't go on somehow, but it would be less living than merely existing. I might as well be adrift at sea the rest of my life, for that was how lonesome I would feel.

Impulsively, I reached down, pulled the leaves off my tattoo, then smeared the milky white remnants of our union into my still-bloody tattoo. It stung, but I didn't mind in the least. I placed the leaves back against my skin, pressing as hard as I could. Now it wouldn't only be my Guardian Spirit who was always close to me.

Pakim looked surprised, then smiled and nodded.

"Now you," he said, and it was my turn to cry out.

◆

Pakim and I lay on our sides in front of the fire, our bodies tucked together as snugly as a musket in its holster. His hand rested on my thigh, his fingers tracing patterns on my skin. We were still naked, but the fire threw off enough heat to keep us warm. Pakim was the taller, so I lay in front of him, his arm wrapped around my waist. It was most peculiar to be held thus; both pleasing, for I felt secure, but off-putting as well, because I felt weaker, less masculine than Pakim. In a week of new experiences, this was to be one more thing to take account of.

I reached behind me, placing a hand on his hip. There was so much I wanted to know about Pakim afore we parted ways, but I was afraid to ask as I didn't want to pry.

"Do you wish to have children?" asked Pakim. Apparently I wasn't the only one who had questions.

"I think we need not worry about that, Pakim," I teased gently. "I do not believe we have all of the necessary parts for that event to occur."

Pakim laughed as he yanked on my ear. "Spare me, Great Spirit," he intoned, "from this white man who believes he is funny when he is most definitely not."

"You laughed!" I said indignantly. I started to sit up, but Pakim tightened his grip on me and pulled me back to him. My wish to no longer be submissive battled with my desire yet to be held. Eventually, I settled back against Pakim, but not without some trepidation. I did not want to Pakim to think this would always be our custom.

I realized what I was thinking and stopped myself. There would be no "customs" betwixt us, nor anything else, since this was our last time together

"Are you going to answer me, Cole?" Pakim chided, when he realized I was lost in contemplation. "Do you wish children?

What an odd question, I thought, given our circumstances. "I suppose I already have Colette," I said.

"But what of your own children?" he asked. "Do you wish a son to carry on your name?"

Of course I did. What man didn't? Granted, such a wish was

rather at odds with my newfound inclination toward sharing my bed with Pakim. "Yes," I said. "Do you? Want children, that is?"

Pakim stiffened, and I immediately regretted my words. I had forgot he had children, at least some of whom had died. "You needn't tell me anything, Pakim," I said. "I'm sorry I asked."

"It is all right," he said. "I am the one that broached this topic, and it is only natural that you should be curious about me as well. We have shared our bodies. There is no reason we should not share our past as well. I have been married twice. The first time was to Nipahum Nunschetto, Moon Doe. She died giving birth to our first child, who also died. I was joined again to Sedpook Pilkisch, Morning Peach, but we were parted after the blister sickness brought by the white man took two of our children."

"I'm sorry," I said.

Pakim shrugged. "Things are what they are. If only Aunt Snow could understand that, my life would be much easier."

"Would she be upset if she knew about us?" I asked.

"Yes, but not for the same reason I'm given to understand your people would. Amongst the Delaware, there have always been some women who prefer women and some men who prefer men." Pakim reached around and ran his hand through my hair. "Everyone knows this, if not everyone understands or approves. Sometimes such people become our shamans, sometimes not. But no matter how you feel about sex, everyone is expected to have children, to make the village stronger. It is always the welfare of the people that has to come first. But once you have done that, you are free to warm your bed with whomever you please."

"But Aunt Snow still wants you to remarry?" I asked.

"She wants me to have more children," said Pakim. "The village I grew up in as a boy had two hundred souls. It was a beautiful place with many happy people. Now, after the latest attack, we are twenty and will disappear into another clan that is also shrinking. Why should I bring a child into such a situation?" He sat up, grabbed a stick, and jabbed at the fire with it. "A child should grow up feeling safe and loved, surrounded by family and knowing that someday he, too, will hunt and fish in the same woods as his father. Our children grow up wondering where they will be living a year from now, who will die next from disease or starvation. I fear we have no future but misery. That is why I left my people two years ago. Like Brother Eagle, I flew far away."

"But you came back," I said.

"Yes, and now I wish I had not. My people are dying and nothing I can do will change that. When I left, it was because I was angry the elders would not fight. But as I traveled, I saw the ruins of many burned villages, heard many tales of slaughtered tribes. Some villages had tried to be friends with the whites, others resisted. The result was the same either way."

"Why did you come back?"

"I thought maybe I had found a third way for us to survive," he said. "But now I do not think so."

"Are you sure?" I asked, eager to do something to help Pakim. "What is your idea? Maybe I can help."

Pakim shook his head. "My idea was a fool's dream. A child's wish to believe in something that is not real." He sighed with such sadness I was sorry I had asked. "Even if I had found a way, I think it is too late for my people."

I hesitated afore asking my next question, not sure I wanted to know the answer, yet desperately needing to at the same time. "And why are you here now, Pakim? I thought you were to stay with your people in the new village?"

Pakim seemed caught off-guard by the question. "We met up with braves from my mother's clan, and they are escorting Aunt Snow and the others to their new home. I decided to leave and will not return to my people. I cannot watch them dwindle away to nothing." Pakim looked at me, placing his hand over mine. "But I did not come here to interfere with you, Cole. I know you have Rose and Colette. It truly was a coincidence we met again."

"I understand, Pakim," I said, feeling both relief and regret that he had not returned for me. "What will you do now?" I asked. "Where will you go?"

Pakim shrugged, and I thought it the saddest gesture I had ever seen. I wanted to tell him to stay, that his finding me again had to be fate—that I thought I loved him. But I couldn't. If I was ever to be Cold-Blooded Cole, now was the time to let this strange thing between us die for good.

We fell silent, watching the flames together whilst each of us was alone with his thoughts. But almost at once, a ruckus arose outside. We threw on our clothes and dashed out of the cabin. The sentry yelled and gestured wildly toward the dark woods which pressed up against Hugh's Lick with the insistence of a rising tide.

Owen appeared in the doorway of the blockhouse. "Everyone inside!" he ordered. Pakim and I barely made it in afore Owen barred the door. I suspected he wouldn't have been much disheartened had we been on the other side

"There's something out there!" stammered the sentry. "Something not natural! I swear it!"

Armed with muskets and pistols—even a large stone pestle wielded by one ferocious-looking old woman—the settlers gathered by the blockhouse door or peered out the narrow slots cut in the walls for shooting through. I peered through one of the slots myself. The clouds had cleared during the night, and the half-moon sat high in the sky, the full effect of its light shining directly in front of the blockhouse. The wendigo stepped out of the shadows, proving the sentry right. This wasn't the wendigo John and I had just encountered, or at least not in that form. I was yet confused about what shapes it could take or if, in fact, there was any connection betwixt the two creatures. This, however, was definitely the beast that had taken me to the cave by the lake.

The beast stood motionless between two other cabins as if it were waiting to see what we would do. It didn't have to wait long. Without warning, Owen Stern let loose with a blast from his musket. The wendigo jerked to the side and out of sight, but I didn't think it had been hit.

At almost the same instant, something landed on the roof. It was as if the wendigo had leaped over the cabin outside and onto the block-house in a single bound. The men started as if one, several women gasped, and one child cried out afore being shushed. We all stared upward, waiting. For a long moment, nothing, then the sound of scrabbling, of nails across wood. Our heads swiveled in unison, track-ing the noise as it moved. The sound ceased, and we stared at the spot from which it had last come. Scratching commenced from up above. Gentle at first, then harder, faster, the wendigo clawing at one place. Two women who happened to sit huddled beneath the spot suddenly sprang away as if they had been jabbed in their arses with a pitchfork.

A blockhouse, like most frontier dwellings, is built of logs with joints and notches carved into their ends, then fitted together, not unlike a puzzle. And like a puzzle, it can be taken apart again, given sufficient strength. Unfortunately for us, I suspected the wendigo had sufficient strength for that effort. Especially since the quality of work here looked rather suspect.

The clawing stopped. I felt like a rabbit trapped in its burrow whilst a stoat snuffles about searching for a way in. Pakim stood close to me. The waiting became interminable and the blockhouse grew stuffy. I loosed the breath I had been holding without even realizing I had been doing so. Someone coughed. Everyone peered upward, waiting, imagining a dozen different horrors.

Laughter, cold and sharp like a knife, came from above. One of the logs in the roof suddenly jerked upward a few inches afore falling back down. Men and women alike screamed as dust floated downward. Only Pakim remained motionless, his musket trained on the ceiling. More laughter reached our ears, then the log lurched upward again, and several of the other men foolishly let loose with their muskets when any idiot knew a musket ball could never penetrate these logs. The sound of gunpowder igniting inside the blockhouse was deafening. Acrid smoke quickly filled the small space and people began to cough and wheeze.

The log jerked upward again, farther this time, and I briefly saw the moon shining through. People again screamed as more muskets were fired, then I felt the cool wash of fresh air. In a panic, some fool had opened the door so as to flee. Someone else yelled for it to be shut, but several people had already bolted out-a-doors. Others followed, whilst the rest yelled for everyone else to come back. I stayed near Pakim, both of us watching for the wendigo to make its next move. Nothing more happened, though. In fact, the wendigo seemed to have left as abruptly as it had appeared. Nonetheless, several minutes of confusion and panic ensued amongst the rattled settlers. It was a wonder no one had been shot during the melee.

Pakim and I ventured outside. A severely rattled Owen Stern stood frozen just outside the doorway whilst one of the women tried unsuccessfully to herd everyone back into the blockhouse.

"Enough!" yelled Pakim. "You people have less discipline than a flock of turkeys fleeing a fox. Get back inside afore someone is hurt."

Soon he had everyone rounded up except for one thin, wild-eyed woman anxiously looking for her little boy. Her gray hair had come loose from its bun and whirled around her head as she turned all about.

"Roan?" she called. "Has anyone seen my Roan?"

No one had. Pakim and I organized a cursory search around the perimeter of the blockhouse. The boy's mother had to be restrained from rushing into the dark. Either the child had got lost during the confusion—or the wendigo had taken it. Perhaps that was the reason its attack had ceased so abruptly. Whatever the others thought, they kept their opinions to themselves.

The woman pleaded with the men to go after her boy, but Owen Stern, having finally got a grip on himself, told her that wasn't possible. Even Pakim didn't offer to go out into the night. Someone got the keening woman something potent to drink, then the other women gathered around her in a protective cocoon and took her to the back of the blockhouse.

After the door was barred and a sentry posted, the others settled down to attempt to get some sleep.

Pakim and I rejoined John, and all of us shared a single

bearskin. John lay facing the wall, and I thought it best to let him be. I fell back exhausted, but sleep didn't come. How could it when a wendigo was on the loose and Palmer and Rose were missing? They could have been anywhere—lost in the storm, already dead, or yet with the wendigo, and God only knew where that might be. A lair somewhere deep in the woods, I supposed. Perhaps it was holed up in a den or—

How could I have been so blind? *I* had been to the wendigo's lair. I knew where it resided. It was proof of how tired I was that I hadn't thought of this sooner.

"John," I whispered, excitedly. "John, are you awake?"

"Leave me alone, Cole," he said.

"I know where Palmer might be," I said. "I know where we have to go."

John sat up. "Where?" he asked.

"The first time the wendigo attacked me, it took me to a cave. I think that must be where it's taken Palmer and Rose."

"How can you be sure it took them there?" asked John.

I felt sure because of all the bones laying about from the wendigo's previous victims. Clearly, that was where it took all of its prey. Telling John that, however, didn't seem like such a good idea. "It was its lair," I said. "Its home. Where else would it take them?"

John's eyes came back to life as he warmed to the idea. "Thank you, Cole," he said. "I know we're going to find them! I know it!"

I could only hope it would be more than their bones that we found.

chapter fifteen

Despite the fact that it was the dead of night, not to mention freezing and snowing, John was prepared to set out that very minute.

"Do you think you can find the way back to the cave?" he asked.

That was a bit of a conundrum. At the time the wendigo had taken me there, I had been like a fish hauled from a lake—dazed, unexpectedly near death, and borne away to some place with which I had no familiarity. And later, when I had finally fashioned my escape, I was so battered as to nearly be insensible. But when Pakim took me to search for my supplies, he had also shown me the spot where he had first come across me. That couldn't have been too distant whence the wendigo dwelled as I had been too injured to have gone far. I queried Pakim if he knew the area north of there, up by the great lake.

"I am sorry to say I do not," he said. "I was quite far from my tribe's customary hunting grounds when I found you."

Even so, I thought I could find my way back to the cave starting from the spot Pakim had discovered me. "Maybe Gwennie could help," I suggested. "Didn't you say from planting her trees she knows the countryside as well as anyone?"

John nodded.

"Well, the cave was in a pretty distinctive area," I said. "If I describe it to her, I'd wager she can help us find it. Too, there were ruins nearby as well. Maybe she knows those."

"What sort of ruins?" asked Pakim.

"I'm not sure," I said. "A fort, I think. Whatever they were, they were quite old, as most of the walls had fallen down. All that really remained was a cellar filled with lead bars. That was why I thought it might have been a fort, but it just as easily could have been a blockhouse."

"Were there a lot of lead bars?" asked Pakim.

"Enough for me to stack high enough to climb out of the ground," I said. "Why?"

"I had not heard of a fort north of here, so I am puzzled," said Pakim. "And this fort is near where the wendigo lives?"

I nodded.

"Then let's go," said John, springing to his feet.

Pakim placed his hand on John's arm and held him down. "We will go at sunrise. We do no one any good if we get ourselves killed in this storm."

John looked as if he were going to argue, then thought better of it. It was a good thing, too, because I was exhausted. In fact, I didn't think I could stay awake a minute longer.

◆

But I did stay awake. We all did. No one slept during that damnable night, or at least they only dozed fitfully. Fear that the wendigo might return kept slumber at bay for all of us. Therefore, it was barely after dawn that John, Pakim, and I were already prepared to leave, as were the last citizens of Hugh's Lick. Even the rapacious Owen Stern had given up on the fortune he had wanted so badly to wrest from the wilderness.

As the last retreating settler passed by, my friends and I rode away in the opposite direction; we were headed to Gwennie's cabin to fetch her for our trip to the wendigo's lair.

I felt terrible, like I'd spent six weeks on a storm-tossed sea. My tired eyes burned as if potash had been sprinkled in them, and my muscles ached fiercely. As if that weren't enough, my new tattoo itched furiously. Pakim hadn't warned me about that and I feared it would drive me mad. A hollow-eyed John looked even worse. He was deep in thought, terrified, I knew, over what might have befallen Palmer.

The brief respite from the snow ended and, once again, it fell copiously all around us. The already quiet woods grew even more so, muffled by the blanket of winter white that grew deeper by the minute. At least the temperature had risen. It was yet cold, but not nearly as bad as it had been.

Apparently, I had dozed off, for I suddenly found myself jolted awake in front of Gwennie's cabin. John and Pakim dismounted, went to her door, knocked, and went in. As I waited, I pondered how we might defeat the wendigo. Thus far, it had wreaked its will against us without hindrance. Stich Burke, just afore he'd been killed, had even apparently shot it at close range, but to no effect.

I recalled Whitewood Tree's warning that, for a man, killing the wendigo was all but impossible. Yet I refused to believe it *couldn't* be killed without my having to become a cannibal. I simply had to figure out how to do it. Even then, according to the shaman, that wouldn't be enough; its heart had to be burned to ash. Despite my skepticism over Whitewood Tree in general, I knew I would at least do that as instructed. I wasn't a superstitious man, but nor was I one to take needless chances.

In the meantime, what was taking John and Pakim so blasted long? Every minute that passed was another minute for the wendigo to terrorize, or do worse, to our friends. Perhaps John was having a hard time persuading Gwennie to help us. Who could blame her? Had she left for the Firelands when she wanted, she would have been out of harm's way long ago.

"John?" I called out. "Pakim? Is everything all right?"

They must not have heard me. Resignedly, I slid down from Midnight, landing with a thud. Hunger and lack of sleep had left me muzzy-headed.

"John?" I said again, yet getting no answer. I went to Gwennie's door, knocking loudly, for if they were arguing heatedly I had no wish to catch them unawares. Only silence answered me back. I tried to open the door, but it wouldn't budge. That was when I began to get a bad feeling. "Pakim?" I called out more urgently. "John? Is everything all right? Why is the door bolted?"

No one answered. I pushed harder against the door, then threw all of my weight against it. It didn't give an inch. Panic built inside me. Frantically, I pounded on the door, yelling for them to open it.

That was when the screaming started. Whoever screamed didn't stop, didn't even take a breath, just let go one continuous agonized wail. Again and again I kicked at the door, but to no avail. I dashed around Gwennie's tiny cabin, but there were no windows, no other ways in. I again came to the front door as a second scream joined the first, then a third, a cacophony of terrified voices. With growing horror, I realized Palmer and Rose must have come back during the night and were inside as well. Each of them screamed as if being skinned alive. What in God's name was happening?

Abruptly, everything fell silent.

I froze, staring at the cabin, waiting for something to happen. Nothing did, so again I pushed against the door. This time it swung open easily. A gust of fetid air washed over me, rank and ripe, the smell of blood and guts. Dear God.

I stepped inside. At first I could see nothing in the gloom. The smell of blood was so thick that I could taste its copper tang. I felt as if I might retch. Then my eyes adjusted to the light, and I could see the horror afore me. Everyone was there, seated at the table. Pakim, John, Palmer, Rose, the baby, Gwennie. They were all dead. And not just dead, but disemboweled, their guts spilt forth across the table in rank, steaming piles.

I opened my mouth to scream, but no sound came out.

Seated at the head of the table was the figure I had seen on the moonlit trail. He was tall and skinny, swathed in black. Again he wore the peaked, wide-brimmed hat that hid his face from me. He reached forward and extended one impossibly long, bony finger. The terrible man jabbed his finger clear through a bloody heart that lay in front of Pakim. He smacked his bony lips and pulled the organ toward his shadowed mouth. I heard the tearing of the heart as he pulled it apart in long, stringy pieces. He swallowed clump after clump until it was gone.

I couldn't move.

Finished eating, the figure slowly tipped its head back. Blood smeared its chin and lips, and it smiled a horrid smile of blood-streaked teeth. Now I saw its nose: sharp and narrow, two flared nostrils that quivered constantly. Then, at length, I saw its dead, lifeless eyes, and I understood at last. I knew those eyes. They were my father's eyes, my brother's eyes.

Maybe even my eyes.

This time the sound of my voice came when I screamed.

◆

An elbow dug into my side.

"Nice nap?" asked a distant voice.

I jerked awake with a start.

"We're here," said John.

Blinking slowly, I looked around and saw we had arrived at Gwennie's. *Sweet Jesus above,* I thought. My vision hadn't been real—only a dream. It might only have been a dream, but I knew that was the wendigo I had seen in it. I didn't know how I knew, but I knew. It must be able to change shapes after all; if nothing else, at least it could shift between the beast and the black-clad figure. But why had I dreamed that *I* was the wendigo? Why would have I killed the others and eaten Pakim's heart?

"So was it?" asked Pakim, dropping to the ground.

I rubbed my burning eyes and ran a hand across my face. Despite the chill in the air, I sweat profusely. "Was it what?" I asked. My mouth felt as if it were stuffed with cotton-batting. I was desperately thirsty. Ironically, I had to pee as well.

"A nice nap," he said. "You've been snoozing for quite a while."

"Yeah," I said. "Nice."

"Let me talk to Gwennie first," said John. "Getting her to help might be tricky. Do you mind waiting out here?"

"What? No," I mumbled. The dream had been so real, so awful, that I was having trouble shaking free from it. After knocking, John disappeared inside Gwennie's cabin. I slid off Midnight and stumbled toward the woods whilst Pakim tethered and tended to the horses. Out of sight of the front door, I undid my breeches and let loose a mighty stream of piss. Snow dissolved beneath it, but so many more flakes swirled down that all traces I had been here would soon be erased. Finished relieving myself, I went to Gwennie's water bumkin, dipped in the ladle, and drank till I felt bloated.

At last I was starting to feel myself. I wiped my mouth on my sleeve and turned toward the cabin. I noticed Pakim was gone, and it seemed John was taking an awfully long time to fetch Gwennie. A sense of unease tickled at my spine.

"Cole, we're ready," called out John from the other side of the cabin.

I breathed deeply, held it, then let it go, feeling the tension flow from my body.

It was time to find the wendigo.

◆

We were lost in a whiteout—had been for several hours. It was bitterly frigid as well, so cold that it was hard to think straight. In fact, I was the only one who still seemed to be entirely in control of his senses. The others were sluggish and betwattled, so much so that several times Gwennie and John had wandered away like sheep gone astray. Even Pakim didn't seem entirely himself; he was easily distracted and not entirely present.

Our search for the wendigo's cave was not going well.

The protection afforded by the forest lay miles behind us whilst afore us stretched an empty plain shrouded by the snow. Gwennie had said the plain extended all the way to the great lake, where I hoped to find the lair of the wendigo. She had also said it was only a few miles to the lake whence Pakim had found me, but either she was mistaken, or we had been wandering in circles for hours.

In a trice, Gwennie tumbled from Hiccup. I sprang down from the horse and hauled her to her feet. Her lips were blue and she shook without surcease.

"We've got to find shelter!" I yelled to Pakim.

He nodded. "Stay here for a moment."

I watched uneasily as he rode into the storm. Whilst I waited, I pulled Gwennie's collar tight around her neck. I did the same for John. Against the fury of the storm, my efforts were feeble at best. Fortunately, we had brought supplies with us—bearskins, some food, flints, though we had no wood. If we could find a place out of the wind, I thought we could make it through the night.

"Palmer back?" asked John. He slurred his words as if drunk.

"Not yet," I said. "But we'll find him soon. Stay with us, John, all right?"

I peered back into the blowing snow. It would be so very easy to get lost in this storm—even for Pakim, who was as at home in the woods as Brother Bear. I wasn't sure I could bear it if he didn't return. I was about to yell out for him when a shadow loomed up out of the wall of white. For a moment I feared it was the wendigo, but to my relief, it gradually transformed into Pakim.

"This way," he called.

A short time later, we reached a spot Pakim had found on the gently undulating plain. It wasn't much more than an indentation in the ground, a small scoop where the earth had been worn away leaving behind a shallow bowl. At least it lay out of the wind.

Pakim and I set about digging out the snow that filled the hollow. Next we covered our refuge by anchoring a bearskin over the space with several large heavy rocks. Our tiny shelter—perhaps three feet deep and five feet wide—was inadequate protection at best. The only way for us to all fit was to lie flat and side by side, but even so, I thought it might yet save our lives.

Whilst Pakim stood with John, I goaded Gwennie inside, laying her out, then covering her with another bearskin. Next I brought in

John, got him settled, then called out for Pakim to join us. It truly was going to be a tight fit. In fact, with the four of us inside, there would be no way to completely keep out the wind. We would simply have to make the best of it. By the time I had myself situated, Pakim had yet to enter. I assumed he was tying the horses together so they could at least share their body warmth. When a few more moments had passed, I lifted up the edge of the bearskin, peering out into the darkness.

"Pakim?" I called out. "What are you doing?" When I still got no response, I scooted back out into the howling wind. Elizabeth and Hiccup stood tethered to a rock, but neither Pakim nor Midnight was anywhere to be found.

"Pakim!" I yelled. "Where are you? Follow my voice!" I yelled again and again until I was hoarse, but the only answer I got back was the mournful dirge of the wind.

◆

Heated by our three bodies, the little space soon grew bearable, if not actually warm, and I knew we would yet live. I lay on my back, one tiny corner of the shelter open so I could watch for Pakim. Too, I strained to hear anything over the lashing wind of the storm. Had I been alone, I would have gone looking for him, but doing so now would have meant leaving Gwennie and John unattended, not to mention the fact that Rose, Colette, and Palmer were yet in the hands of the wendigo. I nearly went after him anyway.

The warmth must have at last reached John for he stirred next to me.

"Am I dead?" he asked, understandably confused as to his where-abouts.

"Not unless I've died with you," I said.

"Is that you, Cole?" he asked. His hand found my arm and squeezed.

"It's me," I said.

"That's a relief," said John. "I thought I had died and been buried." I heard him move about some more, then he asked, "That's Gwennie to my right?"

"'Tis indeed," I said.

"Is Pakim next to you then?" he asked.

It took me a moment to speak. "I'm not sure where Pakim is," I said. "I couldn't find him." I hoped my voice sounded even, free of the anguish I felt. So much for being Cold-Blooded Cole again.

"Bloody hell," said John. "So it's the three of us left?"

"Afraid so," I said.

"Pakim will be all right," said John. "He's an Indian. He can survive far worse than this."

"I'm not worried," I lied. "The same goes for Palmer. I'm sure he's fine."

"The wendigo has him, Cole," John said bleakly. "He isn't fine."

"But he *will* be," I insisted. "We're going to find him, or he's going to escape."

"He wouldn't leave without Rose and Colette," said John. "He would sacrifice himself to save them. I'm as certain of that as I am my own name."

John didn't sound particularly happy about that.

"Do you know what made me most angry about the settlers in Hugh's Lick?" he asked.

"What?"

"That they didn't understand how extraordinary Palmer is," he said. "No one did. Not even his family. He *always* put the welfare of others ahead of his own. Sort of like you."

"Me?" I said, startled by the comparison. John obviously had the wrong idea about me.

"Sure," he said. "Your marrying Rose is clearly not what you want. It's a selfless thing you're doing. Noble, even."

I doubted that. I had always imagined doing something noble would make me feel good. Taking care of Rose and Colette was a burden and one I resented. Truth be told, I would have done almost anything to get out of it. If that made me noble, then the word didn't mean what I thought.

"Frankly, it sometimes exasperates me how good Palmer is," said John. "He always overlooks the bad things people said about him. About us. Whereas I couldn't. I would fume and stew for hours over any slight. And if anyone needed help building a cabin or cutting firewood, Palmer was there to offer it. They always took his help, too, the filthy whoresons—even if they later talked about us behind our backs. Of course, now that Palmer needs their help, they only disparage him and wouldn't so much as mold a musket ball to save him."

"Well, we'll manage on our own," I said.

"Would you believe that afore I met Palmer, I had never been to a raising?" asked John.

A raising happened whenever a family settled into a new place and the neighbors all pitched in to help "raise" a cabin for them. This was most often followed with music and dancing, and many a future spouse were met at such events.

"Were you not invited to any?" I asked John.

"Once or twice," he said. "But I wasn't what you would call a social person. I'm sure that comes as quite a revelation to you."

Despite the grimness of our situation, I laughed.

"But Palmer couldn't get enough of other people," said John. "He was always wheedling me to go off with him and help some new family. Believe it or not, I actually found I enjoyed raisings. That was how I met Marda Witt, and learned that not all settlers are gold-plated bastards. Plus I got to dance with Palmer, as there are never enough women to go around. After we went to a couple, I truly started to feel different, less cynical and bitter."

"Makes me glad I didn't happen across you any sooner," I said with affection.

"Palmer used to tease me that he doubted I could be more overwrought if I were sitting on a powder keg with a fire lit beneath it." John laughed at the happy memory afore the sound seemed to suddenly catch in his throat. He fell silent, and again I heard nothing but the wind gently tugging at our shelter. Reassuring John that Palmer would be fine seemed pointless. He was worried and had reason to be.

I peeked back out into the storm. The wind and snow had lessened considerably. The eastern sky was lightening as dawn pushed her way up from the horizon.

"I think it's time to go," I said.

◆

We reached the wendigo's cave at last. We had climbed over the final knoll and now peered down onto the stony beach that tumbled from the mouth of the cave. It was early yet, and I hoped we might even catch the beast yet slumbering. That was presupposing that shape-shifting demons had to sleep, or that it was even here. We remained hidden for near to ten minutes, watching and listening for any sign of the wendigo. We saw nothing and all we heard was the sound of the wind skating in over the lake, and, once, the "hoot, hoot" of an owl which should have already taken up its roost for the day.

Of course, I immediately thought of Pakim's calling me Gokhotit.

As quietly as possible, we made our way down the hill until we stood next to the mouth of the cave. There were no signs of the beast inside or out. I strained with all of my might to hear any sound from within the yawning mouth of its lair. I heard nothing.

With my musket at the ready, I sidled inside whilst John came behind with the torch. The cave was as dank and fetid as I remembered—and as packed with bones. Truly, this place was an ossuary. John's eyes widened with horror as he saw how many others had died here. Fortunately, there were no fresh signs—no blood, nor scraps of flesh—that anyone else had recently been killed and eaten here.

A sudden memory of my nightmare came to me unbidden. Again I saw my friends, dead and disemboweled, as the wendigo speared glistening organs with its long, bony finger. I forced the thoughts away.

I did make one interesting discovery. Scattered amongst the bones were epaulets, brass belt buckles, and buttons made of metal.

Many of them had rusted over, but with a little scraping, I uncovered a fleur-de-lis stamped into one of the epaulets. At least a few French soldiers had died here.

"I had heard talk there was an old French fort in these parts," said John, when I showed him the epaulet. "It was supposed to have been abandoned fifty years ago."

"It looks that old," I said. "But why do you think there are soldier's bodies in the cave? Surely the French would bury their dead, not throw them here."

John shrugged. "I don't know. Maybe something happened. It's possible Whitewood Tree is wrong. It might be that the wendigo has been in these parts a long time and attacked the soldiers and the fort the way it has attacked the Indians and settlers. That might be the reason the fort was abandoned. Frankly, I don't care. Not unlessen figuring that out gets us any closer to finding Palmer. And Rose."

"We should check the ruins," I said. "It's unlikely, but perhaps Palmer or Rose made the same journey through the caves that I did." I nearly tossed the epaulet away, but then I thought of my mother, herself French, and the stories she told of growing up in Lyon. Now that I had lost all that I owned, I had nothing to remember her by. I slipped the epaulet into my pocket.

We quickly climbed back over the hill and made the short hike to the fort, but the ruins were as empty and forlorn as when I had last been there, all the more so because there were no signs of our friends.

◆

We rode southward as hard as we could. Each of us hoped that we would return to find Palmer and Rose safely back in the cabin. John spun elaborate tales that explained how Palmer might have evaded the wendigo, then found shelter from the storm. Each sounded progressively more far-fetched and desperate. I, too, was fearful about Pakim's fate, but chose not to engage in such useless musings.

Someone *had* come calling whilst we were gone, but it wasn't Palmer or Rose, who were yet missing. Gwennie's tiny abode had simply been kicked to the ground. Everything that could be broken had been. Gwennie's face gave way naught of what she felt inside. She briefly picked through the rubble, then went back to hiccup. And John's cabin had been burned to ash. We sifted through the smoldering ruins, but all that could be saved were a tin pan and a bag of apple seeds. The only other things we had left were what we had taken with us for our trip north in search of the wendigo—some cornmeal, pemmican, bear fat, lead balls, rope and gunpowder, and not much at all of any of it. As for weapons, we had my musket, the hatchet I had taken from Rose's, and a knife that John carried.

Our situation was grim, and that was like saying a bear was slightly on the hairy side. We had almost no supplies left, and we were less than halfway through winter. We were the last people left for God only knew how many miles. And our friends were in the hands of what was possibly an evil Indian demon that so far we were helpless to defeat.

So much for my new life on the frontier.

chapter sixteen

It was Gwennie's idea to set a trap for the wendigo.

"Are you daft, woman?" asked John, kicking the blockhouse door in frustration. We were back in Hugh's Lick, having elected to return there in hopes of finding shelter. "You do comprehend, Gwennie, that it's not a simple beaver that we're after? It's a wendigo that so far has outfoxed us at every turn. Besides, there isn't time to build a trap that could capture it. How could you not see that? Palmer and Rose and quite possibly Pakim are in trouble, and we have to do something *now*." At last John stopped his harangue.

Gwennie stared at him expressionlessly. "I not say it *good* idea, Geb Tschaat," she said at last. "Only that I *have* idea. You have suggestion yourself?"

"What is Geb Tschaat?" asked John suspiciously. I, too, was curious as to what Gwennie called him. Something told me it wasn't Good Friend Whom I Forgive for Being an Absolute Son of a Bitch.

Gwennie regarded John with the impassiveness of a cooking pot. Frankly, I thought he had a far better chance of getting a pot to answer him than he did Gwennie.

John must have gathered that as well because he said, "Yes, I have an idea, Gwennie. We go look for them. We ride through the forest. We search every valley, every mountain until we find them. *That's* my idea."

"Wait a minute, John," I said. "Perhaps we should at least think about Gwennie's suggestion."

John exhaled loudly in frustration. Gwennie snorted in annoyance. And I was caught between them.

"Chasing all over has gained us nothing, John," I said calmly. "Shouldn't we consider alternatives?"

"No!" shouted John. "There are no alternatives! You don't understand! Palmer could be dying this very moment, and I will not stand about laying plans for some ridiculous trap when I could be looking for him! Neither of you understands at all!"

With that, John grabbed Elizabeth's harness, swung himself into the saddle, and raced off into the woods.

I went to go after him, but Gwennie stopped me. "Let John be," she said. "He be back in a bit."

Gwennie and I stared after him until he vanished from sight. Finally, I turned to her and said, "Well, Whitewood Tree said the only way to kill the wendigo was with fire."

"Maybe we can lure wendigo somewhere we can trap and burn it," said Gwennie.

"The blockhouse," I said with sudden inspiration. "We can trap it inside, then burn it to the ground."

"Good," said Gwennie. "But how to get it to come?"

"That's easy," I said. "We use bait: namely, me. It called my name, after all."

"I should be bait," said Gwennie. "It also call my name."

"Why you, Gwennie?" I asked. "I'm willing to do it."

"You are bigger, stronger than I," she said. "Better if you surprise it after it in trap. No surprise if you are bait."

I knew she was right, though I was loathe to put her at risk. On the other hand, we were already in peril as it was.

◆

Once we had settled on trapping the wendigo in the blockhouse, we needed to make sure it would burn as fiercely as possible. With that in mind, we scoured the cabins abandoned by the settlers when they had fled the day afore. Fortunately, they had left in such a hurry that there was no shortage of combustible material to be had: ticking stuffed with straw for sleeping platforms, kindling and stacks of wood, chairs, ratty blankets, cloths stiff with bear fat, even several sacks of gunpowder.

We were in the midst of gathering it all together when John rode up to us. He slipped off Elizabeth then said, "There's no excuse for how I spoke to either of you. I'm sorry."

Gwennie and I exchanged glances, then she said, "Carry gunpowder to blockhouse, John? We plan to lure wendigo there, then burn it."

"That's a fine idea," he said.

The three of us proceeded to stuff the blockhouse with everything we could find. Once we finished that, we weakened the back wall by hacking a hole in it, then tied ropes around the bottom-most logs. The ropes snaked out of the blockhouse to where we kept Elizabeth and Hiccup tethered. The idea was twofold. First, Gwennie was going to need an avenue by which to escape once we had lured the wendigo inside. Second, we were going to pull the burning blockhouse down upon the wendigo's head. Hopefully, it wouldn't be able to escape, but if it did, I would be ready to drive it back.

Now all we had to do was to lure the damn thing to us.

◆

To make our plan work, we had to split up. John was by himself on the far side of the blockhouse with the horses, waiting to pull the back wall down once I yelled for him to do so. He hid as best he could and would fire his musket if attacked. Gwennie's role required her to sit on the side of the blockhouse near the front door whilst I was in the cabin directly across where I could keep an eye her. We had found a lethal-looking fishing gaff left behind in one of the blockhouses; I insisted Gwennie keep it close at hand in case she had to defend herself.

All we needed now was the wendigo. And if crowns grew on trees, then every man would be king.

Hidden inside the cabin, I watched Gwennie as the time passed. As a hunter, I was used to long hours sitting motionless near a salt lick or watering hole until game came within musket range. I had thought I was quite skilled at waiting, but Gwennie made me look an utter tyro, freshly pressed into military service. I swore she hadn't so much as moved a jot since she sat down. I had seen carvings that seemed more lifelike than she.

I once dared to speak long enough to tease her the wendigo might mistake her for a statue and pass her by. Even then, she didn't so much as blink.

Late morning gave way to afternoon and still nothing happened. I picked up a stick to fiddle with. I supposed it was stupid of me to expect the damnable wendigo to simply saunter up because we were ready. Who knew if it was even in the area? Or worse, what if it knew exactly what we were up to and had no intention of coming at all? But it had driven everyone else from Hugh's Lick as well as the Indian village. I had difficulty imagining it was going to let us remain here unmolested.

I glanced out the door, saw Gwennie sitting there, still looking as if she hadn't so much as taken a breath. As always the past several days, I was exhausted and starving. I wondered how much longer I could go on without getting a real night's sleep or eating more than a handful of cornmeal and a bit of pemmican.

To occupy my mind, I turned my attention back to the grotty, abandoned cabin in which I found myself. Frankly, it wasn't that much nicer than the hovel in which Rose had lived. A tilted, shoddy-looking table stood in one corner, a broken chair in the other. A chamber pot sat perched on the edge of the bed platform. I hoped it was empty. The place was rank with the smell of bear fat—a smell to which I had grown unaccustomed whilst traveling out-a-doors for so long. It was sad to think this dismal place had only recently been someone's home.

Something bounced off the roof. I froze as I stared upward, then glanced out the door as a pinecone fell to the ground. I swung my eyes back to the ceiling, waiting for something else to happen. I kept waiting even as my neck began to throb from staring upward for so long. Perhaps the wendigo was in a tree and had knocked the pinecone loose. Or perhaps it had been naught but a pinecone breaking free. After all, they were known to do that every so often.

I checked again on Gwennie, then went back to playing with the stick. Hungry, I searched about until I found a strip of venison jerk along with a piece of hard biscuit that had been left behind. Both had moldy bits that I trimmed away. I washed down the jerk with hard cider.

I hoped John held up all right. With any luck, tending to the horses would keep him from thinking too much about Palmer. Which, of course, prompted me to speculate about Pakim. He had been gone for twenty-four hours now. Had he survived the storm? He had to have.

Something skittered across the roof. It was softer this time and definitely not a pinecone. I reached for my musket, my eyes tracking along with the sound. Due to the thickness of the logs, it was hard to judge how large a creature might be up there. The clicking moved toward the front of the cabin and the door, then stopped. I edged closer, pressing myself tight against the wall. I stole a glance at Gwennie to see if she had seen or heard, but she only sat there staring straight ahead. I strained to hear the wendigo's raspy breathing, but heard naught except my own.

Fearing the wendigo would strike at any moment, I burst out the front door, spun about, and aimed my musket directly at…a squirrel.

The gray rodent chirped once in surprise, turned, scampered back up the roof, then jumped onto the low-hanging branch of a pine tree and disappeared. The branch swayed about looking like nothing so much as a head bobbing up and down with laughter. It was only then that I realized my nerves sang like a ship's rigging in a gale. So much for being back to Cold-Blooded Cole.

I turned toward Gwennie to make a joke at my expense.

She was gone.

How had she gone so quickly and quietly? And *where* had she gone? Warily, I circled about, but saw no sign of her.

"Gwennie?" I called out softly. I got no answer. I crept around the perimeter of the blockhouse. Finally, I returned to the back of the blockhouse with yet no sign of Gwennie or the wendigo. It would be just like her to up and go without saying so much as good day.

I went to where John lay in wait. "Have you seen Gwennie?" I asked.

"No. Why?" he asked, instantly alarmed. "Has something happened?"

"I'm not sure," I said. "Nothing, I pray, but I can't find her.

"Bloody hell," he murmured.

"I only looked away for a moment and she was gone," I said.

"Did you try to follow her footprints?"

"There's nothing to follow," I said. "So much has happened here the past several days that the ground is a mishmash."

"Let's think for a moment. Perhaps she went to find something to eat."

"We should check the cabins."

The cabins lined each side of the town's single road. Each cabin had a slanted roof so that the snow would continuously slide off, with mud-brick chimneys perched on top that resembled solitary birds roosting.

In front of most of the cabins were truck patches—large gardens—that were dead now. Had things gone differently, come spring the truck patches would have been filled with green shoots of all sorts—carrots and peas and radishes and so forth. Some women probably would have planted flowers as well, anything to bring a bit of color to the drab place, But now only brown, broken stalks of corn dotted the ground like a volley of arrows fallen to earth.

Beyond the cabins to my left were the frozen waters of the river whose name I had not learned. To my right were the ever watchful woods, yet seeming to bide their time. And at the far end of the road stood the blockhouse, resolutely watching over the abandoned cabins.

We searched each cabin, but found nothing. John kicked at the ground furiously as we exited the last one. "The wendigo has her, doesn't it?" he asked.

"Maybe," I said. "Maybe not. There might be another explanation."

"Like what?" demanded John. "She just up and walked away to take in some fresh air? Not damned likely. The wendigo has her, and it's all my fault for making her stay. First Palmer, now Gwennie. Blast it! Blast it! Blast it!" John seized a fallen branch and attacked one of the cabins as if doing so might force the building to tell all it knew.

"Calm down," I said, exasperated with him. I knew how upset he was about Palmer's disappearance, and now Gwennie had gone missing, but frankly, he was only making things worse. "Let's think about this. Where else might Gwennie have gone?"

"Maybe she thought now would be a good time to inspect her apples," he said sarcastically

Clearly, John was of little use in a crisis. I had an idea. "Did you check the outhouses?" I asked. "Maybe something happened on the way there or back."

We hurried off to the closest outhouse. It was empty. The next one was the one farthest from town, and it was empty as well, but fresh tracks were visible coming and going. Only Gwennie could have made them. To our dismay, however, the footprints didn't head back to town, but instead went north toward the river.

"I don't understand," said John. "Where would she have been going?"

"Perhaps she saw something?" I suggested

"Palmer!" John exclaimed. "She saw Palmer!"

I was less certain of that, but it was possible. As John scurried toward the river, I gamely followed. Gwennie must have had a good reason for going off on her own with a wendigo lurking about. Maybe she had seen Palmer.

John and I followed Gwennie's footprints to the river, but we lost her trail shortly thereafter.

"Damn it to hell!" exploded John. "Where the fuck did she go? Where is Palmer? What is going on?"

I ignored John's rantings as I scoured the ice for any further tracks.

"Do you see anything?" asked John, once he had calmed a little.

No matter how hard I tried, I didn't. The frozen surface of the river provided few opportunities for a footprint to be left behind. "I'm afraid not," I said.

"Clearly, she was headed north," said John, with more hope than logic.

I disagreed. As far as I could tell, she could just as easily have turned have around and headed south, or left the river at any point and gone God only knew where. Perhaps she had simply had enough of all this and decided to head for the Firelands on her own. But John kept moving northward along the river, his eyes searching hopefully for some sign, any sign, and I suspected that were I not here, he would continue on till night fell and he eventually froze to death.

I kept an eye on him as he moved further away whilst I contemplated what to do next. Without Gwennie, our plan to trap the wendigo was severely hindered, not to mention the fact we had no idea what had happened to her. Honestly, I was buggered if I knew what to do next.

I verged on calling to John to head back when he suddenly started waving and calling to me. I ran to his side as he gestured at a thin trail of black powder heading northward right down the center of the frozen river.

"It's gunpowder, I think," he said excitedly.

I wet my finger, dabbed a bit onto the tip, then tasted it. "It's gunpowder all right."

"Gwennie must have left it for us to find," he said.

How that followed, I wasn't certain. Anyone could have left it here, either on purpose or by accident. Maybe it was Gwennie. Or maybe a bag had leaked when the settlers fled, though I doubted they had come this way. This time I truly didn't know what to think. John and I followed the trial for another ten minutes, and John would have kept right on going if I hadn't stopped him. But the next half-mile of the river was clearly visible to us and appeared as devoid of people as the moon. I saw no sense in proceeding on foot.

"Why are you stopping?" asked John. "The gunpowder hasn't stopped."

"We have to go back and get the horses and supplies," I said. "Then we'll come back and keep following the trail."

"But there isn't time!" said John. "Palmer and Gwennie could be right around the next bend. They could be in trouble this very minute! We don't have time to go back!"

I grabbed him by the arm. "John, you're not thinking clearly."

He pulled away from me, hurrying north. This time I chased after him.

"I know how strongly you feel about, Palmer," I said. "But you have to start behaving sensibly if you're to help him. You keep acting foolishly, and, even worse, you aren't thinking."

"What do you know about how I feel?" he said. "You don't even know how you feel."

"What is that supposed to mean?" I asked, taken aback.

"Never mind," he said. "I don't have time for this."

"I want to know," I said.

John stopped and turned to face me. "It means that you can't own up to how you feel about Pakim."

"You don't know what you're talking about," I said. "I feel for Pakim what I feel for all of my friends. Affection."

"I've seen the way you look at him, Cole," said John. "If that's only *affection* I've seen on your face, then it must only be *concern* I'm feeling now for Palmer."

"You don't understand," I said. "I have obligations. Rose and Colette need me."

"That's nothing more than an excuse to avoid Pakim."

"It's no excuse," I said. "They do need me."

"How convenient," said John. "Rose needs you to marry her. Do you marry every woman that needs marrying? Surely, Rose isn't the first."

An image of Rebecca flashed through my mind. Damn John for making me think of her.

"I've known men like you afore, Cole Seavey," said John. "You're tough and nothing rattles you, but you have no idea who you truly are because you're afraid to look. In my book, that makes you a coward."

How dare John accuse me of being a coward or, even worse, of hiding behind Rose to avoid how I felt! It tore my insides to pieces to give up Pakim, but it was the right thing to do. "I may be a lot of things," I said, "but I'm no coward." I felt the heat rising in my face. "And you best watch your bone box, John Chapman."

"Or what?" sneered John. "You going to force me to mind my mouth because you're so tough? You think you're brave because you can shoot a bear? Well, here's a revelation for you, Cole: a lot of men can do that. Why do you think there are so many bearskins around? You're so proud of being calm and collected, aren't you? You're Cole Seavey, so much better than your brother. You're not half as special as you think."

I took a step toward John, who flinched but didn't back away.

"Are you trying to scare me?" he asked. He stepped close, then shoved me hard. "I'm afraid I don't scare that easily. Not after the life I've lived."

He shoved me again, and I staggered backward. "I'm warning you, John," I growled. "Do that once more, and you'll be sorry."

"No sorrier than you," he said. "No matter how many bears you shoot, you're still going to be afraid of what you really feel inside. Don't think for a minute that I'm not as tough as you, Cole. Because I am. And I'm not the least bit afraid either."

When he shoved me again, I made sure it would be the last time. I pushed him so forcefully he flew backward, landing so hard on his ass that the ice cracked beneath him.

chapter seventeen

Without waiting for John to get up, I turned and went back to fetch the horses. I was ashamed of myself. Not because I had shoved John—he had deserved that and more—but because I had been goaded into losing control. And all over words—somebody else's opinion of me. I wasn't supposed to care about that. I wasn't supposed to feel furious over anything, much less this. A week ago I wouldn't have, I was certain. But much had changed in a week. And I had been a fool to think I could change back any more than a chick could return to the egg whence it came.

As for John, if he wanted to be a fool and keep going on foot, it was of no consequence to me.

I heard snow crunching behind me, then John fell in alongside me. Neither of us spoke; each was embarrassed with himself yet angry with the other.

We were soon on horseback and headed north up the river. We had been riding ten minutes when I spotted hoofprints perpendicularly traversing each side of the river. Someone had passed this way in the not too distant past.

"The horse was going full-out," I said, once I had had a moment to examine the prints.

"It's of no concern of ours," said John. "Gwennie wasn't on horseback. Those hoofprints must have been left by one of the settler's horses."

"I'm not so sure, John," I said. "Perhaps Pakim and Midnight came this way. Or maybe Gwennie met up with whomever was on this horse."

"I suppose," he said. "Though I doubt it. I'll wait here whilst you have a look. But don't be long or I shan't wait."

I bit my tongue and left without saying a word. If John had gone by the time I returned, I wouldn't be sorry.

At first the riverbank sloped gently away from the river, but then it rose abruptly where the earth had been washed away in a flood. It had to have been one determined—or frightened—horse to have climbed it. Finally, I reached the top and looked onto a meadow. Bang-smack in the middle of it lay a stallion on its side.

"There's something here, John," I called back. John nodded to indicate he heard.

I decided not to wait for him as I headed into the snowy field. As I approached, the horse lay unmoving on the cold earth. From the way it lay with its hind legs bent horrifically, I strongly suspected it would not rise again. I saw no sign of the rider or his fate.

With my musket at the ready, I crept forward, prepared for anything, including for the bloody horse to turn out to be the wendigo if this whole thing was nothing but a trap.

I drew a little closer, espying a rabbit burrow in the ground. Had the horse been galloping hard, it was easy to imagine it stepping in the hole, snapping its leg, then pitching forward wildly. The only question was what had happened to the rider. The answer became apparent a moment later when I spotted a pair of feet sticking out from underneath the horse. The rider had been trapped when the horse stumbled and crashed to the ground. Yet being wary, I edged closer until I could peer over the horse and see who lay pinned beneath.

"I'll be a son of a bitch," I said, when I saw the familiar face of Owen Stern. "Can't say I was expecting to see you here."

Owen, in obvious pain, only grunted. "Get the bleedin' horse off of me, would you, Seavey?" he asked.

John caught up with me. "I'll be a son of a bitch," he said, and I laughed.

"That's what I said," I told him.

"What befell you?" John asked him.

"My horse got tired and inquired whether he could ride me for a while. Unfortunately, I slipped on the ice," said Owen. "What the bloody bollocks do you think happened, Chapman?"

"Right then," said John, turning to leave. "I see we have no reason to stay here."

"Wait!" cried Owen. "That wasn't called for. I'm sorry, John." He almost sounded sincere. "My horse bolted. Something frightened her, and I couldn't get her to stop. If she hadn't stumbled, we might have been in the Shawnee Country by now."

"Too bad she stumbled then, though I'm unable to fathom what the folks in Shawnee might have done to deserve the likes of you," said John.

"Come on, then," I said to John. "Let's get the horse off him so we can get going."

John's bitter laugh held not a trace of humor. "I wouldn't help that son of a bitch, if the fate of the world depended on it," he said, hurling Owen's words back at him with all the invective he could muster.

"We can't leave him here to die, John," I said.

"I most certainly can," said John. "Don't forget, Cole. This is the same bastard who wouldn't lift a finger to help look for Palmer. I don't owe him a damned thing."

"Of course you don't, John," I said. "But you still can't leave him to die."

"And why not?" asked John. "Besides, who knows what he'll get up to once we free him? I'd trust a rabid dog not to bite me afore I'd trust this treacherous backstabber." John spun about and walked away.

"If you leave, John, then you're no better than Owen!" I called after him. "We both know that isn't the case. Besides, leaving Owen to die isn't what Palmer would do."

John froze.

"Come on," I said. "Let's get this over with."

A moment later he joined me.

"Much appreciated, Chapman," said Owen. "I'll—"

"Not another word, Owen Stern," said John, with barely contained fury. "Or I *will* leave you here to rot, no matter what Cole might say. All I want from you is to know that I'll never see your pathetic countenance again."

Owen fell silent as I walked around him and the dead horse, trying to decide how best to free him. The horse was a big black stallion that was not going to be easy to move. "What do you think, John?" I asked.

John only glared at me, and I knew he was going to do no more than provide muscle. First, we tried to free Owen by digging beneath him so that we could pull him out. But the ground was hard and stony and we had nothing to dig with but our hands. At a loss for anything else to try, we finally tied a rope around the dead horse's rear legs, then looped the other end over our shoulders. Despite the fact that the stallion had to outweigh us by at least twice as much, I was hoping we might be able to lift enough weight off Owen to allow him to slip free.

"On the count of three!" I yelled to Owen, having instructed him to push against the horse whilst we pulled. The horse only budged a little at first, but gradually it slid forward enough for Owen to free his legs.

Whilst John looked on with disgust, I went to see if Owen had been badly injured in the fall. The man lay on the ground, writhing in pain.

"God's balls, but it hurts!" he moaned.

"Hold still!" I ordered, going to his side. I examined his legs, but found no evidence they were broken. "It's the blood flowing back that's so painful. It'll pass in a bit."

"I'm leaving," said John. "Are you coming?"

I hurried to his side. "In a moment," I said. "I want to make sure that Owen can at least walk." I glanced backward, but couldn't see Owen since he lay on the other side of the horse.

"Fine," John said with evident disgust. "But if you're not there in five minutes, I'm leaving without you. And you best not bring that breathing sack of shit with you." With that, John strode purposefully away.

"Well, Owen," I said, walking back. "I suppose it's too much to hope that you're going to a bit more civil after this."

Owen was gone. Immediately, I acquired a bad feeling that somehow there was going to be a wendigo involved in this.

"Owen?" I called again. I looked about for my musket, but it was gone.

"Right behind you," he said unexpectedly, and I started so hard I heard something pop in my neck.

"God Almighty, man," I said, turning to face him. "You about near made me..." My voice trailed off when I saw that not only was he standing right behind me, but he had my musket aimed dead at my heart. On the other hand, at least he wasn't the wendigo.

"Many thanks for helping me," he said.

"Certainly," I replied. "Though usually it's customary to *not* point a gun at those to whom you are grateful."

"If you say so," he said. "You really should have listened to Chapman, you know. He may be a sodomite, but he's smarter than he looks." With that he pulled back the hammer on the musket, intending to shoot me.

The sound of black powder igniting erupted in the quiet of the glen. To my surprise, Owen rose upward as if being lifted under his arms. At the same moment, a crimson opening blossomed in the front of his coat. Mouth agape, he staggered backward several paces, shot a quizzical look at me, then toppled over dead.

"He was right, you know," said John, holding a musket as he appeared amidst the dispersing cloud of smoke. "I am smarter than I look."

◆

"Come on," said John urgently. "We've got to find the others afore it's too late. Unlessen, of course, you think we owe it to Owen to give him a proper burial."

I hurried after John, marveling at both my close call and what a treacherous bastard Owen had been up to the very end. Even now, I could scarcely believe he had intended to kill me. "You knew he was going to do that?" I asked John.

"Like I know a pig will squeal if you pull its tail," he said. "I may not always think things through clearly, but I'm not a total bungler either."

It seemed I had underestimated him. "Look, John, I—"

He held up his hand, cutting me off. "If two dogs bite each other, Cole, they both know they've done wrong and don't need to make amends."

I smiled at his comparison. "Did you make that up, or is that something you heard somewheres?" I asked.

"That depends on what you think of it," he said. "Now let's go."

We rode speedily northward, following the trail of gunpowder along the river. We had traveled another ten minutes when John said, "Look."

I glanced where he pointed. The trail of gunpowder veered to the right, proceeding to follow a frozen tributary about half the size of the river. The creek wound away from us, working its way up a narrow basin.

John followed. "Do you yet think the powder was left by a settler?"

I had to confess it seemed unlikely, as I could think of no reason for someone to venture that direction.

"Maybe this is where the wendigo dwells now," said John. "Maybe this is where it brought Palmer and the others."

"Could be," I said. "Let's go find out."

The stream narrowed further, trees and bushes crowding in against us. Soon both John and I were compelled to ride hunched forward, pushing tree limbs out of our way.

"I've got a bad feeling about this," said John.

I grunted in assent. The way soon became so overgrown that we were forced to dismount and proceed on foot, leading Hiccup and Elizabeth behind us. It very much reminded me of the night we had stumbled onto the wounded grizzly. But the gunpowder trail continued leading us onward; we had no choice but to follow.

The vegetation abruptly gave way, and we reached a pool of water with a waterfall cascading into it, though both were currently frozen. Everything in and around the pond stood coated in ice, as if it were being preserved for the ages. The waterfall itself had been caught in spectacularly unlikely shapes—whorls and curves that no human hand could hope to carve.

"The gunpowder runs out here," said John.

More precisely, the trail of gunpowder across the ice ended halfway up the face of the waterfall. It simply disappeared, almost as if the wendigo had been climbing up the frozen falls when the powder ran out. If so, then we had no way to track it further. I couldn't accept that. I hadn't gone through all of this for it to end with nothing but our turning around and going back defeated.

"What in God's balls do we do now?" asked John.

"Is that an opening in the falls?" I asked, peering up.

John came and stood next to me. "Where?"

"There, by that boulder split in two. I would swear there is an opening and that the trail of gunpowder doesn't vanish but goes inside."

"You know, I think you're right. But that's at least twenty feet up. Do you think we can climb that high?" John asked uneasily. One of us had to, and I supposed it would be me. From the blanched look on his face, I suspected John wasn't so good with heights.

"I'll go," I said

"I'll come with you," John said, and I appreciated that he at least made the offer.

"Somebody should stay with the horses," I said. "Besides, I'll need you out here if something happens." What I didn't tell him was that I also had a bad feeling about this, that it seemed like a trap. If we were both caught—or killed—up there, then the others would have no hope at all.

John didn't argue. "I'll come straightaway if you need me."

I wrapped my hands in strips of cloth, keeping my fingertips free for gripping. I couldn't see a way to both climb and carry a musket, so the musket stayed behind. Doing so made me feel as naked as if it were my pants I was leaving behind. Instead of my musket, I had to content myself with the hatchet, a torch, and a small knife for protection. Given how slick the ice looked, I thought to make good use of the hatchet for hacking out handholds. "See you in a bit," I said.

John smiled tightly, then gave me a boost up. The ice was slicker than I expected, but to my surprise, I actually found the climbing easy, for the ice was riddled with irregularities and crevices that made for good handholds. Surprisingly quick, I found myself just below the opening we had spied from down below. A large branch jutted out from the frozen water, affording me the perfect outcropping upon which to perch and hoist myself inside. Providing I was careful not to slip, of course.

The opening was narrow, taller than it was wide, though I would still have to proceed by crawling on my knees. I peered into the blackness, but could make out naught more than a few feet into the cave.

I boosted myself up and in, then turned and sat facing outward. I lit the torch, then using my flint, after waving to John, crawled inside on hands and knees. The narrow opening curved to the right and out of sight. Should the wendigo be waiting somewhere ahead, it would have all the advantages.

No attack occurred, however, and the opening gave way to a large cavern in which I was able to stand. Stalactites and stalagmites coated with ice reflected torchlight back at me. I held the flame higher, entering cautiously. Each time I exhaled, a puff of white floated up in front of me. Farther in, the walls were coated with ice, as even and uniform as plaster laid by a skilled craftsman. The light bounced around crazily, a cavalcade of dancing luminosity.

The gunpowder trail went straight backward afore again veering right and out of sight. I followed after it, rounded the corner and immediately knew my suspicions had been right. This was a trap, but not the one I had expected. There was no wendigo waiting to pounce on me here, only the half-empty sack of gunpowder that had been used to lure me inside. No doubt, the wendigo was outside and most likely had already struck.

I spun about, sprinting for the front of the cavern. I wriggled through the narrow opening so rapidly that, once through, I nearly skidded off the precipice afore coming to a halt. Unfortunately, I was too late for the wendigo was already there. Nonetheless, I yelled out, "Behind you, John! Behind you!"

John looked puzzled for a moment, then either understood or sensed the wendigo approaching. He spun about as the towering creature sprang forward, seized him, then dragged him into the bushes.

John's scream reverberated off the ice. I immediately started down the frozen waterfall. Glancing over my shoulder, I briefly caught sight of the wendigo pushing through the bushes on the opposite side of the frozen pool, but then, only seconds later, I saw movement on the other side. How in the blazes did the damn thing move so fast? Or was that John? But then how did *he* get over there?

John screamed again, impelling me to move faster. As I scrambled downward, with perhaps six or seven feet to go, I lost my grip and fell the rest of the way. My ankles barked with pain as I landed, but I ignored the stinging ache, stumbling toward where I had last seen movement. I was halfway there when John's anguished voice called out, "Stop, Cole! You're not to come any closer. Please!"

John sounded in so much pain that it was all I could do to make myself halt. I peered into the thick bushes but saw nothing. "Are you all right, John?" I asked.

I heard crying, mumbling, then, "No."

"Tell me what I should do." My eyes scanned the clearing looking for my musket. There! It sat against a tree no more than three long strides from where I stood. I had turned only slightly toward it when John screamed again. "Oh, my God! Please stop!" he yelled.

I froze, uncertain whether he meant me or not.

"Cole, it says you're not to move again," sobbed John. "If you do, it will kill me."

"Who, John?" I asked. "Is it the wendigo?" The damn thing could talk?

I heard more mumbling, then John said, "Yes." There was a long pause, then a sobbing John said, "No! Please don't! Not that!"

Not what? I wanted to yell. What the hell was going on? I felt furious, yet impotent to act. The bushes directly in front of me started to thrash wildly. I heard a dull thud, like the sound of a cleaver biting into meat being butchered.

"No!" sobbed John. "No! Why are you doing this?"

I verged on taking action despite the wendigo's admonition not to move. There was more thrashing amidst the bushes, then they briefly parted. I caught sight of a spray of blood arcing through the air, and heard a horse whinnying in terror and John screaming. Then the bushes closed again, and I heard John holler, "No! I won't! I swear to God—" His voice was cut off replaced by the sound of gagging and I could wait no more.

I took one step forward when I was struck from behind. The last thing I saw was the frozen earth rushing up to meet me.

chapter eighteen

Something tugged at my arm. I opened my eyes to find I lay face-down in a frost-coated bed of moss. I grimaced from the pain emanating from the back of my skull. It hurt so badly I felt fortunate my skull hadn't been stove in. The tugging came again, and I slowly turned my head until my eyes came to rest upon a good-sized raven. It was the bird tugging on my arm—or more specifically, on the bright brass button affixed to my jacket—that had awakened me. Awakened me from what? I wondered, for my head throbbed so powerfully, I couldn't remember what had happened.

As I pushed myself upright, the raven hopped away, but not afore issuing a rancorous protest of *Caw! Caw!*

"You could at least wait until I was dead," I muttered. "Although I suppose I do owe you something for awakening me afore I froze to death." I gripped the button, then gave it a sharp yank. "Here," I said, tossing it to my animal guide.

I looked about, again wondering what had happened. Had I been attacked? Or thrown from a horse? At the thought of a horse, everything snapped into place. The wendigo had attacked John, then me.

"John?" I called. "Where are you?" I got no answer back.

The sun had scarcely moved, so at least I knew I hadn't been unconscious long. Ten, perhaps fifteen minutes. That meant the wendigo had a small head start, although the thing seemed capable of moving so fast it could have been leagues away by now. And this

236

time I knew there would be no trail of gunpowder for me to follow, cunning ruse or otherwise.

"John?" I doubtfully called again, forcing my way through the bushes as I searched for him. "John?" There was no answer, but I was brought up short by a bright bloom of blood coating the snow afore me. I supposed that was an answer of sorts. "Sweet Jesus," I muttered. What had the wendigo done to him?

The bloody streak stretched deeper into the bushes as if something had been dragged away. Expecting to find a disemboweled, dismembered John, I followed and did, in fact, stumble upon a body. But it was Elizabeth, John's horse. Her killing was what I had glimpsed through the bushes. No wonder John had sounded so distraught. He loved that horse very nearly as much as he loved Palmer.

John had sounded badly injured himself and, looking at the bloody remains of the horse, I worried what violence had been perpetrated on him. Something small and pink and not very horse-like caught my attention. It turned out to be two fingertips, each cut off at the first knuckle. Now I understood why John had sounded in so much pain.

I searched further but found nothing else. At least I had hope that John yet lived. But why had the wendigo taken him? Why had the wendigo taken everyone but me? Was that coincidence or on purpose? Either way, I was alone now. In fact, I was the last one left in the whole damned valley. All of the settlers were gone, the Indians as well, and now each of my friends had been taken, too. I had been so certain, so cocky that I could defeat the damned wendigo, yet had been proven wrong at every turn.

The bushes off to my left stirred. As deftly as possible, I slid my knife from its sheath, then spun about slashing as furiously as a Hessian soldier. Hiccup, wide-eyed and skittish, neighed indignantly as she scooted backward. Fortunately, I hadn't intended to kill, only frighten, otherwise Gwennie's poor pony would have already been bleeding to death.

"Sorry about that," I said as the brown-eyed horse regarded me reproachfully. Her expression seemed to say she expected no better from someone who had been bested by an opponent so many times already.

I hurriedly gathered my rucksack, and what supplies I could find. Unfortunately, my musket had been shattered and was now useless. I mounted Hiccup and headed back toward the river, pushing the little pony as hard as I dared. She seemed to feel the same sense of urgency, and we quickly reached the river with no further incident. Once there, however, I found no signs indicating the way John and the wendigo might have gone. Whichever way I chose was as good as a guess.

Nonetheless, a choice had to be made. I was about to steer Hiccup north when the little pony suddenly snorted, backing up into the shadow of the forest. I let the horse do as she wished and was glad of it a moment later when the wendigo suddenly hove into view. This was the gryphon-like wendigo, not the black-clad one with the hideous teeth I had seen whilst searching for Rose and Palmer. I was glad it took this manifestation and not the other, for it was that wendigo-form I seemed to fear most.

To my dismay, the wendigo was alone. Whether John was dead, a prisoner somewhere, or had escaped, I had no idea. Picturing Elizabeth's bloody remains, I was greatly troubled by the most likely answer.

The south-bound wendigo was a quarter mile north of me, having rounded a bend in the creek. Whence was it coming? Where was it going? There was something odd about it, the way it walked. Predators not on the hunt (and what was the wendigo but a predator?) normally moved through the forest with indifference, even swagger, knowing they had little to fear. But now the wendigo hugged the opposite bank as if fearful and hiding from something. Too, it moved oddly, in a halting, shambling manner. Had John managed to injure it?

I knew not how to account for the creature's seemingly odd behavior, but I was grateful for any small advantage afforded to me. It seemed tired and dispirited, and I took encouragement from that, hoping it might prove easier to kill. The longer I watched, the more

I wondered if the beast might not be badly injured. It favored one leg and I doubted it could run far, if at all. Perhaps fortune was finally on my side.

The wendigo stopped and sank down onto a rock. I quickly tied Hiccup to a tree, then crept closer. The wendigo abruptly stood. Thinking I had been spotted, I froze, expecting it to fly wildly at me. But it only resumed its way south, stumbling forward, head down. I grew impatient with waiting, now confident I could overpower the wendigo in this condition.

As much as I wanted to kill it, I needed the damned thing alive, at least until I found out what had become of the others. After finding a sturdy tree limb, I picked my way over the frozen river, steadily drawing closer to the shuffling wendigo. At any moment, I expected the beast to whirl about and attack me. It must have finally sensed me, for it paused, slowly turned and caught sight of me. Rather than attacking me, however, it squealed as if alarmed, then shuffled rapidly away.

I sprang forward, striking it across the back of the head as hard as I could with the tree limb. I was prepared for the wendigo to do anything: roar in anger, attack in a fury of slashing claws, even disappear in a flash of light. What I most certainly didn't expect was for the thing's head to pop off like a cork from a bottle of ale. But that's precisely what happened. And after the head came off, the rest of the body fell face first, so to speak, to the ground.

I watched in disbelief as the head rolled a few feet afore coming to a stop. I hadn't hit it *that* hard.

For a moment, I stood there trying to comprehend what I witnessed. I expected the body to flail about or copious amounts of blood to flow over the ice. But the wendigo lay motionless, and there was no gore at all. What deviltry was this? Heads weren't supposed to simply come loose, though perhaps things worked differently for wendigos. Remaining wary of the body, I made my way to where the head now rested, nudging it with my foot. I think I expected it to spin about and try to bite me, or perhaps fly into the air. It only lay there as a decapitated head should. I kicked it again, harder, and this time it tipped over. The inside was empty.

Baffled, I turned to where the rest of the now-headless body lay. I thought I heard crying, of all unanticipated things, though how a headless body could cry, I had no idea. Warily, I stepped around the motionless bulk so I could see for myself.

My gaze fell upon the face of a white man with long blond hair and a beard, both of them ratty and tangled. So the wendigo yet had a head after all, just not the head I was used to seeing. There was something in the man's mouth that looked like a horse's bit but without the reins attached. His eyes were closed, though tears coursed down his cheeks as he sobbed greatly. The rest of him was clad in what was apparently some sort of outlandish costume.

Someone had gone to great pains stitching bear paws onto what looked like arms covered with feathers. The torso looked to be made of wolf fur and the head was, well, I didn't know what the hell the head was. It was enormous, with a pronounced brow, a jutting jaw filled with sharp teeth, and the whole thing was covered in black fur but for the very center of its face. The entire outfit was the most extraordinary thing I had ever seen.

Given the bit the fellow wore, I suspected he wasn't dressed thus willingly. I realized the man was huge, easily the tallest individual I had ever come across. I recalled the day of our first encounter, the shock I had felt upon laying eyes upon the beast. If he was outfitted this way today, could he have also been the creature I had seen the other night? Then he had been clad in that black cape and wore the peaked hat. Both creatures had been the same size and it seemed to make sense they were one and the same. If he had one costume, why not two?

Sensing my presence, the fellow opened his eyes, saw me, and tried to scream, though the horse's bit effectively prevented him from doing so. He also struggled wildly trying to push himself away from me. Something very fishy was going on here. I caught the fellow by his leg and pulled him to a stop, getting a whiff of the stench that hovered around him. It was every bit as rank as the first time I had encountered him.

Advancing slowly with my hands out to my sides, I came near, and said, "It's all right. I mean you no harm." These had to be the last words I had expected to utter upon finally facing the wendigo. The man reacted as if I were about to devour him. He thrashed about, straining to yell and get away. Given that only moments afore, I had struck him hard enough to dislodge his false head, I could hardly blame him. Clearly, the poor man was terrified even though he was so much bigger than I.

"It's all right," I said. I grabbed ahold of his head, quickly freeing his mouth from the bit.

Again, I wasn't sure what I expected, but it wasn't for him to speak French. Granted it was a hysterical, nearly impossible-to-understand French, but it was French, and I thought he was begging me for his life.

"Can you understand me?" I asked the man in the broken French I had picked up from my immigrant parents (and which Father had always berated me for not learning fluently).

He stopped babbling and briefly looked at me with surprise. I went to pat him on the shoulder to try to reassure him, but this only drove him into a frenzied panic. Whilst backing away, I kept talking in my broken French, always speaking softly, never coming any closer.

"My name is Cole," I repeated several times. "What is yours?"

He eyed me with a mix of wild-eyed fear and suspicion, as if he were a slave and I was his master who, after a long history of having beaten him, had suddenly grown kindhearted and solicitous.

"I've no intention of hurting you, I swear," I said, trying English. "Won't you at least tell me your name?"

He mumbled something in French I couldn't understand.

"Could you say that again?" I asked gently.

"Sebastien," he said.

"Greetings, Friend Sebastien," I said, thinking dolefully of how Pakim had put me at ease with that appellation. "If I may inquire, why are you clothed so oddly?"

Sebastien began sobbing. They were great, heaving sobs, and in between them I heard him say something about traveling with furs, something else about ill-luck, and how he had been captured.

"Do you know who captured you?" I asked.

Either he did not know, or my French was not clear, for he sobbed and said in hurried, confused English, "I want back Marseille town of beautiful praying churches, to fish like birds happy at midnight, and to swim in the sun that fills me like the sea heavy with tide."

Or at least that was what I thought he said. Clearly, I wasn't getting his entire meaning, but the gist of it was unambiguous: He wanted to go home.

"Did your captor make you dress this way?" I asked.

"Yes," he said. "Scare people. I not want to do terrible thing that make me bring fright that people go far away."

"Did he also make you scare others by wearing a black cape with a tall hat?" I asked.

Sebastien stared past me, eventually shaking his head.

"Are you sure?" I asked, uncertain if he had understood my question. "You wore a hat that hid your face."

Sebastien barked something at me in French that I didn't get, but clearly he was angry.

"I'm sorry," I said. I decided to change tack. "Have you escaped? Are you running away?" Sebastien looked puzzled, so I rephrased the question. "Is someone chasing you now?"

Sebastien stared past me, then slowly knelt forward until his head touched the earth. To my dismay, he repeatedly banged his head against the ground. I wasn't sure if that meant yes, no, or neither. Perhaps it was nothing but a sign of his despair.

"No, Sebastien!" I said, grabbing him by the shoulder.

He jerked violently away from me, yelling, "No touch! No touch!"

"All right," I said. "I'm sorry. I won't touch again."

"Not allow me taken by them away not where I not want go," he said crying. A rivulet of fresh blood ran down his forehead and onto his nose where it mixed with tears and snot. Several times he gestured anxiously up the river and I guessed that was whence his pursuer was coming.

"I won't. I promise," I said, regarding his woeful countenance. What had been done to the poor fellow? And by whom? It was then that I noticed his feet were shackled, a chain binding them together, but with enough slack that he had been able to shuffle along. His hands were also bound, iron manacles clamped around his wrists.

"Do you remember the first time you saw me?" I asked. "It was after a terrible windstorm. There was another man who tried to shoot you."

He regarded me with confusion, but recognition must have come at last for he nodded. "You I want help me away get. I take you to hide place. You run away not helping me."

I nodded slowly. "Well, Sebastien, things looked rather different from my end. I didn't know you wanted my help. Fact is, I thought you were going to eat me."

"Other find me. Take me back, make do more things bad."

"Sebastien, do you know where my friends are?" I asked. "The man you attacked a little while ago. Where is he now?"

Sebastien only stared at me with utter dejection and hopelessness, looking for all the world like an ill-treated child who knows he has no control over his fate. "How about an Indian woman?" I asked. "Have you seen her? Or a white woman with a baby? Her name is Rose."

The Frenchman forlornly wiped his nose on his shoulder.

"Come on, Sebastien," I said, annoyance creeping into my voice. "You have to tell me what you know."

But I got no answers, only more tears, and I knew Sebastien was to be of no use to me. The man was ruined, a horse pushed past its breaking point. I did feel bad for what had been done to him, but I was running out of time. Even now I wasn't entirely certain what was going on. Were Sebastien's captors responsible for all that had happened during the past week? The Frenchman seemed to know nothing about my encounter with the black-clad wendigo, but it was hard to believe there was a second giant man dressing up and lurking in these woods. I was yet quite uneasy.

Sebastien suddenly grew frantic, as if he sensed someone approaching. I glanced back along the river. I saw no one, but I did hear the sound of whistling floating around the bend. I had to act fast. I needed to hide, but first I needed to free Sebastien so he could escape. Knowing he could never outrun his pursuer as long as his feet were manacled, I jerked a rock from the ground, then smashed it against the iron chain that bound his legs. The rock shattered on the first blow. Frustrated, I grabbed the chain and pulled on the links as hard as I could. All I got for my effort were two scraped palms.

Obviously, I wasn't going to free him this way. He would have to hide with me. I stood, grabbed his hands, and tried to pull him to his feet. He was so frightened that he only sat there uselessly staring toward the sound of the whistling.

"Come on, Sebastien!" I urged, trying to pull him up. He was so huge, it was like trying to pull a cow to its feet. When he didn't budge, I crouched down next to him. "Sebastien, I don't want to leave you behind, but you have to help me."

He finally turned his petrified gaze to me, but he seemed not to even realize I was there. I knew then he was beyond saving. Perhaps I was as well, for now I heard the crunch of approaching footsteps. I spied a stand of cattails fifteen feet away. I scrambled to reach them, throwing myself among the stalks as a solitary figure came marching around the bend in the river. I lay motionless amongst the cattails, uncertain whether or not I had been seen.

When no cry of alarm was raised, I allowed myself a deep breath to steady my nerves, then studied Sebastien's pursuer. He was bundled up so tightly against the cold, I couldn't tell who it might be even though there was something familiar about his short, stocky profile. But, truth be told, it could have been near about anyone. The man, for I presumed him to be such, stopped once to take a long draught from a flask he carried and that was when he spotted Sebastien and hurried forward.

As he approached the fallen Frenchman, he suddenly paused, looking all about as if sensing my presence. I pressed myself closer to the cold ground. The man's eyes traveled the bank, crossing and recrossing the spot where I lay. Satisfied, there was no one there, he continued on to where Sebastien waited.

He undid the scarf wound around his face and said, "You keep running away, Sebastien. I'm afraid we're going to have to do something about that."

It was Stich Burke.

chapter nineteen

Stich was, as usual, drunk. He was also, much to my complete and utter astonishment, alive and uninjured. So much for his having been dispatched by the wendigo. He circled Sebastien's kneeling form as if he were livestock being considered for purchase. The big man whimpered, which was rather astounding as I doubted Stich Burke had made many people whimper in his life. Unlessen Stich Burke wasn't the milksop I had believed him to be.

As if to prove my point, he kicked Sebastien hard in the side. The Frenchman grunted, then fell over.

"Tsk, tsk, Sebastien," said Stich. "You don't learn, do you? The last time you tried to run away, we warned you what would happen if you did it again. But you did it anyway. Now what should I do about that?"

The crying Frenchman tried to crawl away. Stich didn't stop him. Instead, he trailed along and said, "Mind you, once we were done with you, we certainly had no use for you. You never struck me as especially bird-witted, so you probably knew that, *oui?*" Stich laughed.

Stich bent down toward Sebastien, and I nearly started yelling. But instead of killing Sebastien, Stich undid the shackles. "But I'm a merciful man, so go on. We've no further use for you. Get out of here," he said.

Sebastien looked nearly as surprised as I felt. I was certainly glad I hadn't given myself away. Sebastien hesitantly stood. He was a giant, towering over Stich by near two feet. For all that, Sebastien cowered as if he were a vole and Stich a snowy owl.

"You better get," said Stich. "Afore I change my mind. Oh, wait. Too late." Stich roared with laughter as he whipped a knife from its sheath on his belt. With a speed and strength that belied both his drunken state and the weak man I had thought him to be, Stich slashed the Frenchman's throat from one side to the other. Sebastien's mouth formed a startled "O" shape as he staggered backward. For a moment, there was no blood, then all at once it flowed profusely. I need not look twice to know the blow was a mortal one.

Sebastien clutched at his neck whilst yet trying to flee. Blood seeped between his fingers, bright drops splashing onto the snow with each step he took. Whether by accident or not, he staggered toward my hiding place. I prepared to bolt, but Sebastien swooned, sank to his knees, gasped a final time, and toppled over. Stich sauntered over and perused the dead man's body, all the while slowly licking Sebastien's blood from the knife. Little did I know that worse was to come.

Stich crouched next to the body, cut away one of the pant legs, then carved out large gobbets of bloody flesh that he tossed onto the snow. When he had finished, Stich wrapped the hunks of meat in leather, then slid them into his coat pocket. Duly outfitted, he turned and headed down stream. The fact that he was leaving almost didn't register, as I was so aghast at what I had witnessed.

I was confused as well. Clearly, Stich was a cannibal. Did that mean he was also a wendigo? I didn't know; I didn't know anything! By God's balls, I'd never been so at a loss in my entire life.

My eyes followed the drunk bastard as he walked away. Instead of heading north as I had expected, he went south, toward the now abandoned Hugh's Lick. But why? There was nothing there, was there?

Once Stich was out of sight, I hurried to Sebastien's side, crossed myself and said a prayer. I only hoped it did him some good.

Leading Hiccup behind me, I trailed Stich from the opposite bank, staying hidden in the thick foliage that lined the river. Stich staggered along the riverbank, drinking from a leather flask. It was hard to believe this was the fellow who had outsmarted and defeated me at every turn. Either I had far too low an opinion of him or far too high one of myself. Actually, I had underestimated Stich even more than I realized. It hadn't been an accident my friends had vanished one-by-one until I was the last one left. Only now did I grasp that Stich had done it on purpose. He had done it to get back at me for having taken Rose from him.

I furtively trailed Stich for half an hour, until we finally reached Hugh's Lick. After secreting Hiccup in the woods, I crept into town, searching for wherever Stich had gone. Quiet as a viper, I passed Rose's former abode, moving from cabin to cabin until I heard Stich talking. I prayed it was to John and the others to whom he spoke. Finally, I could get no closer without risking his spotting me. He continued to talk, but I heard no one responding.

I was beginning to think Stich was alone after all when he growled drunkenly, "Stop your squirming whilst I undo your gag, you unruly woman. There now, isn't that better?"

"Yes, Stich," stammered Rose. I couldn't see her, but she sounded frightened and exhausted.

"I've brought dinner home with me," said Stich as something heavy thudded onto the ground. My mind flashed back to the dead Frenchman. "What's the matter, you lousy doxy? You think Cole would provide any better for you? You think because he's handsome and strong he'd make a better husband?"

"No, Stich," said Rose.

"You don't sound like you mean what you're saying, Rose," said Stich. "Try it again, but with a bit more sincerity this time. Would you rather have Cole for a husband than myself?"

"Of course not, Stich," said Rose emphatically.

Apparently it wasn't sincere enough because Stich began yelling, "To Hell with you, Rose! You think you're better than everyone else. You're just like that son of a bitch Cole, ain't you? Well, he's not here to do you any good, which is too bad because I'm going to beat you like the stinking slattern you are!"

When I heard the sound of a fist striking flesh, I could remain still no longer. I yanked my knife from its sheath and sprinted around the corner—right into the barrel of a musket.

"The fine Mr. Seavey," drawled Stich, as cool as a pail of milk fresh from the creek. He held the gun aimed straight at my heart. "I thought you were somewheres nearby. How about you drop the knife?"

My eyes darted to where a tied up Rose lay on the ground. One cheek bore a red mark as if she had been punched. John, Palmer, and Gwennie, bound and gagged, sat in a row, their backs against the wall of the blockhouse. Colette, swathed in fur, lay on Gwennie's lap. A large fire blazed ahead of them, yet they huddled together as if freezing. My relief at seeing them was great, but to my consternation there was no sign of Pakim.

"I said, Drop the knife, Cole."

I did as instructed.

"Good fellow," said Stich. He took a sip from his flask, then set it on a stump. "What do you think, Rose? Should I kill young Mr. Seavey now or later?"

Rose mumbled something I couldn't make out.

"Now, you say?" said Stich. "Well, if you think that's best."

"You certainly have surprised everyone, Stich," I said, trying to stall him. "Especially Murdock."

"What's that supposed to mean, Seavey?" he asked.

"Surely you of all people must know what sort of reputation you have in Hugh's Lick," I said. I needed to rattle Stich, to get under his skin. And I needed to do it afore he put a hole in me the size of a plate. "You're probably the last person anybody would have imagined trying to pull off this sort of feat. It's not as if you're the same ilk as Ben Franklin. Yet somehow *you* emptied out the whole town, not to mention the Indian village. Even your brother fled like a Boston matron in a whore house."

It was only as I spoke that I truly understood the enormity of what Stich had been up to. He hadn't been taking out his revenge on just me, not by a long shot. Stich had avenged himself against the whole town, as well as his family, all of whom had treated him like the drunk imbecile he was.

"And even though you're looking down the barrel of my musket, you still think you're better than me," said Stich.

I shrugged. "It's going to take a while to get used to thinking of you this way, Stich. Hell, even Rose, a woman starving and desperate, wouldn't come near the likes of you. How pitiable is that? And you should have heard what your family said about you after they thought you'd been captured by Sebastien."

Stich sucked in a breath, then fired the musket. I dove toward the ground. As the blast of the gunpowder reverberated off the block-house walls, I was up and running for Stich. He tried to fend me off with the musket, but it was going to take more than that to bring me to a halt. We collided hard, like a hammer striking an anvil. Both of us went sprawling.

"I'm not surprised you missed me, Stich," I said, scrambling to my feet. "After all, your mother said you missed the wendigo, even though you were practically right next to it."

Stich rose a bit more slowly. "You know damned well I missed on purpose, Seavey. It was all part of the plan." The musket lay on the ground, useless to either of us since neither of us would have long enough to reload it. Leaning against the blockhouse was the fishing gaff Gwennie and I had found when we were planning to trap the supposed wendigo. If I could get ahold of it, I could run Stich through like a sturgeon.

"Yet," I said, trying to rattle him, "your family wasn't the least bit surprised that you did miss." As we slowly circled each other, I judged whether I could make a grab for the gaff.

Stich smiled. "Whereas yours would be to learn you're a sodomite, eh? And you lay with Indian braves no less."

Stich knew about Pakim? I tried not show my surprise. Did that mean Stich had captured him? Where was Pakim now? Was he—

Stich feinted toward me, and I realized he'd been trying to rattle me. What's more, it had worked. "What really embarrassed your family, Stich, was the way you screamed and carried on when Sebastien attacked you. 'Just like a girl,' they said."

"Again, all part of my act, Seavey," said Stich, calmly. But his eyes were hard with anger. "I bet you weren't acting when you lay in that polluted brave's arms, were you? A decent man couldn't fake a hard cock with another man's in his mouth. Where else did that Indian put his cock?"

My face flushed despite myself. I glanced at Rose to see if she had heard. Stich used the chance and charged. He hit me in the gut, causing me to double over. As I gasped from the pain, he grabbed the knife he had made me drop earlier, then pinned me against a cabin wall. I seized his wrist afore he stabbed me, but he was startlingly strong despite being drunk. Little by little he drove the knife toward me.

"Maybe I did lay with Pakim," I said. "But you're still envious of me, aren't you, Stich? You always wanted to be the hunter everyone admired. You wanted to be the man Rose picked to marry. But you weren't, and you never will be. In the eyes of decent folk you'll always be lower than even the sodomite."

Eyes ablaze, Stich bore down on the knife. The point sliced through my clothes, then pierced my skin. I grunted from the shock of the pain, which encouraged Stich to press all the harder. Bit by bit, the knife sank deeper until the entire blade was buried in my shoulder. At last I screamed from the searing pain.

Satisfied, Stich smiled and stepped away.

At least I had my knife back. Granted, there *were* better ways I could have retrieved it. Tears filling my eyes, I slumped against the wall as if utterly defeated, sinking lower and lower until my legs were folded beneath me like springs. I left the knife where it was lodged. Removing it now, would only provoke Stich to attack again. I had something else in mind.

"That was too easy Seavey," said Stich. "I guess you're not as tough as you thought."

Groaning, I continued to feign defeat whilst Stich stepped toward me as if to finish the job. As soon as he was close enough, my legs catapulted me upward. I caught his chin with the top of my head, driving him backward. I heard his mouth snap shut with a tooth-jarring crunch. He stumbled backward, holding me in an awkward embrace. Each time he bumped the knife, a jolt of searing pain shot through my shoulder.

I felt the heat of the campfire only an instant ahead our reaching it. Afore I realized it, we had passed into and through the fire. As soon as we reached the other side, I spun about, gripping Stich by the shoulders. With all my might, I shoved him back into the flames where his feet got tangled in one of the logs and he went down in an eruption of sparks.

Stich rolled out of the fire, trying to put out the flames that already rippled over his arms and chest. At first I was puzzled by how readily he burned, but then I recalled how much liquor he had spilled on himself. At once, I thought of the flask of whiskey from which Stich had been drinking. I grabbed it, found it half-full, then rushed to where Stich lay rolling about. At first he didn't realized what I intended, but when I tipped it toward him, he bellowed and scrambled away.

Most of the liquid splashed harmlessly to the ground, but enough soaked into Stich's clothes to send the flames higher. For a minute, it looked as if his whole upper body were aflame and I moved away, driven back by the heat. Bit by bit, however, he beat the fire down. Exhausted and crippled by yet more pain, I doubted I possessed the strength to wrestle him back into the flames.

Even then, I looked about for his musket or the fishing gaff, but afore I could act Stich stood and threw himself against me. For a moment he pinned me against the cabin wall. His still-smoking clothes scorched my skin, and the stench of burning hair flesh was intensely nauseating. Stich's eyes were so wild with pain that he seemed unable to think clearly. Finally, I managed to shove him away. As he staggered backward, he seized the knife handle yet lodged in my shoulder and pulled.

I screamed from the ungodly pain.

Stich staggered a few more steps afore righting himself. Clutching the bloody knife, he smiled maniacally, then scuttled drunkenly toward me. I twisted about, hobbling away as fast as I could. We were both badly injured, but Stich chased me the length of the town until I could go no further. Turning to face him, I backed up until I collided with the wall of Rose's cabin.

Stich raised the knife and charged. I steeled myself for the blow when he jerked to a sudden halt and glanced down at himself. My eyes followed and saw that the sharp hook of the fishing gaff had burst through his chest. Stich barely had the chance to look at me one final time afore he flew backward and was flung to the ground. There his smoking body at last lay motionless. For a moment, I stared at him uncomprehendingly, then I turned my gaze upward to see who had saved me.

It was my brother, Gerard.

chapter twenty

A ghost. I was seeing a ghost. Gerard was dead, frozen in the wilderness months ago. Yet here he stood right in front of me, looking as hearty and hale as the last time we had been together. Had I at long last been wholly undone by pain and hunger and exhaustion? Was I suffering delusions like a madman lost in his own mind? I knew not how else to explain what I saw.

"Cole?" Gerard asked, apparently as surprised as I. "Can that truly be you?" Dumbfounded, I nodded, studying my brother. He looked unchanged from two years earlier. He was slighter than I, but shared the same lean frame with muscles more powerful than they looked. Where my hair was brown, his was blond, and he had my father's rough-hewn features. A high forehead and sober expression gave him a more intellectual air than he actually possessed, though he was anything but bird-witted.

His blue eyes, though, were his most striking feature. They were of a shade, light yet vivid, that most women seemed helpless to resist, at least until they ascertained the rogue lurking behind them. Most times that was too late to do them much good, not that they oft spoke of their experiences. Gerard loathed it when anyone spoke ill of him, but he especially detested it when women did so. He had ways of encouraging them to hold their tongues.

Gerard sprang forward, seizing me in his arms. He hugged me so hard it was difficult to breathe. "I thought never to lay eyes on you again!" he said.

I hugged him back, grateful, if surprised, by such an effusive reaction. "You as well, Gerard," I said. "But how is this possible? I thought you died months ago."

"I'm happy to report that isn't so," said Gerard, thumping himself on the chest. "As you can see I'm yet alive, although I've had more than one close call of late." Gerard glanced down at my shoulder. "You're bleeding, Brother." He looked about as if searching for something. Apparently not finding it, he took off his moccasin, pulling a handful of moss from inside that had been used to keep the cold out. "'Tis not the most fresh bandage," he said. "But I believe it shall do for now."

"But how is it possible that you're alive?" I asked, as he placed the moss over my wound. "Stich said you froze after your canoe sank."

Gerard glanced toward Stich's corpse. "I believe it's safe to say Stich's word was not to be trusted. Alas, I did not discern that about him when we *first* met." Gerard turned back to me, his blue eyes seeming to twinkle from the sheer happiness of seeing me. "It is true that our canoe did sink," he went on, his expression again growing somber. "Took with it every one of our supplies, and all we had to eat was gravel and ice. We grew weaker and weaker, and I had made peace with our fate when Stich did something truly abominable." Gerard looked away for a moment, then said, "Stich killed Thomas Lloyd and ate him."

So that was how Stich first acquired his taste for human flesh. "Did you…" I couldn't bring myself to finish the question. It was none of my business how Gerard had survived.

"Lord, no, Cole! I didn't partake of Thomas's remains," said Gerard. "What more foul sin could a man commit than to do such a thing? When I refused, however, Stich got furious. He said I would tell the others, and he would be hung. He was right, too, although I claimed otherwise at the time. Thomas Lloyd was a good, decent man. Never have I wanted to see a man brought to justice more than I did Stich."

"Justice has been done now, I suppose," I said, looking at Stich's corpse. "So what happened? How did you get off the island?"

"We were stuck for another three days after Thomas' murder," said Gerard. "I grew so hungry, I passed in and out of consciousness. Stich had Thomas, of course, but Thomas was a skinny man and even that supply began to run low. Frankly, I worried that I would be next to grace Stich's plate. That was when we were spotted by a French fur trapper named Sebastien Langlois. Smashing fellow— I owe him my life. Stich, however, wasn't quite so happy to see him."

"But why?" I asked. "Without rescue, Stich would have succumbed to the cold eventually."

"When Sebastien saw that Stich had become a cannibal, he told Stich that the natives believed that anyone who partook of human flesh became an evil spirit the Indians called a wendigo. Sebastien warned Stich that he would change and, for the rest of his life, would never again be fit company for man, woman, or child. Hearing that was more than Stich, already an outcast, could stand. He grew furious and struck Sebastien. He vowed to kill Sebastien if he ever spoke of it again."

I nodded as I listened. It wasn't difficult to imagine Stich's being so upset.

"Sebastien was right, though. Stich had changed," said Gerard, ominously. "After eating Thomas' flesh, Stich became hateful and suspicious and devious. His eyes grew cold and dead, and every time he looked at me I shivered.

"The night after our rescue, as we journeyed back to Hugh's Lick, Stich attacked Sebastien and myself whilst we slept. He kept us both prisoner whilst he pondered what to do next. In the end, he decided he was going to take vengeance on all those who had ever wronged him. He decided that if eating human flesh was supposed to make him a wendigo, then that was what he would become. At least sort of. You see, Stich had grown so devious he conceived a plan to terrorize the settlers by forcing Sebastien to pretend to be the wendigo. He made Sebastien dress in a costume that Stich made from the very animals Sebastien had trapped."

"Even that head?" I asked. "Surely that came from no animal in these woods."

"No," said Gerard. "That is the head of something called a Great Ape. A creature from Africa. Sebastien acquired it from someone who could not pay his debt."

"So Stich was behind all of this? I said, yet astounded that Stich Burke was capable of such deception.

Gerald shrugged. "I know it's hard to believe, but Stich was far more clever than he let on."

"How did you get away from him?"

"I escaped one night when Stich loosed my hands so I could relieve myself. Even then I was lost, badly injured, and starving. I wandered for days until a trapper found me. He took me to his cabin and nursed me back to health. I only became strong enough to leave him a week ago and arrived back here the day afore yesterday. Right away, I went to check on Rose, but she was gone, as were most of the others. I could sense something strange was afoot, so I stayed hidden."

"I have bad news, Gerard," I said. "Sebastien is dead. Stich killed him."

Gerard nodded solemnly "I'm not surprised to hear it. Stich wanted Sebastien dead from the beginning."

"I have more ill tidings, Brother," I said. "Father is dead as well."

"I've expected that cheerless news for some time," said Gerard. "Even so, it's not an easy thing to hear. Had he died afore my letter arrived?"

"No," I said. "And he was so pleased to hear from you, Gerard. Relieved to know you were alive." I paused, then said, "We never were able to figure out why you left, why you never wrote."

Gerard looked chagrined. "Embarrassed, I supposed. Was there ever a bigger jackdaw in peacock's feather than myself?"

I lay a hand on my brother's arm. "Don't be so hard on yourself, Gerard," I said, even though it was true. Gerard had been a braggart, a scoundrel, a man of generally ill repute. Yet he was charismatic, could be generous, and never lacked for friends—at least until he cheated them. Father had remained devoted to him until his dying day. I'm glad Father had not known how low Gerard had sunk in the past couple of years.

"No need to gloss things over, Cole. If everything King Midas touched turned to gold, everything I touch turns to shit. That was partly why I left two years ago and why you hadn't heard from me."

"But you did finally write," I said.

Gerard shrugged. "Aye. I thought that by the time you got my letter, I might have finally set things right."

"But they aren't?" I asked, again thinking of Rose and the baby.

Gerard didn't answer. Instead, he asked a question of his own. "How is Rebecca?"

I tried not to show my surprise. Why was he asking about her? He couldn't know we had been engaged and that I had abandoned her, could he? "I imagine she is fine," I said hesitantly. "What makes you ask?"

"Up until I left, I'd been courting her for a year," he said. "Did you not know?"

I shook my head. "I'd no idea, Gerard. You courted so many women."

Gerard smiled mischievously. "Well, you know how much the ladies liked me. And I liked them well enough, but Rebecca was the only one I wished to marry. At least until she broke off seeing me."

"I'm sorry, Gerard," I said, taken aback by the news we had been seeing the same woman. "I had no intimation that you cared for her, much less that things had gone awry betwixt you. Do you know what came about to cause her affection for you to lessen?" I suspected I knew the answer already: most likely, Rebecca had realized what a scoundrel my brother truly was; that he would never provide a stable home; that he would get her with child and then leave her to fend for herself.

"She went sweet on you," he said. "Did she not ever tell you?"

"What?"

Gerard nodded. "That was why she broke it off with me and, truth be told, much of the reason I left. After all, how could I hope to vie with the ever-reliable *you* when it came to marriage? She said she hadn't yet told you how she felt, but I thought maybe she did so after I'd gone."

"There is nothing between Rebecca and me," I said. Far from it, I wanted to add.

Gerard shrugged. "It matters not. I hold nothing against you, Brother. After all, I am married to Rose now. I was curious, is all."

Rose! And the others! I'd completely forgotten about them. "The others are yet tied up!" I exclaimed. "We have to set them free."

I started to rise, but Gerard caught ahold of me sleeve. "Wait. There is something else you must know."

I looked at him perplexedly, for setting the others free seemed to me the of utmost importance.

"I'm sorry to tell you this," said Gerard. "But one of them was in league with Stich."

"What!" I exclaimed. "I don't believe such a thing!"

"You best consider it then," said Gerard. "Do you really believe Stich could have done all of this on his own? He had to keep Sebastien, not a small chap, his prisoner and make him dress up in that outfit, not to mention carry out all of the attacks on the settlers. Someone *had* to be working with him."

"Do you know who?" I asked, skeptically.

"I briefly saw someone yesterday," said Gerard. "But it wasn't a good look. It could have been any one of them."

"If one of them was working with Stich, why are they all tied up?"

"Treachery," said Gerard. "Now that Stich has got rid of everyone else in Hugh's Lick, he has betrayed his fellow conspirator as well."

Perhaps Gerard had a point. It was hard to imagine one person pulling off so many feats by himself: the attacks on both the settlers *and* the Indians. Just the slaughtered livestock at Marda Witt's bespoke of the work of several people. After capturing Sebastien, hadn't I suspected as much myself? And that would explain how the wendigo had seemed to move so quickly. Instead of one wendigo every time the creature appeared, it had actually been two or three people causing the mayhem.

Who, though? I could see Owen or Benjamin Carson being involved in such a scheme, but my friends? "It can't be, Gerard," I said. "I refuse to believe such a thing. Besides, what reason could any of them have to do such a thing?"

"Plenty, truth be told," said Gerard. "You may not know this, Cole, but John and Palmer are sodomites, and the whole town was aghast at their illicit relationship. They weren't going to tolerate their presence much longer. Perhaps John realized that and elected to take matters into his own hands."

John was decent and good, if prickly as a hedgehog. He might confront those who spoke ill of him, but kill them? No.

"One time," said Gerard, "I even heard John make a threat about getting rid of everyone else in Hugh's Lick. Beyond doubt, he did not like the place. Perhaps he only meant to frighten people and didn't intend for things to go this far."

I abruptly recalled my first day in John's cabin. When I asked about Hugh's Lick, he had said any place with more than four people was a boil needing to be lanced. Judging from his tone, he had been serious. Could he have been more serious than I had understood?

"So you claim it was John and Palmer who were working with Stich?" I asked.

"I don't know that for certain," said Gerard. "Though they are the most likely. Which isn't to say Gwennie didn't have her reasons as well. After all, she is a redskin and the settlers hated her worse than a rattler in their bed. Some coveted her land as well. I also know for a fact that she hates white people. When she was yet a child, her entire family was killed by white men whilst she watched. That woman's more bitter than a barrelful of spoiled vinegar. You wouldn't believe some of things she said to me the first time we met."

I, too, had been on the receiving end of some of her sharp comments. No, Gwennie unquestionably wouldn't have minded seeing Hugh's Lick emptied of settlers. Even I had to admit that. Furthermore, John had told me she was none too fond of the other Delaware either.

But no! This was too hard to accept! Could Gerard be lying to me? I saw no reason for that either. But somebody *was* lying.

"I'm not even sure about my own wife," said Gerard, his eyes cast down as if embarrassed. "Rose tricked me into marrying her, Cole. I'm not certain that her child is my own, or if Rose ever had any real affection for me. Besides, she had her reasons to hate the other settlers as well as much as John or Gwennie. From the day she arrived, everyone in Hugh's Lick treated her as if she had the pox or sold herself as a doxy. Then not *one* soul lifted a finger to help her even whilst she and her babe starved. Not even your John and Palmer." Gerard turned back toward where the others were tied up. "Do you truly know any of these people, Cole? You were always justifiably proud of how ruthlessly rational you are. I always admired that about you. Does your logic now rightly tell you that you should trust these people—these strangers—with your life?"

Gerard was right: I didn't know any of the others that well. But I did know Gerard, probably as well as anyone. Yet even I had almost fallen for his deception. How could I have doubted my friends after all they had done for me? And how could I have believed my brother after all I knew about him?

"You look like you've thought of something," said Gerard.

I had. It wasn't one of my friends helping Stich. It was Gerard. Furthermore, I'd wager anything Gerard wasn't merely helping either. He had been the instigator behind the whole affair. He'd always been the schemer, the charlatan looking to make an easy fortune, though this was beyond the pale, even for him.

Like most liars, Gerard always had to push things a little too far. If he had settled with creating some doubt in my mind, I might never have seen the truth. It was his story about Rose that tripped him up. The fact of the matter was the only way he could have known how miserably the other settlers had treated her was if he had seen it himself. But only a short time ago, he had said Rose had already disappeared by the time he had recovered enough to return. That meant he had been back longer than the one day he claimed.

A lot longer, if I wasn't greatly mistaken. In fact, he had never been anywhere else other than lurking nearby, pulling strings and wreaking havoc upon settlers and Indians alike.

"I have thought of something," I said to Gerard. "I believe I know who was working with Stich." I willed myself to stay calm, to again be Cold-Blooded Cole. Everything now depended on me, on my living up to my nickname, for at the very least Gerard was an accomplice to murder. Somehow I expected he was far more than that.

"You do?" asked Gerard.

Rising, I nodded. "Let's get back to the others."

"Who do you think it is?" asked Gerard.

"Palmer," I said.

"What makes you so sure?" asked Gerard.

"Because of what you said. You understand people well, don't you, Gerard?"

Gerard looked rather pleased with himself. "But why exactly do you suspect Palmer?"

"Because every single time something happened, Palmer conveniently wasn't around," I said. "John and I left him with Rose, and when we came back, she and Colette were gone, but somehow Palmer had escaped. Then he *happens* to disappear in the dark when no one can see, and we all believe the wendigo has him. After that, Gwennie vanishes, then John. I was with John and Gwennie when their cabins were destroyed. It has to be Palmer. No one else had the opportunity."

"But why would he have done it?" asked Gerard. "Especially to John?"

I thought a moment for I needed a convincing reason. "He was jealous. Of Gwennie. Anybody could see he didn't like how close she and John were. You know how covetous those sodomites can be."

Gerard sighed deeply, as if distraught by such treachery. "Well, if you're sure," he said.

"Oh, I'm sure, all right," I said.

"What should we do with him?" asked Gerard.

"There is only one thing to do," I said. I looked about until I located the knife with which Stich stabbed me with. Spotting it, I strode purposefully over and retrieved it. It surprised me that Gerard let me have a knife so readily; he must have truly believed that I thought Palmer the traitor.

"What are you doing?" Gerard asked nervously. He backed away from me, and I saw he didn't trust me that much.

"I'm going to kill Palmer," I said, heading back to the blockhouse.

"You are?" Gerard couldn't hide his surprise.

"What choice do we have?" I asked, walking as fast as I could. "We know he's a murderous bastard and probably a cannibal to boot. There is no sheriff or garrison to mete out the justice he has coming. Besides he deserves to die, don't you think?"

"Well, if you think it for the best," said Gerard, sounding almost gleeful.

It occurred to me that this was what Gerard had intended all the while: for me to turn on my friends, maybe even kill one of them. He was playing a game with me, had been all along. It wasn't simple-minded Stich's idea to capture my friends one at a time, although I'm sure he was more than happy to go along with the plot. It was Gerard behind the whole thing. Gerard getting his revenge on me. But for what reason? Because of Rebecca? That was hard to comprehend. Gerard never actually cared for the women he courted. They were entertainments, diversions, as easily changed as a pair of shoes. Whatever the reason, I knew what I had to do.

We reached the others. Gripping the knife, I crossed over to where Palmer sat. "I know it was you behind all of this, Palmer Baxter. And for that, you're going to die."

John and Palmer both looked surprised, then alarmed. Clutching his hand with the amputated fingers, John tried to roll between Palmer and myself, but I roughly pushed him away; Gerard had to keep believing I truly intended to kill Palmer. There was fear in Palmer's eyes, but resolve as well. Crouching down in front of him, I said, "May you rot in hell, Palmer Baxter." Then I silently mouthed, "Trust me."

Palmer looked startled, then nodded slightly and pretended to struggle. As fast as possible, I tried to saw through the ropes that bound his hands.

"What are you doing?" asked Gerard. "I thought you were going to kill him?"

"I am," I said. "I'm going to hang him. I want him to die slowly."

"Then why are freeing his hands?" asked Gerard. "Get away from him, Cole. Did you hear me? Cole, I said, get away from him."

I had nearly severed the ropes around one of Palmer's wrists when I moved away. As I left, I slipped Palmer the knife.

When I turned back to Gerard, I found myself staring down the barrel of a pistol.

"Very good, Cole," sneered Gerard. "Who knew you were an actor worthy of a London stage? Much better than I would have expected. I *almost* believed you were going to kill Palmer."

"What are you doing, Gerard?" I asked, still hoping to bluff him.

"Enough with the games, Little Brother," he said. "As soon as I let slip the fact that the other settlers had watched Rose starve, I knew you would figure the truth out. Even you aren't that dim."

I considered playing dumb, but saw nothing to be gained. "But why, Gerard? All of this to get back at me? That's excessive, even for someone with your vanity."

Gerard erupted in anger. "You self-absorbed little prick!" he yelled. "Of course, you would think this was all about you. Everything always was about you. Well, for once, it's not."

"Then what? Your doing this makes no sense." I considered with whom I was dealing and thought perhaps I understood. "There has to be money involved, doesn't there?" I asked. "Even you wouldn't let your own daughter starve for no reason." Gerard was self-important and could rarely resist showing off. I counted on those traits now, for if I was right, I thought he would brag about his plans. If he did so, I hoped there might be a way to use it against him.

He eyed me smugly, then gestured toward the woods. "Somewhere out there is a fort full of gold that was abandoned fifty years ago. Ten soldiers were left to guard it, but two of the soldiers betrayed and killed the others so they could have the gold themselves. Something happened to them afore they could move the gold, so it's stayed there all these years. And now I'm going to find it. First, though, I had to get rid of the rest of the lowlifes in this shit-hole of a settlement. I wasn't about to share it with the likes of Murdock Burke or Owen Stern."

"Or Stich, for that matter," I said.

Gerard spat, a look of visceral hatred lighting up his face. "Stich had outlived his usefulness. Besides he was drinking himself to death anyway. Apparently he felt *bad* about our having eaten Thomas Lloyd to survive. Why should I risk his one day inadvertently telling the truth whilst drunk?"

There was yet something about this foul business that didn't completely make sense. I didn't doubt Gerard was after money—he was always after money—but something else was going on as well. "If you wanted to get rid of everyone, Gerard, then why did you capture John, Palmer, and Gwennie? And why didn't you kill me straight away? Your not doing so makes no sense."

Gerard glared at me. "Yes, it does," he said. "But if you can't see why, perhaps you aren't as clever as you think."

"Clearly, this *is* about getting revenge on me," I said "Did I wrong you somehow?"

"Shut up," growled Gerard. "It has nothing to do with you."

Obviously, I was getting under his skin, and that was good. If he got angry enough, he might make a mistake of which I could take advantage.

"Is it because of Rebecca?" I ventured.

"I said shut up!" Gerard bellowed.

"But I didn't even know about her rejecting you," I said. "Nor did you know I was coming here. It must be something I've done since I arrived. Is it Rose? Because I was to marry her?"

"No," said Gerard emphatically. He raised the pistol at me, and I suspected I was right about Rose. "I'm warning you, Cole."

"But I thought you were dead, Gerard. I wasn't trying to steal her any more than I was Rebecca. Although, it is true Rose told me what an awful husband you were."

"To hell with you!" shouted Gerard.

"You never could bear to be thought of as less than perfect, could you? In fact, it drove you berserk. But you didn't know what Rose had told me. Unlessen...you overheard her telling me." I recalled that first day I had met Rose, her spotting someone lurking outside the cabin, and my suspicion Stich had been eavesdropping. But it hadn't been Stich. It was Gerard. And for the second time, he had heard a woman rejecting him in favor of me. And not just rejecting him, but disparaging him, the thing he hated most. "This *is* about me, isn't it, Gerard? Good Lord! Just how pathetic are you?"

Afore I could react, Gerard swung the pistol, clubbing me upside the head with it. I staggered under the blow as hot blood filled my mouth. At the same instant, Palmer, having finished cutting his bindings, shot forward, trying to stab Gerard with the knife. Gerard seized Palmer, knocked the knife from his hand, and sent him hurtling to the ground. He then unleashed several brutal kicks that caught Palmer square in the gut.

I sprang forward, tackling Gerard. He lashed out at me with his feet as I tried to scramble upright, but one of his boots caught me in the head. I tumbled backward, landing hard on my ass. Next to me lay the knife Palmer had dropped.

"I'm going to kill you!" yelled Gerard, throwing himself at me. I barely managed to grab the knife afore Gerard was on top of me. Unfortunately, he grabbed my wrist sooner than I could drive the blade into his guts.

"Let go you half-witted, deformed issue of a misbegotten whore!" he bellowed.

I spat in his face, which only infuriated him that much more. He bore his weight down upon me, placing a forearm against my throat. For such a lean man, he felt incredibly heavy. Little by little, he choked off my air until I was forced to release the knife. Desperately, I clawed at him, trying to shove his arm off my Adam's apple.

Suddenly, he relented, but only to seize the knife which he then pressed against my jugular.

Despite the cold, we were both ruddy and sweaty. I gasped for air and was so dizzy with pain that it was hard to think clearly. Gerard glared at me, then said, "This has been entertaining, Little Brother, but I think I've had quite enough of you. Give Father my—"

Gerard was cut off mid-word as Palmer whacked him upside the head with a skillet. "It's been anything but entertaining, you son-of-a-bitch!" swore Palmer.

Gerard seemed unfazed by the blow, however, and even laughed out loud. He spun about, grabbed Palmer by the wrist, yanked him close, and drove the knife deep into Palmer's belly. Horrified, John screamed wildly through his gag. The skillet clattered loudly to the ground as Palmer gripped the knife sticking out of his gut. He moaned in agony, his eyes losing their focus as blood poured out of him. He gasped once and tumbled face first into the dirt, where he lay unmoving.

I couldn't comprehend what I witnessed. This wasn't supposed to happen. I was supposed to have found a way to save him. I always found a way. I was Cold-Blooded Cole, and I didn't fail. But I had. Terribly. And a good, kind man who deserved better was dead.

If this was what caring about people led to, I wanted no part of it. I wanted to remain apart and aloof. I wanted to stay Cold-Blooded Cole. I had another more terrifying thought: If losing Palmer hurt this much, how would it feel if I learned Pakim was dead as well? The very thought paralyzed me, and I lay unmoving on the cold earth, waiting to see what my brother would do next.

Gerard's eyes were disconcerting—unnaturally clear and bright—as if he had just woken well-rested from a deep sleep. It sounded like he hummed a song as well, something cheery and light. Despite the blood trickling down his face, Gerard seemed strengthened somehow, as if this mayhem were invigorating rather than sapping him of strength. In fact, he was enjoying himself.

I knew I should act, but my whole body throbbed with so much pain I wasn't certain I could rise, much less fight Gerard again.

Besides, I had not a single idea about what to do next. Nor was Gerard going to give me time to figure something out. "I was going to kill you first, Cole," he said. "But I think it best if I save you for last so you can watch. It seems to horrify you so." Gerard smiled as he turned to the others. "Any volunteers to be next?"

"Let them go," I said, trying to think of something to stop him. "Keep me, Gerard. I'll help you find the gold, and you can have it all."

"But of course I can. Who's to stop me? You?" he asked derisively, then laughed. "So, no volunteers to die next? Then I guess I'll just have to pick. Let's see. Well, I never did much care for Indians what with all that scalp-lifting and whatnot."

Gerald took Colette from Gwennie, placing the infant back on Rose's lap.

Gwennie was going to die, and I was helpless to save her. I couldn't let myself give up, though—I had to try. I wracked my brain trying to come up with something, my eyes searching the ground for anything to use as a weapon.

I heard Gerard yell and looked up to see him hopping on one foot. Apparently, Gwennie had kicked him afore he could kill her.

"You're going to pay for that, you red-skinned bitch," yelled Gerard.

Think, Cole! Think! I needed an idea, some kind of leverage over Gerard. Something about Father? I could think of nothing to say that might stop him. And then I had a notion. Or at least the start of one. "I know where the gold is!" I yelled. It was a lie, of course, but I was desperate to buy time. "But if you kill anyone else, I shan't tell you."

Gerard regarded me skeptically. "Somehow I doubt you're speaking the truth, Brother."

"I am," I said, my mind racing. I breathed deeply, trying to concentrate, to think of what to say next.

"All right, then," said Gerard, seizing Gwennie by the hair. "Where is the gold?" He pressed the knife against her throat.

My mind was yet blank, then I blurted out. "A fort. It's in a fort."

Gerard scowled, pressing the blade hard enough against

Gwennie's throat to draw blood. A tiny squeak escaped from her. "*I told you that, Cole*, and that leads me to suppose you are lying to your own flesh and blood. Prove otherwise quick, or she dies."

A fort. I had to think of something I could say about a fort. But the only fort I knew anything about was the one through which I had escaped from the so-called wendigo—the one where I had found the bars of lead.

Good Lord! It all became clear to me in a flash. Those hadn't been bars of lead I had found in the ruins! They were bars of gold, for that was the very fort for which Gerard searched. And I had been there! I could take him there.

"It's a French fort you're looking for, isn't it?" I asked.

Gerard looked startled, even let the knife drop from Gwennie's throat. "How did you know that?"

"Because I've been there," I said. "In fact, I've seen the gold myself."

He scrutinized me intently. "I don't believe you," he said, though it was clear he desperately wanted to.

"It's true," I said, rummaging through my pocket. I finally found what I was looking for and held it out to Gerard. At last I was beginning to think there might be a way out of this.

Gerard approached, hesitantly taking the epaulet I had picked up in the cave. He stared down at it as if unable to trust his own eyes.

"It's a soldier's epaulet," I said. "From a French soldier in a French fort. Who else would have the fleur-de-lis on his epaulets?"

Gerard threw the epaulet to the ground. He grabbed me by the collar and pulled me to my feet.

"Take me there!" he ordered.

"Free the others," I said calmly.

"If I free them," said Gerard, "then you'll have no incentive to take me there. Something tells me you're going to need an incentive."

"But you'll kill us when you're done," I said.

"You have my word I won't," he said. "I swear on it."

Despite our dire situation, I actually had to stifle a laugh. Gerard offering me his word? Hell, his word was worth less than Benedict

Arnold's, but I knew it mattered naught in the end. I only needed to keep everyone alive until I got Gerard to the fort and then…

Well, I didn't yet know what I would do once there, but I would come up with something. I also knew I couldn't simply agree to take him, or he would be suspicious that I was laying a trap for him. "Your word, Gerard?" I said derisively. "After all the lies you've told, your word holds less worth with me than wampum in an English bank."

"You best watch your tongue, Little Brother, afore I cut it out of your accursed head. As for whose word is better, at least I'm no sodomite." The shock I felt must have been apparent upon my face, as Gerard laughed, then said, "That's right, Little Brother. I know about you and the Indian, so I'd think twice afore I go feeling all superior. Imagine how such news would have weighed upon poor Father. Now take me to my gold, or I scalp this worthless squaw." He yanked Gwennie close to him, once again.

I pretended to think it over, then said, "Fine." I tried to sound as defeated as possible.

Gerard hauled Rose to her feet, forcing her to stand next to Gwennie. Rose looked dazed and battered, and clutched Colette fiercely, clearly worried Gerard would seize the infant from her. Gerard next went to John and tried to pull him to his feet. But each time he did so, John only slumped back to the ground. "Get up, you pathetic sodomite," ordered Gerard. "Or I'll kill you and leave you with your perverted friend."

John was so catatonic I wasn't certain he even heard Gerard.

"As you like then," said Gerard, drawing his knife.

"No!" I said. "If you kill him, I won't take you to the gold."

"Then make him get up," said Gerard. "Because I'm not leaving him behind alive."

I went to John and knelt by his side "Come, John," I said. "Let's go."

He slowly turned his eyes toward me.

"This isn't what Palmer would have wanted," I cajoled. "He would want you to live and help save Rose and Gwennie and Colette."

John's eyes swung back to where Palmer lay. I had been about to haul John to his feet when he held out his good hand to me. I took it and pulled him upright, then turned my cold gaze toward Gerard. "Best none of you try anything," he said. "Or I kill the baby."

Rose looked as if she were about to run. I glared at her, my resolute eyes warning her not to try anything. No one else was going to die. Not today. Not whilst Cold-Blooded Cole yet breathed.

chapter twenty-one

I went ahead of the others. My hands were tied together, but otherwise I was unrestrained as I rode Hiccup. The poor horse carried not only me, but all of the supplies Gerard had originally thought he might need in his quest for the gold: torches, a shovel, rope and pails for hauling dirt and rocks if digging for the gold had been necessary. My brother had come well-prepared.

John, Gwennie, and Rose came behind me, all yet gagged and bound together like prisoners of war. Last came Gerard clutching a pistol and carrying Colette.

The ruins of the fort lay around the next corner of the trail, but I had yet to conceive of a plan. The most I had come up with thus far was clubbing my shitter of a brother with a bar of gold, not exactly a strategy for the ages, but I was trying to work with what I had at hand.

When we reached the first of the fort's fallen walls, Gerard ordered everyone to stop.

"This is the fort?" he asked.

I nodded.

"And where is the gold?"

I verged on speaking the truth when a way to gain the upper hand occurred to me. "There are more ruins like these on the other side of the bushes," I said. "The gold is there."

"Just lying out in the open?" Gerard asked suspiciously.

I shook my head, making up the lie as I went. "Of course not. A bunker overgrown with bushes stands there, though there isn't room for the horse. I happened upon it by pure chance whilst I searched for shelter."

Gerard weighed my words, then nodded. "Will we need light?"

If my plan went accordingly, Gerard would be the only one needing light. Nonetheless, I thought it best if we brought a couple of torches. After all, how much in the past week had gone accordingly? "The gold is rather far back in the bunker," I said. "We should probably bring a torch for each of us."

"Light them," said Gerard, after untying my hands. "You best remember not to try anything or someone else will die."

Someone else was going to die all right, but it wasn't who Gerard thought. As I set about doing as instructed, I said, "The others have to come with us."

"You think so, do you?" sneered Gerard.

"It's safer if they stay with us," I said.

"You're obviously up to something," he said. "The question is do you really want them with us, or do you want them to stay here?" He thought for a moment then said, "Rose and Gwennie stay here. John comes with us, but I want his hands bound behind his back."

Gerard hadn't said what he intended to do with Colette, and she was my real concern. As long as he carried the infant, I couldn't execute my plan without great risk to her. I elected to hold my tongue for fear that saying more would give away what I truly wanted.

Gerard ordered me to separate John from Gwennie and Rose, and then to bind the two women together at the base of a tree. There was fear in their eyes, but I squeezed each of their arms reassuringly.

After tying up the women, I turned to see what Gerard would do next. He yet held Colette in one arm whilst carrying the pistol in his free hand, not an easy feat to manage. He aimed the pistol at me, but it was clearly awkward to do whilst holding an infant. At that moment, Colette, bless her soul, began to cry and squirm about.

"Bloody hell," muttered Gerard. He glanced at me, but I remained impassive, trying to give nothing away. Finally, Gerard strode to where

Gwennie and Rose were tied up. He lay the crying Colette in Rose's lap, then turned to John and me.

"Come on then," he said, picking up the second torch whilst leveling the pistol at me. "I've already waited far too long to be a wealthy man."

My eyes searched the ground ahead as we walked. The opening to the chamber was square in shape and not especially wide, perhaps two feet on each side. Such was its small size, I was having more difficulty spotting it than I expected, and for a heart-stopping moment, I feared we had already passed it by. Convincing Gerard to backtrack would be parlous at best. Then I spotted the hole not far ahead. As if things weren't tricky enough, John was going to walk right into it if I didn't do something.

As subtly as possible, I moved toward John, who instinctively adjusted his path farther to the right. It looked as if he would now miss it. Gerard was five feet behind, his pistol, I knew, aimed right at my heart. I thought about throwing my torch at him, or even using it to drive him toward the hole, but as long as he held that pistol, I didn't dare. I needed some other way to lure him close enough to the hole to knock him in.

Earlier Gerard had said I was a better actor than he had expected. Now was time to find out how much better.

I stumbled, sprawling face forward. I hit the ground without breaking my fall. I even managed to split my lip on a rock.

Rolling onto my back, I regarded Gerard with as dazed an expression as I could muster. Hopefully, the blood running down my chin made my appearance that much more convincing. Holding my hand to my lip, I struggled to sit up. "I'm hurt," I said.

"You're an oaf is what you are," said Gerard. "Well, it's only blood. Now fetch your torch and get up afore I show you what pain truly is."

I nodded, pushing myself upright. I made it halfway afore I feigned a wave of dizziness that nearly brought me back to my knees. In fact, I was so battered, I scarcely had to pretend I couldn't stand.

"For God's sake," said Gerard, jabbing his torch into the earth afore finally stepping forward to help me. That was when I launched myself at him.

Gerard reacted at once, swinging the pistol back toward my chest. But it was already too late. Using both hands, I grabbed the barrel, forcing the pistol upward as I dug my feet into the earth, pivoted, then swung with all my might. I had counted on Gerard's refusing to relinquish his grasp and he didn't disappoint. That allowed me to propel him directly toward the hole.

He stumbled forward, his eyes widening in surprise as he saw the opening beneath his feet. At the instant I felt certain he would fall in, I let go. Gerard stumbled, looked as if he were about to plunge into the hole, then caught his balance long enough to leap across the gap.

He landed awkwardly, falling to one knee. Cursing my luck, I leapt over the hole, grabbing ahold of Gerard's arm as he turned to face me. He swung his free arm, catching me upside the head with the pistol. Even though I could have sworn I heard my skull crack, I stayed upright and threw myself at him. Gerard staggered backward as we fought.

I seized ahold of his wrist, wrenching it back and forth until he was forced to drop the firearm. Gerard seized me by the throat with his now freed hand, then grabbed me by my belt with his other. With a display of strength that shocked me, he slowly lifted me up until I was nearly above his head. Carrying me thusly, Gerard steadily moved toward the opening in the ground. I caught a glimpse of John who, although he looked right at us, seemed no more cognizant of me than did the trees beyond him. Realizing Gerard planned to drop me through the hole, I seized a handful of his hair and pulled with all my might.

Gerard screamed, stumbled, then hurled me at the opening. He just missed, but when I slammed into the frozen ground, it hurt as if I had fallen from the top of a blockhouse. My accursed brother yet swore as clutched his bloodied head and I realized I had lifted a fistful of hair from his scalp. Gerard flew into a frenzy of yelling and kicking at the earth. In fact, I could feel the very ground shake beneath me. My torch lay next to me, its flame holding steady, and I thought to defend myself with it.

Then the earth gave way beneath me. I scarcely comprehended what happened as I plunged downward amidst a cascade of dirt and rocks. For the second time in mere moments, I slammed into the ground. More dirt came crashing down as the cave-in spread. I heard Gerard yell, caught a glimpse of him plummeting downward, then heard him cry out as he, too, landed with a bone-breaking thud. As I lay there, my addled mind realized that the ground above the chamber must have given away beneath the weight of our struggle. Recalling the rotted beams I had seen here afore, I wasn't surprised.

Spitting dirt from my mouth, I forced myself upright, knowing I had to act whilst I had the chance. Dust swirled wildly through the already gloomy air as I looked about. My torch, miraculously yet lit, rested ten feet from me, whilst Gerard lay on his back, dazed. The second torch sputtered near his feet, then went out. My eyes scanned the ground for the pistol, but all was a chaos of broken boards, dirt, and rocks. Then I realized I did not see something else I should have seen: the gold!

There should have been a stack of it, which we should have practically landed on top of. Instead, there was naught but dirt and rocks. I didn't understand. Nor did I have time to puzzle it out, for Gerard began to come to his senses. I debated attacking him, trying to finish him off, but I doubted I possessed the strength. I needed to escape, and here I possessed the advantage, for I knew there was a way underground that led back to the cave where Sebastien had first taken me. Gerard couldn't know this and would either stay here trapped in this chamber or might, if he followed after me, get lost and die. It heartened me to have something so fine to hope for.

As I grabbed the torch, Gerard sat upright, saw what I was doing, and lunged for me. He missed, and I turned and hurried toward the back of the chamber.

"And where might you be headed, Little Brother?" he called out after me.

Without answering, I plunged into the dark.

◆

The ground quickly sloped downward beneath my feet. The cavern, cool and dank, had a ceiling so high that I need not worry about striking my head. At least not yet. Soon enough, I knew, it would narrow afore it branched off into the maze through which I had already wandered once. I did not relish the idea of venturing back there, but it seemed I had little choice. I hoped Gerard, consumed by his greed, might search the chamber for gold afore he came after me. At least then I might have a bit of a head start.

Better yet, this time I had got Gerard away from the others, which meant they were safe, even if I should perish down here. Or were they? Hadn't they all still been bound and gagged? True, John had been able to walk, but with his hands bound together and his wits addled by Palmer's death, he was of no use to himself, much less the others. No, if I didn't get out of here, then Rose and Gwennie and the baby might yet die.

"I know what you're up to, Little Brother," Gerard called out from behind me. He had followed sooner than I expected, and I feared I wouldn't find the right tunnel afore he caught me. "You've hidden the gold down here, haven't you? But afore you retrieve it, you're hoping to get me lost."

If only such were true!

My mind raced, trying to come up with something else down here that I could use to defeat him. There was the river farther in. I would have to follow it for some ways afore I reached the turn back to the cave where Sebastien had taken me. Perhaps I could lure him to it, then drown him. That was too good for the likes of Gerard—the idea of drawing and quartering the bastard held enormous appeal—yet in the end I would happily settle for letting him die peacefully in his sleep if only to be done with him.

I wracked my brain for anything else I could use. There was also the body I had found after escaping from the the cave. I had been so addled at the time I hadn't even bothered to search it. Might the body have a musket or at least a knife that I could use as a weapon? It was worth investigating.

"Bloody hell!" cried out Gerard as he stumbled and fell. I hadn't realized he was so close behind me. My injuries slowed me more than I knew. If I didn't do something soon, he would catch up with me, and all of this would have been for naught.

I came to the fork where the chamber separated into two parts. Despite my best effort to recall, I had no idea from which way I had come the first time. Trying to prod my memory, I looked about. All around stalactites and stalagmites shone in the torchlight, some nearly as wide around as I, some no thicker than my wrist. A flicker of light appeared in the darkness behind me and I realized Gerard had managed to relight the other torch. I had to choose a fork now, afore he reached me. But the odds were fifty-fifty that Gerard would pick the same fork as I. And if the fork I chose didn't lead in the right direction, then not only had I gone the wrong way, but I would have Gerard blocking the way back behind me as well.

God's balls! I need a third choice. Quickly, I examined the walls around me, but saw nothing useful, no place I could hide. I glanced upward, following the graceful flow of the stalactites hanging from the ceiling like an upside down forest of stone tree trunks. And the sight gave me an idea. It meant extinguishing my torch, but I felt I had no choice. I had made it through here in the dark once afore. I thought I could do so again.

I snuffed out the torch, then hid it behind a stalagmite. Next I went to the lowest hanging stalactite that looked able to support my weight, grasped it with both hands, and pulled myself up. My injured shoulder throbbed furiously, but I forced the pain aside. Once I had climbed high enough to reach the other stalactites, I used them to support myself as I worked my way higher. Soon I was tucked up amongst them like a bat at roost. And not a moment too soon.

A panting Gerard appeared below me. I froze, daring to not so much as breathe. His torch easily illuminated me, but he would spot me only should he look straight up. Already my arms and legs trembled from the effort of wedging myself against the ceiling, and I prayed he would be quick in choosing which fork he took. Instead, he looked about, as if he knew I was up to something.

"Damn it to hell," he muttered, clearly annoyed. Brandishing the torch in front of him, he wound his way in and out of the rock formations. I hadn't counted on his doing so, and prayed he wouldn't spot my torch. Beads of sweat popped out on my face as Gerard's light danced and flickered, casting eerie shadows all about.

Then Gerard returned to the fork in the trail, looked back and forth a final time, chose the one to the right and quickly vanished from view. Not a God blessed moment too soon, as I didn't so much fall as slide down the stalactites, whereupon I landed with an echoing thud. I feared Gerard might have heard, but he didn't reappear.

Exhausted, I knelt there, recouping what meager strength I had left. I felt not a little discouraged, for Gerard had not only come after me sooner than I had thought, but he looked scarcely injured at all, even after our fall. Whence did his strength come? He seemed as nearly unstoppable as an actual wendigo. Nor, I thought, was that the only way in which he was like a wendigo. Whitewood Tree had said a wendigo was a man whose heart had turned to ice. Clearly that was true of my brother: Only one with such a heart could commit the acts of which my brother was guilty.

Whitewood Tree had also said the only way to defeat a wendigo was to become one. Well, I knew now there never had been a wendigo, only my wendigo-like brother and his heart of ice. But perhaps only someone else with such a heart could kill him. In which case, maybe I was the perfect one to defeat Gerard, for in a sense I was almost as much a wendigo as was my brother. I was Cold-Blooded Cole, after all. And if I encountered Gerard again I was prepared to do whatever it took to vanquish him.

◆

I thought to retrieve my torch, then remembered I had no way to relight it, so I left it where I had hidden it. Since Gerard had taken the right fork, I took the left, having no desire to encounter him afore I was ready. Already I thought I heard the rush of the river, but I had no idea where I would come out upon it.

At that moment, I spied light up ahead and froze where I stood. Gerard stepped into view, apparently crossing the tunnel down which I descended. This place was even more of a honeycomb than I realized. Thank God Gerard's back was to me as he halted to look about. His head pivoted back and forth as if deciding which way to proceed, and I prayed he did not look toward me. I thought he was about to continue forward when he did turn and look directly toward me.

It wasn't Gerard! It was Pakim and, despite myself, I gasped out loud. But it couldn't be Pakim! He had vanished in the storm. I had even thought him captured by the wendigo, quite possibly dead. Clearly, he wasn't, but what was he doing down here? Was he lost? Looking for me?

Apparently, he couldn't see me from so far away. I nearly called out, only staying my tongue at the last moment for fear of alerting Gerard to our presence. I had to warn Pakim about Gerard, but without giving ourselves away. Unfortunately, Pakim moved out of sight afore I could do anything. I hurried down to the junction hoping to catch him. I was too late, however. Pakim had already vanished down one of the passageways. Now I had to worry not only about saving the others but also making sure Pakim escaped as well.

From here, I was certain I heard the rush of fast-flowing water. Moving carefully in the dark, I made my way forward until I felt the cool layer of air invariably situated over a river like a blanket. I picked my way along the rocky bank. The stones were slick and I took great care, for if I were to fall into the rushing water, I doubted I would be able to climb back out afore my brains were dashed out upon the rocks.

I had gone perhaps forty or fifty feet when a gust of tainted air reached my nose. The odor recalled the foul-smelling tributary I had encountered my first time here. Only this time, the smell was familiar, for it was the same stink given off by Pakim's sacred burning waters. Was that what Pakim was doing here? Was this another of the Delaware's sacred places?

Another scent assaulted my nostrils. This was the smell of death emanating from the body I had found my first time down here. I moved forward carefully, not wanting to trip over the dead man. After my foot kicked his leg, I knelt next to him. A life of hunting had left me accustomed to dead things and their more gruesome aspects. Yet I did not relish what I needed to do now.

The odor of the body was quite foul, though somewhat masked by the stink of the tributary flowing past me and into the river. Starting near the feet, I felt all about in case the dead fellow had dropped something useful when he perished, say, a sword or a British cannon. Alas, I found nothing but cold, hard rock. Next I turned my attention to the body. His feet were clad in moccasins, cold and slimy to the touch. Even down here where it was cool and there were few animals, a body wouldn't last long. The flesh felt unsettlingly spongy beneath the deerskin, and I concluded the man hadn't been dead for more than a week or two.

My hand moved higher, encountering bare skin, then a breech-clout, and I realized this was not a white man, as I had assumed, but an Indian. I felt all about his waist in hopes of locating a knife or tomahawk. I found nothing. The rest of my search revealed the Indian had worn a beaded hunting shirt and had a bandolier bag slung over his shoulder. Alas, the bag was empty.

I sat back on my heels pondering my situation. Was there a way I could use the body to trick Gerard? Perhaps if I dressed it in my clothes, I might be able to fool Gerard into thinking it was me, and then…

Try as I might couldn't come up with anything to do next. Well, I did think of one thing, though it wasn't very cold-blooded and in no way helped me to defeat Gerard. I could bury the Indian, or at least entomb him in rocks. I would have wanted the same done for me. That would have to wait until later, however. With that in mind, I decided to drag the body away from the river; in case I had to come back this way in a hurry, I had no desire to trip over it. And as fate would have it, as soon as I slipped my hands under the dead Indian's shoulders, I found my weapon.

It was a bow and arrow. I hadn't thought to search under the body, but that, of course, was where an Indian wore his bow, slung across his back. As gently as possible, I rolled the Indian onto his side, then slid the bow off his body. The wood was unbroken, and the cord felt whole. Hesitantly, I slowly pulled back on it, fully expecting the cord to have rotted and snap at any moment. To my relief, it held, and its tautness promised great power. Next I found the quiver, and there my luck was very much less, for in it there remained only a single arrow. It seemed I was to have only one chance when I encountered Gerard. But that was one more than I had had afore.

The bow was not a weapon with which I could claim much familiarity. I thought now a good time to quickly acquaint myself with it. Of course, I couldn't actually fire my single arrow, but I could notch the arrow to the cord, then pull back and pretend to aim (since I couldn't see in the dark). There wasn't room where I stood to fully draw back the cord, so I stepped back around the body onto the riverbank. I drew the cord back several times, getting used to gauging the tension necessary to fire an arrow. It was not inconsiderable by any means, and I thought I understood whence Pakim had come by at least some of his strength.

Still familiarizing myself with the bow, I pulled the cord all the way back to my ear, then happened to turn and face the way I had come.

Gerard saw me at the same instant I saw him. He stood perhaps twenty-five feet from me, a pool of light from his torch encircling him like a bull's eye. I did not remember consciously letting loose the arrow, but I did it at the same moment my brother raised the pistol and fired. Guided more by instinct than wit, I threw myself to the ground. At first I thought I had been struck by the lead ball, for my already-injured shoulder abruptly pained me greatly. The pain soon dulled, though, and I realized I had landed on a sharp rock, far preferable to being ripped into by a lead ball.

Gerard, it seemed, was not so lucky. He screamed as if mortally wounded, then the sound abruptly vanished as if he had fallen into the rushing water. Clutching my throbbing shoulder, I sat up and scanned along the riverbank. The torch Gerard had held lay flickering on the ground, whilst smoke from the pistol's discharging drifted unhurriedly toward me. Of my brother, I saw no sign.

Yet grasping the bow, I cautiously made my way upstream. With each step I hoped to see Gerard's body caught in an eddy or wedged between the rocks. I saw nothing but black, rushing water. I reached the spot where he had been and retrieved the torch. I held it up, peering onto the river, then over to the other side. I even scouted the rocks directly behind me in case an injured Gerard had managed to crawl to them. There was no sign of the bastard.

I turned back to the river that had apparently swallowed my only brother. The iron-gray water looked brutally cold which, I supposed, made it a fitting grave for the cold-hearted prick. I again wondered if I wasn't very much the same, if the blood that coursed through my body wasn't every bit as cold as the water rushing past me. And was that how I truly wanted to live? I was no longer so certain, but somehow I doubted I could ever be anything but Cold-Blooded Cole.

I wondered if Gerard deserved a prayer even if he were bound straight for hell. I hardheartedly thought not. Then, in spite of myself, I made the sign of the cross. Maybe I wasn't so cold-blooded after all.

That was when a voice behind me said, "Perhaps that was just the slightest bit hasty, Little Brother."

◆

I spun about, not wishing to believe my ears. But there was no doubting it: Gerard yet lived. Afore I could react, he rushed me, and we tumbled to the ground. I landed on my stomach whilst my brother was perched on my back. Water rushed by only inches from my face. Gerard seized me by the hair and plunged my head into the freezing river.

The absolute iciness of the river shocked me. In an instant, my entire face fell numb. My hands grasped at Gerard's, my nails digging into his flesh. He used one hand to hold my head underwater, the other to fend off my attack.

Water surged up my nose and down my throat. I gagged instinctively, convulsions wracking my chest. Seconds ticked by, and the roar of the river yet filled my ears, but it slowly became muffled, as if it were moving further away. My chest ached with the need to breathe, and it was all I could do not to inhale. Over and over, I clawed at Gerard's hands, but his grip did not loosen.

I fought on, but my arms felt as if they were carved from rock and my chest burned as if on fire. Even so, I tore at Gerard's hands, though I suspected my hands now did more flailing than clawing. Little flashes of light like sparks from a fire went off afore my eyes, and I grasped I was going to die. And once I was dead, I literally would be Cold-Blooded Cole.

That was when I realized I had been wrong all along. I wasn't Cold-Blooded Cole, not really. That notion was nothing more than a myth I had created about myself, a mask I presented to the world. I did care about others: Rose and Colette. John and Palmer and Gwennie, too. I had even felt concern for that dead Indian I had found.

Then there was Pakim. I loved him, even if I now only understood how much. My blood didn't run cold; I was no wendigo. I understood something else as well. The way to defeat Gerard wasn't to become like him. It was to match his chilled heart with a fiery one, to bring life and not death, to meet hate with love. It made me angry to learn such an important lesson at this instant, only moments afore I was to die. Such knowledge had come at too great a cost never to be put to use. Indeed, I refused to allow that to happen.

Yet on my stomach, I pulled my legs forward until they were under me as if I were kneeling. Gerard halfheartedly tried to force them back down, but he must have been exhausted himself, as he couldn't do it. He choked me furiously, but with the last of my strength I thrust my legs up as hard as I could and tumbled both of us forward into the river.

Again I felt the shock of its utter iciness, but this time it was invigorating rather than sapping, and it was I who experienced a surge of strength. I felt Gerard roll over me, scrabbling to keep ahold of my throat, but the water was too powerful, and he lost his grip. My legs banged against rocks on the river bottom as I fought for the surface. Finally, I popped above the water. Gasping for air, I reached for an outcropping to keep from being swept away. I caught ahold of one, barely managing to keep my grip.

For a long while, I simply hung on, coughing and sucking in mouthful after mouthful of air. Of Gerard, I saw no sign. When I started to shiver, I knew I had to get out of the water even though doing so seemed impossibly hard. Little by little, however, I pulled myself out of the river and finally crawled onto the bank.

Gerard's torch lay on the ground. I held it up looking down the bank for my brother. I didn't have to look long. Thirty or so feet down the river I spied his shadowy figure rise up. Water cascaded off him in long sheets. Gerard spotted me, snarled, and staggered along the stony bank. Instinctively, I lurched to my feet, hurrying as fast as I could in the other direction. Gerard had no torch, and I hoped that if I could get far enough ahead, he wouldn't be able to follow my light, and I might lose him down here.

It was as I reached the outflow of stinking water that a knot of pain blossomed in the back of my right thigh. Dropping the torch on the ground, I reached around with my hand until I touched the handle of a knife. Seeing his throw had struck home, Gerard called out in triumph.

Crying out, I pulled the blade free. Slick blood coursed down my leg, but I had no time to bandage it. I took a step, but my injured thigh seized up in a spasm, and I knew I wasn't going much farther. I looked back and saw Gerard coming.

Retrieving the torch, I swung it about, searching for some place to hide, but saw nothing other than the river, rocks, and the stinking flow of the smaller tributary running past me. That stream shimmered in the torchlight with a sheen not unlike the glossy shell of a beetle. Watching it, I recalled how hotly the oily surface of the similar stream near Pakim's sweat lodge had burned.

As fast as I could manage, I scrambled alongside the stream.

Stepping around and over the oily waters, I prayed I did not trip and end up immolating myself by setting the water aflame. Grimacing from the accumulated pain of my injuries and sweating from the effort of clambering alongside the stream, I soon reached a large pool of water whence the stream flowed. Stinking bubbles languorously burst in the center of the pool, and I realized this was the source of that foul-smelling water. Taking extra care to keep the torch away from its surface, I made way around it. Just as I reached the far side, a voice called out, "By God Almighty, what is that stink?"

"Perhaps it's your soul, Brother," I said, my eyes stinging from the water's fumes.

"Don't you think you're clever and brave making quips," sneered Gerard. "How long are we going to keep this up, Cole? I know you put the gold somewhere. Wouldn't it be easier if you told me where?"

"Easier for who?" I asked.

Unaware of the pool afore him, Gerard walked toward me. "I know you're badly injured, Little Brother. Eventually, I *will* get you."

"I suppose you're right, Gerard. But I kept that knife you threw at me. Perhaps I might kill myself afore you can do so."

"You wouldn't do that," said Gerard, but I heard the alarm in his voice. "Be reasonable, Cole." I watched him come closer. "Let's talk about this. Can't we—blast it," swore Gerard, when he walked into the water. "These were my last good moccasins, Cole. Do you realize how bloody hard it is to get good footwear out here?"

"Haven't really had time to think about it, Gerard." Now nausea accompanied the burning in my eyes, and I wondered how long I could stand it this close to the oily water.

"This is your last chance!" yelled Gerard, and I could hear how incensed he was now. "Tell me where the gold is, Cole!"

"About that, Gerard," I said. "I may have been mistaken."

"What are you talking about?"

"In point of fact, there is no gold," I said. "Never was. I lied."

"No, that's not true!" he said, panic verging in his voice. "I had been told there were bars and bars of it."

"There probably were—once. But they're long gone now."

"You son of a bitch," snarled Gerard.

"Sorry," I said. "But I had to get you down here away from the others."

"You're going to pay, Cole."

Hadn't I already done that many times over? "I'm ready to do just that, Gerard." My words slurred slightly. I realized I was growing dizzy and feared the stink from the water would overcome me afore I could act.

"I'm going to cut you like a deer!" Gerard exclaimed with rage. "Do you hear me, you whore's son? Do you?" It took him a moment to regain his composure, then wading through the water toward me he said, "I think you're lying, Little Brother. I think that gold *is* down here, and I'm going to make you a deal. You're going to throw down that torch and back away so I can look for the gold. I'm going to let you live and give you a chance to find your way out of here. If you don't oblige me, I'll not only kill you but the others as well."

"You want me to throw down the torch, Gerard?" I asked. By now I was reeling and felt as if my arms and legs were very far away.

"That's what I said, isn't it?" he asked.

"All right, Brother. If you say so." It seemed to take a long time for my hand to open, the torch to fall, the water to ignite. But once it did, the reaction was instantaneous. The water exploded, eerie blue flames racing toward Gerard. He bellowed once, turning and sprinting for the edge of the shore. Inky smoke swiftly surged up from the water giving me only glimpses of his flailing form as I, too, staggered away from the heat. I watched the fire catch him as he clambered onto dry land, but to my dismay he beat out the flames.

Yet the heat from the burning water must have been overwhelming, for he howled and spun about looking for a way to flee. But he was only feet from the fire and had come up against a rocky wall that provided no egress. Amidst the smoke, I lost sight of him for a moment, then spotted him trying to scale the cave wall.

The thick, tarry smoke enveloped me now, stinging my eyes even worse, clogging my throat. I realized I had to escape as well, but how could I flee if Gerard yet lived? The heat scorched my exposed flesh, and I realized I had to go or die. My brother I would deal with later. Afore I could move, however, an icy blast swept over me. The heat vanished, replaced by an intense cold I had only felt once afore—the night in the woods when I had encountered that strange creature as I searched for Rose and Colette. Too, I tasted that strange metallic taint in my mouth. As afore, I couldn't move; again, I felt my chest being punched into and my heart being squeezed by some terrible force. Immobile, I strained against the unseen might that gripped me. Then the pressure and the cold vanished, and I slumped against the wall.

Dizzy and nauseous, I glanced up and saw Gerard climbing even higher through the swirling smoke. Then, to my horror, he must have reached an outcropping for he suddenly pulled himself upright and turned back toward me. I watched his eyes search until he spotted where I stood. Blue light from the fire below bathed him as a malevolent smile spread across his face until another upwelling of black smoke obscured him again. When it next parted, Gerard had gone immobile, with a puzzled expression on his face. As the haze from the fire swirled about him, he suddenly clutched at his chest. Then the heat around me grew even more intense and I was forced to move on, desperate to reach the river and cooler fresh air.

When he was next visible, Gerard was no longer alone. Or at least I thought not, though between the dizziness yet hounding me and the smoky light it was hard to be sure what I saw. I had the impression of a tall man struggling with Gerard, whose face was contorted with rage. It could only be Pakim up there with him.

Gerard suddenly screamed and I watched his body plunge into the fiery water. Despite the heat, I froze in my tracks. Aflame, Gerard rose from the burning water and stood there openmouthed, as if he were unable to believe what was happening. The pain must have hit him then, for he let out a shriek that was utterly inhuman. He spun about, wildly beating at himself. No matter which way he staggered, the fire followed, leaping about and encircling him, almost as if holding on to him. The flames swirled about him in a terrible column and for an instant it wasn't Gerard I saw, but a black-clad creature, its terrible mouth open in a silent scream. An instant later, it was Gerard again.

For a brief moment, his pain-crazed eyes locked on mine. He turned toward me, arms outstretched as if begging me for mercy. He took several steps in my direction, stopped, screamed a final time, then collapsed.

My eyes darted back up to the outcropping, searching for Pakim, but there didn't seem to be anyone there.

"Pakim!" I hollered. "Pakim, are you there?"

No one answered.

My head swam with the stink of the smoke and the heat of the fire. My eyes burnt and my throat felt so scratched and raw I could scarcely breathe. To stay was to die, but I couldn't leave without Pakim. "Pakim!" I yelled again. Again, he didn't answer back.

I prayed that if he had found a way up there, he could also find his way out.

Gasping for air, I reached the river and staggered along the bank. I had covered perhaps fifty yards when a terrific explosion erupted from behind me. The last thing I remembered was flying forward, then all was dark.

epilogue

Something cold and immensely pleasing trickled through my lips. A soothing hand touched my brow, and a cloth caressed my skin. I opened my eyes and recognized the gaze that met my own.

"Hello, Gokhotit. It is about time for you to wake up and stop leaving the work to the rest of us."

I smiled and said, "Is that truly you, Pakim?" I had feared he might not have escaped and had, in fact, died in the explosion. I wondered how he had gotten away.

"You were expecting George Washington perhaps?" he asked with a laugh.

I tried to smile back, but my face hurt. In fact, I didn't think there was a single part of my body that wasn't either cut, bruised, burnt or, quite possibly, all three. I finally looked about and saw we were back in the blockhouse yet again. Lord, I was sick of this place and, for the life of me, I couldn't recall our having returned there. But I knew my ordeal was over at last. I had seen Gerard die.

"You killed him, didn't you?" I asked.

"Killed who?"

"Gerard. I saw you shove him off of the rocks into the fire."

Pakim looked at me with concern. "Have you hit your head?" he asked, peering at my face.

"Yes, several times at least. But I still saw you kill Gerard. Back in the cave."

Pakim studied me dubiously.

"I know you were in the cave," I said. "I saw you."

"This is true, but I did not kill Gerard. At the time, I did not even know he was down there. I yet believed he had died exactly as Stich claimed."

I tried to sit up, but dizziness kept me from doing so. "You mean to tell me you didn't fight Gerard up on an outcropping, then knock him into the burning water?"

"That is so," said Pakim.

"I don't understand," I said. "Besides me, you are the only other person who could have been down there."

"Perhaps you should tell me exactly what you saw," said Pakim.

"All right." But first I told Pakim about everything else that had happened since he disappeared—Gwennie's vanishing, John's capture, the truth about the wendigo being Sebastien, Gerard's murder of Palmer. Then I cast my mind back to my final confrontation with Gerard, but already the memories seemed distant and disjointed. I had been so injured and dizzy, and there had been so much smoke. Too, it had all happened so fast. Nonetheless, I described the tall figure, their struggle, Gerard's fall. Even to my ears, I realized I could have been describing almost anyone.

"Is there nothing else you can recollect?" asked Pakim.

I pondered for a moment until I remembered that terrible icy pressure in my chest. I described the sensation to Pakim.

Pakim listened, nodded, then grew reflective. "Earlier you said I was the only other person who could have been down there with you. Person, yes. Something else, no."

"You mean a wendigo," I said. "But we know the wendigo wasn't real, Pakim. It was only Gerard and Stich forcing Sebastien to pretend to be one."

"It may be true we know Gerard was behind the earlier incidents, but that does not mean wendigos do not exist, Cole. It does not mean that one is not in these woods as we speak. Maybe Gerard and Stich were not responsible for all that has happened."

"I don't believe it," I said. But could I be so certain I was right?

How could I explain all I had seen, much less that icy claw that gripped my heart whilst I was in the cave? I had experienced that only once afore: the night in the woods when I had been chased by the black-clad figure. There had been something else odd that night. I had heard my name called. Actually, as I thought about it, what I had heard was "Seavey," and I now realized that could have meant either Gerard or myself. Might it have been a real wendigo I had encountered that night?

And perhaps I had seen it again. I recalled Whitewood Tree having said that a wendigo couldn't stand the presence of another. My brother had certainly done enough terrible things to prove his heart was of ice. He had even become a cannibal. Perhaps he truly had become a wendigo. Had another wendigo sensed my brother's transformation? Was it searching for Gerard when it seized me that night in the woods, examining my heart to see if it was made of ice?

Gerard had fallen into the fire right after I had seen him clutching his chest. Perhaps the wendigo had examined Gerard's heart as well—found that my brother was no longer human—and killed him.

This was ludicrous! It had been windy that night in the forest, that's all. What I had heard wasn't my name being called, but the wind in the trees. The pressure in my chest was fear, nothing more. And it had been John riding Elizabeth chasing me, not a wendigo. Yet I glanced uneasily toward the blockhouse door and the woods beyond.

Pakim followed my gaze and said, "Indians know these forests far better than anyone else, Cole. I do not think it wise to dismiss all that they believe."

I was quiet for a long moment, then asked, "How is John?"

Pakim shrugged equivocally. "John is having a very hard time," he said. "I think it will be a long while afore he will be himself again. Perhaps never."

The old Cole, the cold-blooded one, would have expected John to simply move on. But looking at Pakim, feeling so grateful he was alive, that he was with me again, led me to believe I understood at least a little of what John felt about Palmer's death. And it must have been nearly unendurable. In fact, it was too painful to even think about, so I asked, "How long was I out this time?"

"Three days."

"Three days!" I exclaimed. Not again. That's how long I'd been unconscious the first time I had been rescued by Pakim and taken to John's. This was threatening to become a habit for me.

"Now I think you should rest, Cole."

Whether he thought me too injured to talk or not, I had a torrent of questions. Afore I could ask even one, however, the clatter of approaching hoofbeats reached us. A moment later, Gwennie and John appeared in the blockhouse's doorway.

"You are awake," said Gwennie. "This is good. I would be sorry if I not say goodbye."

So she was going at last. My eyes traveled to John, and I wondered if he was to accompany her.

"Hello, John," I said. "It's good to see you."

"You, too," he said, flatly. His face gave away nothing—no hint of pain or anger or sadness—and I feared he was to be the cold-blooded one now. Perhaps that was the only way he could survive. "Are Rose and Colette ready?" he asked.

"Are they ready for what?" I asked.

"To go home," said Rose, as she stepped into the blockhouse. She cradled Colette in her arms. "To go back to my parents and set things to right with them."

"But what about our getting married and my taking care of you?" I asked.

Rose looked at me as if I had announced a newfound ability to fly, and I realized she knew about Pakim and me. "I'm not going to pretend I understand, Cole," she said. "But you risked your life to save all of us, and I won't judge. Nor will I saddle you with a life that is most certainly not one that you want."

"But Rose," I objected. "I yet—"

She held up her hand. "You can't grow watercress and corn in the same place, Cole. No matter how hard you might try."

"Well, I know you're not a woman to brook disagreement, Rose. So I'll offer none."

"There's a Moravian missionary village south of here," John said. "Gwennie and I will take Rose there, and they'll make sure she gets home."

"Will you come back here afterward?" I asked him.

John shook his head. "I think not. I've kept Gwennie from the Firelands long enough, so I'm going to accompany her there."

"Will you stay with her?" I asked.

John's eyes took on an unfocused, far away look. "I'm not sure where I'll settle," he said. "Do you yet wish to venture there, Cole? If so, you may join us if you like."

"I don't know what I want to do," I said. *That wasn't true, of course,* I thought, glancing at Pakim. I knew what I wanted all right. It was less a matter of what I wanted than what I could have.

"Should I choose not to stay with Gwennie," said John. "I'm thinking of going farther west." He patted a bulging sack on the table. "This bag of apple seeds and a tin pot are all that survived the fire that burnt our cabin. But I think that will be enough to keep me going. Perhaps I'll start planting apple trees in Gwennie's stead. I think Palmer would like that." John considered his words for a moment, then said, "In fact, I'll do it for him, in his memory."

"Apelishi Mingw," said Gwennie. "Appleseed John. That shall be new name for you."

Gwennie's nickname was sweet and all, but it wouldn't keep him warm. "You can't go provisioned so poorly, John," I said. "Even your feet are bare."

He looked down and shrugged as if he had neither noticed nor cared. "I'll make do," he said, taking the apple seeds and going outside. I followed him and found a pleasant surprise—Hiccup, Gwennie's horse, yet lived.

John patted her nose, but absentmindedly and with the none of the affection he had previously lavished on her and the now-deceased Elizabeth. In fact, he hardly seemed to notice she was there, and that worried me. I feared John might wish to take his own life, but rather than shooting or hanging himself, he planned on killing himself slowly.

"Do you at least have a musket?" I asked.

"No muskets," John said, adamantly. "Neither knives nor pistols. No weapons at all. I've seen too much killing." He seemed angry now, but at last he was showing some emotion.

"How will you protect yourself then?" I asked. "What if someone attacks you?"

John thought for a moment, then reached around to the back of Hiccup and removed the tin pot he had saved. He placed it on top of his head, which made for a remarkably good fit. "I'll wear this," he said. "It's sure to keep me safe from musket balls and toma-hawks." He couldn't quite smile, but I could see he was at least trying to make a joke, and that made me feel somewhat better about his future.

Pakim touched the tin pot, then his eyes fell on the apple seeds. "Appleseed John is a good name. One with promise for better things tomorrow."

"You can't go yet!" I said excitedly, for thinking of the future had made me think of the gold. "There is gold somewhere back at the fort! That was what Gerard was after. We just have to find it and you'll be set for life. You won't ever want for money again."

John shook his head. "No. There is only one thing I covet, and gold can't buy it."

I knew he spoke of Palmer, and my heart ached for him. "For Rose and Colette then," I said. "At least they should take some back with them."

Pakim placed his hand on my shoulder. "It is already taken care of, Cole. Rose and Colette have a bar each."

"How?" I asked. "The gold was gone. Someone had been there and—" Understanding came to me and I said to Pakim, "That was why you were down there. You were taking the gold."

"Why did you not say something when you saw me?" asked Pakim.

"I was afraid Gerard would hear. I was afraid he would kill you."

"Well, I did not see you, or I would have come to find you afore the explosion rather than afterward, when you had nearly expired."

"You found me?" I asked.

Pakim nodded. "I heard the blast, and when I went to investigate, I all but trod upon you. I carried you out."

"But how did you even know the gold was here in the first place?" I asked.

"You told me," said Pakim. "At least sort of."

"Me?" I asked, unable to recall having done so. "I couldn't have, Pakim. I didn't even think about it until Gerard told me he was looking for a fort. Until then, I had only thought the bars to be made of lead."

"But I also had heard rumors of an abandoned fort with gold," said Pakim. "And during the night we spent in the blockhouse after Palmer disappeared, you told me you had come across some ruins filled with lead bars. You thought the ruins were from a blockhouse, but said it could have been a fort as well. That was when I knew, or at least suspected, the gold was there."

So I had told him without realizing it. "The gold was the way you thought you could help your people, wasn't it?" I asked, solving another small mystery. "That was why you had come back to them."

Pakim nodded. "I had heard about it whilst I journeyed away from my people. I considered it more likely to be wishful thinking than anything else. But by then wishes were all I had, so I thought I would at least look for it when I returned. But until you mentioned having found a fort, I had no luck in locating it. In fact, the day I first found you, it was whilst I searched for the fort."

"Why didn't you tell me about the gold when you suspected I had found it?" I asked. I wondered if Pakim had said nothing because he wanted to keep it all for the Delaware and feared I would demand a share. The thought saddened me, for I had thought we were closer than that.

"With the others missing, we had more important things to worry about that night," he said. "I believed it would have been unseemly to discuss searching for gold whilst our friends' lives were in danger."

"I see," I said, once again feeling the horse's ass for even suspecting him.

"It is all right, Cole," he said. "It would be suspicious to me as well. Do not feel bad for wondering about my motives."

Could he read my *every* thought as easily as a moose's trail through a meadow? If so, then he would know I truly felt terrible for having doubted him. When we were alone, I would apologize.

"I thought you died in the blizzard," I said. "I almost went after you. What did happen to you, Pakim?"

"Midnight wandered away whilst I tethered the other horses," said Pakim. "I followed after, but by the time I found her, I could not find my way back to our shelter in the whiteout. I eventually stumbled onto the ruins of the fort you had described. You had said the wendigo's cave was near there and was connected to the ruins by an underground passage that you used to escape through. I had gone down hoping to find you, and that was why I was down there when I heard the explosion."

I smiled and said, "And here I was thinking I never had any good luck."

John and the others were ready to go. I offered to hold Colette whilst Rose climbed onto Hiccup. As I did so, another question occurred to me, something I had wondered about from the first time I had met my niece. "Her name really isn't Colette, is it, Rose? You only said that the first day to earn my affection."

Rose studied me for a long moment, then held out her arms for the baby. "Colette is her name, Cole, and shall always be."

Smiling, I handed her the baby.

"Wish us luck," said John.

"All the luck in the world to you, John Chapman," I said fervently. "You as well, Gwennie."

Gwennie kissed us each on the cheek, and though she surely would have denied it with her dying breath, I saw her eyes were wet with tears.

Pakim and I stood side by side watching them ride away. I wondered if I would see any of them again.

"Are you going to take the rest of the gold to your clan?" I asked Pakim.

"Some," he said. "It will keep them fed and warm for a long time. But if I take too much, it will only attract the attention of others and bring trouble to my people. You can do whatever you want with the rest."

I thought about the gold and the depths of depravity to which my brother had fallen in pursuit of such riches. I thought of the ruin and misery that had been wrought on Hugh's Lick, of all the dead: Palmer, Addy Lobb, Benjamin, Sebastien, and the others. Did I truly want any part of that? "I think it should be left where it is," I said. "Well, most of it anyway." I smiled and Pakim smiled back.

"Why don't we go fetch some then," he said. "Once my clan has it, we can decide what to do next."

"We?" I asked, unable to hide my surprise.

"I thought that perhaps with Rose and Colette gone you might feel differently about our situation," he said. "But if you do not, I—"

"No!" I said. "Or yes. I do feel differently." Did I ever. Not long ago I had thought I had to go to the Firelands to be the person I wanted to be. And in a way, I had done just that; the old me had burned away in the conflagration of my brother's hateful and evil nature. I was no longer Cold-Blooded Cole, unemotional and detached. I was just Cole now, and I didn't need to go anywhere else to be my true self. As long as Pakim was with me, I was already there.

"So will you come with me, Little Owl?" asked Pakim.

"A whole army of wendigos couldn't keep me from staying with you, Pakim," I said.

"Goodness," he said. "Let us hope we do not have that experience yet awaiting us."

I hadn't yet expressly apologized for all but accusing him of plotting to steal my share of the gold. "Pakim, I implied you wished to cheat me. I'm sorry for that."

"Well, you have upset my feelings, Friend Cole," he said woefully. "Very badly, I might add."

Pakim sounded so dismayed that I felt terrible and couldn't bring myself to look him in the eyes. I wondered if there was anything I could do to make it up to him.

Pakim must have sensed my compunction because he said. "If it will help assuage your conscience, there is a Delaware ritual of apology you can perform. First, we must find a tree stump and some feathers. And you do remember how to gobble, I hope?"

I looked up as he burst into laughter. "Welcome home, Friend Cole," he said, kissing me.

And everything was exactly as it seemed.

THE END